FOXFIRE

Amanda had always breathed the incense of male
attention. She was not beautiful, but she had known
since she was fourteen how to appear so. She was five
feet five, small-boned and small-breasted, so that clothes
became her. Bathing suits did too, for her legs were
exquisite, and years of tennis, swimming and dancing
had long ago vanquished an adolescent pudginess.
Her fine, curly hair had been abandoned by nature to a
light brown exactly the shade of a wild mink fur-piece,
then rescued by beauty parlours to tints of rich and tawny
gold. Her face was squared at the jaw and temples,
belying a childishly soft and appealing mouth, which
Amanda enlarged to a vivid scarlet.
These allurements and an aura of shining cleanliness she
shared with many other American girls of her age and
background, but it was her eyes which arrested attention.
They were large and green-blue, set beneath straight dark
brows. They held an expression of direct and friendly
interest, tinged with laughter and a hint of coquetry.

Foxfire

Anya Seton

CORONET BOOKS
Hodder Paperbacks Ltd., London

Copyright © 1951 by Anya Seton
First published June 1951
Fourth impression 1963
Coronet edition 1964
Second impression 1967
Third impression 1969
Fourth impression 1969
Fifth impression 1971
Sixth impression 1972
Seventh impression 1973
Eighth impression 1974

Printed in Great Britain
for Coronet Books, Hodder Paperbacks Ltd.,
St. Paul's House, Warwick Lane, London, EC4P 4AH,
by Richard Clay (The Chaucer Press), Ltd.,
Bungay, Suffolk.

ISBN 0 340 02488 7

CHAPTER ONE

THE steep mountain road narrowed again, twisting upward on a hairpin curve. The battered little Model T sputtered as Dart shoved the throttle and spark lever, and pushed the pedal into low, while the yellow head-lamps dimmed flickeringly over the dirt road ahead.

They were still climbing, towards El Capitan Pass, on the eastern slope of the Pinal range. Outside of the car there was nothing but an immense brooding darkness. The dark of the cliff on the right, faintly tufted with the chaparral growth of the foothills. On the left, a deeper blackness of the canyon. Night seemed to fall so swiftly in Arizona, and tonight there were no stars.

The sombre enigma of the mountains held Amanda silent. Nor had Dart spoken since they turned south off the Globe highway a few miles back. His calm eyes scanned the road ahead as it rolled in washboard corrugations after each switchback. He was watching for rockslides or the distant lights of a descending car. There were few good places to pass. Still, they had seen no other cars since sunset, when they were driving through the San Carlos Apache reservation.

Dart drove expertly and without tension, allotting to the process the exact amount of awareness which it required. What undersurface thoughts he might be having Amanda could not guess, deeply though she loved him. Nor was she ever quite sure of his inner life apart from her.

Dart swerved sharply to avoid a chuckhole, the Ford's left wheels bounced within inches of the hundred-foot drop to the creek bed below. Amanda held her breath and stared ahead until the middle of the road jiggling resumed. "How much farther now, Dart?"

"Oh, about twenty miles to Dripping Springs, and then twelve more up the Lodestone road. It's pretty rough, but we ought to get into town before midnight."

"Don't you consider this road we're *on* rough?" asked Amanda.

"Why, no ma'am," said Dart, chuckling. "This is a highway to Tucson. Didn't you know that? They'll grade it pretty soon, though, when winter's over. Getting tired, Andy?"

Amanda uncrossed her slim silk-covered legs and buttoned her British tweed topcoat tight under her chin. It pushed up her dark gold curls into a little ruff. It had been stifling hot all day crossing the southern desert, but now it was cold. A few snowflakes drifted down and melted as they landed.

"Not exactly tired," she said. "I'm all keyed up to see Lode-stone, I can't wait, and . . . but, oh, I don't know——" She checked this incoherence, and made an effort to express the not quite unpleasant feeling which had been growing each hour since they had entered Arizona. "I'm not used to mountains, at least not stark, queer ones like these. The country's overpowering. It's spooky. Canyons, cactus, empty, vast, lonely." She laughed. "All the things I've read you're supposed to feel about the south-west. . . . Well, I feel 'em."

Dart didn't answer at once. Then he spoke with quiet amusement. "I think you always obligingly try to feel what books tell you to feel; you're a romantic little thing."

"Well, of course I'm romantic! That's one reason you love me, darling. Temperamental contrast. Dewy-eyed little romantic versus big, silent realist. We complement each other."

Dart made a non-committal sound, then peered through the dirty windshield as a huge red-tailed hawk sailed above the amber lights and disappeared.

I'm being silly, Amanda thought. *Ingénue* and brittle. He hates that. Fluffy badinage that did not mean anything, analysing emotions. A habit developed in sub-deb days and always successful with men like Tim Merrill. Amanda shivered a little, lit a cigarette, and thought about Tim with remote and affectionate tolerance. The image of Tim presented itself to her now in a sort of phony glitter, like a carousel with the painted horses whirling by, the calliope screeching, and with Tim you caught the gold ring every time. She had very nearly persuaded herself that she was in love with him, because they laughed so much, and kept up a line of chatter by the hour, half teasing, half amorous.

Like the night three years ago after the Princeton Prom when seven of them had all piled into Tim's Packard roadster and careered sixty miles to the ocean at Sea-Girt to go swimming at dawn. They'd kidnapped a little Italian accordionist somewhere along the way, and he had played "O Sole Mio" for them on the beach, while they dashed in and out of the freezing surf in their evening clothes. Crazy but fun. That was the night Tim had first asked her to marry him. But even then, long before she met Dart or dreamed of the dark, profound compulsions of real love, she had not wanted to commit herself yet. Tim had scarcely listened to her groping refusal. He had kissed her on the nose, rubbed sand into her hair, and they had drunk together from his flask of imported gin. Tim had plenty of money to pay the best bootleggers. He still had.

"Look, Dart—isn't that a man standing there ahead by the road?" Amanda asked, suddenly pointing and clutching his arm.

"That's a cactus, my girl," Dart answered patiently. "A saguaro. We're getting down in desert country again."

Amanda said, "Oh," and laughed. "You must bear with your tenderfoot bride."

"I do," he said, and though he did not move his hands from the wheel, she felt the pressure of his arm against hers. She sighed voluptuously, resting her head on his shoulder. Her heart beat faster, and she thought of these past nights since their marriage. The surroundings had not mattered too much. She thought of the tourist court outside Harrisburg on her bridal night, a shabby little cabin, straw mattress, and dust on the carpet. But there had been beauty in the dingy cabin with them. Fulfilment. No doubts then, and no regrets. She thought of the note she had written to her mother from St. Louis.

"I'm so happy. Don't ever worry about me. Marriage is a gorgeous, wonderful thing."

This note was for reassurance in answer to her mother's misgivings during the weeks before the wedding. Mrs. Lawrence was worldly and realistic; she was also a pleasant woman and a tactful one, inclined to talk in worthy clichés, since they saved trouble and were never misunderstood. On the whole, she had managed to keep most of her doubts to herself once she had been forced to accept the strength of Amanda's desire for Dart. This time, however, she had voiced her worry. "But, baby, you hardly know the man—shipboard flirtations don't really count— nor is he an easy man to understand—such different background from yours, too. And the life of a mining engineer's wife is no bed of roses. It isn't as though I could help you out either, unfortunately. . . ." She sighed and cut across Amanda's protests, "Oh, I know, dear, money doesn't mean much to you; you haven't really had to face that yet—and I'm not so calloused by middle age that I don't know the strength of young love, but——" Here Mrs. Lawrence had smiled to soften the anxiety of her blue eyes under their frowning, carefully plucked brows. "Well, there is the fact of Dart's rather—rather peculiar parentage."

Amanda had laughed. "Oh, if that's all! It adds to his charm. I think it's exciting."

Mrs. Lawrence shook her head. "Marriage is a hard enough job at best, without adding extra handicaps."

The flivver jounced through the bottom of a dip up on to a comparatively level stretch, and Dart pulled a cigarette from his pocket. He scraped the match with his thumb-nail and the flare lit his face. Amanda looked up at his profile. Not handsome by her mother's standards, too rough-hewn, but so completely male. His frontal bones and black eyebrows were very heavy above a straight, thick nose. His flexible lips were sharply defined and held firm at the corners, even when his rare smile showed fine square teeth against his sun-browned skin. His eyes were grey, and their steady, often ironic gaze was hard to interpret. He was six feet two, his body loosely knit and angular, like a Scottish Highlander. That's what I thought on the boat when I first saw him standing by the rail. That he was Scotch. . . . Did I actually fall in love with him at first sight, or was it that other night at the Captain's dance?

Dart jammed on the brake, and the Ford shivered to a stop.

"What is it?" she asked, peering ahead at a rippling band of black just beyond the headlights.

"This wash is running," said Dart, opening the door. "Been plenty of rain or snow in the mountains. I'll see how deep." He jumped out and returned after five minutes. "We'll have to wait a bit," he said. "She'll be down enough to cross in a while."

"You mean, we can't cross?" she asked incredulously, remembering all the dry creek beds.

"Never did teach the flivver to swim," he said, laughing.

"How long, Dart?"

"Oh, about an hour, I guess. You'd better take a nap." He

pulled a dusty old steamer rug from the back seat, which was piled high with their luggage, and spread it over their knees. He stretched out his long legs, leaned his head back and fell asleep at once. Amanda looked at him with envious amusement. Already she knew his gift for complete relaxation, turned on and off like a light switch. His body always obeyed his will. Hers, however, did not. She sat beside him in the dark little car, listening to the gurgle of the wash, and the sporadic distant screech of some night bird. An uneasiness seeped through her and a loneliness which she tried to rationalize. They had been so close to each other while they crossed the East's rolling green hills, and later on the mid-western plains. Friends as well as lovers, sharing the tiny incidents of the road, exploring with mutual excitement the unknown countries in each other's personalities. Why, then, should this uneasiness have crept in? The scenery, she thought. A sinister quality in the landscape, the weird rock formations, the stark granite mountains bare of all softening green. A sinister quality in the giant cactus, sharply grooved and towering against a burning copper sky. Grotesque shapes in the rocks and in the plants. The prickly pears, thick fleshy paddles armed with hostile spines; the snake-like ocatilla, the vicious cat's-claw and mesquite, but especially those giant saguaros, rearing themselves brutally phallic into the dusty sunshine. A male country, eternally disdaining the soft, pliant female.

Freudian nonsense! she thought. Let's get it straight. It isn't so much the scenery. It was that damn historical marker . . . and maybe those Apache wickiups we passed today.

Dart stirred a little and raised his head. "How are you doing, Andy?" he said, seeing the light of her cigarette and the tense lines of her body. "You're not scared, are you? Nothing to be afraid of."

"I know," she said, after a moment. "I'm not afraid with you. I never could be."

He grunted and went to sleep again. She thought of her last remark and knew that it was true. That quality of quiet strength she had felt in him from the first hours on the boat. She had wanted it for herself to lean on, to sink into luxuriously. For she had never known any man like him, and the difference between them had but added glamour. Until for a moment today there had been the shock provided by the historical marker.

It stood by the highway as they passed the Peloncillo Mountains just after entering Arizona, and Dart at her request had stopped the car so that she might read it. It said, "Site of Apache Raid in October 1881. An entire wagon train of white settlers was massacred here. 30 men, women, and children."

"Heavens!" she had cried, shuddering and staring at the bland mesquite-studded desert. "How ghastly. It's so hard to believe."

Dart nodded. "Tanosay was one of the war chiefs in that raid. He never told me much about it, though."

She had been silent while it seemed that a chill wind blew off the desert between them. Dart had started the car and they continued on their way.

"Was that THE raid?" she asked, very low. "The one when your grandmother——" She could not finish through the tightening of her throat, though at home she had often questioned him.

"No," said Dart. He was not on the defensive, he seemed indifferent to anything she might think. He had stated a fact, bluntly, as he always stated them, and she might do what she liked with it.

Yet that night on the *Bremen* she had thought him defensive, and she had glowed with impulsive sympathy.

Amanda snapped on the flashlight and looked at her tiny gold wrist-watch. Fifteen minutes had passed. Ahead the wash still gurgled darkly, beside her there was even, steady breathing. She pulled the blanket up across her chest, nestled close to Dart, and tried to sleep. But her thoughts would not still, and over and over, as if for reassurance, her mind unreeled again those days on the boat, and after.

They had been a gay crowd of young people in Tourist Third on the *Bremen* last September, mostly students returning to college after happy vacations in Europe, though some, like Amanda, would not be able to continue their studies, but must go job-hunting, an uncertain prospect in that fall of 1932. Amanda had rationally accepted the new poverty which engulfed her family in 1929, but except for passionate rebellion against her father's resultant death from a heart attack, the shadow of insecurity had not touched her emotionally. There had been enough money salvaged from life insurance for her to complete her sophomore year at Vassar, and to provide Mrs. Lawrence with a tiny income and three-room flat in New York. There had been a few hundred dollars left to Amanda outright, and these she decided to spend on the student trip to Europe before facing the "grim realities" of life. This was Mrs. Lawrence's own phrase, often expressed. Let Amanda have what fun she might while she could, poor child, and thank heaven that Jean, at least, was provided for.

Jean, six years older than Amanda, had in 1928 married a solid young man called George Walker. His solidity, though worthy and unencumbered by imagination, might not have en-sured Jean's security during the panic years that followed, but his position as vice-president in his father's Gelatine Products Company did. George's income had shrunk, of course, but Jean still had her house in Greenwich, her Buick coupé, and a nurse for little Sally Lou.

"Maybe," Mrs. Lawrence had said, laughing at the flavour of hopeful Victorian mamma which underlay her thought, "on this trip to Europe, Andy darling, something will turn up. You never can tell. Thank heaven, you've still got some good clothes. Or," she added wistfully, "maybe you'll make up your mind about Tim. I think he'd make you happy and you *would* be so well taken care of."

But, not at all in accord with Mrs. Lawrence's hope for Amanda's future, it was Dart who had turned up.

Amanda had first noticed him just after they left Cherbourg on the voyage home. He was standing by the rail, his hands in his pockets, gazing out over the ocean towards the setting sun. She noted first that he was very tall, and that he was a little older than most of the students. His clothes were nondescript, a cheap and rumpled brown tweed suit, but the position of his body, leaning slightly forward against the wind, suggested an easy strength. So did his hands, she thought, as she watched him lighting a cigarette, and his blunt, thin profile interested her.

In the steamer chair next to Amanda's, Peggy Gordon, her cabin mate, had giggled. "I wouldn't bother to make a play for him, Andy. He looks pretty grim—inhibited, I'd say. Cere-bretonic type." Peggy was a psychology major at Vassar.

"I don't think he's grim exactly. There's something about him. . . ." Amanda had paused, trying to analyse the quality

she felt in this tall, rangy, and quite unexceptional young man—
was it a lack of self-consciousness? An inner poise? "I think he's
attractive, anyway," she finished a trifle defiantly.

Dart had then turned, throwing his cigarette into the water,
swept the two girls with an indifferent stare, and walked off
towards the stern.

Neither Amanda nor Peggy was accustomed to indifference in
a masculine eye, especially on shipboard. Amanda, especially,
had always breathed the incense of male attention. She was not
beautiful, but she had known since she was fourteen how to
appear so. She was five feet five, small-boned and small-
breasted, so that clothes became her. Bathing suits did too, for
her legs were exquisite, and years of tennis, swimming, and
dancing had long ago vanquished an adolescent pudginess.

Her fine, curly hair had been abandoned by nature to a light
brown exactly the shade of a wild mink fur-piece, then rescued
by beauty parlours to tints of rich and tawny gold. Her face was
squared at the jaw and temples, belying a childishly soft and
appealing mouth, which Amanda enlarged to a vivid scarlet.

These allurements and an aura of shining cleanliness she
shared with many other American girls of her age and background, but it was her eyes which arrested attention. They were
large and green-blue, set beneath straight dark brows. They held
an expression of direct and friendly interest, tinged with laughter
and a hint of coquetry.

Amanda was predisposed to like people and showed it. Nor
had she as yet, in her twenty years, been met by anything but
warm response. Her self-confidence was therefore ingrained and
unassuming. She was also a romantic. The combination had led
her into several love-affairs besides the one with Tim, and led
her out of them again. For the romance always unjelled, rapidly
melting, it seemed to her, into a sticky mess of sexual byplay,
and though bred on Freud and accustomed like all her genera-
tion to the frankest possible analyses of sex, her passions were
still unawakened. This was before she met Dart, and despite
Peggy's jeers she continued to watch for him while she played
shuffleboard or lay in deck-chairs with the other young people.

"Probably a shoe-clerk, married, with three children in Brooklyn," said Peggy.

"Maybe," answered Amanda; "but I'd like to meet him. I
think he looks lonely."

Peggy snorted, and it turned out that she was right. Dart was never lonely, at least not in the usual way.

Amanda did meet him that night, as they all sat in the lounge and drank rich Bavarian beer. Some of the German exchange students clustered together and began clinking mugs and singing. Dart was sitting by himself in a corner, and, emboldened by the fruity sentiment of "Alt Wien," Amanda walked over to him, smiling. "Don't you want to join us?" she said, indicating her own group. "We thought we might set up a rival chorus when they've finished over there—the 'Missouri Waltz,' or something."

Dart laughed. "Thank you, no. My bullfrog bellow would lead you all into international hostilities. I was just going to turn in, anyway."

"Oh, I see," she said, flushing a little. She was startled by his voice. Whatever he might aver as to his singing, his speaking voice had unusual richness, and the intonation was that of cultured New England. Not a Brooklyn shoe-clerk, anyway. She saw Peggy watching her sardonically, and smiled at him again with gentle directness. "I thought you might be lonely."

"Did you?" he said. "But I'm not." He smiled back, answering her friendliness with equal candour, and almost sparing her the implication that she was trying to pursue him. He had been pursued a good deal by women, and he did not like it.

Amanda, unused to rebuff and caught by a pull of attraction stronger than she had expected, could not quite hide her dismay. "I'm sorry," she said, flushing again. She added lightly, "Well, if you change your mind . . ." And walked back to her table.

"Misogynist?" asked Peggy with interest. "Impervious to female charm?"

"My charm, anyway." Amanda sank down on the cushioned bench between the two Cornell seniors, who received her with delight and amorous sparring, in which she carried her part without effort.

The wind blew up in the night, and the next morning it was rough. The *Bremen*, large as she was, pitched convulsively, and Tourist Third in the stern got the full benefit of the motion. Peggy remained in her berth, nor did most of the other passengers appear. Amanda, however, was immune to seasickness. She wandered up to her deck-chair and began to read *Shadows*

on the Rock, which she had found among the novels in the ship's
library.

She was unconscious of Dart until he sat down in the vacant
chair beside her and said without preliminary, "Willa Cather, is
it? Has she got a new book out? *Death Comes for the Archbishop*
was a magnificent job. One of the few novels I ever enjoyed."

Amanda jumped. She looked from his face down to the book
on her lap. So we have a literary discussion now, she thought,
amused. She was happy that he had stopped, and therefore wise
enough not to make reference to last night's rebuff. Moreover,
she knew instinctively that this was not a belated gambit. He
was interested in Willa Cather, he had not been interested in
the singing, and in her as a pretty girl or even an individual, he
had as yet no interest at all.

"I've forgotten *Death Comes for the Archbishop*," she said.
"It came out some years ago, didn't it? Wasn't it about the
West?"

"Yes," said Dart. "New Mexico. She got some of the real
feel of the country. Few people do."

He had dark-grey eyes, rather the colour of the leaden waves
beside the ship, but, as he spoke, his eyes reflected light.

"You know the West?" she asked.

"Certainly. It's my home. Arizona. I was born there."

She considered this with surprise. His voice was typically
eastern. Cultured and well-bred, her mother would have called
it. And Amanda, like most people who had never travelled past
the Alleghenies, had a vague mental montage of the West,
pasted together from bits of Bret Harte, Zane Grey, *The Vir-
ginian*, and cowboy movies.

"You don't sound like—I mean . . ." She stopped and laughed.
"I thought you were a Yankee or a New Yorker."

Dart smiled, but he withdrew a little. "My father came from
Massachusetts," he said, getting up, and for a moment she
thought he was going to leave her like that. They were alone on
the deck except for a scurrying steward, and she had no wish to
be thus consigned back to her book. With anyone else, she
would have suggested that they walk around the deck together.
With Dart she dared not, but she gave him a look of unconscious appeal. He responded to it after a moment, held his hand
out, and pulled her up from the chair. "All right," he said, as
though she had spoken. "We'll get some exercise."

Amanda had read a great deal about electric thrills running between man and woman, and now, while Dart held her hand to pull her out of the chair, she felt one. It frightened her, and as they walked as briskly as possible, teetering from one side to the other on the heaving deck, she scolded herself, trying thereby to regain an inner balance.

Physical appeal, pure and simple, she told herself. One-sided at that, since he seemed to feel nothing at all. Humiliating and ridiculous. At the second turn around the deck it occurred to her that she did not even know his name, and this reflection annoyed her into decisive action.

She stopped dead, saying, "I've had enough exercise, thanks. I'm getting chilly." And turned to leave.

It was then that Dart first really saw her as anything but a pretty and self-assured little eastern girl, ripe for shipboard dalliance.

There was gallantry and unconscious dignity in the way she held herself braced on the deck, her dull gold hair whipping about her head, her nose and cheeks pink from the biting, salt wind. Under the straight, dark brows, her clear eyes looked up at him with direct honesty, the coquetry had vanished. Her mouth, almost bare of lipstick, quivered a little, and he had a sudden impulse to kiss it which startled him.

He smiled suddenly, half at himself. "Well, come on into the lounge if you're cold," he said, laughing. "I'll buy you a drink."

His amusement, which she did not understand, made her feel childish and flat. She would have liked to punish him by disappearing, but she was sure it would not punish him, that he would have returned into the self-contained solitude which he obviously enjoyed.

He was, however, by no means a recluse, she found after she had followed him into the lounge. He talked easily and well when he wished to, and though reserved about himself, she did learn that he was a mining engineer. That he had just been recalled from an unfinished journey to the Transvaal because the American mining company which had sent him had suddenly collapsed, unable to weather the depression.

Later, Peggy and the two Cornell seniors drifted wanly up from their staterooms and joined them. Peggy was too feeble to express surprise when she saw Amanda sitting with Dart, except to growl that smugness could apparently draw people together

when nothing else could, and that people who did not get sea-
sick deserved to be drowned.

Dart laughed, and ordered her a brandy, and remained with
them chatting until lunch-time.

From then on he joined the other young people at times, and
they all liked him, though the boys deferred a little to his five
years' seniority. Dart was twenty-seven, it developed, and had
graduated from the Arizona College of Mines at Tucson. Since
then he had worked in mines in Colorado, in Mexico, and this
recent brief abortive job in South Africa. Other biographical
data appeared casually in the course of conversation. His name
was Jonathan Dartland, but he had been known as "Dart" since
prep-school days. He had gone to prep school in the East, to
Andover. Here a Williams junior pricked up his ears and said
that he'd thought the name Dartland was familiar. "Didn't you
win the interscholastic track meet for Andover once?"

Dart said briefly that he had and changed the subject. The
Williams boy, who had attended Andover several years after
Dart, looked puzzled, as one who is trying to remember. He
mentioned this to Amanda later. "Something about that guy—
something else I heard at Andover, I mean, beside his name being up in the gym—something sort of screwy, but I can't get it."

Amanda did not encourage him. She wanted to know all about
Dart, but she wanted no possibly unsympathetic comments from
the sidelines. Nor was their relationship progressing. Dart,
when he now joined their group, was pleasant with everyone.
He did not single out Amanda for special attention. He even
seemed to assume that she was paired off with one of the Cornell
seniors, and devoted what impersonal gallantries he showed to
Peggy, or a little redhead from Memphis who had drifted somehow into their crowd.

On the next to last night out there was a gala dance, humbler
replica of the Captain's dance, taking place three decks up in
First Class, and Amanda, while she batted balloons and drank
inferior champagne, was actively and consciously miserable. The
ship had entered the Gulf Stream now, the air was balmy, and
Amanda had worn the most filmy and seductive dress she
owned. It was of peacock-blue chiffon trimmed with gold, both
colours designed to enhance her eyes and hair. Its effect on the
other young men was instantaneous, but from Dart it evoked a
long, thoughtful look. From this look she took what comfort she

could and prayed that he would ask her to dance. Her prayer was answered presently: because all the others were dancing they were left alone at the table, and there was nothing else for him to do. His reluctance prompted her to schoolgirl gaucherie.

"It won't be so painful . . ." she said crossly. "The dances aren't long. You aren't by any chance afraid of me, are you?"

Dart considered this remark. Then he laughed. "Sorry if I seem rude. I'm not afraid of you, but I guess I've always been wary of your type."

This remark would have annoyed a saint, and Amanda snapped, "I'm not a type, I'm me, you dope. You have the most insufferable——"

Suddenly Dart put his arm around her, and she felt the faint pressure of his chin on her hair. "Shut up and let's dance," he said.

Unlike many tall men, Dart had lightness of foot and perfect muscular control. He also had a superb sense of rhythm. Amanda had little time to note this before she was swept by more compelling emotions. The physical contact with him overpowered her. Her body terrified her by a sensation of melting into him, of identification. The saloon and the other dancers, the lights and the coloured streamers, the gentle creaking of the ship, the honeyed strains of the "Pagan Love Song," all receded to an opalescent blur. She knew nothing sharply except the feel of Dart's hand on her waist, of his body against hers.

Surely this violence of physical response could not be one-sided. The very essence of a feeling so primitive was reciprocity. She looked up into his face, and knew from the expression of his eyes as they met hers that she was right.

When the orchestra stopped they both turned silently and went out on deck. Other couples had had the same impulse, and all over the scanty deck space there were murmurs and giggles from the shadows. They moved towards the taffrail and stumbled over Peggy and somebody sitting behind a stanchion, their arms and faces commingled.

Amanda made an involuntary sound of revulsion, and leaned against the rail watching the foaming wake flow back into darkness. Dart put his arm around her and also leaned against the rail. "I'm quite willing to neck too," he said, "if you want to. I'm sure we'd both enjoy it."

"Yes," she said after a moment. "But no. Cheap. Wasn't

there more than this"—she gestured towards the entwined couples behind them—"while we were dancing? It felt beautiful to me—deep—was I wrong?"

Dart glanced at her, removed his arm and lit a cigarette. "No. You weren't wrong. You're a sweet thing, Andy."

"That surprises you?" she said, smiling faintly. "You haven't liked me, have you? But I liked you from the minute I saw you. I don't know why exactly."

Or do I?—she thought. Because, though he isn't technically handsome, he's physically so attractive to me? Because he's different from any man I've met? Deeper, more mature? Because I can't dominate him? But you shouldn't analyse love. That's what it is, she thought. Love, but not like the other times I've felt it.

Dart, when he chose, had intuition. He said now, "You've been in love quite often?" And the edge of indulgent amusement had returned to his voice, cutting the deeper intimacy.

She sighed. "Oh, in a way. The sort of thing everybody does in their teens. And you?"

"Girls—women from time to time. Not love. 'One word is too often profaned for me to profane it,' I guess, and, anyway, I don't much like spilling emotions around. Untidy."

"Do you have any emotions to be untidy with?" she asked bitterly.

Dart laughed. "Yes," he said. "I think I do.—Come on, let's go in and sit some place, unless you'd like to try that German gallop that's going on in there."

They did not dance again, nor did they go out on deck, but they stayed together for the rest of the evening, drinking a little and talking of desultory things. Amanda was content with what she could get, and tried not to batter herself against the barrier he had again raised against her. And despite the barrier, there was an encouraging change in their relationship. She knew that he was aware of her now, and twice their eyes met in a long, searching look. This happened late in the evening, after the orchestra had vanished and several of the usual crowd had joined them in a corner of the lounge. One of the German students, a pimply youth in horn-rimmed spectacles, started a beery exposition of the virtues of Aryanism. The Williams junior was a Liberal and said so. He cited the names of famous Jews—what about Mendelssohn, Einstein, Freud? The German countered with contempt. Peggy, looking rumpled and self-conscious, reappeared alone from outside and jumped into the discussion. She brought up the mass psychology of social problems.

Amanda listened vaguely while the arguments ran along familiar tracks. Exceptional Jews but—the follies of racial mixture, and what about the Negro problem? asked the German, with that air of triumph Europeans reserve for this question.

Peggy replied hotly that all intelligent Americans were perfectly aware of it and, anyway, all this racial pro and con was a matter of half-baked emotion, not logic.

Whereupon the Williams junior turned to Dart, who had been sitting silently next to Amanda, and said, "What do you think about all this, Dartland? Which side are you on?"

Dart uncrossed his legs, and Amanda was aware that his body stiffened, but he spoke with amiable calm. "I don't know that my opinion on racial problems would be very objective, seeing that my mother is a half-breed Indian."

There was a moment of silence. The German's jaw dropped. They all stared at Dart. Amanda's heart jumped. So that's it— she thought—oh, poor darling . . . and she burst into speech.

"But, Dart, that's so different. *Indian* blood. That's romantic."

Dart lifted his eyebrows. "More romantic than Jewish or Negro blood?" he asked.

"But of course it is!" she cried. "People are proud of Indian blood. Think of all the people who boast about being descended from Pocahontas!"

"That's true," said Peggy judicially. "Though it's rather hard to analyse. It's the only racial mixture that's respectable in this country. Maybe because we subjugated them, and part of the 'Lo the poor Indian' complex, perhaps. Excuse me, Dart. But it's interesting."

"Yes, it is," Dart agreed placidly. "Particularly as it was not at all respectable fifty years ago when my grandfather, Tanosay, murdered my white great-grandparents and abducted my grandmother from a wagon train. Tanosay actually married her, Indian fashion, after a while, but he was an Apache, and neither the Apaches nor the Arizona whites considered the match in the least romantic." He glanced at Amanda. "My mother, Saba, was born to them, and was raised among the Apaches."

"Himmel!" said the German student continuing to gape at Dart. "Apaches! It's fantastic. One has read of them, naturally. So vicious—and how you say—ferocious."

"Quite," agreed Dart. "The 'tigers of the desert.'"

"But that's ridiculous!" cried Amanda. "There must have been lots of nice ones. Besides, the Americans did dreadful things to the Indians, too. Everybody admits that now."

She subsided, flushed and disgruntled, because Dart laughed. He patted her hand and said, "Bless you, my child," but he showed no special appreciation. And yet Amanda had sensed the faintest bravado in his presentation of his Indian ancestry. Had felt that he must have been hurt by it sometimes, and that he had brought out these lurid facts now for her—as a warning.

The German, and the Williams junior, who looked embarrassed, having now recaptured the additional fact about Dart's Andover background, both fell silent; but Peggy, whose clinical interest was aroused, continued to question eagerly.

"Please forgive me, Dart, but it's really such an unusual heritage. You weren't raised on a reservation, were you? What about your father?"

Amanda thought for a second that Dart, having proved whatever point he had set out to prove, was not going to answer, but relapse into his habitual reserve.

"I'd like to know, too," she said softly, looking up at him.

Dart nodded after a moment. She saw his long body relax.

"Okay," he said. "Brief biography. My father was Jonathan Dartland, born in Ipswich, Mass., educated at Harvard, became a history professor at Amherst. He was a bachelor, caught T.B., and was sent to the Arizona desert to get well. That was in 1901, when he was about forty. He took an adobe cottage on the desert, and hired an Indian girl from the Indian school to housekeep for him. That was Saba, my mother. They fell deeply in love and got married. I was born in 1905 and educated at home, by my father. When I was thirteen, Father began to fail, the old T.B. broke out, he wanted to see the East again before he died, and he wanted me to go to an eastern school. So the three of us came East. . . ." He paused a moment. "Father put me in Andover. They went back to Arizona and he died. After my graduation I went to the College of Mines at Tucson. And that's that."

From this bold recital Amanda garnered two things. In the

slight change of tone as he said, "They fell deeply in love," the only emotional phrase he had used. So he does believe in love, she thought, and he loved his parents. Especially Saba. She did not know how she knew this, but in the middle of Peggy's comments—"All that Yankee scholastic strain mixed with the primitive adds up to a definite plus factor, unless of course the environment——"

Amanda said, "I'd love to meet your mother, Dart. I've a feeling she's a wonderful woman."

Dart looked startled for the first time in her observation of him, and turning his shoulder on Peggy, he looked down into Amanda's frank and sympathetic eyes. "She is," he answered seriously. "The Indian half of her predominates. She doesn't see life as white women do. Lots of things they think important, she doesn't. She's very simple, and strong."

"Do you see her often?" asked Amanda timidly.

"No. She lives on the reservation with her people because she wants to. We don't need to see each other often, we understand each other. With Indians the silver cord is cut early and thoroughly."

Peggy, who had been trying to overhear, caught enough of this to branch forth into the Œdipus complex, but Dart got up and held his hand out to Amanda as he had on their first deck meeting. This time she clung to it, unashamed.

"Let's walk around the deck before we go to bed," Dart said to her, "or let's not go to bed at all. I've just realized how fast this tub's steaming towards New York."

"But you'll stay in New York awhile, won't you?" she asked very low as they stepped through the companionway. "I do hope you will."

Amanda, dozing on Dart's shoulder in the Ford, heard a dull thump before she saw a long, greyish shape outlined against the darkness of the wash.

"Dart!" she whispered.

He awoke, instantly alert, and simultaneously reached for the flashlight on the seat between them. In the circle of light two little green lamps glared at them, then disappeared.

"Bobcat," said Dart, switching off the light. "Too small for lion."

"Oh," she said. Eyes watching from the darkness. The

crouching wilderness filled with invisible life. But to Dart not invisible, not menacing. He understood it.

"Don't you wish you'd had your gun handy?" she asked, thinking of her father's delight in hunting expeditions to Canada and duck-shooting in Carolina.

"Why, no," said Dart, yawning. "I've got nothing against that bobcat. There's no point in killing except for food or because you're in danger. That's the law."

"What law?"

"The law of the wild," he said, chuckling again. "Live and let live."

"How about fishing?"

"For food only," he answered, and she knew that he was laughing at her, but under the laughter there was an inflexibility.

"I don't see what's wrong with hunting and fishing for sport, for just plain fun," she said crossly. "You're sometimes so set about things. So—so Spartan."

"My Indian blood, no doubt," said Dart lightly. "Let's see if the wash is down enough." He got out of the car with the flashlight, and when he came back he started the engine. "We'll just about make it."

The Ford slithered and chugged and pounded through the soft sand of the creek bed, the water lapped the running boards, but they pulled through and up the other side of the dip.

"Thank goodness, that's over!" cried Amanda. "On to Lode-stone." She nestled against him again, ashamed of her momentary irritation. "I find I keep thinking about bed in a shameless way. I hope our bed's decent. Not all straw and lumps like that horror at Lordsburg last night. Beds are so important."

"Oh, I guess it's okay," said Dart, watching ahead for the next wash. If *one* of them was running, likely there'd be more down here in the valley, though this he forbore to tell Amanda. "I didn't notice the bed. Was so damn glad to find us any kind of a shack to live in."

And so was I, she thought. And so damn glad when I finally got those letters from him. Their love had fruited and ripened by letter. After they landed he had lingered five days in New York before going back West. And he had, of course, met her family, Mrs. Lawrence and Jean and George. Each morning Dart had appeared at Mrs. Lawrence's cluttered little apartment on the edge of Beekman Place, and he had hardly concealed his impatience to get out of it again as quickly as possible, with Amanda.

Poor Mamma, thought Amanda with impatient affection—trying to crowd the treasures garnered through all the affluent years into a three-room walk-up. Most of the contents of the big Greenwich home had had to be sold, of course, but Mrs. Lawrence had clung to the Chippendales and Bouguereaus, the Chinese teakwood tabourets, and the Oriental rugs, and particularly the walnut bedroom suite which she had always shared with her husband.

Dart, Amanda had soon realized, was extraordinarily indifferent to possessions. Indifferent to many things which she had accepted as the natural fabric of life, like shopping and fine restaurants and theatres. During those days in New York they walked miles together. Dart enjoyed walking, and so—after discarding her high heels for a pair of Oxfords—did Amanda, happy to be with him, exploring Central Park and the East River, Chinatown or the Battery, eating at any time or place when they felt hungry, and talking a lot. There was love between them, but little love-making. Only twice during those five days did Dart kiss her, and she, though puzzled and finally a little frightened, had understood that in him reserve and a great strength of passion would permit of no casual intimacies. And she had been—almost—content to wait.

She had suffered through a bitter week after he left for the West, with no word from him except a non-committal postcard received from Chicago.

On the seventh evening after Dart's leaving, she had been in despair, and Mrs. Lawrence, who had been watching and worrying all week, finally spoke. "Andy darling, PLEASE stop moping. Get dressed and go to the Merrill's dance with Tim. . . . He wants you to so much. . . . Dart's an interesting young man, but he isn't worth all this. . . ." There was much more delivered in Mrs. Lawrence's sweet, incisive voice. The voice of common sense and convention. She ran down at last, sighed, and glanced at her daughter. She patted her bobbed, still-brownish hair nervously and added, "Besides all that, too. . . . Well . . ."

"And besides all that," said Amanda, "he hasn't actually asked me to marry him."

"You're so pretty, dear," said Mrs. Lawrence quickly. "You

ought to be having lots of gaiety and fun. If only that horrible crash . . . and when I see those Merrills going on the same, not scratched—just because Roy Merrill developed some sort of a sixth sense or something in September of twenty-nine and got out of the market, while poor Daddy . . ." She shut her eyes, then shook her head. "There's no use going back over things, but when I see the Merrills giving a dance like this at the Waldorf . . ." She broke off and listened to the buzzer in the hall outside. "I guess that's Tim now, dear. Please be nice to him."

Amanda had always been nice to Tim and she was still very fond of him. He was a gay and personable young man in his evening clothes, a white carnation winking in his buttonhole, his blond hair gleaming like a helmet above his narrow, pinkish face. But he had gone out of focus for her, and there was no gaiety in her to respond to his, nor any deeper chord of answer for the question in his eyes. She acceded at last to the combined urgings of her mother and Tim, and went off dispiritedly to dress. It was while she was pinning on the lavish orchid corsage Tim had brought her that the phone rang. Long distance from Globe, Arizona. And Dart's voice, amidst the crackles and fading of the connection, said, "Andy—jobs are mighty scarce out here now, but I think I've got one lined up as mine foreman. Shamrock Mine at Lodestone, fifty miles from here, in the Dripping Spring Mountains. Will you marry me?"

"Yes," said Amanda after a second of silence. Her hand shook on the receiver, and her mother and Tim watched her with identical expressions of dismay as she added, on a breaking quaver, "Did you have any doubts that I would?"

His deep voice answered slowly through the wire, "I wasn't sure. I can't offer you much, my dear. Lodestone's nothing but a tough mining camp. I don't know if you can be happy."

"I can," she said. "If you really want me."

"I want you." Then he added, with his usual bluntness, "I had to get back here to be certain. This is my country. I see clear here, but I don't know if you can."

"I'll chance it," she said.

So she had not gone to the ball with Tim, after all. She had apologized abjectly, and cried a little at the hurt bewilderment in his eyes.

"I can't, Timmy. I know I'm a beast, but I want to be alone."

"My God!" said Tim. "You just going to sit here and moon

over that guy? He's in *Arizona*, for Pete's sake. Honey, you can still dance, can't you—even if you are"—he swallowed and flushed—"engaged?"

"I know," she had said gently. "But I don't *want* to go. Forgive me. You'll have fun, anyway. You always do."

And he had, apparently, for she heard later that Tim and his special crowd had closed the Stork Club and then taken a ferry ride to breakfast in Staten Island.

During the months before Dart came back East for the wedding, she lived on his letters. They were brief and almost devoid of the endearments which had sprinkled her other love-letters, but there emerged from them, nevertheless, a strength and assurance that made her happy. Once only he mentioned his mother. "I went to see Saba yesterday at San Carlos and told her about you. She was glad I had found a woman I want at last. She seems not very well. I tried to persuade her to go to the Agency doctor there, but she won't, I'm afraid." Upon reading that, Amanda had thought—Oh, poor thing, I'll soon fix that when I meet her; I can persuade her. And yet today, as they had come through part of the reservation, Dart had checked her suggestion that they call on his mother with a brief, "No. Not now."

Dart came East after Christmas, and they were married on New Year's Day in Greenwich, Connecticut, at the Walker home.

Mrs. Lawrence, after some weeks of dismay, had achieved resignation, and put her considerable efficiency into giving Amanda the best possible wedding. Over Amanda's vehement protests she sold the Chippendales and a gold-mesh evening bag which dated from her own honeymoon in Paris. George Walker, badgered by Jean, finally permitted the use of his Greenwich house for the wedding. George was careful of his possessions and of his standing in the community, and he found his sister-in-law's choice of a husband unpleasantly bizarre. During one of the pre-wedding family conferences he was moved to express his opinion.

"Good Lord, Amanda, if you've got to marry a western miner who's part Indian, why couldn't you pick one of the Oklahoma Osage boys with an oil-well, at least? This guy'll never make a nickel. No ambition."

"I don't mind being poor," said Amanda, smiling and politely

sipping George's bathtub-gin Martini. Nothing from the outside affected her during this time. . . . She dwelt in a golden
secret room with her love.

"You don't know a damn thing about it," snapped George.
"You've never been poor—yet."

Neither have you, thought Amanda, looking around the
Walker's pine-panelled living-room.

"We don't want the papers to get hold of this Indian thing,"
said George, pouring himself another Martini. "People'd think
it very queer."

"They did get hold of it once," said Mrs. Lawrence, smiling.
"Here's a letter I just got from Aunt Amanda."

"You told her about Dartland!" exclaimed George, frowning.

"Of course. I asked her to the wedding—with slightly venal
motives, I admit. She ought to do something handsome for
Andy, after we inflicted that name on the poor baby."

Jean had been upstairs reading Sally Lou a bedtime story; she
entered the living-room in time for her mother's speech. "Aunt
Amanda never has crashed through yet," she said, pouring herself a cocktail. "I wouldn't count on it. George, you look cross.
What are you worrying about now? I said we'd take care of all
the wedding arrangements. You won't have to bother." Jean
was a brisk and handsome young matron, who ran her house without effort, played excellent bridge and golf, and never neglected
her duties towards her husband and child. Only Amanda suspected that she was sometimes devastatingly bored.

"Here's the letter—" said Mrs. Lawrence, and began to read
from the sharp spidery writing. ". . . I found your news about
little Amanda most interesting. I had some acquaintance with
Professor Dartland years ago when he was teaching at Amherst
College, and was later dismayed, as were all his friends, by his
extraordinary marriage. I met the woman once when he brought
her East just before the war. Some of the ladies on Beacon Hill
'took her up'—as a novelty, I dare say. Mrs. Ransome gave a
reception for her. I'm bound to admit that there was nothing
outré about Mrs. Dartland, no feathers or strange costume. She
wore a plain black dress. She was tall and very quiet. We all
urged her to give a little talk about her strange life and Indian
customs, but she would not.

"She did not seem to enjoy the party, and as I remember they
left very early, which I thought most ungracious. I enclose a

clipping from the *Transcript* about her. I do not consider the Dartland boy a *suitable match* for Amanda (though I have no expectation that my opinion will be heeded), but I'm bound to admit that on his father's side the background is impeccable. The Dartlands came over with the Winthrop fleet in 1630. I thank you for your invitation to the wedding, but my age and sciatica make it quite impossible for me to leave Boston."

Mrs. Lawrence folded the letter and there was a silence.

"Well," said Jean, "that's that. No dice. No present either, I guess. Let's see the clipping, Mother."

Mrs. Lawrence extracted a yellowed column of newscript. It was headed "Indian Princess visits Boston." There followed a highly sentimental account of Professor Dartland's marriage to a tender-hearted Indian princess called Saba, who had nursed him devotedly and saved him from the perils of the desert. Saba, the paper said, was the daughter of a great Apache king, who had in his turn rescued a little white girl from his savage retainers, whereupon love had shown him the error of his evil ways, so he had married her and become a devout convert to Christianity. Saba was described as being "quite dainty in her beaded buckskin costume, and lisping in charming broken English, her wide eyes dazzled by the wonders of civilization." The whole flight of fancy was characterized in the last paragraph as a "touching romance linking blue-bloods of the white and red races."

"Thus producing a revolting shade of purple," cried Amanda violently. "How Dart must have hated all that. And poor Mrs. Dartland."

"Well, I don't know . . ." said George thoughtfully. "It makes it sound better, though thank heaven there's no question of Dartland's mother coming to the wedding. But if anyone asks questions, we can show them that clipping."

"We will not," cried Amanda. "It's a sickening mess of sticky lies. It makes Saba sound like a half-witted freak. Tanosay, her father, wasn't any king; he was one of many chiefs, he didn't do any rescuing, and he never was converted to Christianity. Dart's told me that much."

"So much the worse, then," said George. "But I see no reason for not putting the best foot forward. I'm not intolerant, I believe."

"Oh, well—stop fussing, old boy," said Jean rising. "It'll be a very small wedding. Andy seems to love him, so that's that. And Dart's very nice."

Amanda looked quickly at her sister and then at George. Had there been a note of unconscious envy in Jean's voice?

The Ford bumped around the corner of a cliff, and Amanda opened her eyes and stretched her cramped legs.

"There's the Gila, down there," said Dart, and his voice expressed an affectionate satisfaction which surprised her, though she was later to find how personal and beloved were the few Arizona rivers.

"Where?" she asked, craning over him to see nothing but a drop of black canyon on the left. "I guess I was asleep. I was dreaming about our wedding."

"Lot of speculative faces and too much champagne," said Dart laughing, and pushing into low for the steep climb through the canyon. "Thank God, it's over."

"Didn't you get any exalted moments out of it at all?" she asked after a moment. "How about our nuptial vows?"

"The vows are fine, but I don't much like labelling my feelings in public. Mating is a private business. . . . Here's the Lodestone turn-off." He threw the flivver into reverse, backed to the edge of the cliff, then turned right, apparently into the mountain.

At once the jiggling to which she had become accustomed turned into bounces. The dirt road, fortunately dry, narrowed to the width of a car and a half, and pointed straight up into the sky. Amanda bit her lip and clung to the top of the car door. "Is this the only road to Lodestone?" she asked after several tense moments.

"Sure," said Dart. "The ore trucks make it every day, unless it's wet."

"What happens if you meet another car?"

"Oh, somebody backs up to a turn-out. You'll get used to the mountains."

"Yes, of course." Only twelve miles of this, she thought, why, that's nothing—and a hundred more back of this since we've seen a town, added a sharp little voice in her head. It certainly would be good to get there, to get to Lodestone. After all, six hundred people lived there. There would be lights and houses and shops, a self-contained little island in the mountains. There

was even a hospital and a school and a Catholic chapel, Dart had
told her. These things made a nucleus of civilization. She had,
in New York, been almost disappointed to hear of them, detract-
ing as they did from the thrill of pioneering. A long twelve
miles, with the Lizzie in low most of the time, though, and
around each corner she strained her eyes to peer ahead for the
lights of Lodestone.

But when they rounded the last curve and the little canyon
widened a trifle, and Dart said, "There she is," she saw no
lights yet. She saw the dim shapes of little shacks, higgledy-
piggledy in the gloom of the hillside. Some of them seemed to be
made of adobe and some of wood. Their corrugated-iron roofs
gleamed dully in the car lights, then flattened into darkness and
silence.

"Is this all?" she whispered. "They look so deserted."

"Some of them are," said Dart; "though the real ghost town's
up the canyon towards the mine. But we'll run down Creek
Street, so you can get the lay of the place. It straggles, you
know; no room in the gulch for neat city planning."

Amanda was silent as Dart drove slowly down the main street.
Here there were a dozen buildings, slightly larger than the
cabins they had passed, but exhibiting the same air of dilapidated impermanence. There was one two-story building which
said, "Miners' Union Hall" in black letters across the front of a
false gable; next to this a smaller frame box labelled, "Pottner's
General Store," then a dimly lit saloon, unlabelled in deference
to Prohibition, but from the back room there came the only
sounds in Lodestone: men's voices uplifted in argument, the
ping of slot machines, and the feeble jangle of a piano playing
"The Sheik." Then another string of dark fronts and another
saloon, whereupon the road ended in the mountain-side and a
thicket of cholla cactus.

"Thriving metropolis," said Amanda, trying to laugh. "I
guess I won't get lost. And where is our particular mansion?"

"Up the mine road a bit—we'll take a short cut through
Back Lane." Dart turned the car, and they jounced over some
well-worn ruts on the desert floor, then climbed a sharp rise.
"This lane's not respectable, by the way," said Dart, laughing
suddenly. "Don't ever walk through it alone, you might get con-
taminated."

"Why?" she said, staring at four tiny cabins set in a prim row like toy houses; above each miniature doorway there hung a red bulb.

"Cribs," said Dart. "Where the ladies of the town take care of the miners' needs."

She stared at the four little cabins with the fascinated interest harlotry arouses in the purest female breast and, momentarily diverted from her growing dismay, she said, "But their lights are all dark, too."

Dart shrugged. "Miners mostly don't have any money except on pay-nights." The Ford turned west and climbed a block. He waved his hand towards another huddle of greyish shapes. "Bosses' Row—town society lives in these. That bigger one on the corner is the Mabletts'—mine superintendent."

She registered a change in his voice as he mentioned this name, but her entire intelligence was marshalled to combat an engulfing bleakness. It was not precisely because the town and these "best houses" were so small and starkly unpainted, dwarfed, not only by the mountain wall behind them, but even by the giant saguaro cacti which towered above them like menacing fingers pointing to the blacker sky.

It was more of a loneliness, a forlorn helplessness to withstand the vast impersonality about her. Lodestone, from which she had hoped so much, had not withstood. This huddle of puny shacks and silence did not constitute even a toehold against the encroachments of the alien force. I'm too tired, she thought, and hungry. This terror, this loneliness, is physical. Things always look worse at night.

"Buck up, Andy," Dart said, putting his hand on her knee. "You'll get used to it."

"Yes. Yes," she said, comforted at once, for how could she be lonely when she had Dart, who understood sometimes when you least expected it.

"The place was much bigger, of course, during the boom before 1900," he went on half apologetically; "up the road another half a mile there's lots of big houses still, all falling to pieces. That's the ghost town where Madame Cunningham lives in her thirty-room mansion."

"Oh?" said Amanda.

"I wrote you about her. She's been a good friend to me. Strange old lady, used to be a Creole singer. Her husband, Red Bill Cunningham, struck it rich here, located this mine. He built her a palace in the wilderness. She won't leave it. She's not really so strange though," he added thoughtfully. "She has vision."

Amanda sighed. "Dart, dear—aren't we nearly to our place?"

"Yes. Right beyond the Company hospital there."

She looked at the Company hospital, and saw a two-story, unpainted six-room house, with a light in an unshaded downstairs window. A man was sitting by the window in an arm-chair. His head was thrown back and he seemed to be asleep.

"That's the doctor. Hugh Slater. Probably drunk," said Dart indifferently. "He often is. But a swell guy when he's sober."

"That's nice," said Amanda. She saw the little square wooden shanty with a slanting stovepipe that was the only dwelling beyond the hospital, and prayed that it wasn't theirs. Dart stopped the car in front of the shanty and opened the car door.

"You're supposed to"—she said—"carry the bride over the doorstep——" She heard her voice rise high and shut her mouth tight. Dart grinned, picked her up, and carried her up the path. He kicked open the door and set her down on a linoleum-covered floor. Then he lit a kerosene lamp. "Electricity doesn't run past the hospital yet, but it's a strong, well-built little shack; only decent one I could find for the money. Someday I hope we can get some plumbing in."

"There isn't any plumbing?" she asked in a small careful voice.

"Oh, there's a sink with a hand pump in the kitchen, but I'm afraid there's also an outhouse in the back." He looked at her ruefully.

"That's all right," she said. "I've used those camping in Maine. I hope it has a crescent in the door." She walked very slowly around the two rooms, while Dart held the lamp. In the kitchen there was an iron sink, a kerosene two-burner stove, and a chipped enamel table. In the other room there was a bureau, a red overstuffed rocker with a tattered antimacassar, an enamel chair from which the paint had peeled in leprous scars, a round table, and the bed. The bedstead was of brass, with one knob missing from the headboard. The mattress lay exposed in all its nakedness of lumps and stained ticking.

Amanda sat down on the edge of the bed and looked at Dart. He put the lamp on the table and sat beside her. "It does look pretty bad. I'm sorry." He leaned over and kissed her on the mouth.

She caught her breath and gave him a wan smile. She was thinking of the embroidered table linens her mother had given her, of the three pairs of monogrammed sheets Mrs. Lawrence had insisted on including in the trousseau. Suddenly she stiffened, peering at the walls by the flickering light of the lamp. "What are those, Dart?" she cried; "those pictures on the walls? It looks like a girl with bloomers, and a woman in corsets."

Dart examined the wall. He came and sat beside her again. "I'm afraid, my child, that our house is papered with pages from the Sears Roebuck catalogue."

She stared at his rueful face, then at the walls again, then she fell over on the bed, shaking with laughter. "It's all right, darling——" she choked. "It'll be all right tomorrow, we'll transform the place. It just needs paint, and some new furniture . . . I know."

Dart looked down at the flushed face and wet eyes under the childish tousle of short gold hair, and neither his love nor his keen sense of justice prevented a flash of misgiving. So she was, after all, disappointed in Lodestone and in the home he had provided for her; she did not know how scarce was any decent housing in a mining camp, where uncertainty and impermanence pervaded every act and thought. She had no appreciation of the importance of his job, or his luck in finding one so challenging now when most of the mines were shutting down. She did not know that no matter how much one does oneself, paint and furniture still cost money, and that a salary of $160 a month will not cover extras, when there is a loan to be repaid and living costs are so high in isolated mining towns.

He had told her these things, and she had agreed with the enthusiastic charm which was one of her greatest attractions, but she did not know. She would learn, of course. He sighed, regretting that a creature so delightfully compounded of emotion and romantic illusions must be tethered. The word "tethered" echoed unpleasantly in his mind. He put his arms around her, holding her close to him. Her little hysteria had passed and they were both silent, pressed against each other for a long moment. Then he went back to the car to start the hauling in of their luggage.

CHAPTER TWO

AMANDA awoke to crisp sunlight, the chill of the mountain air, and a feeling of buoyancy which soon evaporated.

She had expected Dart to prolong his vacation another day so as to help her with the heaviest unpacking, and explain to her the idiosyncrasies of the hand pump and kerosene stove.

Dart, however, was dressed and ready to leave when she awoke at seven He had made coffee, and he stood by the bed with a cup in his hand, looking down at her. "Good-bye," he said gently. "Take it easy today, I'll be down off the hill by six. Never mind about fixing supper, we can get something at Mrs. Zuckowski's hotel. Here's ten bucks for supplies. You remember I showed you the General Store in Creek Street?"

"I guess so," she murmured, reaching her arms up around his neck and pulling him down to her. "But surely you don't have to go to the mine today; they can manage without you one more day."

"I hope not," said Dart, kissing her warm, sleepy mouth, then straightening. "I fear I'm not indispensable, but there was plenty of trouble when I left, and I think I can deal with it better than the shift boss who's been pinch-hitting for me."

"Trouble? What kind of trouble?"

"Discontented men, bad timbering, too much water seepage." He grinned at her expression, and put the coffee cup down on the dusty table. Normal mining troubles, my child, and fun to lick 'em. . . . By the way, if Mrs. Mablett turns up, don't let her get your goat; she's the mine superintendent's wife, and Mablett hates my guts."

"Why?" asked Amanda, sitting up and staring at him.

"Because we don't see eye to eye on anything." Dart frowned and started buttoning his battered leather jacket, but seeing her worried eyes, he reluctantly explained further. "He's lousing up the mine and the men too, and poor old Tyson's not strong enough to stop him."

Tyson's was the only name Amanda knew in Lodestone.

Alexander Tyson, general manager of the Shamrock Mine, was an elderly widower who lived alone near the mine and suffered from a heart condition, but whose reputation, gained from forty years of mining engineering, had been so outstanding that Amanda had actually heard him mentioned by one of George and Jean's Greenwich friends. It was also Mr. Tyson who had lent Dart two hundred dollars for his trip East to marry her.

"Could Mr. Mablett fire you?" she asked nervously.

"Not without Tyson's okay. He would if he could, I dare say. 'Bye, Andy love, I've got to hurry. See you tonight."

Amanda jumped out of bed, and in one of her bridal night-gowns of rose crêpe de Chine and Chantilly lace, she peered through the dirty window, watching Dart get into the car. It was then that she realized what had puzzled her about his appearance. He was dressed to go underground, knowing that he would not have time to change today before the shift began. He was wearing stained blue jeans and short rubber boots. The ancient leather jacket which he would discard in the mine had matted into oily patches. He looked taller than ever and more boyish, his dark wavy hair glistening with an almost reddish cast in the bright sun. She was conscious of slight shock, for he did not look like the Dart she knew, he looked like a hired man her family had employed one summer in Vermont when they had thought farming might be fun.

She watched while the Lizzie balked as usual, then coughed, and finally bumped off up the dirt road towards the mine three miles away.

He forgot to wave, she thought.

She looked across and up the dry, stony creek bed towards a low red-brown mountain tufted with the dark green of creosote bush, prickly pear, and cholla. The mountain had a limestone cap, faintly rosy under the slanting rays of the sun. I suppose that's pretty, she thought, but there was no thrill of awareness. The mountain cast a shadow black as a cave across the canyon, and the saguaros towering above the pebbly desert floor seemed to her as hostile and distorted as they had by night.

She turned back into the cluttered cabin. She looked at the rumpled, lumpy bed. So close they had been there together in each other's arms last night, and yet this morning he had hardly been aware of her, had shut her off into a separate compartment, not thinking that she might be appalled by unfamiliar chores, by his totally unexpected hints of "trouble," by people she had never heard of—by homesickness.

Amanda sat down on the bed and stared at the fitted leather dressing-case Mrs. Lawrence had given her. "I know, darling, it's an extravagance, but I want you to have it." The dressing-case lay on the linoleum floor, its open cover resting on a rough two by-four riser. The gilt and tortoise-shell fittings sparkled from their blue satin pockets. She looked at the crystal bottle which her mother had so carefully filled, drop by drop, with Chanel No. 5 toilet water for her, and burst into tears.

After ten minutes her sense of proportion began to return, and because certain truths which fitted her repentant heart had been much better formulated by others, quotations gleaned from years of English classes flitted more or less appropriately through her mind.

> *Man's love is of man's life a thing apart;*
> *'Tis woman's whole existence.*

Byron . . . always smugly patronizing about women, but maybe he had something there. "Men must work and women must weep. . . ." Who said that? But it doesn't matter. Stop wallowing Amanda. She got off the bed, knotted a blue silk négligé firmly around her waist, and carried Dart's coffee cup back to the kitchen. Think of the pioneer mothers, she said to herself. You wanted to pioneer. Her spirits recovered after a cup of Dart's leftover coffee and some dry bread. She sat down and made a list of supplies to be bought, feeling matronly and efficient. The mess in the cabin must wait, *had* to wait until she got soap powder and—and—ammonia, she thought, trying to remember what her mother's cleaning women had used.

Anxious to make a good impression on Lodestone, she dressed herself in a flecked mauve heather wool suit and a pink cashmere pullover, both products of the trip to Scotland last summer, and sallied forth on to the road. It was dusty and hard walking on the myriads of small stones, in her thin Oxfords. And I thought there'd be sidewalks, she thought, laughing at herself.

As she passed the Company hospital she examined it with determined indulgence. What if it was only a rickety unpainted cottage reminding her of shacks along the railroad tracks outside of New Haven? They were lucky to have a "hospital" at all. And there were always the big towns, Phœnix or Tucson, for anything serious, of course. Only seven hours' drive to Tucson, Dart said, not much more to Phœnix. As she started on past the hospital, the door opened, and a man came down the two wooden steps. He sauntered up to her. "Hello," he said, without enthusiasm, "I suppose you're Dartland's bride—I'm Hugh Slater."

"The doctor?" she asked uncertainly, her eager smile dying as it met no response. His small, greenish eyes stared at her with disapproval. He was a stocky man in his late thirties—only an inch or two taller than Amanda. From his sandy hair, sharply receding at the temples, to his blunt-toed leather boots, he gave an impression of squareness. He wore a small clipped moustache, like an English subaltern, and it looked like dry straw against his freckled skin.

"Well, I've got a degree . . ." he said sourly, answering her question. "What I actually am here is a goddam combine of mid-wife, bonesetter, and veterinarian." He shrugged his heavy shoulders and lit himself a cigarette without offering her one. As he did this she noticed his hands: square, freckled, and covered with coppery hairs. They shook with a faint tremor.

Hangover! she thought, enlightened. Of course. And she smiled vaguely, preparing to walk on.

"Lodestone society'll be charmed by all that lipstick and those bloody finger-nails . . ." said Hugh. "Just like Big Ruby's in Number Three crib."

Crib? thought Amanda, then she remembered the four little cabins with the red lamps. She raised her eyebrows, and then she laughed. "You can't be true," she said. "I've read you in a hundred stories, the surly woman-hater, the embittered doctor, drowning his troubles in bad temper and drink. Underneath there beats a heart of gold." She saluted him and walked on.

Hugh opened his mouth and shut it again, staring after her.

Amanda continued down the road towards Pottner's Store, where she encountered more hostilities so foreign to her experience that she had trouble in recognizing them.

Her shopping expedition was unsatisfactory for several reasons. In the General Store, she was at once confused by the absence of brand names she knew, the scarcity of fresh vegetables, and any meat but pork, uncertain what to buy and appalled by the high prices. The ten dollars, it soon developed, would cover only the dullest staples. And in all innocence she offended Mrs. Pottner, the owner, who was serving behind the counter in a white butcher's apron. Amanda responded pleasantly to Mrs. Pottner's greeting, smiled at jocular remarks about newly weds, but she treated the lady with no more warmth or intimacy than she would have one of the clerks in the corner grocery at home. Pearl Pottner, however, was one of Lodestone's social arbiters and instantly resentful. It was some time before Amanda came to understand, first, the democracy of a western mining camp and, second, the wariness which the label "New Yorker" aroused in the female bosoms. Amanda, intent on her difficult purchases, did not notice the disappearance of Mrs. Pottner's smiles, nor guessed that her exclamation, "Heavens, I had no idea butter would be so dreadfully expensive," grated on her hearer in its entirety. The clipped eastern voice, the "lah-di-dah" choice of words, the complete unconsciousness of Mrs. Pottner as a person, above all the implied criticism induced a mottled purple to spread across Pearl's fat face.

"My butter's a fair price," she snapped, closing the little butter jar with a thud. "MOST folk are pleased I handle it at all, what with having to truck it in myself from Tucson when the road's open. MOST folk don't expect luxuries, and are pleased when they find 'em."

"Oh," said Amanda, "I'm sorry, I didn't mean . . . I'm not much of a housewife . . . in fact," she added with her quick and lovely smile, "I'm not any kind of a housewife at all, I'm just beginning to realize."

Pearl thawed only a trifle. "You'll learn——" she said. "We all have to." But not with painted finger-nails and baby-pink sweaters and gold wrist-watches, she added to herself, much as Hugh had predicted. Pearl had a spinster daughter, Pearline, who gave music lessons in Globe, and the thought of that daughter's pinched face and nervous eyes peering through thick lenses at an unresponsive world added maternal jealousy to the counts against Amanda.

Unconscious of having offended, but appalled at the task ahead of her, Amanda walked home, negligently accompanied by little Bobby Pottner to help carry her parcels. The noon sun poured liquid fire from a cloudless sky, and her body inside the

woollens which had been so comforting this morning now
dripped and itched. She thought with passionate longing of a
cool, tiled shower-bath.

Bobby flung his parcels on the kitchen table, accepted the
dime she fished from her nearly empty change purse, then he
stared around at the two-room shack. "Jeez——" he said
dispassionately, "what a mess. You goin' to live here like
this?"

"Not like this, naturally!" she snapped with a sharpness not
meant for him. "But I've got to have some help. Bobby, could
you stay and help me for a while? I'll be glad to pay you. . . ."
She paused, remembering the thirty-five cents remaining in her
purse, but Dart would give her more tonight when he understood. "I'll pay you a quarter."

Bobby's alert face grew blank, then cleared. "Two bits," he
translated for her. "Nope. No soap. Mom'll give me hell effen I
don't git right back to the store." He turned to go, but he
thought Amanda very pretty, and his eleven-year-old heart was
not lacking in chivalry, so he paused on the doorstep. "I don't
know who could help you," he said, "except mebbe one of the
crib girls. They don't do nothin' all day."

The crib girls. Amanda, despite her sophistication and college
background of long theoretical discussions of sex, blushed a
vivid red. She perceived, however, that to Bobby the crib girls
were a sociological fact, no more interesting than the miners,
tradespeople, or any other segment of Lodestone.

"Well, thank you," she said, smiling. "Maybe—I'll see."

Bobby departed down the street whistling "Hallelujah, I'm a
bum," and pausing at the corner past the hospital to hurl his
jack-knife at the giant seven-branched saguaro cactus. The knife
rebounded and fell in the dust. Bobby picked it up, a daily ritual
performed, and continued around the corner. Amanda turned
back into her shack, set her jaw, and prepared to cope with the
mess. She removed the woollen suit and sweater, and her satin
and lace trousseau slip. She hunted through her suitcases until
she found one cotton dress with short sleeves. Nobody at home
had dreamed that it would be hot like this in January. The
dress was a mass of wrinkles. Iron—she thought. Have to buy
one. Then how did you heat it? She stared at the little kerosene
stove. Courage, my girl, one thing at a time. *Petit à petit,
l'oiseau fait son nid*—"It's dogged as does it." My education will

be useful for providing cheering maxims, if nothing else. She picked up the broom and began to sweep.

After his encounter with Amanda that morning, Hugh Slater had stood for a moment watching her swing off towards town. Her shoulders were held high, her beautiful legs flashing in nude silk, her short golden hair blowing in the desert wind. Maybe she's not so dumb at that, he thought, without much interest. The mud-black depression which always accompanied emergence from the periodic binges settled down on him again. He flung the cigarette at a passing tomcat and re-entered the hospital.

The three ground-floor rooms were deserted, office hours wouldn't start until afternoon. From the second floor there came the methodical groans of a woman in labour, one of the Mex women. Usually they didn't bother with the hospital, but she lived with a mid-European miner she was terrified of, and when her pains started she'd run here for refuge. A good thing, too, Hugh thought with the corner of his mind which nothing, not even liquor, quite obscured. She's going to have a breech. He went to the dispensary and mixed himself a stiff bromide, at the same time glancing at his wrist-watch. The groans were still ten minutes apart; anyway, Maria was with her. Maria. . . . God, he thought, what a nurse! Miss What's-her-name, back at the Washington General, should have tried her infallible training methods on *this* one.

He lit another cigarette, slumped down in the big chair in the waiting-room, put his feet up on the rattan couch, and yelled for Maria. After the usual interval, in which Maria adjusted herself to any new idea, he heard her scuffling down the wooden stairs in her huaraches. She appeared in the doorway wearing her usual look of sulky dishevelment. The stained white uniform had lost a button and been fastened together with a bent hairpin. The gap showed a patch of brown breast. The winged nurse's cap perched rootless on top of Maria's enormous bun of glossy blue-black hair. Maria was very proud of her uniform, and wore it off duty whenever she dared. It was a badge of aristocracy, and set her far above the crib girls, to whose number she had once belonged until Hugh, desperate for help and finding her moderately seductive, sent her to Phœnix for a three months' course in practical nursing. Maria was a half-breed, half Mexican, half Pima Indian, and the mingling had proved æsthetically successful. She was small and skinny, but with beautiful breasts, and straight bronze features like Gauguin's Polynesian girls.

"Yes?" she said to Hugh. "You call?—You not drunk no more?" she added, surveying him with mild surprise. "You want I fix some eggs, mebbe?" Her brown hands were adorned with several flashing rings from the five-and-dime store in Globe. She put her hands on her hips and, arms akimbo, leaned against the door-jamb, waiting patiently.

Look at her, thought Hugh, a very caricature of a nurse. And I'm a very caricature of a doctor, according to Dartland's wench. Yes . . . well . . .

He scowled furiously at Maria. "Stand up straight, can't you, and sew a button on that thing you're wearing. No, I'll fix my own eggs, later. I want you to boil up my instruments, the ones from the delivery kit."

Maria stood up a fraction straighter and raised her eyebrows.

"De-livery kit," she repeated, and stared around the waiting-room. Her limpid eyes returned to Hugh.

"Oh, Christ!" he said through his teeth. "I've showed you a hundred times. The black bag in the dispensary. It's labelled 'Delivery Kit.' You *can* read, can't you?"

"Sure I can. You know it." She thrust her underlip out, her pride hurt.

"Then take out all the instruments and boil them for twenty minutes in the white enamel pot. *Now!*" he shouted. "And leave them in the pot. *Don't* touch them afterwards. Then come up to me and the patient."

"Sure," said Maria. Suddenly she ran across the room and rubbed her cheek against Hugh's. "You no want to make love some more? You better have another drink."

"Oh, for God's sake——" He jerked his head away and shoved her violently. Her cap fell off and she picked it up, holding it tight against her breast like a baby. Then she hunched her thin shoulders and walked towards the kitchen.

Hugh went upstairs to the labouring woman. She gave him a look of animal terror and moaned, shutting her eyes.

"You're okay," said Hugh, sitting down by the iron cot. "Pretty soon I'm going to put you to sleep." Where's that damn rubber sheet? he thought, and saw it lying crumpled by the window. He made a noise in his throat, picked it up and smoothed it under the woman's haunches. So much for Lister, Semmelweiss, etc., he thought, "scrupulous antisepsis in the Delivery Room—Doctor Slater's certainly a stickler for that, Miss Burns—a regular martinet."

His head throbbed, and he leaned it back against the white-washed plank wall. That Dartland girl's maybe brighter than she looks, he thought morosely. But you wouldn't think a guy like Dart'd fall for a smooth little eastern job with a Park Avenue accent. She won't stick it two months in Lodestone. Then she'll go high-tailing it off for greener pastures. Like Viola. Funny—still pain at the thought of Viola. That's one from the books too, isn't it, my dear? Besides the heart of gold, the surly, embittered, frustrated doctor has a broken heart. Broken golden heart.

He looked down at the woman on the bed. The contractions were getting stronger, but not ready to put her under yet. A tiny louse ran out from her matted sticky hair and scuttled across the pillow. Hugh pinched it between thumb and forefinger and dropped it on the floor. He shouted down to Maria to hurry with the instruments, received in return a vague "Pronto, pronto." He lit another cigarette and sat down again, and began to think quite dispassionately about himself.

Hugh Slater, born thirty-eight years ago into a pretty good Virginia family. Wanted to be a surgeon ever since he could remember. Why? Sensitive hands—mechanical ability—flair for drama—sublimated sadism they'd call it nowadays, no doubt. But was there more than that once? Had there been a period of high dedication, the thrill of alleviating suffering? A thrill, even, out of the old Hippocratic oath? Anyway, that thrill hadn't carried through the war. France, 1917–1919, and an undedicated shambles of gas and gangrene and mutilations and expendable human life. He had returned to Johns Hopkins for his diploma. Internship next year at the Washington General, going to specialize in surgery, poor as Job, but it didn't matter—until Viola turned up one day as a patient in the west ward. She had had an appendectomy, and even as she struggled damply out of the ether, her extraordinary beauty was little dimmed. She had soft hair, with auburn lights in it, and it curled all around her heart-shaped face. Really heart-shaped, because a widow's peak cleft the white forehead. The face was still childish in its porcelain skin and delicacy of bone, but her eyes were woman's eyes, large and slumberous and aware, golden-hazel between curling black lashes. Viola had never for a moment doubted her destiny, and even then, besotted with love as he was, Hugh had wondered that she could envision marriage with him instead of any one of her other innumerable suitors. Perhaps she had really loved him for a while, certainly the first months of their marriage had been ecstatic. But he had seen so little of her, enslaved as he was by the hospital, and their poverty had been grinding. She had not complained, that was not her way. But he later discovered she had been preparing herself all the time, taking secret lessons from an infatuated drama teacher, and sending her photographs to the various studios. He had felt the change in her before he knew any cause except their ghastly poverty. It had frightened him into the first mistake.

He had done some minor surgery for a Greek restaurant owner in the latter's home, and accepted a fat fee for it. Fortunately, the head surgeon who found out kept his mouth shut, for it was a penal offence to practise medicine unlicensed. Viola had accepted the three hundred dollars he brought her with a sad little smile. At her suggestion they blew part of it on a superb week-end in New York. A farewell week-end, it turned out, for she took the rest of the money and went off to Hollywood with it, leaving a little note. "I love you, Hugh, but I *know* I am a great actress, and I must do it. I don't mean just the movies. More than that. Forgive me."

And she was right. Viola was the one in ten thousand who makes the grade in Hollywood. In three years she had become a star, and long before that she had divorced Hugh, who never communicated with her in any way. Two years ago she had tried her luck on Broadway and met with unusual indulgence from the critics, though the play had only a moderate run. And at thirty-two, her beauty was richer and deeper than it had ever been, judging from her pictures. She had not married again.

Hugh's disintegration had not come fast, after Viola left. He had managed to wall off the memory of her and concentrate on work. He moved to New York State when he was ready to practise, because the doctor who had shielded him had nevertheless not forgotten and kept a watchful eye on him. He had spoken to Hugh one night over a beer in a speakeasy near the hospital.

"Watch your step, young man; you're a good doctor, but you've got some sort of queer streak in you. I overlooked that business with the Greek because of your war record, but there've been other things. I know about that extra shot of morphine you sneaked old Billings. He bribed you for it—didn't he?"

"He needed it," said Hugh sullenly.

"I don't agree. Anyway, he's my patient—and my orders were plain on his chart. Look, Slater, you're too brilliant a medico for shady ethics. Too nice a fellow too, actually."

Hugh was both grateful and resentful, and he got away from the older man as fast as possible. In the New York suburb where he started practice he had bad luck. Jealousy from the already entrenched surgeons, and then a rich patient died on the table through no fault of Hugh's. His practice fell off, and one day he admitted an hysterical woman to his office at eleven at night. She wanted an abortion which Hugh refused from prudent, not moral, reasons, and he referred her to a man in West End Avenue in New York. Here the woman had the abortion and hæmorrhaged after getting home. Terrified by her condition and also by the threats of the actual abortionist, she called another local doctor, and accused Hugh of performing the operation against her will.

This case came into court, and though Hugh was eventually cleared, his reputation was irretrievably damaged. He moved out West, drifted from town to town, finding increasing difficulty in getting a practice, since he also became a periodic drinker. The last solution was the mining camps. Isolated mining camps with scant funds and facilities must often content themselves with the dregs of the profession, and ask no questions. So Hugh landed a year ago at Lodestone, where the population of six hundred apathetically accepted his ministrations when he applied them, and did without when he was drunk.

The woman on the bed gave a convulsive heave and a shriek. Hugh started, opened his eyes, jumped up, and applied the ether cone in one swift motion. He poured the first drops from the can and said, "You're okay. Just let go, and breathe in." Her frantic thrashings stilled a little. She stared up at him with terrified appeal, and her fingers fastened on his arm. "All right, all right," he repeated. "Take it easy. . . ." Her eyelids drooped, her breathing slowed under the white cone.

Maria shuffled in with the potful of instruments, looking

scared. She obeyed his curt instructions, and took his place at the head of the bed, pouring a drop of ether when he told her to. Hugh pulled on sterile gloves, fished out the instruments, and in five minutes started a delivery which managed, before it was accomplished, to present him with most of the standard textbook complications.

An hour later he oiled the squalling purplish baby, and put it down beside its mother, who still slept heavily. Saved 'em both; now let's wave the flag for Dr. Slater, the wonder boy of Lodestone. The sanctified surgeon of Shamrock Mine.

"They okay?" asked Maria importantly; "or shall I get Padre?" She had twice performed this interesting errand, running down the main street of Lodestone to the corrugated-iron chapel on the edge of town.

"They won't need the Padre," said Hugh, peeling off his gloves. "But they need a hell of a lot of other things they aren't going to get." Aside from the probability that that Bohunk, the brat's father, would kill them both in one of his psychopathic rages.

They'd both have died here and now and painlessly, if I'd let 'em, Hugh thought, and everyone would have been happier.

"I'm going to get out of this blasted shack for a while," he said to Maria. "If anybody shows up for office hours, tell 'em to wait. You stay right here"—he indicated the sleeping woman—"until I get back."

"You goin' to the 'Laundry'?" asked Maria wistfully, referring to Lodestone's most popular speakeasy and gambling hall, and so affectionately named because its patrons always emerged "cleaned."

"Nope," said Hugh. "And neither are you!" He gave her a look from under his bushy blond eyebrows, which effectively quelled Maria's tentative plans. She thrust out her lower lip and sat down. The Doc was a lot more fun when he was drunk, even when he called her names and hit her. Most men did like that. But when he was sober he was cold and sharp like a knife. Always picking in a mean biting way you couldn't answer back. . . . And what's he want to keep a magazine picture of that movie star for? thought Maria, reverting to a problem which had given her some hours of jealous pondering. In between his only two good shirts he kept this torn picture of Viola Vinton. She was sitting on a chair and staring at some books, a kind of goofy look on her face. And Viola Vinton wasn't so much, either; her pictures never came to the Miners' Hall in Lodestone, and you hardly ever saw anything about her in the movie magazines. Maria herself had a picture of Ramon Novarro up on the wall of her room at the Garcias', but that was different; besides, it wasn't hid like she was ashamed of it.

She'd asked the Doc about the picture once, and he'd got awful mad, called her a goddam nosy bitch, yelled at her never to open his drawers or touch his things again.

Maria rested her chin on her hand, morosely contemplating her quiet patients on the cot. I wish I hadn't got this lousy job, she thought, but without real conviction. The Garcias, where she boarded, and even the Padre kept telling her how lucky she was to have it. Though the Padre kept bawling her out, too, and giving her penances for living in sin, so now she didn't go to confession. . . . I wish I had a real nice lover, she thought, would show me a good time, take me to California maybe; *un rico*, she thought, reverting to the language of her childhood, *muy elegante y amoroso*. . . . She sighed, her head fell forward and slipped down until it rested on the pillow beside the woman and the baby. Maria slept too.

Hugh had flung out of the hospital bearing a gun and a small volume of Schopenhauer, whose pessimistic philosophy pleased him. Hugh ignored both hunting seasons and licences, but as there was no big game down in these arid mountains anyway, nobody ever questioned him, and when the mood was on him, he shot indiscriminately at birds, rabbits, snakes or squirrels, or, indeed, anything that moved. This, too, gave him pleasure. One more symptom of my degeneration, no doubt, he thought, as he passed the Dartlands' cottage and saw Amanda's golden head inside near the window. He saw another head, too, unmistakable because of its bird's-nest of coiled brown hair, surmounted by a round blue hat.

So the Mablett's calling on the bride already, he thought with malicious amusement. Hope that fool girl can keep from making trouble for Dart. Dart's the only decent guy in this dump.

He strode on up the mine road, flattening himself against the cliffside as one of the ore trucks came grinding down in low. It was filled with concentrates from the mill, destined for the big smelter twenty-five miles south at Hayden.

But with the price of copper shot to hell at six cents a pound,

it was not the concentrates which kept the Shamrock Mine
fighting for its precarious existence. It was the slender vein of
gold-bearing ore, and it was also the Boston stockholders and
their dogged and glittering hopes for better production soon.
God, if only the price of gold *would* go up, thought Hugh, or
if those rock-hounds up on the hill could only find something
really good in their mole tunnels, the blasted old Shamrock
might get into the black for a change, might even put a little
paint on the hospital, let alone raise my salary a nickel a month.
He gave an exasperated sigh, and whipped his gun through a
clump of cholla cactus, morosely watching the vicious little
spined segments break off and roll over the road.

"You shouldn't do that, Doctor," cried a wheezy and re-
proachful voice. "Susan gets them in her paws."

Hugh turned to see Old Larky dismounting from his burro
and shooing his dog, an obese spaniel, away from the scattered
cholla. "Sorry," said Hugh. "How come you're down from the
mountains so soon? You found your lost mine or something?"
He surveyed the old prospector with amusement. Like many
another of his kind throughout the West, old Larky lived alone
some place in the mountains near a spring, he appeared once a
month for supplies in Lodestone, and departed again with his
two burros and his dog after a visit to the post office, where he
invariably received a letter from England. Old Larky was a
British remittance man, and only Hugh, who had saved his eye-
sight after a virulent dose of wood alcohol, knew that the usual
romantic speculations in this case were true. Larky was the
younger son of an earl.

He had shown Hugh a picture of the magnificent Warwick-
shire castle where he had been born, but his true name or the
particular misbehaviour which had caused his exile forty years
ago Hugh did not know.

Old Larky had blue eyes rimmed with white around the irises,
which appeared to swim in a viscous red fluid, but through them
he surveyed Hugh with dignity. "No, I have not found my lost
mine yet, but I have no doubt I shall eventually. I came down
early because Susan there will soon be whelping."

"You don't say so," said Hugh, eyeing the dog with distaste.
"She find a lustful coyote up there?"

"Indian hound," said Old Larky sadly. "There's some
Mescaleros camping not far from my cabin. I think some of the

bucks are working in the mine. Those damned Apaches—I
tried to shoot that hound dog, but he was too quick for me."

"Too bad——" said Hugh, and turned to go.

"No, Doctor, wait." Old Larky seized Hugh by the arm, exhibiting a row of white china teeth in a smile as anxious as the
swimming eyes. "Susan, she's a bit old for a first litter; I've
always been so careful of her. I thought perhaps you'd just——"

"Oh, my God. No!" shouted Hugh. "At dog obstetrics I
draw the line."

Old Larky's lips trembled. "Doctor, I beg of you—look, I'll
pay you well. Look—look at this." He fumbled in his saddle-
bag, and held out on his shaking palm a round gold coin.

"Gold?" murmured Hugh, startled. For a second it seemed
as though there were a spot of seductive, infinitely beckoning
light floating on the seamed old hand. "Where'd you get this?"
he said angrily. "You didn't offer to pay me when I pulled you
through that bout with the melted Sternos."

"It's a gold sovereign," said Old Larky. "The only one I have.
I brought it from England. You pull Susan through and you
shall have it."

"I don't want it." Hugh thrust his jaw out, and he turned his
back on Old Larky.

"It'll buy a lot of Payson Dew, Doctor Slater," said Old
Larky softly. "You like Payson Dew."

Hugh turned back; he looked at the pleading bleary old face,
he looked at the pregnant bitch with her mournful swimming
eyes like her master's—and he burst into a sharp laugh. "Okay,
I like to deliver dogs so I can get money to get drunk, so I like
to deliver dogs."

The old man nodded and climbed on his burro with Susan in
his arms. "We'll go to the hospital when the time comes.
Thank you, Doctor Slater." He lifted his lumpy old Stetson,
clucked to the burro, and they ambled down the road towards
town.

Private room for Susan, said Hugh to himself as he walked
on, and it's not, Mrs. Dartland, that I have a heart of gold melting over the pathetic old prospector and his whoring little dog,
I assure you, it's just plain gold. He walked on glumly, staring
down at the rough road until he reached the original Lodestone,
the ghost town abandoned when the Boston company bought the
old mine fifteen years ago and had optimistically founded a

new town site with more room for expansion, and nearer the Gila River, from which much of the water must be pumped.

The ghost town presented the appearance of romantic desolation peculiar to all ruins. There were piles of rubble, a few backless façades, two or three crumbling skeletons of large houses, and an enormous painted wooden sign flanked by giant saguaros fallen against a flight of wooden steps which led into mid-air. The sign said "Opera House" in dim red and gold letters, and a small lizard lay basking on the letter "H." In the vanished opera house behind this sign, Lotta Crabtree and Adelina Patti had performed, and here Mrs. Minnie Maddern Fiske had played to one of the most enthusiastic audiences of her entire career, for during its brief glory in the 'eighties and 'nineties, Lodestone had rivalled Tombstone and even Leadville as a boom town.

Hugh was not interested in the ghost town, crumbling under the silent sun, and he skirted all the rock and adobe foundations where rattlers loved to lurk, but he paused by a large mesquite to look up a trail between fallen timbers, a trail which had, over thirty years ago, been a broad avenue flanked by stunted everailing palm trees. A hundred yards up the mountain-side, on a platform hewn out of the rock behind, there stood the Cunningham mansion.

Nobody had ever viewed this mansion without a shock of disbelief, thus fulfilling the desire of Red Bill Cunningham when he built it in 1888 for his bride. Red Bill's exploits had always aroused disbelief. Bill Cunningham had been a flaming red giant of an Irishman, and he had brawled and roistered his way as a boomer, or tramp miner, through most of the western mining camps until the day when the luck which never deserted him had made him lose his way in the Dripping Spring Mountains of Arizona's Gil Country. This was in 1882 when he was forty, and he had just spent a few weeks working as a mucker in the Old Dominion Mine at Globe. Globe, however, had begun to quieten from its first wild boom days, and Red Bill, powered by a recurrent urge to move on, was attracted by reports of Tombstone, which was still enjoying a turbulence that appealed to him.

One morning at dawn he set out on horseback, south over Pioneer Pass, and far too drunk to be worried by the threat of wandering Apaches. In fact, he saw no hostiles, but by nightfall he was drunker yet, and had lost the trail some miles back. He cursed, took a final swig, tumbled off the horse, and fell asleep where he lay between a stunted mesquite and a large bisnaga cactus.

The pitiless September sun finally awoke him at noon the next day. He sat up and groaned and looked for the horse, and also the water canteen which was tied to the saddle. The horse was not in sight, and Red Bill staggered to his feet and tried to produce a whistle with his thickened tongue and cracked lips. He saw that he was in very rough mountain country. The pinkish diorite rocks huddled thickly around him, above loomed the glaring white of limestone cliffs. He was standing on a slope in a broad gully near the top of a dull reddish mountain. No use investigating the bottom of the gully, it'd be dry. There'd been no rain for weeks. He tried to whistle again, and the sound was like a mouse's squeak against the thunderous silence. He sat down on a rock, and the sun blazed down on his fiery hair. Holy Mother, he thought, this is a tight one. No horse, no water, and he couldn't even get direction from the sun straight overhead. He licked his lips and pulled out his rosary, mumbling familiar words. After a minute he shifted the wooden beads to one hand, and fumbled in his breast pocket to bring out a small tin locket. Inside the locket there was a dried shamrock, given to him by his mother in Cobh the day before he stowed away on the brig bound for America. The locket slipped from his enormous fingers and fell between two rocks. He picked up one of the rocks to release his locket, and paused, startled by the weight. He bounced the rock in his hand, his aching eyes focusing on it gradually. "Holy Mother of God," he whispered. "I'm dreaming for sure." He picked at the rock with his finger-nail, and a minute gleaming fleck came off on his dirty nail.

It was thus, from a piece of high-grade float, that Red Bill Cunningham located the Shamrock Mine, and his luck and native shrewdness thereafter overcame all difficulties. As he feverishly piled up a cairn to mark his claim, he noticed the bisnaga beside which he slept. A twofold saviour, this barrel cactus, to all those lost in the desert wilderness, and now that his wits had cleared he made use of it. Bisnagas always leaned roughly south, so his best chance of hitting the stage road again would be over there to the west. And the bisnaga pulp provided water. He hacked the top off with his hunting knife and macerated the green fibres with a mesquite stick until they yielded a quart of watery fluid, which he sucked up feverishly.

Red Bill never found his horse, but, unlike many other dis-coverers of fortuitous minerals, he found his mine again two months later, made good his claim and, for the sixteen years of the Shamrock's first productivity before the original vein pinched out, he amassed a fortune. And all of it flowed from his free-spending hands as fast as it came in. Ninety thousand dollars of it went to build the mansion at which Hugh was gazing. Every foot of the materials which composed its thirty rooms had been dragged in by mule team from somewhere else. The pines which formed the main wood of the structure came from no farther than the forests near Flagstaff, but the mahogany banisters and the oak parquet floor in the ballroom, the silver hardware and bathroom fixtures, the crystal chandeliers, the rosewood furniture, Turkey rugs, and glass for the windows and conservatory, had travelled from San Francisco, New York, and even Paris.

Crazy-looking monstrosity, thought Hugh, still staring fascinated at the weird ruin of an Irish immigrant's dream of magnificence in the Arizona desert. Pigsty Gothic, with imita-tion turrets from which the gingerbread fretwork dangled in broken strips. The leaded green and red windows were starred from the impact of long-forgotten stones, when there were any panes left at all—most of the windows were boarded up. In all that vast and mouldering mansion there was no sign of life. And yet, there was life in there, in the two corner rooms to the west, where purple velvet portières covered the windows. Here Calise Cunningham, Red Bill's widow, lived alone, as she had for thirty-three years. Alone—except for a ghost.

She's nutty as a fruit-cake, Hugh thought, half resentful of the impression she had made on him, the one time he had seen her. She had been Calise de Barnay, a French Creole singer from New Orleans, an orphan, of good family and high intelli-gence, who had, nevertheless, run away from the aristocratic Louisiana convent where she had been reared, to plunge herself into the turbulence of the West. Her true musicianship and rich lyric voice caused no great interest in the mining camps, but her extreme youth and dark beauty got her a job with the troupe. And then Red Bill Cunningham fell violently in love with her on the first night of her appearance in Lodestone.

She had been seventeen and he forty-six, and in view of that disparity, and also of subsequent happenings, it would seem unlikely that Calise had reciprocated the huge bellowing Irishman's passion. She had certainly married him, though, and a few old-timers could still remember glimpses of her galloping through town on an Arab gelding, and dressed in the maroon velvet riding habit Red Bill had had made for her in Denver.

Yet not five people in the new Lodestone had ever seen her. Once a week the scared little Pottner boy hauled his delivery wagon up to one of the mansion's dilapidated side porches, unloaded a standing order of provisions, and picked up five silver dollars which were laid on the step for him, before scampering pell-mell off to safety. The great silent house was well known to be haunted.

Mrs. Cunningham wished no company, though she made an exception of Dartland apparently, and it was because of Dart that Hugh had once visited her. Dart had met her by chance wandering alone at dawn in the mountains one morning, and they had talked a little. That was when Dart had first come to Lodestone and had as yet found no place to stay except the mine boarding-house. Calise had offered him the use of one of her myriad empty rooms, and shown him a side-door he might use. She had also made it clear that he must confine himself to the part of the house she indicated nor ever disturb her privacy. This suited Dart admirably, and he had lived there some weeks, oblivious to the curiosity of the Lodestone matrons.

Dart had come to Hugh's office one Sunday morning and asked him to walk back to the mansion.

"I'm afraid Mrs. Cunningham's sick," Dart had said. "I heard crying and moaning from her wing last night, and she hasn't been out in days. I want you to look at her, if she'll let us in."

Eventually the two men had climbed the twelve broken steps to the great front door and pulled the giant silver knocker shaped like a shamrock. Red Bill had never forgotten the symbol of his luck.

They waited a long time, and pulled the knocker again before they heard soft footsteps inside, and Dart called out, "Mrs. Cunningham, it's Jonathan Dartland—please open the door."

A bolt slid back and the door swung slowly inwards. The woman who stood in its shadow was tall and slender, dressed as nearly as Hugh could make out in a froth of cream lace and scarlet ribbons. Her shoulders and arms were bare, and he had the impression of jewels on her wrist and bosom.

Dart said quickly, "Please forgive me for bothering you, but last night—I thought I heard—I thought you were sick."

She moved a little from the shadow, though she still held the doorknob in her hand. Hugh stared with astonishment. Her hair, which must still be very long and thick, was crystal white, like the chandelier in the dim hallway behind her. It was coiled high on her small head in the fashion of the 'nineties. Her cheeks were touched with delicate rouge, and above them her large dark eyes surveyed Dart with a remote sadness. She ignored Hugh. She was fifty-nine, but her olive skin, at least in the dim light, showed few lines. She gave no impression of false youth, and the elaborate négligé, the rouge, and the perfume which floated from her laces were not incongruous, for there was a regal quality in her carriage, and a fatefulness.

"You promised never to intrude," she said to Dart, and her low voice, with its French intonation, seemed to issue from far behind her pale lips.

"I know, ma'am," said Dart with a confused earnestness which surprised Hugh, who had never seen Dart anything but self-possessed. "I'm sorry, but if you were sick here alone . . . I brought the doctor."

"Yes . . . well . . ." she said gravely. "I am not sick. It is only that Raoul is coming again tonight. *Ça recommence toujours, la tragédie. C'est la punition que je dois subir.*" Her lids lowered over the brilliant eyes, she began to shut the door. "Go away, please," she said. "You can do nothing." The door clicked into place, and they heard the bolt pushed home.

Both men silently descended the steps, and then Hugh burst out with a laugh. "My God, Dart—I thought you said she always wore black!"

"She has when I've seen her before."

"And who the hell is Raoul?"

They had picked their way down the trail between the vanished avenue of palms and reached the fallen opera-house sign before Dart answered. "Raoul is her dead lover, I believe. Old Blevins, the hoistman, was here when it happened, and he insisted on telling me the story once."

"Well, tell me, then," said Hugh.

Dart frowned, but after a moment he said, "There's not much

to it. Raoul came from New Orleans as she did, and was her lover. Her husband came home unexpectedly one day and found them together in one of the bedrooms up there." He gestured towards the house. "He murdered Raoul, and had some sort of a stroke himself and died pretty soon, but she's stayed there ever since."

"And what's she all dressed up for now?"

"I gather that the tragedy is re-enacted at certain times. She's dressed as she was on that night."

Hugh nodded. "Completely bats. She's a psychopath."

"Maybe, in a way. But usually she seems strangely happy. She has a piano in her rooms, and she sings and plays a great deal. Good stuff—Scarlatti, Bach, Mozart. And she reads a lot."

"Reads what, for the love of Mike? Ghost stories?"

"No. She never invited me into her suite but once, and the books I saw then were mostly religious and philosophical. She's a sort of mystic, I think; she lives for the spirit. I don't know——" He added half to himself, "Maybe she really sees things other people can't."

"Holy smoke!" cried Hugh. "You don't think she entertains her dead lover, I hope!"

Dart had stopped then and looked down at Hugh, his grey eyes had hardened and were devoid of the ironic affection they usually held for his friend. Then he shrugged. "It would be a most terrible punishment," he said. He sketched a salute and walked rapidly up the deserted street to the mine road.

Queer reactions in Dartland sometimes, Hugh thought now, as he turned his back on the Cunningham mansion and set out up a trail. Dart was a cultured man, the only other really intelligent man in Lodestone, but suddenly you'd run into a snag like this. Superstition. A soft spot. The Indian blood? he thought with astonishment, for he had forgotten this completely. He considered it now for a moment. He had had little contact with the Apaches, though there were a few of them working in the mine, but they never came to the hospital or called a doctor. They disappeared, went home to the reservation most likely. Nobody knew much about them. They were very good miners, but a sullen and taciturn lot, who kept to themselves, and resented the slightest indignity, especially when drunk. Apaches went hog wild when they got drunk. But there'd been less trouble with them since Dart had become mine foreman. Well, Dart's a good guy, he thought, no matter what, if that little Park Avenue babe he's married doesn't ruin him.

Hugh caught a flicker of motion behind a creosote bush to his right, sighted the gun, and forgot the Dartlands.

CHAPTER THREE

By three o'clock that afternoon, Amanda had swept the lino-leum floor, which looked as grimy as ever, scrubbed the kitchen table, and put her scanty groceries into the one cupboard. She had also discovered how to pump a trickle of water into the rusty sink, and managed to coax from the kerosene stove burners a shower of sparks and foul-smelling smoke.

There was a sharp rap on her front door. Amanda said, "Damn!" pushed her hair back from her face with dirty hands, and went to open the door.

Lydia Mablett stood outside, dressed for calling. Her small plump body was sheathed in a silk print, black daisies on a greyish ground. She wore a Navajo Indian silver brooch and two strings of artificial pearls from the department store in Phœnix. A large black pocket-book dangled from her arm, and her hands were encased in white cotton gloves. Her brown hair, sparsely threaded with grey, had never been cut, and she had "ratted it back" with a comb into a pile on top of her head rather in the shape of a small beehive. On the apex of the beehive there perched a round, navy-blue grosgrain hat. She wore small square glasses with silver rims, and through these she surveyed Amanda's dishevelment with astonishment. Then she extended her cotton-gloved hand and said, "Mrs. Dartland, I believe?" in a tone of forbearing sweetness. "I'm Mrs. Mablett. I've come to welcome you to Lodestone."

"Oh yes," said Amanda, smiling nervously. "How nice of you. . . . I'm sorry I'm not fixed up, the house is in dreadful shape. . . ." She clutched the doorknob tight, determined not to expose the shambles within.

But Lydia was very good at managing people. She had been a social worker in Des Moines before she married Luther Mablett.

"Oh, I quite understand—but I do so want us to get acquainted."

Amanda, without knowing how it happened, found that Mrs.

55

Mablett was inside the house. The shining spectacles flashed from side to side, and behind them there gleamed an energetic light which would have been recognized by many a case family in Des Moines. Lydia's tongue made a very slight clucking noise. She swooped down and removed a stack of Dart's shirts from the chair to the bed, and seated herself on the vacant place thus provided. Then she turned upon Amanda her look of determined sweetness.

"You do seem to have rather a lot of things, don't you," she said, looking at the fitted dressing-case, the overflowing suitcases and bed. "As an older woman with quite a lot of experience, might I give you a little teeny-weeny word of advice?"

Amanda, who had been longing for help and friendly counsel, now followed the example of most recipients of Lydia Mablett's advice and found herself bristling.

"Of course," she murmured.

"Adaptability," said Lydia in her high, unexpectedly cooing, voice. "One must adapt oneself to—to circumstances. You won't be able to live here as you did at home. I've lived in different mining towns for twenty years, and Mr. Mablett always was so surprised that I could make a sweet little home for us, no matter where. I always said I had just one secret—adaptability."

"Lovely," said Amanda, just managing to smile. "I shall try very hard to be adaptable, but I don't know just where to begin yet. We need a good closet very badly. Have to get one built, I guess."

"It's a pity Mr. Dartland could not have found a larger house," said Lydia; "but dwellings are so scarce here."

"We couldn't afford a bigger house on his salary," said Amanda, and saw the other's face freeze.

"I believe he gets a very fair salary for a mine foreman, and a new man at that. I seem to remember Mr. Mablett remarking upon it."

Oh Lord, thought Amanda, Dart warned me. "Yes, no doubt he does," she said brightly. "I don't know a thing about it. I'm so sorry I can't offer you a cup of tea, or something."

"Quite all right," said Lydia, all sweetness again. She rose, but instead of leaving walked into the kitchen. "You don't mind if I just see the rest of your little home? And, my dear, no matter what else you do, do put up good nutritious lunches for Mr. Dartland. It's so important, especially for the men who go underground a lot, like your husband. I have a little book on dietetics I'd be glad to lend you. Oh, I see. . . ." She pounced on a small domed black box which Amanda had not before noticed. It was lying on the window-sill. "He didn't take his lunch today?"

"No," said Amanda, and shut her mouth. No, he didn't take his lunch, because I didn't know he was supposed to, or that I should make it, or that that thing was a lunch-box.

"Little brides must never neglect their hubbies," said Lydia, smiling. She opened the peeling cupboard door and ran her eye over Amanda's purchases. "Canned asparagus?" she said. "I always feel that's such a luxury; I said to Pearl Pottner when she stocked it, that I thought it was foolish of her. She'd never sell it."

"I like asparagus," said Amanda. "Mrs. Mablett, I'm awfully sorry, but I've got to get this place straightened up before Dart gets home. But please do come again some other time."

Lydia hesitated, much too thick-skinned to take offence. She was rather bored by her visit, but there were things she wanted to find out and she hesitated no longer. "Mr. Dartland is such an interesting kind of man," she said. "He's had a strange life, hasn't he? Isn't his mother an Indian?"

"His grandfather was an Apache," said Amanda, moving towards the front door.

"Goodness, weren't you brave to marry him! Mr. Mablett always says the Apaches were so cruel and dangerous. Of course not now, on the reservations."

"Do you think Dart is cruel and dangerous?" said Amanda.

Lydia Mablett looked startled. She was not used to combat. "Of course not, dear," she said, laughing. "But I do hear he's a teeny bit opinionated. Still, now he's married, I'm sure he'll—er—tone down. Wives can do so much to help."

"Yes, indeed," said Amanda. Years of her mother's social training enabled her to give Lydia a pacific smile, and to take the white-gloved hand with sufficient cordiality.

So Lydia finally left. Amanda returned to her labours. At dusk these were again interrupted: by a scratching, tapping sound. She whirled around, and saw the doctor's square, sardonic face peering through the window-pane. "Hey!" he called. "D'you want a rabbit?"

Amanda gave vent to another expletive. Her back ached,

discouragement pressed heavier every minute. Privacy, among other virtues, seemed to be lacking in Lodestone, and she felt unequal to parrying more hostility. "Go away," she said in the general direction of the window.

Hugh opened the door himself and walked in. "Glamorous veneer sure wore off fast," he observed, inspecting the girl. Her short hair, no longer sleek, stuck out around her head in duck-tails; across her face, innocent now of make-up, there ran two dirty streaks. A treacherous nail had torn a tri-cornered hole in the wrinkled cotton dress. "Life in Lodestone is a great leveller, I always think," he added, helping himself to some tissue paper from the nearest open suitcase. On it he deposited a small dead rabbit.

"Peace offering," he said. "Embittered doctor demonstrates heart of gold."

"Thank you very much," she said coldly. "Though I haven't the faintest idea how to cook it."

"Dart will show you," said Hugh with equal coldness. "But I only hope you learn to pull your own weight pretty soon. Dart's got a big, man-sized job to do, without nurse-maiding you along as well."

Amanda gasped. A flame ran up from the pit of her stomach. "You're so beastly unfair! I've been here one day, I'm trying all I can. I can't help it if I just don't know things—I——"

"Unfortunately," said Hugh, "ignorance is no excuse. Even legally." He lit himself a cigarette, crossed his legs, and leaned against the Sears Roebuck-papered wall. "You're used to soft, sentimental values. You think people should like you and help you just because you're a pretty, well-bred girl, that they should make allowances for you. I don't doubt that you've got a lot of fuzzy, sloppy ideas about love, too. They won't wash with Dart, not for long. I'd bet a thousand bucks you haven't the dimmest idea of the sort of man you married."

Amanda's eyes flashed, but she spoke with control. "Doctor Slater, is there any particular Lodestone law that forces me to join you in a discussion of my shortcomings?"

Hugh laughed. "You've had a tough day, haven't you! The Mablett give you a good going over? You better be nice to her though, my pet. Dart has enough troubles at the mine without petticoat skirmishes down in the town." He gave her a mock salute and left, as abruptly as he had come in.

Well, I've got troubles here too, she thought with hot anger. If Dart hadn't left her alone today, this one day. If only he'd come back soon, take her in his arms and comfort her. Then the muddle wouldn't matter, or the unaccountable jibes from strangers, or the rudeness of that impossible doctor.

But it was nearly seven o'clock before Dart came "down the hill" and she heard the Lizzie's characteristic sputter and snort outside. Cleansed in cold water, powdered, perfumed, and freshly dressed, Amanda flew out to meet him.

"Darling, I'm so glad you're back! It's so late," she cried. He responded absently to her kiss, and strode ahead of her into the house. She followed, feeling deflated.

"Still pretty much of a mess," she said nervously, indicating the room. "I've made a list of things to be done, that we'll simply have to get." She took her little list from the bedroom table. It said, "Closet, hangers, mirror, another cupboard in kitchen, paint," and continued down the page.

She held it out and saw that Dart was not listening. He sat on the chair, pulling off his boots and frowning into space. Amanda put the paper down. She had violated her mother's No. 1 rule, "Never bother your husband at night until he's fed."

"Tired, dear?" she asked.

Dart shook his head impatiently. As a matter of fact he was never tired. He had endless endurance and complete indifference to bodily discomforts. Nor, as she had already discovered, did the physical weaknesses of others interest him. He might be indulgent, but he did not understand them.

"Was it hard today at the mine?" she persisted. He went to the kitchen and began to pump water. He sluiced it over his face and neck and hair. Gradually her question penetrated his thoughts. He looked at her with astonishment, seeing someone who had the right to question, someone whose desire to question must be gratified.

"That damn fool is ruining the mine. We'll fold if he goes on like this. But I won't let him."

"Mablett?" she asked slowly. "What is it he does, Dart?"

"Gross incompetence, coupled with petty jealousy and megalomania."

"How?" she asked, puzzled. "How can one man hurt a big mine?"

"It's not a big mine any more, it's a marginal enterprise with

great possibilities. This guy is mine superintendent, and he has
the power to bungle every single operation because poor old
Tyson's not well enough to stop him."

Amanda frowned, trying not to feel annoyed at this recurrent
theme which she did not understand. How little she had ever
actually envisioned Lodestone or the mine. Her speculations
and fantasies had never travelled past Dart himself and his
relation to her.

Nor did Dart seem eager to enlighten her. "Come on, Andy—
or Mrs. Zuckowski won't have any grub left for us."

She nodded, then said involuntarily, "No tie?"

Dart had changed the blue jeans for a frayed pair of flannel
pants and an open khaki shirt.

He laughed. "No tie. The Imperial Hotel is not the Ritz."

She walked along beside him in the crisp evening air. The
stars, larger than she had ever seen them, shone like silver lamps
against the blue night. The street was silent, the town had
regained its air of expectant mystery, as though it awaited a
revelation—fear or beauty from an ancient splendour poured
down by stars and mountains free from human taint, hostile to it.

Amanda slipped her arm through Dart's, wanting to share
with him, to pull him back into close communication. "Are the
nights always like this?"

"Like what?"

"Big—and—frightening—thinking how silly and little we all
are."

Dart paused a second in his even stride. He turned his face up
to the sky, and she saw the starlight flash across his upturned
eyes. He's part of it, she thought, and uneasiness returned to
her. He's apart from me, and part of it.

"You mustn't be afraid of things," he said, gently.

I'm not, she thought, startled and a little hurt. She thought in
swift refutation—swimming, sailing, riding, physical courage for
which she'd always been praised. And yet, she knew that was
not what he meant. "I'd bet a thousand bucks you haven't the
dimmest idea of the sort of man you married."

"Dart—I don't like Doctor Slater," she said. "I haven't told
you yet about today, but he was"—she laughed a little—
"obnoxious."

"You'll get used to him," said Dart. "Here's Mrs. Zuckowski's."

They turned into a two-storied frame building with a towering false front. The lobby smelt of stale tobacco juice from the cuspidors, and overcooked cabbage. Dart and Amanda sat down at the long table in the chilly dining-room, where two commercial travellers and a man from the Hayden smelter were finishing their supper.

Dart and the smelter man fell at once into unintelligible conversation—concentrators, flotation, tonnage. Through this ran a graver note of possible shutdown, of mounting loss, of the deplorable copper prices. "You're lucky you got some gold here," said the smelter man, shaking his head, and Dart's face tightened. "Such as it is," he answered.

Amanda listened absently, trying to avoid the sly disrobing stares of the two salesmen, trying to cut the blackened, greasy pork chops. She longed for the moment when she could be alone again with Dart, could tell him some of the day's annoying little incidents, sit on his lap, and have him soothe and pet and make love to her until she forgot all niggling discomforts and was reassured.

On the following Saturday morning, little Bobby Pottner appeared at Amanda's door with a note. It said:

"Mr. and Mrs. Luther Mablett are holding a card party and collation at their home in Creek Street at seven o'clock tonight. The favour of Mr. and Mrs. Dartland's company is requested."

The note was written in green ink, and there was an embossed cluster of gold apple blossoms in the upper left corner.

Amanda read it twice, then burst into youthful giggles.

Bobby, who was groping under the door-stop after a chuckwalla lizard which had eluded him, looked up. "What's so funny?"

"Royal command," Amanda said, still giggling. "And I thought it said 'collection.' Visions of Mrs. Mablett passing the hat. What *is* a collation, Bobby?"

He returned to the lizard. "Grub, I guess. Mom's been cooking stuff for it all morning. . . . Well," he said impatiently, "you gotta write sompthin' back, you know—she's waiting."

Amanda frowned. "We certainly haven't any previous engagement," she said half to herself; "I don't know if Dart will approve, but I suppose we ought to go."

"You gotta go," said Bobby, astonished. "Everyone does."

Amanda retreated to the kitchen table, and composed a brief acceptance in Mrs. Mablett's own words. Bobby departed, and she returned to her chores, her curiosity mildly piqued. Any party, even a Mablett one, might be fun if only Dart were not annoyed by her acceptance. Still, there was no way of consulting him. She saw so little of him, for he spent six days a week at the mine. It was hard. In fact, everything was hard.

The shack was tidier and more habitable, since Dart had knocked up a large plaster-board closet for her off the kitchen. And they had painted the walls of both kitchen and bedroom a soft sage-green. Other improvements must wait, because there was no money to pay for them. As it was, the plaster board and paint had been charged at the Mine Supplies Store, and not without protest from Dart, who had a horror of debt.

Amanda had inherited her mother's optimism, a comforting certainty that "there was always a way," and when you really needed something, the Lord would somehow provide.

On paper Dart's salary had seemed adequate. She and her mother had discussed it several times in the long evenings before Dart came East. "You'll have to be careful, baby," Mrs. Lawrence had said buoyantly, "but things out there will be cheap, and, of course, you've got all your clothes and things. You'll manage."

But things out here were not cheap. A mining town was expensive. The far-eastern depression prices in the winter of 1933 scarcely affected it at all.

Food and rent were exorbitant for the value received, and by the time they paid out insurance, fuel for the stove and the car, and a portion of Mr. Tyson's loan, there was nothing at all left for "sundries."

Already Amanda was discovering how dear to her heart were the "sundries," and how shamefully she missed them. The latest magazines, new books and music, an ice-cream soda, a box of caramels, new cosmetics to try, the hairdresser and manicurist, above all the movies. Once a week on Saturday night the Miners' Union Hall showed an old Grade B Western, so that that deprivation was not very significant. But how strange not to be able to afford to go if they wanted to.

Amanda, trained from babyhood to be a good sport, had made valiant and unnecessary efforts to conceal her recurring dismays from Dart. The sundries of life meant nothing at all to him, nor did it occur to him that they were important to her. He recognized her right to a slightly improved house and provided it. For the rest she must be self-sufficient. If one could not pay for things, one did without. He knew that he was lucky to have a job at all when so many mines were shut down, and he considered the salary fair, especially in view of the minimum wages Mablett was paying the miners.

"I wouldn't take a raise now if they gave it to me," he said to Amanda with finality, the once she had broached the subject of his prospects. "For the mine's sake. Every penny counts, and we have enough to get along until things get better."

She had been conscious yet again of annoyance, resentment of the mine which took so much of his life. He answered her questions reluctantly, knowing that she could not understand, and she had gained only the dimmest picture of the complexities and conflicts which seethed on the hill.

Two days after their arrival she had asked innocently, "When will you take me up to visit the mine, Dart? You know I'm dying to see it."

"You can ride up with me any time, but there isn't much you could see."

"Why, Dart—of course there is! It'd be thrilling to go underground, see where you work, learn something about what you're doing."

Dart shook his head, smiling. "My poor Andy. You can't go underground. You can't even stick your head down the shaft."

"Why not?"

"Because you're a woman. Women are forbidden in most mines. It's a strict taboo."

"How perfectly ridiculous!" she snapped. "What could I do to your old mine, curdle the gold or something? Idiotic Mex superstition, I suppose."

"Mexican, yes, but they all share it: the Cornish Cousin Jacks, Slovaks, the Polish—it's in every hard-rock miner's soul." He added imperturbably, "Women bring bad luck underground."

"And you believe it too?"

"Not particularly, but I respect the men's belief."

Her eyes had stung with sudden tears, and she had flung out at him, "Oh, don't be so noble and inflexible. I don't care so much about seeing your old mine, but don't shut me out of your life. It's—it's *lonely*!"

Ah! then, thought Amanda, remembering the scene now while she washed the breakfast dishes, he had been sweet. He had been startled by her tears. He had taken her in his arms and held her gently like a child. The way her father used to do, long ago, when he had denied her something and she had sobbed with disappointment. But Daddy had always given in at the end, and accorded her whatever it was she cried for. Dart did not. He would pet her, and later, as their mutual passion mounted, she would feel that they were one in understanding as well as body, and yet he did not give in.

"Not an easy man to handle," Mrs. Lawrence had once said, laughing ruefully.

"I don't want a man I can handle," Amanda had rejoined laughing too, "I love masterful men." But she had not really believed that she could not always cajole him if she wished.

The psychologists said that all human beings had mixed masculine and feminine traits, no matter what their sex. But not Dart, she thought. He was all male, he had no feminine traits at all. He would be just, but he would never comply out of sentiment or a desire to please.

She was relieved, when he came down the hill at six o'clock, to find that he considered Mrs. Mablett's collation to be a necessary evil. "They want to look you over, I suppose, and I think Tyson'll be there. I want to talk to him."

"Bobby Pottner says everybody goes. Who's everybody?"

"Lodestone society. Everyone who speaks English, more or less. You'll see." He ran a comb through his thick, dark hair and rummaged in the drawer. "It'll be quite different from anything that's ever happened to you. Andy—do I *have* a clean shirt?"

Amanda had been standing by the western window carefully applying lipstick by the waning light. She turned slowly, staring at him with stricken eyes. "Oh, darling, don't you? Isn't there one left in the suitcase? I tried to wash this morning, but everything still looks sort of grey, and I don't seem to be very good at ironing."

She sighed, thinking of the rumpled pile of half-cleansed laundry which she had stuffed in the bottom of the kitchen cupboard. It still seemed to her incredible that the laundry could not be sent out. Incredible that so many women knew how to cope with the wooden tub of water which must be first pumped, then heated, and with the heavy flat-iron which alternated without reason between a scorching cherry red and the blackness of cold stone.

"Well, never mind," said Dart kindly, "I guess I can make this one do. You'll learn."

She nodded and stifled a little voice which cried, "But I don't want to learn," stifled, too, all thought of tomorrow's chores, and finished dressing. Then she went to him and smiled at him with assured coquetry. "How do I look, Dart?"

She had set her hair in the morning, and the short, tawny curls clung to her small head like a shining cap. Her afternoon dress of mist-grey crêpe had come from Paris, and was ingeniously cut, so that it emphasized her small breasts. There was no trimming or ornament, except a strand of cultured pearls and pearl-button earrings. Her eyes, between slightly mascara-ed lashes, shone vivid like the blue-green of a summer wave; her cheeks were delicately pink; her mouth a more subdued scarlet than she would have made it at home, and she smelled delightfully of Coty's Emeraude.

She awaited with assurance for Dart's verdict, knowing that this self which she had achieved would have produced instant admiration in any masculine eyes she had ever challenged. Dart's reactions, however, were never predictable.

"You look very sophisticated, I guess," he said. "But they may think you haven't dressed up much."

"But don't I look pretty?" she faltered. "It's for you, Dart. You must be so sick of seeing me all frowzy and dishpanny."

He started to say something, then stopped. She saw a flash of the look which she dreaded in the back of his eyes. A weariness, the look of an indulgent parent whose patience is tried.

"You look beautiful, baby," he said and kissed her.

They set off for the Mablett party. They were late, and Mrs. Mablett met them at the door, cooing a welcome, but her eyes behind the square spectacles were guarded. Her plump body was clothed in magenta lace, which consisted of a great many draperies and floating ends. There was a bunch of artificial daisies on her shoulder, and clanking silver and turquoise Navajo jewellery on her wrists and in her low décolletage. The magenta lace was an evening dress. All the other ladies were in full evening dress. Everyone stood up in a long line embracing the small, cluttered living- and dining-rooms. They stared at

Amanda, while her hostess ushered her competently around.
"And here's our little bride, Mrs. Dartland. This is——" The
names slipped through Amanda's ears and out again, though
she repeated each one at the time, and smiled her charming
smile. The men said "How d'you do," and "Pleased to meet
you" in grave accents. The ladies murmured indistinguishably,
and withdrew their limp hands in a genteel way from Amanda's
cordial handclasp.

Hugh Slater stood in a corner of the dining-room and watched
her progression. He had fortified himself from a bottle of
Payson Dew, and almost achieved an agreeable contemplative
detachment. His early afternoon hours had been requisitioned
for Susan's accouchement, but the spaniel had needed none of
Hugh's assistance, and presently produced three amorphous little
monstrosities for Old Larky's passionate admiration. Old Larky
had been as much of a hovering nuisance as any male in these
circumstances, and Hugh had accepted his gold sovereign without compunction, and leaving Old Larky to brood over the new
mother, had fled to the smoky comforts of "The Laundry" and
two hours of concentrated oblivion. He was now by no means
drunk, though he intended to be later, and he extracted from
Amanda's introduction to Lodestone a rich enjoyment.

The girl had a polished smooth sparkle in contrast to the
other women, all of whom fluttered and jingled. She was
rather like a gem, aquamarine in a trayful of rhinestone baubles,
he thought, pleased with his simile. And Viola? The thought
surprised him, but it revealed the exact stage, half-way, of his
intoxication. Her memory seldom jumped at him like that at
other times.

Well, what would Viola have been like here? A ruby?—rich
and deep and glowing, not transparent and palely blue like the
aquamarine; no, a flame—a crimson rose, and *she* would have
won them all in spite of themselves. You're a fool, dear Dr.
Slater. He turned his eyes from Amanda and looked at Dart,
who had greeted everyone with a brief smile and "Good evening," and now stood quietly by Alexander Tyson's chair, chatting a little. Those two men were withdrawn from the buzzes
and murmurs and bowings, and yet it seemed to Hugh that they
dominated the room. Dart, sloppily dressed, his hair too long
and falling over his forehead, his tall body arched over the
general manager's chair, yet gave an impression of complete

composure. His face, as usual, was inscrutable, but to Hugh, who knew him well, it seemed that Dart no longer shared in the quality of ironic detachment which had made them congenial. There was purpose now in the set of the flexible lips, a crystallization of some sort, a feeling that Dart was biding his time. Mablett! thought Hugh, suddenly enlightened. Of course.

He looked around for the mine superintendent, and found him by the sideboard ladling into punch glasses the revolting temperance mixture of canned fruit juices, cinnamon, and Karo syrup, which was all that Lydia Mablett served at her collations.

Luther Mablett was built like a bull. He reminded one of an unpedigreed Hereford, the same massive shoulders encased in a brownish wool suit, the same belligerent downward curve to the mouth, the same prominent and suspicious eyes, the same tight curling hair of nondescript yellowish-white. The Herefords' faces were white too, however, and Luther's was of a dull choleric red. He was spilling a good deal of the punch as he ladled, and scowling over his task. Sneaked a few quick ones, some place, Hugh thought; can't blame him.

Hugh moved his speculative gaze back to Dart and the general manager, and for a moment professional interest sharpened it. Old Tyson's colour was leaden—the lips faintly cyanosed, respiration shallow and rapid. Hope he's got those ampoules with him, thought Hugh; looks like we're going to have trouble. Still, you never could tell with cardiacs: either they'd conk out without reason, or they were a hell of a lot tougher than seemed possible.

Alexander Tyson was pretty tough, for all his frailty, for all his seventy years and appearance of a gentle and ascetic monk. "Last Chance" Tyson they used to call him, all those years when his reputation was international. He'd put a hundred crumbling mines back on a paying basis, taking over often a month or so before what seemed inevitable shutdown, and pulling the tearful stockholders through and back to dividends. He had no special secret, if you expected intuitive intelligence and the ability to learn by experience; sometimes he located a new vein, sometimes he improved equipment and cut waste, always he had provided heightened morale, and the indefinable greasing of the machinery which spelled good management. But he can't seem to do it at the Shamrock, thought Hugh; he's lost his grip, and he ought to retire. But the Company would not let him retire, nor did they know how ill he was. To hell with the Company, thought Hugh; they can stand it if the mine folds. It's *us*—damn it. Every soul in the magnificent metropolis of Lodestone.

"Doctor Slater. Hello! Aren't you going to speak to me?" cried Amanda, having run the gamut, and being now deserted by her hostess with a murmur about seeing to the refreshments. "Thank God for a familiar face," she added, sinking down beside him. "I feel like a new girl the first day at school."

Hugh nodded. "Probation period. We're a right tight little group and we're careful about outsiders."

"Yes. Yes, I know. And I'm frustrated because I don't understand who anybody is. I want so much to be a helpful wife to Dart—you know, polish the right apples, further his career, but they don't seem to like me. Why don't they?" She had forgotten her own dislike of him, and spoke with a mixture of wistful humour and genuine dismay.

Hugh shrugged. "Well, you better not polish this apple, my dear," he said; "I'm of no use whatsoever to Dart's career. You might go and bat those eyelashes at your host, if you fancy yourself as a Mata Hari."

She laughed ruefully and looked at Mablett, who had now walked over to join Dart and Tyson. The three men seemed to be chatting casually, but Amanda caught something of their tension. "Listen," she said seriously to Hugh, "what is it all about—the 'trouble' at the mine? Dart doesn't like to talk about it, he doesn't talk much anyway, but I know he's worried. . . . Maybe I really could help, though you think I'm such a dope."

There was a pause, while a tiny fourteen-year-old Mexican girl, dressed in a black satin uniform with an embroidered white apron, appeared from the kitchen, seized the heavy tray of punch glasses, and staggered around among the guests with them. Amanda took a glass and sipped. "Gosh," she said, and hid the glass beneath her chair. "Oh, for a Martini!"

This remark softened Hugh, who had just decided to disappear to the bathroom, where he could get at his flask, and he paused to answer her appeal. "I don't know exactly what's going on at the mine, except that Dart thinks Mablett is taking risks with the men. Inadequate ventilation, flimsy timbering, second-grade powder—that sort of thing. And Mablett bullies them all, too. He won't let them play the practical jokes on each other that miners have always used to relieve strain, he won't give them long enough rest periods—petty tyranny. And I know he's paying about the lowest wages in the West."

"Why do they stand for it then?"

Hugh shrugged. "I suppose because the poor devils know they're lucky to have any jobs at all in this year of Grace, because we're a very isolated camp and have always run on our own, and maybe because they have faith in Dart. I don't know. I do know that Mablett countermands every constructive order Dart tries to give. It's tough. The fight between them stems partly from the classic feud, of course."

"What classic feud?"

"Dart's a technical man, highly educated for the job, while Mablett never got past eighth grade in Butte thirty years ago, and ever since he's been battering his way up from mucker, in what is prettily called the school of experience. Naturally, he thinks he knows it all."

Amanda frowned. "What about Mr. Tyson? Isn't he supposed to—to arbitrate?"

"Oh, go talk to him," said Hugh, suddenly bored, and bound for privacy and his flask. "Maybe you'll understand better. Anyway, you shouldn't be sitting here with me. Sexes are segregated at these parties."

So they were. After Hugh's abrupt departure towards the stairs, Amanda noticed that all the ladies were in one group by the Nottingham-lace curtained windows, while the men clustered in the opposite corner near Tyson. Nobody else was in the dining-room. Mrs. Mablett and the little Mexican girl were clattering around in the kitchen.

She sighed and got up, and, walking slowly past the men's group, she threw Dart an imploring look. He smiled, but made no move towards her. She saw that Mr. Tyson was speaking, and caught a sentence. "No, Dartland—no problems tonight. This is a party. And a red-letter day for me, incidentally. I found a complete Hohokam palette in the ruins today."

This reference to his archæological hobby was gibberish to Amanda, but she saw Mablett give Dart a look of mulish triumph, saw the other men turn away and begin to talk of something else, as though a moment of crisis had passed. That Dart was trying to force an issue her intuition told her, and that Mr. Tyson had gently evaded it. Dart shouldn't do that at

a party, she thought; must have plenty of chance at the mine.
But there she was wrong. Tyson was equally elusive at the mine.
He was often bedridden, and his Filipino manservant guarded
him fiercely from all intrusion.

"May I join you?" said Amanda meekly to the ladies' group
and sat down in the nearest chair, which happened to be next
to Pearl Pottner. They all stopped talking and looked at her in
silence. Pearl's huge satin-covered bosom swelled. She had not
forgotten the affront in her store last Monday, nor missed
Amanda's puzzled look of semi-recognition during the introduc-
tions tonight. In truth, Amanda had not at once associated this
resplendent and becurled matron with the woman in the butcher
apron who sold groceries. She now tried to make amends.
"What a lovely dress," she said wildly, eyeing the yellow satin.
"Just like a French import—Lanvin—my sister has at home."

This was not only untrue, but a mistake. She had meant to
say the most flattering thing possible, and saw that she had only
succeeded in sounding pretentious.

Pearl said "Thank you" in iced tones. "I made it myself.
I'm afraid we know little of French clothes in poor old Lodestone."

Oh dear, thought Amanda. The silence resumed. She glanced
helplessly around the group, and fastened on a face warmer than
the others. A little woman in brown velveteen, with brown, intelligent eyes. Amanda called upon the charming frankness
which had never yet failed her, and spoke directly to the little
woman. "I do feel such a fool, but you know I was so frightened
when I came in, I don't remember anybody's name—except Mrs.
Pottner, of course," she added hastily.

The little woman smiled. "To be sure," she said. "'Tis very
natural. Shall I put you to rights?"

"Oh, please," cried Amanda, startled, for the voice was not
at all what she expected, it had an almost Cockney lilt.

"I'm Tessie Rubrick, the postmistress; my husband's shift
boss at the mine. He's working now. We're Cousin Jacks," she
added, her brown eyes twinkling—"Cornish"—she explained
with a lift to her chin. "Both of us from Penzance fifteen years
back. Mrs. Dartland, did ye not know the Cousin Jacks're the
best miners in the world?"

Amanda laughed, relieved to find friendliness at last. The
others smiled vaguely. They were used to Tessie and her

Cornish pride. They continued to smile vaguely as Tessie re-introduced them to Amanda.

The thin, pinched woman in black was Mrs. Kolsanko, wife of the mill superintendent, and therefore, as Amanda later discovered, theoretically on equal social footing with the Mabletts. The Kolsankos, however, did not aspire to power. He was of Montenegrin extraction, and a shy, quiet man who ran the mill efficiently and kept to himself. Mrs. Kolsanko spoke broken English, and had no interests in life beyond crocheting, and her internal ailments, which she dosed with Lydia Pinkham's.

Besides Mrs. Mablett and Mrs. Kolsanko and now Amanda, there was no other staff wife, for like many small and isolated mines, both staff and miners consisted mostly of unattached men, rolling stones, who had, while the choice of operations was still large, drifted from one mine to another with rapidity.

The remaining ladies of the Lodestone hierarchy turned out to be Mrs. Naylor, whose husband ran the Miners' Hardware and Supply Store, Mrs. Zuchowski, the wiry, meagre little woman who owned the hotel, Mrs. Mattie Thompson, a fat widow who ran the switchboard in her home (ten phones in town and they seldom had night calls, so her niece Cora, over from Ray on a visit, was pinch-hitting tonight), and Miss Gladys Arden, the schoolteacher who was forty-four and afflicted with warts to such an extent that she had escaped the matrimony usually urged on all schoolteachers in the West by the woman-hungry males.

Miss Arden had been to college in Nebraska, she informed Amanda in mincing tones, and she named one Amanda had never heard of. "Where did *you* go, Mrs. Dartland?" she asked; "and what was your sorority?"

"I went to Vassar, though only two years," said Amanda apologetically; "and they—they don't have sororities——" There was another silence. All the pairs of eyes contemplated her without expression, except Mrs. Kolsanko's, who was crocheting, and Tessie Rubrick's, which showed uncritical admiration.

"I fear," said Pearl Pottner, in a stately voice, folding her fat hands together, "that you may find Lodestone sadly lacking in cultural refinement; Pearline always said——"

"Oh no," interrupted Amanda, eager to propitiate; "I mean, culture doesn't really mean very much anyway, does it? There

are always books and things. Mother is going to send me some
of the new ones—I'd love to lend them around—if anyone would
like them." She finished lamely, for she saw at once she had
made another mistake, even before Pearl said with a thin smile,
"Kind of you; but we always receive the latest, most improving
books for our little Book Club through arrangement with a
library in Tucson." And she did not ask Amanda to join the
Lodestone Literary Ladies, of which she was president.

"But we'd be mighty glad to have Mrs. Dartland's books too,
now wouldn't we, Pearl!" cried Tessie, smiling at the discomfited girl.

Pearl gave a majestic and non-committal smile, and rose to
meet her hostess, who was shepherding the little Mexican girl
out from the kitchen with another loaded tray.

Amanda had never been snubbed before, and her heart was
sore. I can't help it if I'm an easterner, she thought. She tried to
chat and laugh with the remaining ladies, but there was nothing
to talk about. Tessie had gone too, to help with the serving.
Amanda subsided into unhappy silence, staring at the Mablett
walls. They were papered in sulphur yellow, lavishly dotted with
chromos and framed photographs of the Mablett family.

The evening dragged on its appointed way. The collation was
impressive. Lydia Mablett belonged to the Woman's Page, or
Hand-painted, school of cookery. Each dish was cunningly designed to look like something else. The salads had little faces
drawn on canned pear halves with pimento features, and marsh-
mallow and cheese hair. The main dish represented nesting
birds, the birds (cut from pork with cookie cutters) nesting on
green-pea eggs. These creations provoked much admiring
comment, and they were certainly very good. Everyone ate
greedily except Hugh. He sat slumped in a corner, glowering
into space.

At nine, Mrs. Mablett gaily proposed a few hands of Auction,
and Amanda, who was a good bridge player, but knew Auction
only by name as an ancestor of Contract was relieved to have
Dart stand up saying, "I'm sorry, Mrs. Mablett, but I don't play.
And I've got to get back up to the mine tonight."

"Tonight!" cried Amanda. All heads turned and looked at
Dart, who stood very quiet, his hand resting on the table, his
head thrown back a little.

"I understand there's been orders to enter the old Shamrock

workings tonight in the graveyard. That there's been orders to start pulling the pillars in the old number thirty-three stope," Dart said pleasantly. He looked at Mablett, then he looked at Tyson. "Now I happen to know the timbering's rotten in there. Any drilling'll start a cave-in."

Amanda saw Mr. Tyson raise his head and frown. She did not understand the terrifying impact of the two little words "cave-in," but she saw a tremor run over the faces of all the men, and a hostility too, as they looked up at Dart. He continued in the same voice, "So I think I better go up and change the orders."

Luther Mablett hoisted himself out of his chair, and thrust his glistening red face towards Dart. "You can't do that. They're MY orders."

Dart's mouth tightened, and his eyes also narrowed to a cold implacability that frightened Amanda. Dart, don't—she cried to him silently—don't make a scene now! Dart merely bowed a trifle. "Then I shall go underground to be there with the men when your orders are obeyed."

"Bravo," said Hugh loudly from his corner.

There was a moment of complete silence. The company sat transfixed, staring at the two big men by the table.

Mablett's ponderous brain reacted slowly. Then suddenly his great hand formed into a fist and came crashing down on the walnut top. Veins stood out on his forehead. "Goddam know-it-all! Will you stop butting into every goddam——"

"Luther!" cried Mrs. Mablett, clutching at his arm. He shook her off.

"Lousy mine foreman with a fancy degree, sucking up to the men, stirring up trouble, sneaking around behind my back, I'll show you who's——"

"Wait a minute, Mablett! Hold on." The thin, weak voice cut between the angry men like a cold knife. The general manager stood on his feet beside them, swaying a little; his head barely reached to their shoulders, but his tired old eyes were steady and authority had returned to them.

"Dart," he said, "how do you know the timbering's rotten?"

"Because I've tested every inch of it."

Mablett scowled furiously. "I say it's not. I say it'll hold up until we get the old stope cleaned out and we need that ore. You know goddam well we need that ore, and fast—if you cared anything about the mine——" He glared at Dart, but his voice was more subdued.

Tyson held up his transparent, veined hand. "Wait, Mablett. We all care about the mine, but we care about the men, too. Now I don't know who's right and I can't get underground to see for myself just now, but as long as there's any doubt, I think you had better hold up work on that stope until everything's shored up."

Amanda saw Dart's muscles relax, and her throat unclosed, too. A rustling sigh fluttered over the room, then there was no sound again but Mablett's heavy breathing. He stood there with his jaw thrust out, his fists still clenched, his bulging eyes shifted from Tyson's face to the carpet, and in them there was an angry bewilderment.

The old man smiled, he put one hand on Dart's arm, the other on Mablett's. "Now look, boys—you're both good men," he said gently. "I'm lucky to have you. I know you can get along. You got to listen to each other a bit more, but Dart—remember he's your boss——" The thin voice paused. Amanda, watching, saw Dart give himself a shake. He looked down at Mr. Tyson with affection not unmixed with indulgence. "Yes, sir," he said, "I know that."

"And, Lute," continued Tyson, turning, "when you got mad just now you said some pretty rough things to Dart. I'm sure you didn't mean 'em."

Mablett mumbled something inarticulate, and Tyson's hands dropped from their arms, he staggered backwards towards his chair. In the old days I'd have made 'em shake hands, he thought; I'd have made 'em pull together somehow, but I'm too tired. . . . Too tired for fights. . . .

The dining-room billowed and darkened around him, the nagging ache in his left arm speared up into his chest. He slumped gasping into the chair. "You got your ampoules with you?" He heard the doctor's sharp voice, and felt fingers fumbling in his breast pocket. Then he smelled the pungence of the broken ampoule in his nostrils, the pain receded, the lights came back into the dining-room. "I'm all right," he said irritably, pushing Hugh away. "Plenty of life in the old dog yet."

"Sure," said Hugh, shrugging. "Cardiacs live for ever if they take care of themselves. You better go home to bed now; your Filipino's here with the car."

Mr. Tyson's attack at least provided respite from the embarrassment of the earlier scene. Amanda stammered the usual courtesies: "Thank you so much . . . delicious food . . ." to a clammily unresponsive Mrs. Mablett. She and Dart escaped, to find Hugh outside in the road waiting for them. He had been helping Tyson into the car. The three of them started walking up Creek Street.

"Showdown," remarked Hugh. "Victory for noble young mine foreman. Except you damn-near killed the general manager in the process."

"Either that or kill three miners," said Dart. "That timbering's rotten."

"So I gather. You made your point. You think maybe dear Luther's going to love you better now and tremble with delight at all your opinions?"

"No. But he may be more careful for a while."

Hugh hiccoughed, and said, "Christ, I sure need another drink. Well, you at least provided some entertainment at last at one of those God-awful Lodestone parties. And I'll bet they're having fun now——" He jerked his head back towards the Mablett house. "Indignation meeting."

"But surely somebody'll be on Dart's side," cried Amanda quickly. "They've got to be, because he's right."

Both men had almost forgotten her. They paused now and stared at her. She looked very pretty in the starlight, her anxious eyes raised to Dart's face. He took her hand and tucked it through his arm. "Poor baby, you had quite an evening!"

"Awful," she agreed, trying to laugh. "But, Dart, *somebody*'ll be on your side . . . that little Jones man with the glasses, the chief engineer, isn't he? He looked nice."

"Maybe," said Dart soothingly, "but Jones doesn't get underground much, he's run ragged assaying, surveying, map-drawing. Anyway, Mablett's his boss, too, you know."

"Dart's a new-comer, my dear," said Hugh, "and has established himself as a purveyor of unpleasant facts. That he may be right will not make him popular as well."

"Nor do I give a damn," said Dart. He lifted his face to the sky in an unconscious gesture.

No, he doesn't give a damn, she thought, but I do. Her heart grew thick and heavy in her breast, and she dropped her gaze to the dark pebbly road. Unpopularity hurt. How could you live

among people who did not like you or admire you. Even before
the quarrel in all that gathering tonight, there had not been
one friendly face, except Tessie Rubrick's. And then later,
during the flustered leave-takings, Tessie had looked confused
and uncertain. But Tessie's husband was a shift boss at the
mine. No doubt she was afraid to take sides. They were all
afraid except Dart. Afraid of what? Of disapproval from the
herd, of insecurity. Oh, I wish—I wish . . .

"Medical Centre," said Hugh, turning at the hospital path.
"Come on in. I've got some rotgut left. You both need a swig."

"Sure do," said Dart. "But I'll pick it up later when I get
down from the mine. Give Andy a drink and then send her
home."

"You're going to the mine, anyway?" she said, her hand
tightening on his arm. "Oh, darling, must you?"

"I'm afraid so—I've got to change those orders in case
Mablett should happen to forget. I want to talk to some of the
men on the graveyard, anyway." He patted her shoulder and
strode rapidly up the road.

"Graveyard," she repeated, watching him disappear into the
night.

Hugh chuckled. "Graveyard is a shift, my girl, from midnight
on. You needn't sound so tragic about it. Come on in."

She followed him slowly into the hospital waiting-room. A
figure in crumpled white unfolded from the rattan sofa.

"What's that?" Amanda said, startled out of her depression.

Hugh made a sound in his throat and pulled the light chain.
"That's my nurse!"

Maria, who had been asleep, returned Amanda's stare with
interest, while she languidly coiled up the long, shining black
hair, which had tumbled around her shoulders, and pinned on
her cap. Something new, Doc bringing girls here at night, and
she didn't like it. He'd had a snootful, all right—but not real
drunk yet.

"Stand up for Chris-sake," said Hugh. "This is Mrs. Dartland."

"Yeah, I know," said Maria, not moving. As if the whole of
Lodestone hadn't seen her trotting around with her nose in the
air, and her pearls and her yellow hair; as if everyone hadn't
been gabbing about the mine foreman's wife from New York.
"What's she doing here? She sick?"

"Oh, shut up," said Hugh. "What did you do with my bottle
—drink it?"

"You locked it in the drug cupboard."

"So I did. Any calls? Not that you'd hear them."

Maria shrugged and stood up. "Well, I didn't hear none."

"Sit down, Andy," said Hugh. "I'll get you a drink."

Amanda, who had been listening to this colloquy in considerable amazement, sat down. She was not experienced enough to
guess the actual situation, she saw only in Maria's insolence yet
more baseless enmity. This enmity Hugh partly dissipated in the
dispensary, where Maria had followed him. "You want I should
go home now, I guess . . . now you got HER," said the girl through
her teeth, watching him pour shots into white enamel cups.
"Maybe she's why you ain't been very loving in a while."

Hugh drained his cup and snorted. "Good God, no! What a
mind you've got, never rises above the umbilicus. You can stay
until I pass out. Go wait in my room."

Maria's brow cleared. She put her arms around his neck. He
shoved her away. "God, you stink, and I'm not so drunk yet I
don't mind. Go take a bath." He pushed her towards his
quarters off the kitchen, and returned to the waiting-room bearing
the enamel cups. Amanda had discovered Susan in a box in a
corner with her three pups, and she was down on her knees
crooning to them.

"My patient," said Hugh, pointing to the dog. "She paid for
this refreshment." He handed Amanda the cup. Amanda got
up, caught by the bitterness of his tone, by the ugly twist to his
mouth under the straw-coloured little moustache. He's not
friendly either, she thought, but he's at least someone I can talk
to. She sipped from her cup, and acrid fire ran down her throat
and up into her brain. She sipped again.

"Hugh," she said, "I'm scared. I feel lost. Nothing, nobody
is like anything I've ever known."

"Well, you haven't known much," he said, lighting himself a
cigarette. "You've lived on cushions."

"Why must Dart hate so, be so unyielding? I know he's right,
but why can't he bend a little, compromise, coax them along?"

"For one thing he's not an appeaser, and for another he's part
Indian."

She winced, and he regarded her with a malicious satisfaction.
"You knew that when you married him. Don't you love him?"

"Oh, I do. I do. More than anything in the world. . . ."

"Well, then, stop beefing. Dart's a better man than you or me. D'ju want another drink?" He stood up swaying a little. She shook her head. "Well, I do. Run along home."

Loneliness swept over her, released by the drink. "Home," she said. . . . "Oh, why do we have to be so—*poor*?"

He paused by the sill, holding on to the lintel. "Yes, that's what Viola thought," he muttered; "but *she* never said it."

Amanda, lost in her own maze, stared at him uncomprehending.

CHAPTER FOUR

As Dart strode up the mine road that night he thought about Amanda. He was more sensitive to her discouragement than she realized. He had not stopped at their home to pick up the car, because there was plenty of time to reach the mine before the men came off night-shift, and always he preferred to walk. Especially to walk alone through the star-flooded night.

For him now, the heavy stillness of the desert mountains shimmered into life with a hundred intimate welcomes. The limestone cliffs far to the west reflected light, and the Teddy Bear chollas glowed like phosphorescence along the margins of their fuzz of spines. The paloverdes, tender-green even at night, waved and murmured in the wind; the little brittle bush, ghost grey along the roadside, sent forth its incense perfume against the sharper smell of the creosotes; and the giant saguaros, their majestic arms uplifted to the sky in eternal invocation, repeated the solemn note of welcome from the dim mountains behind.

His spirit expanded into awareness, and with each exhilarating breath he drew in strength from this country of his birth. It was the stern and mystic land of his India forebears, the Apaches, and farther back than that to the Ancient Ones who had called the Arizona mountains home, even before the Apaches came.

That Amanda felt none of this, he knew. Here, for her as yet, there was no message. She had no shield against the buzzing swarm of small discomforts, or the clashing of divergent personalities from which he could so easily escape. She was still a spoiled and charming child, striving to gild the raw stuff of life with romantic illusion, yearning for the fairy-tale. He loved her, she had sensitivity and humour, and she was a warmly responsive mate. He did not regret their marriage. He had never in his life regretted a decision once taken. He had known, as she had not, the risks involved in their marriage, and he was prepared to be patient with her flounderings, with her initial recoil from a tough and alien environment, from the tough and alien streak in himself. But she must also make her own way and find her own life apart from him, for he despised dependence as much as his nature demanded solitude at times.

Calise Cunningham might help, he thought suddenly. He had entered the ghost town, and he turned from the road up the shattered trail towards the great silent mansion. He saw a thin strip of light between the velvet portières in her ground-floor window. As he mounted the broken steps, he heard the rippling of a piano, and a low clear voice singing. He hesitated, his hand on the silver shamrock knocker until the song stopped. There was silence after his knock, then the door opened a crack.

"It's Dartland," he said quickly; "I just wanted to see you for a moment. May I come in?"

"Oh, it's you," she said, and opened the door. "Come in."

She was dressed in a neat black wool, which hung loose about her slender body. This was the type of dress in which he had always seen her, except the once he had brought Hugh there. Her thick white hair was coiled into a black net on the nape of her neck. Tonight there was no perfume, rouge, or jewels. Except for her grace of movement and the carriage of her head, she looked her full age.

She surveyed Dart with her calm dispassionate eyes, then silently led the way into her living-room. It was not large, it had been only an ante-chamber in the original house, and aside from the velvet portières which shrouded the windows and a wall of bookcases, it was starkly furnished. There was a table and two straight chairs, some fibre matting on the floor, and the piano, nothing else. But on the table there stood an Indian bowl full of desert broom—a common bush Dart had seen a thousand times, but in this bare room it sprang to feathery pearl and olive beauty.

"What is it you want, Dart?" she asked, sitting down on the piano stool and smiling a little.

He hesitated, caught from the impulse which had sent him there by the strength of the impression she always made on him. Bare as the room was, it repeated the same note of order and peace which emanated from her. A crystalline force, almost tangible. She is like a silver bell, he thought.

"I wanted your help——" he said at last.

Calise raised her eyebrows. "Help from a crazy old woman who sees ghosts?"

"You see more than ghosts," he said slowly. "I think you see

into the true spirit behind things—behind people. I think you
have suffered much, and understand much."

She looked at him steadily, the inward, withdrawn look in her
wise, dark eyes. "I have suffered and I have prayed. Often now
I am happy, for God answers me—in music, in my books, in
the mountains."

"Yes," he said. "You've found happiness where so few
could. . . . It's——"

She nodded. "You're troubled about your wife," she said.
"I see it now. You are strong and she has not yet learned to be.
She is very young."

"If you'd let her come up here and see you. Talk to her. She
needs a friend."

Calise laughed then. A warm gay sound. "Ah, Dart, you
choose strange friends for your little bride. Do you know what
I was playing when you came?" He shook his head. "*Don
Giovanni*. 'Il Mio Tesoro'—Listen!"

She turned on the stool and began to sing. "'Take my
beloved in your keeping, console her, drive away her tears'—it's
very apropos, is it not?" She turned, and he nodded, smiling.

"I'll do what I can, Dart," she said, and stood up. "But she
must not come here at the bad times. She would be frightened."

He frowned, suddenly realizing how grotesque his effort to
promote the friendship of this woman would seem to Amanda,
or indeed to anyone in Lodestone. But she's *not* a lunatic, he
thought.

Calise read his thoughts again, and the cool impersonal flame
which nourished her warmed in the sympathy between them.

"It is like this——" she said slowly, groping to express that
which she had never told, the terror of which she tried never to
think until a day or so before it happened, and she was forced to
accede. Then the first sinister premonitions gave way to tor-
ment, then to a mounting agony of the spirit, and she was once
again plunged into the inexorable tragedy.

"It is like the cinematograph—the movie, you call it now.
It comes again and again, never changing, the same in every
detail—except that I cannot watch from a safe seat in the theatre.
I am in it, and I must play my part, as I did the first time." Her
pupils dilated and she turned her head away. "My bitter, bitter
part."

"But it's *not* real—you know that," he said quickly.

"Ah, but it is," she answered in a dull voice. "Look. I've studied much to try to understand." She gestured towards her books. "Time—the other dimensions, the curve we cannot see. It is that Time, for me, has caught itself on a snag; in this one thing it cannot flow on. The past always becomes the present and the future, but by God's grace, usually we do not know it. It is my punishment that I am caught. Not allowed to forget." She raised her thin, white hand and let it drop again; she looked back at Dart with eyes of resignation. "It comes back, you see— and I must feel as I did once, and Raoul must come to me here, young and handsome as he was that night. He was my cousin from New Orleans, and I loved him when I was twelve, even in the Convent from which I later fled—breaking the good sisters' hearts. Raoul must come, and I must take him to my bed as I did then. My husband's bed, the man I never loved, though I married him because he was so rich. Then my husband comes home because he guesses, he finds us, and he shoots Raoul six times, until the head of my beloved is a bloody pulp on the pillow. And he would have shot me, as I begged him to, but something burst in his brain. He fell to the floor paralysed. His body never moved again until he died. I killed them both."

Dart looked at her with a pity she made no call upon. "No, you didn't kill them," he said gently. "And your share, your guilt, you've expiated long ago. After all, it was a tragedy, but something like that has happened often enough before to people who've——"

She stopped him with a strange half-smile. "I am not 'people.' Each one of us is separate in our destiny. Each one of us must struggle on alone, fighting the monsters of deceit and lust and cruelty until at last, some day, somewhere, we reach the top— and peace."

She moved across the fibre matting to the door. "Now go," she said. "I've talked too much. It's not good to talk about these things. But you have in you something which will understand a little. I will see your wife, if you still wish it; but come first yourself to be sure that it is *now* with me and not thirty-five years ago." She smiled and held out her hand, touching his lightly. And in the cool contact he felt the crystal quality of her, and felt, too, the agony it must be, when the unknown compulsion, no matter whence it came, poured into this crystal vessel the ugliness of bloody passions which had been long since spent.

"I don't entirely understand," he said; "but I admire you very much, madame."

As he walked down the trail he heard the piano again. The cool, pure notes of Mozart, and her voice, silver-toned as a bell in the night air. "Take my beloved in your keeping, console her, drive away her tears——"

He smiled a little to himself as he hurried up the mine road. Yes, she might help Amanda, incongruous as it seemed. Because Calise had integrity, that most desirable of all virtues. Even in the recurring storm that racked her there was integration, for she submitted to it with fear certainly, but also with recognition of its mysterious part in a larger purpose. How few people admitted the existence of evil, and yet had wisdom enough to fight it with the only weapons of any value, the beautiful comfort of simple things, like her Indian bowl full of desert broom, or the making of music. How few knew the values of solitude and the quiet persistent search for glimpses of the Spirit.

She is like Saba in many ways, he thought. And a longing came to him for his mother. Perhaps Saba would leave San Carlos for a few days and come to see them. Even as he thought that, he knew it would not be a good thing. Where could she stay? And though she would try to hide it, how deeply Amanda would be shocked by the gaunt silent woman in the flounced Apache dress with the blue tattoo marks on her chin. Nor, with the state of the mine as precarious as it was, could he take time to visit the reservation himself. If the roads were dry, a hurried trip might be made on a Sunday, but he knew that it was wiser that the two women should not meet yet. His mother understood this, as she understood all direct elemental matters of feeling. It was thus in silence, with instinctive wisdom, that she had sustained his father, and himself as a boy, even during the period when he had been East at prep school, and ashamed, not exactly of his Indian blood, but suffering the normal adolescent shame of being different from his fellows. She had known then how to give him strength, and after his father died, she had known how to console his deep grief with a substitute father—Tanosay, her own father, the fierce Apache war chief, who had never repented of any of his actions, who lived out most of his life in a remote rancheria in the Natanes Mountains untouched by missionary or agency, and who became for Dart the rock and the salvation of his turbulent adolescence.

Those were strange years, in which Dart had had a foot in two different worlds: the American boarding-school life in a small New England town, punctuated by Christmas and Thanksgiving with Professor Dartland's spinster sisters in Boston, and the summers in an Apache wickiup in a fastness of the Arizona mountains with his grandfather Tanosay, and Saba. Belonging to both worlds, and yet not quite in either of them, it had been necessary to learn to live without belonging, to develop a unity within the self which needed no support.

Tanosay had had no doubts, ever. For him there were no half-tones. There were friends and there were enemies. The friends you died for, the enemies you killed, and a lying tongue which pretended to be friend and was not should be killed with torture. That was but justice. Though pain and death in themselves were never as important as the Spirit's humiliation. Nothing must ever threaten the essential dignity of the soul. And Tanosay believed in the tangible existence of the soul, as he believed in Usen, the God-Spirit, whose essence pervades all created things.

Tanosay, lean and wary as an Arizona lion, had been a powerful shaman as well as a chief. He was related to the Great Cochise, Chief of the Chiricahuas, and had shared with him and the other Apache tribes much of the forty years' struggle with the white man. A history of violated peace treaties, of corrupt agents, of greed for land and gold, of hysterical fear. And also of an occasional opponent worthy of respect like Crooks, Clum, and Jeffords. These were good men, all too soon replaced by weaker, double-tongued ones, in response to the impatient and vacillating policies of the Indian Bureau three thousand miles away.

It had been in 1882 that Tanosay and many other Apache chiefs travelled the war-path for the last time, and eventually accepted defeat with the stoicism popularly attributed to Indians, though it was really compounded of two more positive factors—recognition of the changing order, and the desire to save their people from extermination. True, Geronimo's guerrilla warfare continued for four more years, but Geronimo was an outlaw among his own people, and his little band of renegades, squaws, and children—though it required five thousand United States soldiers to subdue—never had the support of the wiser Apaches.

Tanosay had justification for his series of raids in 'eighty-two, one of which resulted in the capture of little Nellie Brown, Saba's mother. Tanosay's brother, Na-Klin, had always had friendship for the whites because of General Crook, for whom he had acted as scout against the Mojaves. And yet, after the trouble at Cibicue, in which five scouts were accused of mutiny, Na-Klin, who was innocent, was summarily hanged with the rest.

Tanosay's heart lay like a dark and bitter fruit in his breast while he led his band of Coyoteros on the path of revenge. From the Tonto Basin to the Gila he burned isolated ranch-houses, and clubbed or shot the owners, determined to rid Apacheland of these treacherous white intruders. He was down in Arivaipa country near Fort Thomas, when he spied, from ambush in the rocks, an isolated mule-drawn wagon plodding along the road towards Globe. It was driven by Abner Brown from Missouri, who was lured like many another by the rich silver-mining district around Globe—the mining district which had been arbitrarily grabbed from the Apache reservation as soon as anything of value had been found there.

Abner Brown had with him in the wagon his wife, his grown son, and his sixteen-year-old daughter Nellie, and being of an arrogant and foolhardy nature, he had ignored the warning of Apache uprisings he had heard along the road from Silver City.

Tanosay, whose lust for revenge had now been somewhat sated, might not have bothered with the lone wagon, but he needed ammunition, and the shiny new rifles which the two men carried across their knees.

During the brief fight Abner and his son killed three of Tanosay's warriors, and fought so bravely that by Tanosay's orders and according to immemorial custom, their bodies were not molested after death, nor was that of Mrs. Brown, whose husband shot her through the heart with his last bullet to save her from the Apaches. Little Nellie had fainted, and Tanosay thought for a while that she, too, was dead. When he found that she was not, he picked her up and took her back to his hidden rancheria in the wild Natanes Mountains, along with the bodies of his three slain warriors.

Nellie was a gentle, pretty girl of limited intelligence at best. Nature now mercifully wiped from her mind in a total amnesia the horror which had befallen her family, and all memory of her life before that moment on the Globe road.

Tanosay took her to his own wickiup, and she was kindly received by his wife, Man-tzee, who was a plump and good-tempered woman from the Chiricahuas, though regrettably barren. Nellie was not unhappy, she fitted herself into the domestic life of the tribe, she danced well, she wove baskets, she roasted mescal, and she learned how to brew from fermented corn a tizwin as potent as any in the rancheria. Tanosay grew fond of her and married her. Man-tzee did not complain. The two wives lived together amicably. The next year, when Saba was born to Nellie, it was Man-tzee who received the baby with a soft cry of pleasure, and it was Man-tzee who tenderly nursed Nellie through the ensuing child-bed fever. Tanosay used all his medicinal arts for Nellie—he invoked Usen, the deity, through Tanosay's own particular totem, the white-tailed deer; he sang for Nellie the Purification chant; he sprinkled her with the sacred pollen; and when these failed, he sent for another shaman from Fort Apache across the mountains.

But Nellie died. The baby, Saba, never knew that Man-tzee was not her mother, nor that she herself was only half Apache, until the fall that she was twelve and went to the Indian school at San Carlos. Then it was that Tanosay told her her history and soothed her grief and shock with thoughtful words. "The world has changed, my daughter. The white man now rules this land of ours, and we must accept. One never rebels against the things one cannot change, for that is weakness. It is better that you go to school and learn the white ways which were once the ways of your real mother."

In truth, the arms of the Agency were lengthening each year, and Tanosay had had to bow to compromise. He could no longer keep his people separate and self-sustaining as in the old days when they had ranged over half Arizona at will. If they were not to starve, they must move down from the mountains for the winter months, at least. They must learn agriculture, and they must accept the weekly rations doled out by the patronizing Government. All these acceptances were distasteful things, and though the Apaches bowed to the inevitable, nothing could force them to enjoy a way of life so alien to their natures, nor force them to admire their conquerors. They remained proudly aloof.

Saba, more aloof than any of them, ignored her white blood. None of her teachers, nobody at the Agency, ever guessed it.

Her skin was lighter than some, but Indian skin tones vary as do white ones, and her features were those of Tanosay. She learned English with rapidity, as she learned all her lessons, fast and well, but most Apache children are highly intelligent, and she evoked no special notice beyond a recommendation that she go on to the new Indian school at Phœnix for further education. And it was at Tanosay's insistence that she did so. He loved her, and he was wise enough to wish her to be as well equipped as possible for coping, not only with the new order, but with the inevitable day when her white blood should awake, and she would begin to suffer the humiliation and the loneliness inherent in the term "half-breed."

That day never actually came, for Saba continued to feel entirely Apache, and yet it was no doubt her white blood which contributed to the success of her marriage. Her heart had never been touched until the morning when Professor Jonathan Dartland, wan and thin from the tuberculosis which had sent him to Arizona, came to the Indian school in search of an efficient girl to be his part-time housekeeper. Saba had always thought to marry an Apache, one of her father's band, when this tedious exile should be over, but she fell deeply in love with Dartland and he with her. And for the fifteen years of their marriage until his death, they were happy together and with little Dart in a modern house in the desert near Phœnix. And then, after the funeral and to the disapproving amazement of their few friends and acquaintances, Saba had quietly returned to the reservation and to Tanosay.

"Can you beat that!" people said. "Right back to the blanket, filthy wickiup, no plumbing, raw meat in a pot, and those ridiculous clothes! After all those years with a charming, refined man like Professor Dartland. Once an Indian, always an Indian. Why in the world do we waste the taxpayers' money putting a veneer on them that rubs right off?"

But Saba knew that her Jonathan would have understood. Indeed they had discussed it many times. He knew that when the spirit is filled and dwelling in the climate of its dreams and memories, it cares little about physical conditions. He knew that except for himself and Dart, all Saba's love was given to her own people—to Tanosay.

Dart, rounding the last curve on the mine road, and seeing the head frame over the old Shamrock shaft outlined against the sky, had a sudden memory of his grandfather, a memory of which he had not thought for years.

Tanosay had been old and decaying, too, that last time Dart had seen him, and yet he, too, had looked against the night sky with an imperturbable and rooted dignity. A wonderful old guy, Dart thought. He remembered the tall, brown, and seamed body, scarred from a hundred wounds, the shrewd black eyes which could gaze unmoved on murder, and yet could soften to tenderness for children, especially a grandson. He remembered the old man's rare laugh, chuckling and bubbling like a mountain spring. How few white people realized the keenness of the Indian sense of humour. He had heard Tanosay laugh that day, and he had also seen the old face grow dark and stern as the northern sky when the storm clouds gathered. For Tanosay knew that It-which-must-not-be-mentioned was stealing near on soft padded feet, and soon the women's doleful voices would be uplifted for him in the death dirge. "Listen well, Ish-kin-azi," he had said to Dart, calling him as always by his nickname "tall boy," for real names were never used in conversation. "Listen well, my son, for it is the last time . . ." Dart had listened, but his boy's attention had wandered. He had been deeply impressed, but he had not altogether understood the old man's effort to hand down to him some of the secret wisdom of the "Dinneh," some of the certainties about life and death, and about the Apache holy trinity—Earth, Air, and Water.

Dart now approached the collar of the new Plymouth mine shaft, and smiled a little to himself as he turned right and entered the change house. He knew how Tanosay would have dealt with a man as stupid and bungling as Mablett. The Indians, true socialist, never hesitated to sacrifice one individual for the good of the tribe. But unfortunately the beauties of civilization also entailed such watery virtues as caution and expediency and conformity.

The eleven-thirty whistle blew as Dart climbed into his muddy blue jeans and rubber boots. He hauled aloft on the pulley the suit in which he had dined at the Mabletts'. He hurried up to the mine office to read the order book. Sure enough, Mablett had not been there, and the order to start pulling the pillars in the old No. 33 stope was unchanged. Dart set his lips and erased the order. The men began to straggle off shift and queue up

outside the paymaster's window. Dart lit a cigarette and sat
waiting until the shift bosses came into the room.

The night boss that week, Tom Rubrick, Tessie's husband,
was a wiry little terrier of a Cornishman, with darting eyes
which missed nothing, and a nervous energy which incited his
men to top production. He was an excellent boss, and they
worked well for him. He came off shift at his usual jog-trot,
hurriedly munching a Cornish pasty he had found in his pocket,
and gave a low, surprised whistle when he saw Dart.

"And wot be ye doing 'ere at this time o' night? I thought ye
went to Bull'ead's party?"

"I did for a while. Saw your wife there. I left early for . . .
reasons."

Tom cocked his head and glanced at the order book. He saw
the erasure of a line which had drawn his startled attention as
he went on shift that afternoon. The situation was thus fairly
clear to him.

Dart knew that, alone of the three shift bosses, Tom was
sympathetic to Dart's problems. Tiger Burton on day-shift,
despite his nickname which came from his early predilection for
Faro, or Tiger, was a meagre and colourless man, middle-aged
and sallow. He had known Mablett in Butte days, he owed his
job to him—and he was plainly Mablett's creature.

Big Olaf, on graveyard, obeyed orders with Scandinavian
literalness and complete lack of curiosity. Olaf came in now and
leaned against the lintel, his greying blond head lowered, his
jaws working ruminatively on a plug of tobacco, waiting without
interest for Dart and Tom to finish conferring.

Tom, however, did have curiosity, but he also had respect for
the young mine foreman who, he knew, would not tell him the
story of the changed orders. Dart maintained discipline, and no
matter what the justification, he did not complain of superiors
to subordinates. Tom's curiosity was too much for him, however, and he whispered, "You and Bull'ead 'ave a set-to, tonight?"

Dart's lips twitched, he passed over this second disrespectful
use of the superintendent's nickname, and shrugged.

"Well, 'ow in the name o' 'eaven did ye ever make 'im back
down on them orders?"

"Mr. Tyson was there," said Dart briefly.

"Aow . . ." said Tom, enlightened. He shook his head and

sighed. A mine that had bickering at the top was a bad thing. But the lad was right. Bullhead was for ever taking wicked chances. "You going underground, sir?" he said, glancing at Dart's clothes, and raising his voice to include Olaf, who shambled forward.

"Yes," said Dart. "As long as I'm here, I'll do some sampling. What's the report, Tom?" The conversation became technical as Rubrick reported to Olaf, the incoming shift boss, the mine activities of the last eight hours. They had been working on the 700 level, water seepage was getting worse. One of the pumps had broken down, repaired at 10 p.m. The ore didn't look so good in the new drift, and they were running into heavy ground. Curly Jim, one of the muckers, had dropped a rock on his foot and had gone home, but said he didn't need a doctor.

That's just as well, thought Dart. I doubt that Hugh'll do any doctoring tonight.

Twelve holes had been drilled in the face of the cross-cut, continued Tom, the blasts set for eleven-twenty after the men had left as usual. "Watch out for missed 'oles, though," said Tom; "I've not too much faith in this new lot o' powder Mr. Mablett's got in." He glanced at Dart. "Got it cheap, didn't 'e?"

"I believe so," said Dart non-committally. "You know we've got to cut costs every way we can."

"Sure," remarked Olaf the Swede, in the brief silence, and resumed chewing.

Rubrick cocked one eyebrow and gave Dart a shrewd, affectionate glance. "Well, watch out for yourselves, lads," he said. "There's something don't feel right underground. Me Cousin Jacks've been 'earing the Tommyknockers all evening."

Dart laughed. "Your Cousin Jacks wouldn't have sneaked a little hooch down in their lunch-boxes, would they?"

"No, sir," said Rubrick, suddenly serious. "You know I don't let 'em drink on the job."

"I know," said Dart. He knew, too, how foolish it was to argue with the miners' superstitions. The lamps that dimmed or flickered—an evil portent. The taboo against whistling, against women in the mine. The Tommyknockers, tiny English elves who tapped among the rocks to warn their countrymen of danger. He smiled and stood up. "The Tommyknockers didn't know the change of orders; they thought we were going into the old workings, maybe." He grinned at Rubrick, then turned to

Olaf. "You got it all?" The Swede nodded. "Then we better get going."

They left Rubrick scribbling his report in the order book, and walked outside the office and around a pile of timber to the hoist. The men were already waiting by the cage, a dozen of them, six more than the usual skeleton crew on graveyard, since Mablett had ordered extra men for the No. 33 stope work. They greeted Dart pleasantly. Despite his reserve and the knowledge that he was a "technical" man, he was liked by most of the miners for his industry and his justice, and for his identification with their welfare. The divergences of opinion between the mine superintendent and foreman naturally filtered underground at times, and the majority of the men favoured Dart.

He stood by the cage with Olaf watching them pile in: a heterogeneous lot—two "Bohunks" from Montenegro and Jugoslavia, one Polack, three Mexicans, a Cornishman, an Irishman, a Finn, and the others native Americans, including, as Dart noted with interest, one of the Apache boys whose white name was Grover Cleveland. The Apaches, when complying with the Agency's request for pronounceable English names, were apt to pick at random from the Indian school's textbooks.

Cleveland was a stocky, good-looking young man, quick to laugh and slow to anger. He was an Aravaipa, descendant of Eskiminzin, long-suffering chief who had repeatedly trusted the white man, and as repeatedly been betrayed. Dart had known Cleveland slightly during his boyhood days on the reservation, and often talked with him in the mine, and he was glad to see him tonight. The Indian was an expert driller, a good all-around miner, far better than most of the flotsam and jetsam Mablett insisted on hiring.

"Hello, Cleve," said Dart, catching up with the Apache as they walked down the tunnel on the 700 level towards the new cross-cut. "Glad to see you. I was afraid—I heard you had quit."

"I quit tomorrow, Nantan," said Cleve, using the Apache word for Boss. "I'm going home."

Dart sighed. It would be hard to get another driller as intelligent and trustworthy, and also Dart had a feeling of personal loss. "Is it the money?" he asked. "I'll try very hard to get you a raise."

The Apache lifted his head, and in the light of their two carbide hat lamps they looked at each other steadily.

"It's not the money, Nantan," he shrugged. Suddenly his black eyes twinkled and his smooth brown face creased in a smile. "There'll be big tulapai party next week, at San Carlos, and coming-out dance for my little sister. We'll get very drunk, have big fun."

Dart smiled, too; he knew it was useless to argue, but he knew there were other reasons behind this wish to return to the reservation. "How about the other boys?" he said slowly, referring to the other five Apaches who worked in the mine.

"They go too, Nantan."

"You'll come back though later, after the dance, won't you? I'll see that you get your jobs back."

The Indian did not answer. They walked along through the silent dim tunnel. Their lamps, and that of Olaf just ahead, glimmered like dancing will-o'-the-wisps in the darkness. Three muckers followed them; they were Mexicans, and they chuckled softly and told filthy jokes in Spanish as they walked. The other members of the shift had scattered earlier to other parts of the mine according to their several jobs. There was no sound but the squelch of rubber boots through the deepening puddles, and the tap, tap of dripping, invisible water. Then Cleve spoke suddenly in a low tone, and he spoke in Apache. "We cannot work here, Nantan. Not for this Tiger Burton."

"Burton?" repeated Dart, surprised.

Cleve nodded. "He is not like other men; he is hissing and sly as a serpent. He is crooked as a serpent, too. He is not a stupid bull like Mablett. He is a very bad man. He is crazy."

Dart tightened his lips and sighed with exasperation. He agreed on the estimate of Mablett, but Burton, the shift boss, had always seemed efficient. Dart had seen no special fault in him except that he was Mablett's sycophant.

"Your talk is foolish," he answered, also in Apache. "There are many things not quite right in the world. One must do the best one can in spite of it."

The Indian made a noise in his throat—of indulgence, or derision. Dart waited during another silence. Apache conversation cannot be hurried.

Then Cleve spoke again. "Burton hates the Apaches, Nantan. His mother was killed by Geronimo nearly fifty winters ago. You did not know that, did you?"

"No," said Dart, startled. "I thought Tiger came from Butte, like Mablett."

"Later. But he was born in Nogales. He is Mexican. This he hides. Even if he were not crazy and bad, I could not work under a Mexican, Nantan." Cleve twisted his head to look up at Dart, and again his black eyes twinkled.

Dart grinned, for the Apache resentment towards the white was pale beside their contempt for the Mexicans. "Okay, I know," he said in English. "But I'll be mighty sorry to lose you boys. How'd you find all this out, by the way?"

Cleve lowered his head and shifted his pile of drills to the other shoulder. "I knew him fifteen years ago when my father worked in the Magma Mine at Superior. I was just a kid then; I wasn't sure it was the same man of whom my father told me, until yesterday. We were alone in the stope. He called me a stinking name, and his eyes held murder. I do not wish to kill him, so I go. Watch out for yourself, too, Nantan," he added softly. "He is mad for power and revenge."

"Nonsense!" said Dart in English, and he would have smiled except that Cleve's round face was solemn, and Dart knew that Cleve had made a great concession in giving this lengthy explanation. "Thanks, anyway," he said.

He had discounted all Cleve's story, knowing how touchy the Apaches were, and the thought of personal danger for such flimsy reasons seemed to him ridiculous. If Tiger Burton were indeed an enemy, it was because he shared Mablett's hostility towards Dart, not because of a fifty-year-past trouble with Geronimo. And if he wished to hide his Mexican blood, that was his privilege.

"Oh, Cleve, when you get back there to the reservation—you know where my mother lives up Blue Spring? Please go and see her, tell her I'm thinking of her, will you?"

"Mebbe so," said Cleve. And this universal response, which may mean anything, Dart knew was this time affirmative.

The men reached the cross-cut. It was still filled with acrid smoke and dust from the blasting. Olaf and Dart went ahead, clambering over the piles of scattered rock, Dart's keen ears were alert for the faint buzzing which meant a delayed fuse. But there was nothing sinister or menacing, all the holes had fired. The three Mexican muckers went methodically to work, shovelling the broken rock into an ore car. Dart pulled out his little pick and began to sample. He frowned as he picked and pried the moist dark rocks from the just uncovered virgin depths of the mountain. Copper, yes—plenty of it, in a darker greenish streak through the waste rock. If only it paid to mine for copper, as it used to before the bottom fell out. Six cents a pound now —and three years ago copper had brought seventeen and a half cents. He stood frowning and balancing a small hunk of copper ore in his hand, staring at the rock wall ahead and calculating how many more yards they had to go before they hit the vein again. That slender dwindling vein of gold-bearing ore, on which the mine depended now. *If* they hit it. Little Jones, the chief engineer, was a competent geologist, but he was badly over-worked. Jones, therefore, made mistakes; in fact, all geologists did. Dart put the sample in his pocket and walked away down the drift and back towards the shaft, thinking.

What a strange occupation mining was.

All these divergent personalities, stupid, intelligent, petty, violent, even weary and remote like Tyson, were yet bound tight together by loyalty to the mine. It was more than identification in a shared enterprise; most men felt that for their means of live-lihood, the mine was a beloved entity, as a ship is to seamen.

Even Mablett, stubborn and ill-judged as were his methods, cared deeply about the success of the mine. Give the devil his due, thought Dart. Of Tiger Burton he did not think at all.

Dart shared with most native westerners a large tolerance towards eccentricity. Here, against the vast panorama of moun-tains and desert, each individual became sharply silhouetted, traits intensified, passion more violent. The air itself bred sharper men than the soft and foggy East, where corners blurred into a monotonous smooth mould.

It was not, he thought, now cooled down completely from his anger earlier at the party, Mablett the man whom he disliked so much. Dart could forgive personal vituperation and bluster-ings if the end were gained, as it has been. But he could not overlook the continuing stupidity, the threat to the whole fabric of the mine.

He reached the shaft and signalled to the hoistman, then while he stood waiting in the cool rock chamber there came to him a great love of this earth around him, the preciousness of the primitive return to the great mother, the beauty of the darkness and silence deep in the secret heart of the mountain.

He felt again, as he had earlier out on the surface of the mountain, an extension of consciousness and a clarification.

The cage rattled down to a stop in front of him. "Hello, Mike," he said to the old Irish cager. "Take me up to the three hundred, will you?"

"You going over to the old workings, sir?" asked Mike, surprised. "'Twill be mighty dark and lonesome, over there. The men was glad they didn't have to work there tonight. They said you changed the orders, said the big bosses didn't even know you changed 'em." He winked up at Dart, slyly admiring.

Dart shook his head—thus gossip ran like wildfire through the mine. "Of course, Mr. Mablett knew it," he said repressively. "We'll start re-timbering there tomorrow, so it won't be dark and lonesome any more. You'll be telling me it's haunted next."

"Well, it might be," said Mike. "Them Cousin Jacks keep hearin' the Tommyknockers."

"I'll go scare the little dears away," said Dart, stepping out into the pitch blackness of the 300 level. The cage clanged and rattled upwards towards the surface. Dart bent his head so that his lamp illumined his wrist-watch. Two o'clock already. He thought with contrition about Amanda, lying there alone in the bed waiting for him. Mining's a tough profession, my girl, he said to her, and it's tougher to be a miner's wife. Almost he regretted the impulse that had sent him over here. An impulse that had come while he was waiting for the cage and worrying about the mine's welfare. An impulse born partly of hunch and partly from a subconscious memory.

He hurried, half crouching, along the tunnels of the old drifts. They were not high enough to accommodate his six feet two, and the hard skull-guard hat on top of that. These old workings had been untouched since shortly after Red Bill Cunningham's death in 'ninety-eight, when the Boston Company bought the mine for a song, since Red Bill's original high-grade vein had suddenly pinched out. The new owners started sinking the Plymouth shaft to the west of the old Shamrock, and eventually found just enough gold-bearing ore to keep them going, as it still did in diminishing quantities. No one had bothered with the old workings for years, but now Tyson and Mablett were right. The time had come for recovery, for extracting from the old mine the remnants of ore which had been disdained in the lavish bonanza days.

But that won't take us far, thought Dart sadly, as he crawled up over the rotten timbering to the man-way and into the old No. 33 stope.

He examined the pillars of rock which had been left to support the stope's roof when the rest of the ore was mined out. Not really high grade, might run around fifteen dollars a ton, but at that a hell of a lot better than the stuff they were pulling from the new Plymouth vein. That was running about nine, and not too much of that, at the moment.

They'd show a loss again this month, and the eastern stockholders would squawk, but Mr. Tyson would accompany the report with one of his lucid, beautifully philosophical letters giving them hope for next month, when the cross-cut went through, when they hit the vein again. And the stockholders and the Company president in Boston would be soothed, and wait once more. They had faith in Tyson, in the magic of his name and past reputation. Poor old boy, thought Dart, and yet, despite his deficiencies, the old man still had value to the mine, as a cohesive force no matter how remote, and as a liaison officer with the East.

Dart tucked his sampling pick in his belt and clambered down the man-way again to the drift below. It was not for ruminations about Tyson, nor even for another confirmation of the rotten state of the timbering that he had entered the old workings tonight.

He wanted to examine the far western end of the old 300 drift —the spot where Red Bill's original mine staff had given up some thirty years ago.

On an earlier visit his keen eyes had unconsciously noted some tiny grooves on the rock surface, the slickenside. He found it again now, and the marks made by pebbles when the fault occurred. From the direction and pressure of these marks he suspected that the slip had gone north, and besides, there was the tiny quartz outcrop he had seen on surface, hidden in a hollow beneath a jumble of diorite and cactus.

Maybe only a pocket, maybe nothing, and yet he was almost sure. He'd examine the surface indications again in the morning, but he was as sure as anyone can be in the chancy and romantic science of mining. Drive a blind cross-cut right here, he thought. I think we'd hit something good. That old Shamrock vein didn't pinch out, it side-slipped in some uncharacteristic way, I'm sure, but who's going to listen to me? Not Mablett, certainly, not little Jones, who had natually given this spot perfunctory examination and agreed with the original geologists. Tyson then—thought Dart. I'll make him listen. He nodded, and turned back to stumble through the maze of tunnels. He lost his way once, but went back and retraced his steps successfully, buoyed by a very real optimism.

It would take patience; he'd have to bide his time and pick the right moment for the effort to convince Tyson. And there'd be renewed clashes with Mablett, of course. But there did not have to be, he thought suddenly. If Tyson could be convinced, Mablett need never know who originated the idea of the blind cross-cut. Dart had absolutely no desire for personal glory, and much as he hated subterfuge, he was prepared to do violence to any of his inherent traits—for the good of the mine. Take the odium and the blame later—if the cross-cut were opened fruitlessly, but for the present and in case of the success in which he devoutly believed, keep himself out of it entirely except to Tyson.

He was whistling "My Sweetheart's the Mule in the Mine" when Mike again appeared down the Plymouth shaft to pick him up.

"Jeez, Mr. Dartland," said the skip-tender, his grizzled little face lengthening, "don't be doing that."

"What?" said Dart, stepping into the cage and ducking his head as usual.

"Whistling underground. 'Tis bad luck."

"Sorry," said Dart, grinning. "But I was feeling good. I didn't hear any Tommyknockers either, Mike."

"They've too much respect for you, sir." Mike grinned, too. He turned his head and addressed the cable, "But wouldn't you think a young man'd be out raising hell on a Saturday night, 'stead o' traipsin' around in a mine when he don't have to?"

"Well," said Dart, as they came to the surface and the cage stopped, "there were some things to see to."

Mike nodded, and he twisted his head towards Dart. "You're a mighty good foreman, Mr. Dartland," he said; "I've seen plenty of 'em come and go through the years, and I know."

"Why, thanks, Mike." Dart was touched. How rare and startling was praise. Really undeserved, too, when you had a job you loved, when even the setbacks and frustrations and personal squabbles appeared tonight as challenges, as necessary hurdles set by life on the track to any worth-while goal.

He glanced at his watch as he entered the change house again. Three o'clock now, and if it weren't for Amanda, he would not have left the mine, since at seven-thirty he wanted to be here for the day shift. How much simpler to turn into the bunkhouse for a few hours, as he had often done before their marriage. He could phone from the mine office, doubtless waking up Mattie's niece, Cora, at the switchboard, and then get her to run up to Amanda with a message. Even as the idea crossed his mind he rejected it. He kicked off his muddy boots and yanked down the pulley with his good clothes before starting for the showers.

He raced down the mountain in the cold dawn air, jog-trotting in the effortless gait Tanosay had taught him long ago, and he let himself into his shack just as the gilded flickers began to dart from their nests in the giant saguaros, twittering their tiny "Wake-up, Wake-up!"

Amanda was asleep, but she stirred as he came in and opened her eyes. He saw the traces of tears on her face, and she looked up at him with bewildered reproach. "I thought you were never coming," she whispered.

"I know," he said. "Poor baby." He sat down on the bed and gathered her up in his arms.

She smelled of perfume, and she had put on a new écru lace and chiffon nightgown. It slipped down below her breasts as she slowly, reluctantly raised her arms to him. "You *said* you'd be right back. It was so lonely here."

He began to kiss her, hard and deep, dissolving from her eyes the darkness of resentment, and dissolving from his own heart the first impulse of exasperated pity, as he saw her lying there, waiting to be made love to, perfumed and beautiful, and ready for the act of love which alone seemed to give her reassurance.

They were happy there in the sunrise hours, islanded in content, whispering and teasing a little, floating in the voluptuous aftermath of fulfilment. With tenderness he shared her mood; he let her pretend that Lodestone did not exist, or the mine or its problems, or the cluttered shack and lumpy ill-made bed on which they lay.

He gave her willing respite for those three hours, and when he at last got up and started for the kitchen to light the stove, he laughed softly at her expression of dismay.

"Oh, God," she said, rousing herself from the drowsy peace. "Dart, you're not going back to that damn mine already!"

"Yes, my love," he said, "I must. Get out of the hay, trollop, and put the coffee on while I shave."

She made a face, and touched one foot to the floor, then she turned around and fumbled in the bed. "I suppose I ought to put something on."

He glanced at her through the open kitchen door and snorted. "Well, maybe, until we can buy some shades. But hurry up with the coffee, naked or not."

She pulled on her nightgown and pattered over the linoleum into the kitchen. Dart, already dressed in his khaki pants, was crouching to see in the mirror over the sink while he shaved. The mirror which was hung for Amanda was much too low for him. Amanda, flinging coffee into the percolator basket, looked at him with eyes of deep love. Even semi-crouching, even shaving, Dart had a lean easy grace.

"Oh, darling," she said with a laughing catch in her voice, "I love you so. Can't we always be close together like this? Then I could stand anything."

He wiped his face and hands on the greyish, sodden towel, turned and smiled at her.

"Is there really so much to stand?" he questioned, without reproach, but she flushed and bit her lip.

"No—of course there isn't. I'm a pig. A spoiled brat." She cracked an egg on the edge of the frying-pan, hurrying, and some of the white flipped on to her lace and chiffon nightgown. She dabbed at it while she tried to spread grape jam on bread for Dart's lunch-box.

He leaned down and kissed her head on one of the rumpled yellow duck-tails. "Sweet brat," he said, "you'll grow up, some day."

"I don't want to," she answered, laughing, as she scooped the egg on the plate and gave it to him.

He had been gulping his coffee, but for a second he put his cup down and glanced at her unconscious rosy face. She looked extraordinarily pretty, fussing over his lunch-box, her sea-blue eyes dark with concentration. No, she doesn't want to, he thought.

"I think I'll be down off the hill by six, anyway, Andy," he said quietly. "I'll try not to be late tonight."

CHAPTER FIVE

IT was two weeks before Amanda went up to call on Calise Cunningham in the ghost town, and there made a discovery which profoundly affected her life. Amanda had been interested in Dart's suggestion that she should go to see Calise, but she caught a stuffy head cold, and the resultant lethargy left her no energy for anything but chores.

On the morning of February second, Hugh dropped in as she was pumping water on to the breakfast dishes.

"How are the snuffles now?" he said, sitting down at the kitchen table. "Want some more nose drops? And have you got a cup of coffee left in that funeral urn?" He pointed at the large old-fashioned percolator the Dartlands had found in the shack.

She nodded and poured him a cup. "Snuffles about gone," she said. "But I don't seem to have much pep." She wiped a plate and put it on the shelf.

Hugh looked at her keenly. She was thinner than she had been when she arrived, and pale, though of course without make-up most women looked pallid. "You ought to get out more," he said. "Bustle around. This climate's supposed to be quite healthy, you know."

"Well, I am going to the post office, pretty soon," she said with a faint smile. "Might be letters from home. There isn't much else to do, and at least Tessie Rubrick throws me a kind word now and then."

Lonely and homesick, he thought, but she doesn't make much effort, either. "You might take an interest in the life of the town," he suggested. "It's colourful enough, plenty of quaint characters. Some of them quite nice."

She shrugged, picking at a hangnail on her index finger. "You're a fine one to talk. I can't see you do much mingling with the local colour. Gosh, I wish I could get—or afford—a decent manicure again."

"Dishpan hands?" said Hugh. "How sad."

"Oh, shut up!" She gave an unwilling laugh. "How's business at Medical Centre today?"

"Booming. One miner with a carbuncle, another one with a broken toe, and one of the mill crew with a belly-ache which I trust is not appendicitis, because there won't be time to send him to Globe or Ray."

"Can't you operate yourself?"

"Certainly. On the kitchen table. Maria makes a simply splendid anæsthetist. It happens that I'm rather short of equipment like retractors and clamps, but then I suppose I might use paper clips."

She looked at him, frowning. "Hugh, don't you ever regret—I mean, I know you came from the East—were trained there, this seems so——"

She stopped, confused by the cynical amusement with which he watched her flounderings.

"No regrets at all," he said. "I was kicked out of the East for unethical practices, and here I can be as unethical as I damn please. I can also get drunk when I feel like it, and sleep with Maria."

"Oh," she said. She sighed, for at moments she liked him, and the romantic mould in which she had first tried to fit him seemed appropriate. His deliberate crudities did not shock her, but the sadistic streak which she had seen without understanding in his treatment of Maria did. That and the indistinct recognition of his ambivalence, "two men within my breast." One might be trusted and the other not.

So different from Dart, she thought, and a warm feeling came into her heart. "Hugh, have you ever been in love?" she asked on impulse.

"Repeatedly." Nothing in his square freckled face changed; the little moustache, the green eyes under slightly swollen lids, the thick sensual mouth, all confronted her unchanged, and yet she felt that a warning had flickered far beneath.

She persisted nevertheless. "No, I mean really. With one woman and stuck to her, for quite a while, anyway."

And now the warning flickered up into his eyes, which grew hard as emeralds. "This sort of sentimental questioning, my dear, usually means that the questioning lady has hopes herself. Have you? I'd be most flattered."

She felt herself flush, but a rush of annoyance was at once

tempered by surprise. For perhaps there was really someone. "Oh, don't be idiotic," she said. "I love Dart, and you don't attract me in the least. But I can't help being curious about your love life."

He got up abruptly, and his eyes still were hard and green. The look, if Amanda had known it, which he had turned on Maria the day she questioned him about the photograph in his shirts.

"Thanks for the coffee," he said. "I've got to get back to the hospital." He left Amanda to astonishment. For a moment he had shown none of his characteristic cynicism or detachment. He had shown straight, uncomplicated anger at being questioned. But the doctor's peculiar reactions did not interest her for long. Lassitude descended upon her again. She moved languidly about the shack, tidying a little. She looked with loathing at the basketful of dirty clothes. They could wait until tomorrow. She glanced at the window. That was one thing about this place anyway: no need to take advantage of a sunny day. They were all sunny—and dry. In the corner of the bedroom on the floor there was a little package of recent books Jean had sent her. *Mary's Neck*, by Booth Tarkington; *The Fountain*, by Charles Morgan; *What We Live By*, by Ernest Dimnet.

She had read part of *The Fountain* in the afternoons or evenings waiting for Dart. But she had not finished it. Reading wasn't as much fun as it used to be. She looked at her wristwatch. The mail stage from Hayden Junction never got in until noon, and then you had to allow time for Tessie to sort the letters. But she might as well walk over early. Buy myself a nice cold coke, she thought. That'll be exciting. She looked in her purse. Two dollars and sixty-five cents to last until pay-night. Damn, I thought there was more than that.

She put on her heather tweed suit and fixed her face by the little wall mirror in the kitchen, and was about to leave when she remembered Dart's renewed suggestion that morning. About going up to the Cunningham mansion. He had left a trunk of his up there in the room he had occupied. "I think there's an old blue suit in it that I had at college. I wish you'd look at it and see if I couldn't use it for work clothes, anyway." Poor lamb, she thought, except for the one good suit he'd been married in, his clothes were certainly terribly shabby. "Stop in and see Mrs. Cunningham, won't you?" he had added.

She was faintly amused at his insistence. Mrs. Cunningham was apparently another "character." Arizona seemed to be full of characters, eccentrics of one kind or another of which the natives were proud.

She ran a comb through her hair, and walked outside into the brilliant sunlight. She blinked in the blinding glare, then began to walk slowly down the dusty road towards town. She passed the hospital, but did not see Maria's face in an upstairs window.

Maria stared down avidly with sulky resentment masking her envy of the tall blonde girl in the beautiful suit, like Carole Lombard's in the movie Maria had seen last year in Tucson. Doc had been calling on that girl this morning, too. Maria had seen him come out of the Dartland cabin not so long ago. Bet that poor husband don't know what's going on, thought Maria. She had admired Dart from afar, and only recently heard that he had Indian blood, as she had. There was a real man for you, big and dark and quiet. He'd be good in bed, too; Maria knew from considerable experience in such appraisals. That dope, she don't know her luck, she thought, continuing to stare angrily at Amanda's retreating figure.

Amanda was thinking about nothing at all. The air and the sunshine began to revive her a little. She reached the crossroads by the first saloon on this end of town, a small wooden building with a false front and portico. The windows were shuttered and it was euphemistically labelled "Café" for the benefit of possible prohibition agents. These, however, seldom bothered Lodestone, and when they did, there was always plenty of warning. Nobody worried about them.

From the back room through open windows there came the usual sound of clinkings and men's voices, the click of billiard-balls, the rattle of dice, and the monotonous ping of the slot machines. Somebody laughed, and a voice cried jovially, "God damn it to hell, you old cowpoke, if I don't love you better'n a brother! Set 'em up, Joe!" And there was more laughter.

Well, they were enjoying themselves anyway, thought Amanda. I wish I could join them. She thought of the fun she had had in New York speakeasies with Tim, of the five hundred francs she had won at roulette in Monte Carlo. But here ladies didn't drink or gamble. Here you conformed to Mrs. Mablett's standards, or you were a bad woman. These were still the standards of the old frontier. They had seemed very romantic when you read about them.

Instead of continuing as usual down the mine road, past Bosses' Row where the Mabletts lived, and then veering left to Greek Street and the business block, she turned at once into the canyon behind the saloon, and headed for the forbidden shortcut, Back Lane, where the cribs were. Hugh told me to see the town, she thought.

Three of the four separate little doll's-houses were quiet, with the blinds drawn, their occupants asleep. But Big Ruby was sitting on the steps in the sunlight in front of hers, drying her brassy hair, which was rolled up in kid curlers. She wore a voluminous pink cotton kimono with green parasols printed on it, and her fat white legs were bare above red felt bedroom slippers. She was reading a *True Confession* magazine and smoking. A bottle of home-brew frothed on the step beside her.

"Why, hello," she said calmly, as Amanda, caught by a sudden paralysing embarrassment, hesitated between answering and running by. The latter impulse she quickly vanquished. She stopped and tried for a casual smile.

"You wanted something?" asked Big Ruby, flipping over a page of the magazine. She had seen sightseers before, plenty of them, staring at the cribs and snickering like the girls was a lot of wild monkeys.

Amanda was quite sensitive enough to realize this, and she was ashamed to admit curiosity and defiance as her only motives for walking down Back Lane, so she seized on the lead little Bobby Pottner had given her her first day in Lodestone. "I thought maybe—I've only a tiny house, but the cleaning sometimes . . . I didn't know if—if one of you would——"

She faltered to a stop before Ruby's pursed lips and air of judicial detachment. "I'm Mrs. Jonathan Dartland; my husband's foreman at the mine," Amanda finished in a subdued voice.

"I know," said Ruby. "I seen you downtown. I asked Doc Slater about you, too."

"Oh, did you?" said Amanda faintly.

"Well, I dunno," Ruby smiled suddenly. She had just realized how young the girl was, and Ruby had a fairly maternal spirit. "I used to take day work sometimes, up in Bosses' Row. But——"

Did you indeed? thought Amanda, startled. This was one more anomaly in western society. That the élite could employ Ruby, while at the same time ignoring her usual profession.

"I ain't no chicken any more," Ruby continued, taking a deep pull from the beer bottle. "Mebbe one of the other girls. . . . How much would you pay?"

Amanda flushed scarlet. But she had got herself into this ridiculous situation.

"Well," she said hurriedly, "I don't know just now. I just thought I'd enquire."

Ruby watched with understanding. Though Dart had never visited any of the cribs, she had a very fair idea of what his salary must be, for some of the mining staff were among her clientèle, and talked freely.

"Well, now," she said soothingly. "Later on, if you need help, we can talk about it again. Four bits an hour'd be fair, I think."

"Oh yes, certainly. Very fair." Amanda nodded. We couldn't even afford a woman like this, a—a prostitute to scrub the floors, she thought. It's incredible.

"Good-bye," she said slowly, and she smiled her lovely, friendly smile. "Thank you."

Ruby put down her magazine and stood up. There'd been a lot of talk around town about this girl, how she was so stuck up and full of herself she wouldn't even give you the time of day. But she ain't so bad, thought Ruby. A real lady, you could say that for her, and awful young. They was a nice good-looking young couple, the Dartlands, and it wasn't all roses and honey being just married either. Who to know better than she? Older people ought to give young married couples a few breaks.

"Mrs. Dartland," she said, as Amanda turned to go. "I dunno as I ought to tell you something. But a word to the wise, you know, and you might just put a flea in your hubby's ear. 'Twouldn't hurt."

Amanda stared blankly at the round flabby face under the kid curlers.

"There's a guy at the mine's got it in for your husband. I won't mention no names."

Amanda swallowed. This Mablett thing, even here. Though

Dart said there'd been no trouble lately. "Yes," she said, sighing, "I know."

Ruby shook her head. "I don't reckon you do. This guy
don't talk to nobody but me, and only when he's dead drunk.
He's a sly one."

Could that be Mablett? Getting dead drunk with Big Ruby,
airing his grievances? It didn't sound just right, and yet remembering Mrs. Mablett, maybe it did. And far better not to question, or attach too much importance. One didn't listen to back-
stairs, or in this case "Back Lane," gossip. "Thank you," she
said. "It was kind of you to tell me." She moved definitely
away.

'Well, tell hubby to keep his eyes peeled, that's all. And you
needn't tell who said so. Bye-bye now." Ruby felt her curlers,
decided they were dry, gathered up her magazine, cigarettes,
and beer, and disappeared into her house.

Amanda continued on the canyon road, towards town. Go
West, Young Man, Go West, she said to herself. "Where never
is heard, a discouraging word, and the skies are not cloudy all
day." Hurrah!

Creek Street provided its usual mild noon bustle. There
were two cow ponies hitched to the rail by the portico, and Old
Larky's burro stood beside them. The mail stage was in, standing in front of the post office. The mail stage was a Chevvie
pickup truck, but it encountered enough adventures on its tri-
weekly run from Hayden to justify the continuance of its
pioneer title. It was still a lonely route, and depending on the
condition of the roads and washes, it often took nearly as long
to make the run as it had in the days of horses. And though there
was no longer an Indian scare, there were still plenty of lawless
men with acquisitive interest in the contents of the mail stage.
Roy Kellickman, the mail carrier, always kept a loaded ·44 on
the seat beside him, and packed a 30-30 in back with the mail-
bags. Roy was a stout and social young man, who enjoyed being
a link with the outside world. When Amanda walked into
Rubrick's, which was half post office, half lunch counter and
drugstore, Roy was regaling an appreciative audience with the
tale of his morning's trip. Amanda glanced through the open
window and saw that Tessie, among the canvas bags, had not
yet finished sorting the mail, so she went to the counter and
ordered a coke from the twelve-year-old Rubrick daughter.

The mail carrier's audience and Roy himself paused a moment as Amanda settled herself on a stool in the corner. She smiled in vague embarrassment, never dreaming that they were waiting for her to greet them with a howdy or a hello. They turned their collective eyes back to Roy in a moment, and he continued his story.

The audience consisted of two young cow-punchers who had been hunting cattle strayed down from the range to the north, a welder and a mechanic from the mine, and Old Larky back again from the mountains to collect his monthly remittance. Susan lay with her pups in a basket under his feet.

Amanda knew none of them, and she sipped her coke and listened abstractedly to Roy's baritone drawl while she wondered if there'd be any letters from home.

There was a party of tourists had driven over the cliff in Gila Canyon just north of Winkelman, said Roy. He'd stopped to investigate, but they was all mashed flatter than pancakes, and their bodies could wait until the deputy came along. The car had a California licence.

"Them prune pickers had ought to stay at home where they belong," said one of the cowpunchers. "Or leastways stick to them fancy-pants resorts that'll wet-nurse the dudes so they don't get hurt."

There was a murmur of agreement.

Another jailbreak from the state pen at Florence, said Roy; they'd caught two of them right off heading for the border, but the other one was an Apache boy, and they figured he'd make for the reservation, like the Indians always did. Those Apaches knew every foot of this mountain country, and could melt into the chaparral like they was made of bark themselves.

Everybody nodded. Old Larky wheezed and screwed up his rheumy eyes. "I trust he doesn't come fidgeting around me and Susan up on the mountain. Perhaps I'd better buy me some extra shells."

Amanda looked up startled. An educated English voice out of that filthy old man. Another character apparently. The men all laughed.

"D'you find your lost mine yet, Larky?" asked Roy, winking at the others.

"Any day now. Any day," returned Larky with dignity. "I think I misread my map. I'm working on a new theory now."

The mine welder, who had been silently smoking his pipe, suddenly leaned forward. "Hear anything more about what's going on at Ray?"

Old Larky and the mechanic leaned forward too. The mail carrier's face sobered. "I reckon they'll shut down purty soon," he said. "There's plenty of rumours. That'll mean the smelter, too."

"Jeez . . ." said the welder. "Where'll we send our ore? If we keep a-going ourselves, that is."

"Freight it to El Paso, I reckon," said the mechanic.

"Haulage costs . . ." said the welder, shaking his head.

All this meant as little to Amanda as it apparently did to the two young cow-punchers who had drawn off to a corner and were conferring with each other. It was obvious, from the other men's silence and expressions, that their thoughts were disturbing. More mine troubles, she thought with impatience. There's no end to them. I wish the Shamrock *would* shut down. Then Dart could get a decent job somewhere. This thought, which flashed suddenly through her head, startled her into a lively guilt. Dart loved the mine, he loved his job here, plenty of bitter realizations had taught her that. She slid off her stool and walked over to the window.

Tessie's friendly little face beamed up at her. "Ye got one!" she cried triumphantly. "From New York too!—though I doubt 'tis from your mother by the writing."

Amanda laughed. The bright squirrel eyes were so sympathetic that it was impossible to resent Tessie's delighted scrutiny of every piece of mail. And Tessie was without malice. Though she read every postcard, and speculated about all sealed matter, she had never been known to use the extensive knowledge thus gained to anyone's disadvantage. Amanda glanced at her letter, and saw that it was from Tim Merrill.

Her heart gave a sideways lurch. The large sprawling handwriting which had once been so familiar, and associated with the promise of gaiety and excitement, now produced a dull sense of shock, mostly, though not quite, unpleasant.

" 'Tis not a welcome letter?" asked Tessie anxiously.

"Oh—oh yes, I guess so." Amanda smiled and put Tim's letter in her pocket-book. "I was hoping to hear from my mother or sister, though."

Tessie nodded. "I mind how 'twas when we first came over

from Cornwall. Seems I couldna 'a lived without the post. Ye'll get over the worst of it."

"Yes," said Amanda, and she lingered by the window, warmed by Tessie's friendliness, reluctant to go outside and open Tim's letter.

Old Larky came shuffling up for his remittance with Susan wheezing at his heels. The welder and the mechanic both got letters from home. Others came trickling into the post office, got mail, leafed through the two-day-old *Phœnix Republican.* Amanda glanced over a shoulder at the front page. Somebody called Hitler had just been made Chancellor of Germany. President-elect Roosevelt was in Florida. But most of the news was local. Another lay-off of miners at the Copper Queen in Bisbee. A man in Prescott had shot himself and his starving family.

Why are papers always so depressing, thought Amanda, and turned back towards Tessie.

Bobby Pottner came tearing in on his way from school. "Got anything for us?" he yelled, giving Amanda a shy nod.

"Just a postcard from Pearline," said Tessie, handing it to him. "She says it's been real cold in Globe lately, and she's got a new music pupil."

"Aw, nuts to Pearline—didn't I get my Buck Rogers pistol?"

" 'Tisn't here yet. 'Twill come Wednesday no doubt—Bobby, I see Roy brought your ma a package from the wholesaler in Phœnix. Tell her to save me some sage, will ye? I need it for me pasties."

And still Amanda lingered, until suddenly the door opened and Lydia Mablett, hatted and gloved as usual, swept in.

Oh Lord, thought Amanda, who had managed to avoid her since the disastrous supper party. She rather expected that Mrs. Mablett would cut her dead, but she had reckoned without that lady's firm grasp on mine politics. For as long as young Dartland managed to wheedle occasional backing from Mr. Tyson, open warfare would be inexpedient, particularly as poor Luther was apt to be so headlong and tactless.

So Lydia flashed her spectacles at Amanda and said, "Why, how do you do, isn't it a lovely day? . . ." in her high voice.

Hemmed in by Lydia's short solid bulk, Amanda agreed that it was.

"All settled now in your comfy little home?"

Amanda said, "Yes, thank you." And wondered what the purpose of this was.

"Have you seen Mr. Tyson lately?" asked Lydia, with a playful smile which puzzled Amanda, for there was an edge of anxiety not quite masked by the smile.

"Why, no. I haven't, not since—since your party."

Lydia quite obviously relaxed, the smile became mechanical, and she turned the tail end of it on Tessie, who was waiting with the Mablett letters in her hand. That young Dartland had had two unprecedented and unexplained interviews with Tyson, at his home—Lydia knew, because Luther had been fuming about them. So Lydia had just now laid a horrid suspicion that this bold young woman might also have been trying to worm her way into the general manager's good graces. But apparently she had not. Years of social work had made Lydia a good judge of character. She knew that Amanda had told the truth. Lydia turned now to the more congenial occupation of clucking with Tessie over the morals and filth of the twenty Mexican families who lived at the east end of town beyond the bridge.

Amanda escaped outside to the street. She relegated the incident to a steadily enlarging pigeon-hole which she thought of resentfully as "The Mine Mess," and forgot it.

She walked rapidly back along the street past the Miners' Union Hall and the saloon called "The Laundry" and Pottner's General Store, and the Mine Hardware and Supplies Store, and finally past the overcrowded two-room school-house where Miss Arden of the warts, and a trembling little whey-faced teacher just arrived from Iowa, endeavoured to stuff primary education into Lodestone's children.

A hundred yards beyond the school, where Creek Street climbed up to the mine road and Bosses' Row, there was a paloverde tree which gave some shade. Amanda sat down beneath it on a rock to read her letter from Tim. It began:

"MY STILL DEAREST ANDY,—I continue to miss you like hell in case you've wondered, which alack, I doubt, for your amiable mamma has read me parts of your letters, from which I gather that the little grey home in the West vibrates with marital bliss, and that you're happy as a clam, or whatever simile is appropriate to the Arizona desert. Gila monster, maybe. I'm sure they lead happy, unfrustrated lives. Me, however, I *am* frustrated. I wave the torch for you in all the old familiar places. I wave it at Tony's and I wave it at Twenty-one. I wave it at the Plaza and under the Biltmore Clock. I waved particularly hard at the opening of Cole Porter's *Gay Divorce* (I assure you I mean no particularly snide allusions by hauling in this title), but you would have loved it, Andy. A swell piece of the theatre—and that song, 'Night and Day.' Listen to it on the radio. Fitted my sentiments.

"I'm thinking of running down to the family's place at Palm Beach in a week or so, seeing as the estimable firm of Renn and Matthews have decided to dispense with my services. My dear mother says vulgarly that as we still seem to be well-heeled, it's downright wicked for me to rustle around after another job, when I don't need it, and plenty do. I'm charmed to agree. Playboy Merrill it shall be. I'll flirt with the sun-tanned lassies, fish for the wily tarpon, and exercise the stink-pot up and down the Inland Waterway. Do you remember a certain night on deck last March? I refer to the incident of the champagne.

"Do you laugh like that now, Andy? I miss your laughter— If I get sated with Florida, I'm wondering about the delights of Arizona. Somebody sent me a brochure about a new resort near Tucson called El Castillo. 'Castle in Spain on the desert,' it says. Complete with houris in bathing suits, judging from the photo, and blooded Arabian steeds, and private bootlegger piped in. Tennis, golf, ping-pong and usual amenities on the side. What do you think, Andy? If I came out, would you—and Dart, of course—run down there for week-ends? We could be gay, and I promise to conceal my breaking heart. Write to me. TIM."

There was an enclosure. A Peter Arno cartoon cut from the *New Yorker*. It represented two men in evening dress. One saying, "Gad, but my wife looks terrible tonight," and the other man drawing himself up stiffly, replying, "Sir, you are speaking of the woman I love."

"Oh, Tim, you idiot," Amanda whispered. She stared unseeing at a clump of prickly pear beside her, and it materialized into Tim's narrow laughing face. She saw the cleft in his chin, the sheen of his straight blond hair, the crazy Sulka ties he affected, and she saw the bewilderment in his eyes on the last time she had seen him, the night of Dart's phone call to New York. Tim had not come to the wedding. But that was mostly because

he had been spending Christmas on a South Carolina planta-
tion at a huge house-party. Tim was not one to mourn in
solitude.

She read the letter again, and found there natural balm for
her female vanity. He hadn't then got over her as fast as she
had thought he might. She had never loved him, of course;
there had never been any of the whole-souled and whole-bodied
love which she felt for Dart. But there was a bond between
them, and for a moment, while she re-read the letter picturing
them as they had so often been together, she felt a sick yearning.
Dancing to the "Bye-Bye Blues" at the Biltmore. Baked Alaska
at Tony's, and Tim toasting her with that divine brandy. The
glorious evening of an opening she *had* seen with him. *Of Thee
I Sing*. And the party later for the cast, where she had met
Gershwin.

Tim lived in that sort of world, as she had once.

Amanda moved on the rock, which tipped a little. She flung
out her hand to right herself, and grasped a clump of cholla. A
dozen of the sharp murderous spines embedded themselves in
her palm. She pulled the spines out with sudden fury, which
extended itself to Tim. So rich, and smug. So utterly ignorant
of this kind of life, or anything but social New York and Florida
and summers *de luxe* in Europe.

Listen to "Night and Day" on the radio. There were two
radios in Lodestone, and ninety per cent. of the time all you
could get on them was static, because of the distance, because
of the mountains.

Run down to this El Castillo for week-ends. Tucson was seven
hours' away when the washes were dry, and what about Dart,
who seldom even took Sundays off? And who would pay for a
week-end at a place like El Castillo? Do you think for a moment
Dart would let us be your guests? Do you know what it is to
have two dollars and sixty-five cents—no, fifty-two now after the
coke—in your pocket to last till pay-night, Friday?

She folded the letter and cartoon, and put them back in her
pocket-book. She'd show them to Dart later. He probably
wouldn't be jealous, and anyway, it wouldn't hurt him if he
were a little. Give him something to think about besides his
beloved stopes and drifts or whatever.

Two o'clock. The sun was getting very hot, as usual. When
she reached home, she was strongly tempted to forgo the trip

up to the Cunningham mansion. Lie down and read for a while.
The inspection of Dart's suit could certainly wait a little longer.

But once inside the shack she was restless, visited too by a
compunction. Dart asked so little of her. He accepted amateur-
ish meals, delayed laundry, and forgotten mending without com-
plaint. The least she could do was to fulfil her postponed
promise.

So she set out again up the mine road, walking doggedly,
thinking, in spite of herself, about Tim's letter, and blind to the
changing landscape around her.

The appearance of the ghost town jolted her out of her absorp-
tion. It lay below the present road to the mine, down in a cup
between the mountains on either side of the dry creek bed. The
roofless frame buildings and half-crumbled adobe walls had
weathered alike to a tawny monochrome that melted into the
rocks and the desert floor. She walked down what had once been
the main street, a dusty clearing now, with no life but tiny darting lizards, and she was awed by the brooding, listening silence.
The place had been big once, much bigger than the present
Lodestone. It was easy to follow the outline of many streets not
yet obliterated by the encroaching desert. As she came to the
remains of the opera house with its great fallen sign, a small wild
burro darted out from the cavernous doorway, stared at her, then
galloped pell-mell down the trail away from her. The eerie
stillness fell down again at once like a blanket. She stared at the
dim red-and-gold opera house sign, and the curved flaunting
staircase which had once led to the boxes, and now ended in the
thin blue air. She saw the fragments of the mosaic paving with
which Red Bill had furbished the sidewalk before his opera
house.

"The Lion and the Lizard keep the Courts where Jamshyd
gloried and drank deep," she thought, and the pathos of the
deserted town, the romance of long past things, moved her with
a soft æsthetic thrill—the first æsthetic thrill she had as yet felt
in this country of spines and rocks and harshness. The thrill
deepened when she reached the avenue of vanished palms and
saw high against the mountain-side the huge unwieldy mansion.
It did not appear to her ridiculous with its pretentiousness, its
cupolas and gingerbread fretwork. It was to her like an illustra-
tion from a Victorian fairy-tale, a figment of romance, and thus
subtly reassuring.

She walked up the trail and the broken steps with a sudden childish excitement, and as she banged the silver shamrock knocker her heart beat fast. A princess or a witch? she thought, and when Calise opened the door, she very nearly laughed. For, standing tall and thin in the dark hallway in her black dress, her serene white face shimmering beneath the crystal chandelier, Calise seemed to fit both categories.

"How do you do, my dear," Calise said in her low bell tones with the French rhythm. "You are Amanda and you seem happy. Something amuses you?"

"A fairy-tale," said Amanda, taking the cool slim hand. "The enchanted castle, and you are the witch princess." It occurred to her then that this was an extraordinarily silly speech. She was later to learn that with Calise one usually spoke one's thoughts, or if one did not that she saw them anyway with her cool compassionate eyes that looked deep into the secret heart.

Calise smiled. "You are always searching for the fairy-tale, I think," she said gently. "Come into my rooms. We shall visit together a little."

"Just for a moment," said Amanda. "I don't want to bother you, and I've got to go through Dart's trunk—wherever it is."

"I will show you after we have had some tea."

Amanda smiled and followed Calise into her sanctuary, unconscious of what a concession this invitation was, or of how jealously Calise guarded the quality of thoughts or emotions which she allowed near her.

Amanda was at first disappointed by the simplicity of the two large rooms, when she had expected a Victorian opulence to match the house, but then, as she sat and waited for Calise to make the tea in the little kitchenette behind the bedroom, she saw, as Dart had not, that simple as the furnishings were, they all had rich beauty of line. The bookcases, chairs, table, and the narrow bed which she glimpsed through the door were all hand-made of native pine, amber-brown and glossy from years of beeswax polishing. Only the piano and the carved oak prie-dieu which stood by the bedroom window struck heavier notes in an atmosphere of light and sparkling cleanliness. There was one flash of colour. The terra-cotta red Indian bowl which stood on the bookcase was today filled with a froth of misty rose. A lace-work of elfin grey flowerets on delicate rosy stems.

This Amanda discovered as she walked over to examine them, and from them came a faint pungent perfume.

She looked down at the books below the flowers, and was startled into uneasiness by the titles. Many of them she did not recognize, like *New Model of the Universe*, by Ouspensky; *An Experiment in Time*, by Dunne; *Mysticism*, by Evelyn Underhill; but of the rest some awakened echoes of a college course in philosophy. *The Baghavadghita*, the writing of Lao-Tse, Confucius, Jacob Boehme, Santa Teresa, Saint John of the Cross, the *Religio Medici*, and there were many in French, including the works of Renan and Bergson. There were also two much-worn Bibles, a Douai and a King James.

Heavens, thought Amanda, and as her hostess came in bearing a shining copper tray, she stared at her with astonishment and blurted out, "Golly, Mrs. Cunningham, have you read all those books? I'm stunned."

Calise put the tray on the table and smiled at the girl. "I used to," she said, sitting down at the table and pouring an aromatic greenish fluid into cream porcelain cups. "I have had a long time to read in, you know. But now my search is much clearer, I no longer need books so much."

Amanda sat down and accepted the cup in silence. She was conscious of a strange quality in the room and the composed woman across the table. An intimation of light that was not actually there, of a serenity or peace that was not static, but in some subtle way dynamic and full of unseen motion.

"Forgive me," said Amanda slowly, "but exactly what were you searching for?"

The wide dark eyes rested on the girl's face with a certain tender amusement. "One might call it God," she said. "It has been called many things."

"Oh, I see, of course." Amanda could not prevent an embarrassed recoil. She had been taught indifferent tolerance for all religions; she had been sent to the Episcopalian Sunday School as a matter of course; she had had a few vague spiritual yearnings during adolescence, later satisfactorily explained away by the newer psychology as having been the sublimated sex drive. And at college she had joined with the majority in a comfortable agnosticism in which soul scrapings and serious mention of the deity were left to the unsophisticated.

Calise saw the recoil and understood. She had expected it.

"Do you like my tea?" she asked in a light social tone she had not used in years. "I make it from a bush that grows outside. The Mormon tea, it is called. The Indians use it. It has great tonic properties."

"Why, it's queer but it's good," smiled Amanda, relieved at the change of subject. "Imagine making it yourself!"

"I live very simply. I like to use the growing things that are nurtured in this so beautiful country."

Amanda made a slight face, and Calise laughed. "You have not yet opened your eyes to the beauty. There is purity and strength in the mountains. There is much joy in the lonely places."

"I'm afraid I just don't see beauty or joy here," said the girl. "It's all so violent, and full of prickles, and I hate being alone. At least, I don't like not having any friends. I hate being so poor, too, it—it frightens me." She had intended to say none of these things, and as they burst from her in unconsidered jets, a portion of her mind drew back in shocked bewilderment. What things to say to a stranger, what ill-bred laments. But she could not stop.

"I love Dart so dearly, and he's with me so little. There's things I don't understand about him. The Indian part, maybe —I thought it wouldn't make any difference, but it does, I think. I feel so unprotected, sort of vulnerable here." She gave a little nervous laugh. "I'm sorry to whine so."

Calise shut her eyes, drawing to her all the wisdom she had painfully gained. Turning to the clear light, seeking to become an instrument through which the light might focus to clarify the whirlpool of conflicting emotions in the girl's heart. She saw the groping child reaching blindly back to a remembered security, yearning at once for escape and for the father-image of protection which had once been for it the symbol of ease and pleasure, demanding of no reciprocal effort. She saw deeper than that to a core of hidden strength, dormant as yet, awaiting germination, like a seed buried deep beneath the storms and droughts. Nothing could hasten this germination. It would come when God willed.

"Something special has upset you today, I think," she said quietly. "Do you wish to tell me?"

Amanda felt no surprise; the dream quality and the sensation of peaceful force had strengthened during the moment of silence.

"Nothing really," she said. "A letter from a man I used to know. It's all so silly. I didn't care for him."

"You care for the things he could give you?" said Calise, laughing a little. "*C'est peut-être, ignoble, mais c'est quand même naturel.*"

"Oh no!" said Amanda, after a moment of translation. "I'm not really that ignoble, at least I hope not. It's just that——"

"Why did you marry Dart, my dear?" asked Calise, continuing to smile with amused tenderness.

"Because I loved him. Because he was everything I wanted in a man. Big, strong, very male, different."

Calise nodded. "But, then, you must not at the same time resent the qualities you love."

Amanda looked up startled, uncomprehending. "That's a funny thing to say. Of course I don't."

"No. I should not say funny things." Calise got up with her own fluid grace, and rested her hand for a second on the girl's bright hair. "Now shall I show you where Dart's trunk is?"

Amanda rose too. "Yes, please," she said, a trifle flattened, hurt that the interview had ended so abruptly, embarrassed that she had talked so much to this cool, calm lady, who was a stranger.

"You were admiring my flowers before, I think," said Calise, gesturing towards the cloud of greyish-pink filigree in the Indian vase.

"Oh, yes," said the girl, puzzled. "They're very delicate and beautiful. Where did they come from?"

"From here. They grow all over. They are desert weeds. They grow among what you call the 'prickles and the violence.'" Calise paused, waiting to see if there were any answer in the blue eyes, then she moved to the door and opened it. "This way, Amanda; we'll go up the great staircase, and then back to Dart's room."

One cannot force, one must not preach. Each soul receives only that which it asks for and is ready to receive. God grant that this child may learn without tragedy, as I did not.

Amanda silently followed her hostess up the great mahogany staircase. Scant light knifed through the chinks of the boarded-up windows, but there was enough to show the fraying and moth-holes of the stair-carpeting, and the fine desert dust on carved banister. Here there was none of the immaculate cleanliness of

Calise's own apartment. Nor in the long echoing halls, where gilt-framed pictures hung askew from tattered cords, the glass begrimed with dust and specks. They passed half-open doors with tarnished silver knobs dull in the gloom, and inside there were tantalizing glimpses of massive Victorian furniture.

Calise walked fast, never turning, her slender black figure and luminous hair seeming to float down the dark halls. And it took courage for the girl to break into that preoccupation.

"Please, Mrs. Cunningham," she cried at last, "couldn't I just look into one of these rooms, the house is so fascinating."

Calise turned and stopped. She frowned a little, but she answered with indulgence. "Certainly, if you wish. . . . These were guest rooms."

"So many." Amanda peered hurriedly through open doors, conscious of her hostess's reluctance. "Did you fill them all? You must have had terrific parties."

"Sometimes," said Calise. Yes, for some years the rooms had been filled with Red Bill's friends: miners, gamblers, politicians from Phœnix, once the territorial governor, but not his wife. Yet Red Bill had had social aspirations, he had tried to bribe and bluster his way to acceptance by people he always referred to as "real gents 'n ladies," but he had not succeeded. Nor did I ever try to help him, thought Calise, In no way had she tried to help him. She had accepted his lavishness and his love-making alike with a freezing and subtle contempt, long prelude to that night of climax, the still unblunted instrument of her punishment.

"Why, look, there are still flowers, or at least stalks in that vase!" cried Amanda, pointing to a gilt urn on a rosewood table in the centre of a bedroom. And there were dried, crumbling petals on the purple scarf beneath the urn.

"Nothing has been touched since a certain night in eighteen ninety-eight," said Calise with reluctance. "Those were once roses, American Beauties, packed in ice and brought by train and mule train from California."

Always Bill had kept the house filled with extravagant imported flowers. She had received them as her due, scarcely noticing. On the day that these had arrived, she had left their arrangement to the Chinese servants. Her own mind had been full of other arrangements. The secret plans for Raoul's coming that night. Bill had left for Globe the day before on business to do with the newly completed branch-line railroad there. He said he would be gone four days, and so low was her estimation of his intelligence that she never dreamed of doubting him, or dreamed that he suspected the meetings with Raoul in the deserted mountain cabin.

"What a fascinating life you've led!" cried Amanda. "I can picture this palace in the wilderness filled with flowers and lights and people."

Calise smiled faintly and started walking again.

It must be painful for her, Amanda thought, to tread among the vanished glories, but it was all so long ago, and Mrs. Cunningham was so old, she must be used to it, and surely everyone responded to genuine interest. So she called Calise again, emboldened by the sight of a magnificent shut door at the end of the hall. The door was of walnut, panelled and inlaid with a fine line of ivory. On the centre of the top panel there was a silver shamrock knocker, smaller replica of the one on the front door.

"Mrs. Cunningham," said Amanda softly. "What was in here? Could I see it? Another bedroom?"

"Yes," said Calise, not turning. "My bedroom. I'm sorry, but you may *not* go in." She walked on.

Death and the stench of blood still imprisoned in that bedroom waiting for her enforced participation. The jewels, the lace négligé, the rumpled bed, the smell of her perfume and the roses, the hideous words that Bill shouted as he burst in, the sound of shots, and her own high scream as the blood poured from Raoul's mouth, the bubbling gasps as he died, the dull shaking thud of Bill's fall to the floor, and the glare of his upturned eyes on her face, his eyes the only movement in that great paralysed body.

This horror came now only in memory, softened by long pity, diluted by agonizing repentance. But the night would return, soon perhaps, when there would be no softening, and no memory. A night when the Now dissolved, and that other night became the Now, and her sick and trembling soul be sucked back once again into the lurid vortex of guilt and terror and murder.

Some day she would be freed, when Universal Law had exacted the just meed of punishment. The Law that neither prayer nor God could set aside, for the Law was part of God. This

with increasing clarity she knew, in moments of communication
when the blissful light thrilled through her veins, when for the
space of a heart-beat the Quest was ended, and the glimpse of
Peace which may not be retained yet gave her strength to endure the return to the relentless revolutions of the wheel.

She reached the baize door that led to the old servants'
quarters, and opened it, and at once, through an unshuttered
window, the afternoon sun came streaming. She turned back to
the silent girl, and spoke with soft apology. "I did not mean to
be so brusque with you, my dear. It's natural that you should
be curious. But you must forgive a recluse her caprices, yes?"

"Of course," said Amanda, mollified at once, for Calise's
smile was warm with kindly charm. "I didn't mean to pry.
You've been awfully good to me, listening to all my little fusses.
I see why Dart's so fond of you."

Calise leaned over and kissed the girl lightly on the forehead.
"I return the compliment. . . . Now, here is his room, and there
is the trunk. I will leave you to go through it at your leisure.
When you go you may use the back staircase and door."

"I won't see you again?" cried Amanda, surprised to discover
how much she longed to return to that simple room downstairs
and to talk again to this lady who, despite the two small rebuffs
and certain puzzling remarks, had yet given out a radiance and
a feeling of quiet wisdom.

Calise hesitated. She was touched by the girl's appeal, but she
longed for the privacy of her sanctum, and wished no interrup-
tion of the daily twilit hours of meditation and prayer. Nor did
there seem anything further she could do for Amanda. As Calise
thought this, a faint thrill ran along her nerves, an impression
and a warning. Her eyes seemed drawn as though by a magnet
to Dart's old steamer trunk. Evil for Amanda in the trunk? she
thought: *c'est ridicule*. And yet her highly sensitized perceptions
had telegraphed a message. Not any form of physical danger,
not perhaps danger at all, but a centre of confusion, a focus of
discordant vibration.

"Perhaps you should leave the trunk for another day?" she
said to Amanda. "Come down again with me now."

"Oh no, thanks," said the girl. "I've got to get that suit out
now I'm here, and see if there's anything else useful."

Ainsi soit-il, thought Calise. It is not for me to interfere.
"Then come later, *chérie*," she said, "if you still wish to speak

with me. .... I will help you," she added with a certain grave
emphasis, "in any way I can."

"Oh yes," said Amanda gratefully. But she did not go back
to Calise that day.

When her hostess had gone, Amanda glanced without interest
around the room; a typical servant's bedroom of the 'eighties,
oilcloth and varnished wood, an iron cot, washstand, and straight
chairs. It must have suited Dart's scanty needs very well, she
thought, smiling. She pulled the uncovered pillow off the cot,
knelt on it and opened the low trunk.

Inside there was a pile of jumbled clothes, the accumulation
of any young man's life: a pair of moth-eaten Tuxedo pants, a
turtle-necked sweater marked Phillips Andover Academy, a
tennis racquet with broken strings, an arsenic-green knitted
muffler with a note still pinned on it, "For dear little Jonathan
from his Aunt Martha, Christmas 1919." Dart had had an
Aunt Martha, in Boston, just as she still had an Aunt Amanda;
nor had Aunt Martha been any more lavish with useful presents
than Aunt Amanda, judging from the ghastly green muffler,
thought Amanda, amused, and comforted, too, as reminder of
Dart's Yankee half was always comforting.

She rummaged tenderly among the clothing and abstracted
the blue suit. She held it up to the light. Not too bad; at least,
it looked as though it would still fit. Dart hadn't changed a
pound since his college days. Then she discovered a fuzzy spot
under one sleeve; she picked at it, and it fell apart into a large
moth-hole. "Oh, damn," she said. Her knowledge of tailoring
was sketchy, but she turned the coat over hunting for an extra
bit of material which might be used as a patch. And as she
stared down at the suit wondering how to salvage it, she had a
sudden memory of her father's closet, crammed full of London-
made suits.

How did it happen that the salvaging of a few yards of serge
could have become so important? Amanda threw the blue suit
on the bed, and continued a desultory search through the trunk.

There wasn't much else: a few dog-eared textbooks on min-
ing, a pair of sneakers, some class pictures, a University of
Arizona pennant, and in the corner of the trunk, stuffed partly
in a stiffened old raincoat, there was a round brownish basket.
An Indian basket of some sort, quite small and open at the top.
It was a rather dirty fawn colour, with a zigzag blackish design

woven through it. The kind of basket, it seemed to her, that you saw in all the south-west souvenir shops, and which looked awful when you got them home.

There were several objects in the little basket, and she dumped them into her lap. There was a skin pouch with a draw-string, and inside it some yellow powder; there were four grey feathers, a piece of horn, a sinew on which were strung shells and beads, and a thin coppery disc. Some child's playthings, she thought. There were tiny pictures and tracings scratched on the disc. She studied them a moment without enlightenment, then turned the disc over, to see a paper pasted on the back and a note in Dart's hand, the writing less formed than it was now, but still recognizable as his.

It said, "Map to the Lost Pueblo Encantado Mine. Given me by Tanosay, 1921. But never search."

Puzzled, she examined again the copper disc, then let it fall to her lap. She investigated the basket once more, and found that there were several sheets of thin yellowed paper wedged on the bottom. These proved to be covered with writing in a different hand, and she read some sentences before she realized that they must have been written by Dart's father, Professor Dartland.

"*Notes on the Pueblo Encantado*," said the heading, and next to it, in pencilled parentheses (might work up for magazine article some day). Then the small sharp handwriting continued in ink. "There exists here in this south-western land an inordinate amount of myths and legends referring to so-called 'Lost Mines' and buried treasure. I believe the majority of these lost mines to be as illusory and illusive as the various forms of *ignis fatuus* (will-o'-the-wisp, Jack-o'-lights, foxfire, etc.) which are popularly supposed to guide the gold-seeker to the exact location.

"None the less, during years of enfeebled health and partial confinement to a desert home in Arizona, the study of these legends has furnished me with an agreeable hobby.

"The mass of fact, fancy, rumour, and perennial hope which has attached itself to the more famous of the Lost Mines, such as 'Lost Dutchman,' 'Tayopa,' 'Lost Adam Diggings,' etc., is already so ponderous that one is restrained from adding to it any additional weight.

"There has, however, come to my notice, under rather unusual circumstances the tale of still another and quite unknown lost mine which I venture to believe may present features of general interest. It is in a sense a prototype for the genre, including as it does the traditional trimmings, i.e. Early Spanish discovery, Apache hostility, complete inaccessibility, the reputed existence of a map, and, of course, a gold-bearing vein of incredible richness. These, it must be admitted, are standard ingredients, but others compounded in this legend are not. If, indeed, it *be* only a legend, I must confess to moments of credulity.

"The mine to which I refer is called 'El Pueblo Encantado' (The Enchanted City) and was so named by a Franciscan friar *circa* 1798. He, as far as I have been able to ascertain, was the only white man ever to find it and survive. The Apaches, particularly the Coyotero tribe, have apparent knowledge of the mine as we shall see later.

"Through the kindness of a colleague at the University of Mexico, I have been able to procure from their archives a copy of the Franciscan missionary's report, also that of his superior at the mission church of San Xavier del Bac near Tucson. The MS. is in poor condition and some of the Spanish undecipherable, but the following is an approximate paraphrase."

Amanda looked up from the notes, vaguely amused by the Professor's scholarly and cautious preamble. She thought of finishing them later some time, but the sun was still high, and there was no reason to start back yet, anyway. She settled more comfortably on the pillow, lit a cigarette, and continued.

"In the spring of 1798, two Franciscan missionaries, Fathers Gonzales and Rodriguez, set out north from San Xavier towards the Hopi country. They crossed the Salinas (Salt) River, and thereafter lost their way in 'very terrible mountains' many days north of Los Cuatros Hermanos (which I can only suppose to be the Four Peaks Mountain in the Mazatzal Range). They wandered for days in a malpais of volcanic country, starving and desperate for water, which finally gave out completely.

"The narrative here is very unclear, but in some way they went through a doorway (portal) in a cliff-side, and found themselves in a completely hidden box-canyon.

"High on the opposite side of the canyon they saw a 'little

city in stone' built in a cave, and near it a waterfall. The waterfall, and a rabbit, which they shot, momentarily revived them.
The next morning they investigated the cliff dwelling, which was
of course, deserted and seems to have inspired both men with a
great and strange fear. They report that it glowed in the night—
'like an enchantment,' Father Gonzales, the survivor, says in
the narrative. They persisted, however, and holding their
crucifixes in front of them, they explored the dead city and the
depths of a cave behind it. Here there were corpses (probably
mummies—Father Gonzales says 'Los Muertos') and here also
at the back of the cave they were stunned to see a wall of glittering gold."

Amanda sat up straight, frowning down at the notes. She
re-read the last paragraphs and her breathing quickened. She
tamped out her unfinished cigarette, and bent closer to the
Professor's increasingly cramped writing.

"The two padres thought at first that this golden wall was an
evil hallucination, but they picked off some free gold with their
finger-nails and knives. They were then seized with a frenzy of
jubilation (*frensi alborozado*) and sang a *Te Deum* in the cave,
for the glory of the Church which would profit by these riches.
One gathers that they had less sanctified emotions as well, for
Father Gonzales finishes his account cryptically: 'While we were
in the cave by the wall of gold, the devil came and prompted us
to violent thoughts of hideous attraction.'

"This is the end of the Gonzales narrative. The rest is added
by his superior at the Mission. Father Gonzales was found alone
in September four months later by friendly Pima Indians. He
was wandering half-crazed by the banks of the Salinas, probably
not far from the site of the present town of Mesa. They brought
him back to the Mission, where he dictated a coherent story as
far as the above point, beyond which he could add little. His
mind was obviously affected by his sufferings, and he died soon
after. He did say, in response to repeated questionings, that
Father Rodriguez, his companion, had been mysteriously killed
near the 'enchanted city,' and as they were crossing the box-
canyon. Shot by 'an arrow from the skies.' And thereafter
Gonzales had little recollection of how he got out of the mountains or down to the river, where the Pimas found him. But

his pouch was filled with gold flakes and chunks of gold-bearing quartz richer than any yet discovered.

"Gonzales endeavoured to make a map, but it later proved to be of no use whatsoever, and two expeditions sent forth after his death never even found any of the markings which he said he had seen along the way, and both ended disastrously in the hands of hostile Indians.

"The Superior finished his own account by saying that were it not for the evidence of the gold brought back by the unfortunate missionary, one would think this tale of enchanted cities, glittering walls, and caves of the Dead was but the miserable phantasms of dementia, and that in fact even the evidence of the gold might have some more logical explanation.

"This cynicism from an eighteenth-century Spanish padre it would be well to emulate, and if I persist in the story of the Lost Pueblo Encantado, it is for the purpose of presenting further angles. These comprise archæology, geology, and the history of the Apache Indians, and may therefore have a slightly more scientific turn.

"Perhaps I should first explain. . . ."

That was all. The notes stopped. Amanda stood up, first dumping all the little objects back in the basket except the copper disc; this she held in one hand, while she stood by the window and re-read Professor Dartland's notes from beginning to end in the waning light.

Her heart beat fast, and she was suffused by a warm, delicious excitement. Dart would know the rest of the story, this copper disc almost proved that, for when Professor Dartland had said "reputed existence of a map," he did not then know of this disc so carefully labelled in Dart's firm boyish hand. Besides, Professor Dartland had died in 1919, the disc was dated 1921. She examined the tracings on it again, but they were nothing but a jumble of wavy lines, circles, and little triangles. She put the disc and notes carefully in the basket, flung the blue suit over her arm, and ran down the hall to the back stairway. No thought now of calling again on Mrs. Cunningham, no thought of any delay. She was in a fever to see Dart and question him. She'd walk up to the mine, catch him as he came out, ride back home with him. She let herself out of the back door and ran down the trail and through the ghost town, and up to the mine road. It was five o'clock and growing dusk; ordinarily the loneliness of the unfamiliar mountain road would have daunted her, but she climbed the mile at top speed, lugging the suit and the basket without noticing them, while her mind caressed with fascination the story of Father Gonzales' discovery.

She had been to the mine office with Dart, and had thought the group of dingy frame buildings very ugly, but she was glad to see their lights now, and intent only on finding Dart, she forgot mine etiquette and ran up the steps into the building.

She burst into the general office, and was brought up short by the astonished faces of the two men inside. Luther Mablett sat at his desk smoking a cigar, and he had been talking to a sallow middle-aged man with a knobby head who was lounging on the corner of the desk. This was Tiger Burton, the day-shift boss, though Amanda did not know it, and Dart had been the subject of their conversation.

Mablett's bull face flushed vermilion up to his tight yellow-white curls, and he rose clumsily to his feet. Burton got off the desk; he had little eyes like dull onyx, and they fixed themselves on Amanda's face, unwinking as a lizard's.

'Oh, I'm terribly sorry!" Amanda cried. "I thought Dart'd be here; I could ride down with him."

"Oh—sure," said Mablett, breathing hard, but recovering. "He's still underground, far as I know. Er . . . Mrs. Dartland, meet Mr. Burton—shift boss."

"How do you do." Amanda held out her hand and Burton shook it with alacrity, revealing a few tobacco-stained teeth and many black gaps in an ingratiating smile. " 'S a pleasure," he said.

Amanda, like most people, received from Tiger Burton an impression of nonentity. She perceived only a meagre sweaty little man with nondescript features, a semi-bald head partially concealed by lank wisps of dark hair, and a colourless mouth compressed to an expression of nervous affability. Mablett's toady, she thought, vaguely remembering something Dart had said, and she dismissed him in favour of propitiating the enemy she knew of.

"Mr. Mablett, would I be an awful nuisance . . . I mean, could I wait some place for Dart? You see, I was at Mrs. Cunningham's going through Dart's trunk for a suit"—she pointed to it apologetically—"and I was so near here, I thought

I could get a ride down. I know women don't come to the mine, please forgive me." She instinctively concealed the basket under the edge of the suit, but Burton's hooded eyes had seen it, and at once recognized it for Apache. He effaced himself in the corner of the room and rolled himself a cigarette.

Amanda followed her breathless explanation with a widening of shining blue eyes and her most brilliant smile, to which Mablett was not unreceptive. Dartland was an insubordinate bastard and a hell of a nuisance, but there was no special quarrel with Mrs. Dartland.

His bulging eyes softened. "Sure. Sure. You can wait in the porch. There's a bench. The men won't bother you none. Day-shift's all gone home. . . . By the way, did you say you'd seen that crazy old Cunningham dame?"

"Why, yes," said Amanda, still smiling.

"What's she like?" asked Mablett curiously. "I never seen her, but they say she's batty as a March hare, sees ghosts and stuff. Weren't you scared?"

"No. . . ." Amanda was startled. She thought back to her visit with Calise. It seemed a very long time ago, the impression of it nearly effaced by the far stronger excitement which had followed. "She seemed very pleasant," Amanda added uncertainly.

"Well, you want to watch out who you mix with, a beautiful girl like you," said Mablett with heavy gallantry. "Lots of queer characters in a place like this." He winked and chuckled.

Amanda laughed. "I guess there are." She gave him a small coquettish nod and went outside in the porch. He wasn't so bad, she thought, once you got him away from Lydia. If Dart would only use a little tact, jolly him along. Or far better yet, get away from the whole stupid mess. Her fingers closed tight on the edge of the basket. She sat down on the bench, and after a cautious look round, she lit a cigarette. She gazed down the canyon towards the lights of the mill and waited impatiently.

Inside the office, Burton spoke from the corner. "Nice-looking little bit of tail."

"Yeah," said Mablett. "*She* ain't so bad." He frowned down at the chief engineer's report on his desk. The samplings weren't running any better.

"*He* seen Tyson again, Lute?" Burton spoke casually, his expressionless eyes fixed on the ceiling.

The superintendent hunched his shoulders in sudden irritation. "Jesus, I don't know. I don't think so. Whatever he wanted on them two visits don't seem to've got him anything. But the old man won't talk."

Burton shifted his feet and took a drag on his cigarette. "Like we was saying, Lute, when she busted in—you ought to get rid of him. Sneaking around behind your back, making you look like a fool with the men."

Mablett's chair scraped back, he twisted his thick neck and glowered at his shift boss. "You know goddam well I can't get rid of him just like that. He ain't done nothing out of the way lately, anyhow. Nothing to put your finger on."

In Mablett's slow brain, the familiar baffled anger which this subject caused him exploded in a new direction. He rocked his head from side to side. "You keep harping and harping. He don't interfere with *you* none; you act like *you* was superintendent here. What's the matter with you anyway, Tiger? You been drinking?"

Burton came out of his corner; he put his small hairy hand on his chief's arm. "Why, no, Lute," he said mildly. "I don't mean for to bother you. I just don't like Apaches; they'll get you every time, if you don't get 'em first."

"Oh, for God's sake." Mablett shook off the hand. "That again. You're nuts on that subject."

Mablett's reactions were simple, and he had insensibly become accustomed to accepting the opinions and flattery of his shift boss, but he was not an utter fool. Much as he disliked Dart, he could not picture him as a treacherous physical menace; moreover, Tiger's obsession was getting to be a bore. Dartland was only a quarter-breed after all, and they'd got rid of the other Indian boys.

"You stick to your own job, Tiger," he said gruffly, "and let me do the worrying."

"Sure, Lute. . . . That ventilating pipe on the seven hundred blew loose again; we'll have to patch it . . . like you said."

Tiger knew when he had gone too far. He had plans, but they could wait—wait until everything worked just right. Nor did they need co-operation from this big stupid hulk. An accident, of course. Wipe out the Indian without mercy, like the Indians had wiped his mother out, but no fist fights, no sudden murderous rage like there'd been with that Cleve in the deserted stope. This Indian must be wiped out without anyone knowing how, because besides being an Indian, he was mine foreman. And when that job was open, one of the shift bosses would be next in line. There'd be no trouble about which one, if the whole thing was handled just right. He smiled down in answer to a statement of Mablett's.

"Sure, Lute. You got a great idea there. That'll cut costs all right."

CHAPTER SIX

AMANDA sat in the mine office porch until she got restless, then she got up and wandered down to the parking space below the change house and found their car. She put the suit and the basket on the seat, and decided, since as usual it was getting chilly as soon as the sun set, to walk around. They couldn't really mind that, as the prohibition for women applied only to underground.

Dart would have to come up on top in the elevator thing they called a cage, she knew that much, and she walked over to the jumble of little buildings below the head frame which stuck up like an intricate steel gallows thirty feet into the air, above the shaft. There was a whirring of machinery from the adjacent hoist-house, and she looked timidly inside the open door. Two large Diesels were running the air compressors and the hoist, and Amanda stared at them with the nervous awe the roaring of huge machinery gives to the uninitiated.

The young hoistman and Amanda saw each other at the same time; he was sitting on a platform by levers and an indicator, and he shouted something at her, and beckoned. She picked her way gingerly over to his platform and said, "I'm Mrs. Dartland. I'm just waiting for my husband to come up."

He nodded, showing to Amanda's relief no particular surprise. He was an earnest young man named Bill Riley, who was new to the Shamrock, though he had grown up in the Ray Mines. He was proud of his job, which entailed considerable responsibility, and he was very conscientious. He kept a Thermos full of coffee by his stool to give him extra alertness during the long night hours of watching for signals and timing the hoist.

"That'll likely be Mr. Dartland now," he said to Amanda, as a light flashed and a horn buzzed. "D'you want to wait at the collar?"

Correctly interpreting this as the mouth of the shaft, Amanda picked her way back among the whirring engines, and stood outside. The man-cage clanked up into sight, and Dart stepped off, though for an instant she did not recognize him in the hard black helmet with its single lamp flashing in front like a cyclops eye.

"For the love of Mike," he said, laughing. "Where did you blow from!"

"Oh, Dart—I've got so much to tell you—ask you, I thought I'd ride home with you. Don't mind, do you?"

"I'm charmed." He squeezed her waist, delighted to hear her voice bright and happy as it had not been in a long time. Delighted that she, who had been lying around the house and moping for days, should have found the energy to walk up to the mine.

"Did you see Mrs. Cunningham?" he asked.

"Oh yes, and she's wonderful, but that isn't what——" She stopped. No use explaining all that yet.

"I thought so," said Dart with satisfaction. Calise had helped as he had known she would. "Wait till I change, Andy. I've got to shower, but I'll hurry."

"You sure need one, my gardenia," said Amanda, wrinkling her nose, "but I love you, anyway."

Dart laughed and hurried into the change house. He had had a routine day underground. The usual petty problems to be dealt with, mild vexations, and then mild pleasure when the problems had been solved. The new cross-cut on the 700 had hit a vein finally, but already it was pinching out again, and it was evidently not the main lode, though a few weeks of higher-grade ore had helped. Tyson still was pursuing a waiting policy. Dart's two interviews with him had been inconclusive. He had listened to Dart's hunch about driving a blind cross-cut in the old Shamrock, listened indulgently and agreed not to mention it to anyone. But he had not consented.

"Maybe later, Dart. If we're really up against it. But you know yourself it's an expensive gamble. One of these days, when I feel a bit better, I'll get underground with you and have a look, myself. In the meantime, you're doing a fine job."

So the mine limped along, and Dart, temporarily relinquishing his plan, bent all his efforts to giving the present operating policy as firm a footing as possible. Even to the avoidance of clashes with Mablett, whenever there was no danger to the men involved.

He ran out of the change house and jumped into the car beside Amanda. "Nice to see you, kid," he said, and kissed her.

She snuggled up against him, and they started down the mountain road.

"D'you find the old suit all right?" he asked, as they passed above the mill down in the canyon. The mill lights were off now except for the watchman's. Be nice if we ever could get out enough ore to keep her running steady down there, thought Dart.

"Uhuh," said Amanda. "And I found something else too. Something I think is frantically exciting."

"Not pictures of nekkid ladies, I hope; I can't remember exactly how much of my past's in that trunk!"

"No nekkid ladies. A—a basket."

"Basket?"

She reached around to the back seat, and held the basket near his face. "Here it is—can you see what it is?"

He slowed down and peered through the gloom. "Oh yes," he said after a moment. "That was Saba's, my mother's—she wove it. I'd forgotten where it was, Is that so exciting?"

"Do you remember what's in it?"

"Not very well. I think Saba put in whatever's there." He was puzzled by the tension he felt in Amanda, and a trifle uneasy. He knew that his Indian background did not usually give her pleasure.

"I'll show you when we get home," she said brightly. "By the way—I cooked a stew this morning, out of that cookery book Mamma sent. I don't think it'll be too awful, and there's some left in that bottle of hooch Hugh gave us last week. We'll have a party."

"Fine," said Dart; "but are we celebrating anything special?"

"Indeed we are!" cried Amanda.

After a couple of drinks, the stew and coffee, Amanda cleared the tables of dishes, and brought in the basket with a little air of mystery. Her eyes were shining, and Dart contemplated her with affection and amusement.

"So Saba made the basket?" she asked, putting it on the table between them.

He nodded, smiling. He remembered vividly when it was made, because he had been about seven, and very bored with hunting for "Devil's Claw," the dark pincer-like mountain plant which alone could produce the black design.

"There's lots of queer little things in here," said Amanda,

spreading them on the table, but carefully leaving in the basket the copper disc and the notes. "What are they, Dart? Did you play with them?"

"Good Lord, no!" cried Dart, staring at the buckskin pouch, and the feathers, and the piece of horn, and the beaded thong. "I wasn't even allowed to touch them."

"Why? What are they?"

"They were Tanosay's. He was a great shaman, a medicine man. These were the instruments of—of his trade." Dart spoke lightly, but his eyes were thoughtful. The awe with which these little objects had once inspired him was inextricably mingled with his reverence for Tanosay, who had never doubted their power.

"Tell me about them," said Amanda.

He saw that she was working up to some sort of climax, but also that she seemed to be interested. For some reason the Apache basket had broken through the tenuous barrier she had, since their arrival in Arizona, erected against his Indian blood.

"Well," he said, picking up the pouch, and loosening the drawstring. "These were all used in various ceremonies. This yellow powder is hoddentin, the pollen of the tule, a kind of bulrush that grows in swamps." He showed her a pinch of it, then put the pinch back in the bag. "It's considered very sacred."

He picked up the feathers. "These came off an eagle. Four is the Apache sacred number. They give strength and courage to the fainthearted." He smiled and took up the beaded thong, "This is called the Izze-Kloth. I suppose you might call it a sort of Indian rosary, since it's used for prayers and incantations. And this little hunk of horn was the most important of all to Tanosay."

"Why?" she asked as he paused.

"It's hard to explain. . . . Each medicine man, or woman, dis-covers some object in nature which is his own particular channel through which the great Life Spirit flows. His power, he calls it. It might be lightning or a fox or a snake or a rock—anything. For Tanosay it was the white-tailed deer, because of a mystical experience he had in his youth. This bit of horn came from that deer. He had," added Dart slowly, "great faith in it."

Amanda stared at her husband. She had never heard him use

just that grave and musing tone before. Surely the blunt practical Dart did not also have faith in these primitive fetishes, interesting though they might be as curiosities.

He raised his eyes and smiled at her, answering as though she had spoken. "I don't know, Andy, but I've seen Tanosay make some remarkable cures, after the Agency doctor had given the patient up completely."

"Oh, well, of course," she said after a moment. "One does hear of faith cures all the time. Like Mesmer and—and Coué."

Dart laughed. He began to gather up Tanosay's ceremonial objects. "Let's have one more cigarette and then tackle those dishes," he said.

"Oh no, wait! There's something else in the basket. . . . Look, do you remember this?" She held out to him the copper disc.

"Well, I'll be damned," said Dart, taking it in his hand and examining it with amusement. "The map to the Pueblo Encantado. That sure gave me a thrill when I was fifteen."

"It seemed to give your father a thrill, too," she said, giving him the notes. "Have you ever read these?"

"I don't think so." Dart leafed them over. "Poor old Dad, this sort of thing was a hobby of his those last years when he couldn't get around much. Made him feel adventurous."

"But, Dart," she said, frowning. "Didn't Tanosay give you that map later, after your father died? Didn't Tanosay believe in the Lost Mine?"

"Tanosay wasn't interested in any *mine*," said Dart, beginning to laugh. "Andy, don't tell me——" He stared at her sober intent little face. "Andy, you haven't been bitten by the bug, just like that. . . ."

"What bug?" she said crossly.

"Lost gold fever. Pie in the sky. My poor baby, there're at least four hundred lost treasures in the south-west, and I guess, through the years since old Coronado first got the idea, there's been a million suckers hunting for them."

"I don't care," she said, her eyes flashing. "This is a special one, your father said so."

Dart stopped laughing, and he gave her a keen look. "I guess I'd better read those notes." He pulled the kerosene lamp nearer to him, and bent his dark head over the papers. She sat back and waited. The little kitchen smelled of the kerosene lamp, and of stew and onions. She got up and opened the back door a crack, then came and sat down again tensely.

Dart finished the notes and raised his head. "Yes," he said. "It's a swell yarn. These old Spanish padres come to life, don't they?"

"But what happened next, Dart? The part your father started to write and didn't." She pulled the notes over and looked at the last page. "'. . . the further angles that comprise archæology, geology, and the history of the Apache Indians'. Why didn't he go on?"

"I don't know. But I think he didn't go on because my mother asked him not to."

"Why would she do that?"

Dart pulled out cigarettes, offered her one and lit them. "Look, Andy, I'll tell you what I know about this legend, but really it's nothing to get steamed up about."

She leaned a little forward across the table. "Well, tell me. . . ."

"You haven't seen any cliff dwellings, have you?"

She shook her head. "No, but I've read about them, of course."

"You've read about a whole lot of things, my pet. Well, anyway, there are hundreds of cliff dwellings over parts of Arizona and New Mexico, though the most famous one is probably Mesa Verde in Colorado. They were all built by Indians called Anasazi or 'The Ancient Ones' by the nomadic Navajo and Apache tribes who came to this country later; nobody knows just how or from where. Probably all these Indians came at different times from Asia via Bering Strait, but that doesn't matter to us, though it keeps the archæologists sweating and snarling happily at each other."

"Yes," she said. "Go on; what about this particular Pueblo Encantado?"

"It's a legend in Tanosay's tribe, the Coyoteros. There's a theory that the Coyotero branch of Apaches were among the first to come south into Arizona, and that they intermarried with the descendants of the Anasazi whom they found here. That would probably be in the fifteenth century, though nobody knows that either. The story was handed down by word of mouth to Tanosay back through his father's father's father × number of times. Anyway, one of Tanosay's remote ancestors married an

Anasazi girl whose ancestors had once lived in the Pueblo Encantado, and abandoned it intact for good reasons."

"What reasons?" she said as he paused. "And when would they have abandoned it?"

Dart laughed. "Your avid interest is most flattering, and I'm giving you the best gems culled from Archæology I at Tucson, but nobody knows the answer to that one, either. Why, indeed, some time between twelve hundred and fourteen hundred, did all the Ancient Ones abandon their beautiful fortress cliff dwellings? Drought? Maybe. Disease? Maybe. Depredations by the Navajo or Apache? Maybe. But for the Pueblo Encantado, none of those are the reasons handed down through the tribe to Tanosay."

She waited impatiently as he stopped. He was staring at the copper disc, and he heard once more the solemn voice of Tanosay. He felt again the weight of the old hand upon his shoulder and saw by the light of the camp fire the stern admonishing eyes as they gazed down on the upturned boyish face. He could not now remember the Apache words that Tanosay had used, but he remembered well the tenor of them and the tingle of awe he had felt as he listened.

The City of Spirits lay somewhere in the wildest mountains of Apacheria, said Tanosay. Far north into the turquoise sky beyond the four sacred horn peaks. Long, long before the coming of the Dinneh, by which Tanosay meant his own people, the city in the hidden canyon had been a happy land, where the Anasazi dwelt in joy and contentment. Then evil entered into their hearts, greed and lust stung their bowels like serpents, and the Great Spirit became very angry. He came down to them in a dreadful blast of thunder and lightning and drove them from the happy land which they no longer deserved. He made of it a sacred place, and set mountain spirits to guard it from all earthly wickedness. But when He saw how bitterly the Ancient Ones regretted their lost paradise, and the peace which had once been theirs, He softened their exile by a promise.

If the city and the valley were for ever kept from human defilement, those of the ancient blood might go back there some day and live again in everlasting contentment. And Tanosay so profoundly believed this that the listening boy, in whose blood there was a strain of the Anasazi blood, had believed it too at that time—as Saba did.

Dart became again conscious of Amanda's expectant face; he sighed, and he overcame his increasing reluctance to continue the story.

He resumed the light casual tone in which he had been speaking. "The tradition is a sort of Garden of Eden tale, I suppose. The Anasazi were driven out because they had sinned. But this Coyotero band, though none of them has ever seen it, still think of the place as a kind of heaven. Sacred and inviolate. It is forbidden to go near it. Not that *that* would be easy, since nobody has the faintest idea just where it is."

"But what about the map?" cried Amanda. "The copper thing."

"That was made by an enemy, a Mimbreño Apache, over a hundred years ago, with copper from the Santa Rita mines in New Mexico, I guess. Anyway, the Mimbreños and Coyoteros were at war, and this particular Mimbreño seems to have stumbled on the most infuriating thing he could do to the Coyoteros—invading their sacred canyon. However, he never even got back across the Tonto Creek with his map before the Coyoteros made mincemeat of him."

"Oh," said Amanda thoughtfully. "But why did they keep the map if they didn't want anyone to know where the enchanted pueblo was?"

Dart laughed, tamping out his cigarette. "For one thing, it's a very bad map; look at it—the Mimbreño doubtless meant it only as a guide for himself—and secondly, I suppose, the Coyoteros felt that anything associated with the sacred place became tinged with magic too, and must be preserved. Now, I've told you all I know. Let's get at those dishes, before I fall to snoring."

"But the mine——" said Amanda, not moving from the table. "The wall of gold? You haven't said a thing about that."

"Because I don't *know* a thing about that!" answered Dart with some impatience, "and I thoroughly doubt that there is such a thing."

"The padre said so—Father Gonzales," she said, frowning, "and he had a lot of gold stuff in his pocket."

"Which he might have picked up anywhere in his wanderings, as the other guy, his superior, intimated. Most of those mountains up there are mineralized. Also, he might have stolen the stuff. Andy, for the love of Mike, he was nothing but a crazy old man with a wild story. He had to cook up something to explain the disappearance of his brother missionary, whom he probably murdered."

"But you believe he actually found the hidden canyon, and the lost city—the particular one Tanosay told you about?"

"I suppose so," said Dart, getting up; "the details correspond to Coyotero tradition, general location, malpais, invisible entrance to the canyon through a rock door, waterfall, etc." He put the copper disc and his father's notes into the basket. "I'll carry this back to the trunk some day when I'm near Mrs. Cunningham's. I promised Tanosay to take care of them, though I must confess I'd forgotten all about them."

Amanda got up, too; she walked to the stove and picked up the kettle of steaming water, poured a little over the dishes in the pan, and then she put the kettle down; she turned and looked up at him.

"But, Dart, supposing there is gold up there, gold so rich you can pick it off the walls?"

"Well, suppose there is." He lifted the kettle and poured the rest of the hot water over the dishes. "Gold is where you find it, as people have been saying since the Stone Age went out."

"*You* could find it," she said, very low and distinct. "You know this country, you remember what Tanosay told you, and you could follow that map."

He put down the dishrag and stared at her. "My dear girl, you're not serious!"

She nodded, leaning against the sink, and looking up at him with eyes darkening as he burst out laughing.

"Andy, really!" he said, controlling his mirth under her angry gaze. "Don't you think I have anything better to do than go scrambling around hundreds of square miles of the toughest wilderness in this state looking for pie in the sky? Aside from the fact that I haven't the least desire to."

"You'd rather piddle along in this little two-cent mine, earning barely enough to keep us from starving?" Her words thudded like small stones in the suddenly stilled kitchen. A tightness came into her throat as she saw the change in his face, but she went on in a kind of desperation. "You're looking for gold in this mine here, I can't see what's so different."

His eyes, as they stared unswervingly back into hers, had turned to grey ice, but in a moment he spoke in a controlled voice. "No. I guess you don't see. This mine is a co-operative job, the entire town of Lodestone is dependent on it. It's here and real, a proven enterprise. It's my job in which, though you seem to have difficulty understanding why, I have great interest. And I like to finish things I start."

She moistened her lips which were trembling, but she persisted in a voice as controlled as his, "Yes, that's all very—very noble. But you could *try* to look for it. I know there're always people, prospectors, hunting around for lucky strikes, but once in a while they make one. You can't deny that. You could *try* to find this Pueblo Encantado, Dart."

"No," he said. He turned sharply from her, went and closed the back door, then he walked into the front room. She heard him taking off his shoes, the bang as each one hit the floor. She stared through blinding mist at the greasy pile of half-cleansed dishes. Her breath clotted in her throat. She ran to the bedroom door.

"Why not?" she whispered through her teeth. "Indian superstition? Indians don't care about money, do they? And they don't care about being decently comfortable. Or is it an Indian ghost you're afraid of, up in that canyon—is that it, Dart?"

He raised his head until his eyes rested on her chin. His gaze travelled from her chin, over her mouth and up until it met her frightened, tear-blinded response.

"I didn't mean that, Dart," she whispered. "Don't look at me like that. It's just I don't understand—I—oh, everything's so hard. . . ."

She sank down on the bed and covered her face with her hands.

Dart sat rigid beside her on the bed. After a moment he spoke in a quiet incisive voice. "Do you want to go home. Amanda? Shall we call it quits?"

The shock of his words hit her in the stomach like an actual blow. She gasped, jerking her head up. "No, darling. No!" she cried. "I love you. I didn't mean what I said."

"What you said isn't important. But you obviously aren't happy. And I'm not going to change, Andy. There's no use hoping for it."

"I know," she whispered. "I don't want you to really. I'll be all right. I will be happy. I am when you're with me." She flung her arms around his neck, pulling him tight to her, until he lifted her over on to his lap, and kissed her beseeching mouth, wet and salt with the tears which ran down her face.

"Ah—you don't want me to go home, Dart," she cried in triumph as his kisses grew harder against her mouth. "You do love me."

He rumpled her soft hair, and kissed her eyelids, yielding, as she did, to the sharpened passion of danger passed by.

They slept that night, close in each other's arms, and Amanda waked several times to a voluptuous contentment, as she listened to his deep steady breathing. But when she dreamed, it was of the Pueblo Encantado; she saw herself and Dart running through a glade of pine-trees towards a solid golden wall, yellow as butter in the sunlight. "It's all for us!" she cried to him joyously. "Thank God, now we can buy the Spanish castle ourselves!"

What nonsense, she thought when she awoke, though the dream was one of exaltation and triumph. What did I want with a Spanish castle? It was not until much later that she remembered Tim's letter, and his reference to El Castillo—"Castle in Spain on the Desert." Nor did this interpretation please her much. She had no wish to think of Tim.

She had awakened with a contrite heart and many good resolutions. She would say with King Henry, "My crown is in my heart, not in my head; not decked with diamonds and Indian stones, not to be seen. My crown is called content."

She found, however, that neither good resolutions nor the certainty of Dart's disapproval could prevent her from thinking a great deal about the Pueblo Encantado, though this she mentioned to nobody. Dart did not return the basket to the trunk at Mrs. Cunningham's for several days, and she had ample time to copy Professor Dartland's notes, and make a tracing of the incomprehensible map. Neither Dart nor Amanda mentioned the basket again; it stood in the corner of their closet, until one day he quietly removed it without comment. Nor, when he saw Calise that afternoon, did he mention the basket incident to her, having put Amanda's crack-brained scheme down to some childish or perhaps female emotionalism, best ignored. She seemed happier, and was certainly more efficient around the home, and he thankfully forgot the disagreeable subject.

Amanda soothed a feeling of guilt for the secrecy of her continuing interest by telling herself that, like Professor Dartland,

she was simply pursuing an intellectual hobby which hurt nobody. Two days after the night of her clash with Dart, she
walked down to the town's only filling station and extracted
from the attendant a road-map of Arizona.

She took it home and pored over it, locating, with the help of
Professor Dartland's clues, the Mazatzal range of mountains and
the Four Peaks to the south of them. The Mazatzals on the map
included a square marked "Wilderness Area," which seemed to
lie in just about the geographic centre of the state. Not so far
from here as the crow flies, she thought—not over a hundred
miles. Her immediate optimism was somewhat quenched by the
discovery that it was nearly twice as far as that by road to the
point she judged nearest the area, and after that there were, of
course, no roads at all. Still, burros could get anywhere,
and some trail work was inevitable. The more she studied the
map the simpler the problem appeared. Surely it wouldn't take
any time at all to explore all the yellow-tinted blank spot on the
map marked Mazatzal Wilderness Area. If Dart would only
listen to reason.

She sighed, reminding herself that her researches were only
an intellectual hobby, at present anyhow. She folded the map
and hid it with the copied notes in one of the satin pockets of
her fitted dressing-case.

By March, Amanda, and the rest of the country, had perforce
more pressing things to think about—Franklin D. Roosevelt's
inauguration, and the Bank Holiday, though neither of these
events affected Lodestone as they did less isolated spots. Morning static on the two radios made it impossible to hear the new
President's inaugural address, and thus diluted the sense of
immediate crisis. The Phœnix papers did not arrive via Roy
Kellickman until two days later. He also bore news of the Bank
Holiday.

The Bank Holiday, though startling and heatedly discussed
in the saloons and post office, was of no tremendous significance
to the town. There was no branch bank in Lodestone, nor need
of one. The miners and their families cashed pay-cheques with
the local merchants, to whom they were always in debt, and
therefore seldom recovered much cash. Tessie Rubrick did a
thriving money-order business. In desperate cases, where personal loans could not be negotiated, there was always "The

Chinaman," a sleazy Oriental of unknown origin who lived on
the edge of Mexican town, ran a species of sub-rosa pawnshop,
and charged ten per cent. interest.

The mine itself was fortunate in that it did its banking in
Hayden with the Valley National Bank which reopened promptly
on 16 March.

Two other factors resultant upon Roosevelt's inauguration
affected Lodestone more closely, and produced a mild and long-
absent feeling of optimism. The first was the legal return of
beer, and consequent certainty that total repeal was not far
off. The second was a slight rise in gold prices, and hope that
Roosevelt would decree a substantial rise soon. Dart shared in
the decrease of tension at the mine. They were still pulling
nine-dollar ore from the Plymouth vein, and the rise in gold gave
them a tiny leeway. Mr. Tyson's health seemed improved; he
had not yet gone underground, but he now appeared at the mine
office almost daily, and his presence vastly improved the morale
among the staff. Mablett was subdued, refrained from overt
bullying, and left Dart alone to do his job. Tiger Burton kept
out of the way. He seemed to be running his shift well enough,
he wrote his reports in a sharp legible hand, and made verbal
ones chiefly to Mablett. Dart thought nothing of this; he was
simply thankful that for the moment there was no trouble with
any of the shift bosses or the men. The mine, throughout its
sensitive structure, enjoyed the infiltration of heightened morale.
As the mine so the town, and above ground the subtle sense of
relaxation and hope for better things at last was greatly heightened by the first harbingers of brilliant spring.

Here and there along the canyon clumps of ocatillos, waving
like a cluster of thorny wands above the desert rocks, now turned
a warmer green, and their tips burst into tiny scarlet flames; the
paloverde trees, already green in stem and bark, frothed into
golden flowerets, lacy gilt in the ever more ardent sunlight. The
lavender covenas threw out clusters of mauve stars on the rocky
slopes above Lodestone Canyon. The cacti—the bisnagas and
the chollas and the giant saguaros—all felt the stirring of the
new magic deep beneath their armatures of pulp and thorns and
they shot upwards to their crests the first tender buds, which
would later bloom into startling multi-coloured beauty. Bird
song increased, the cooing cry of the doves, the gurgle of the
desert warbler, the busy twittering of the little cactus wrens

darting in and out of their nests in the chollas—and from the distant hills the coyotes howled their mating songs to the moon.

Nobody was totally unaffected by the blessed recurrence of spring, and the human population celebrated the ancient mystery in its own ways. In Mexican town the doors remained open all day, the brown babies tumbled in the dust outside the adobes, the smell of chili and tortillas lingered longer in the piñon-scented air, and each evening guitars twanged accompaniment to nasal voices singing "La Golondrina" or "Cuatro Milpas."

In Lodestone's Creek Street, the miners walked with lighter feet towards the saloons, which thrived openly, emboldened by the expectation that there would soon be no need for concealment. Big Ruby's girls in Back Lane did a livelier business than they had for months, they put new frilly curtains in their windows, and one day they cajoled an admirer into driving them into Globe, where they descended on a beauty parlour for permanents, and spent happy hours in the five-and-dime store, selecting new cosmetics and ornaments for the enhancement of their charms.

The school-children became yet more unruly; Miss Arden and the whey-faced little teacher from Iowa exerted very inadequate counter force to the call of spring outside, and the new teacher cared little. Already the unacknowledged hopes which had sent her to an isolated mining camp were being realized. She had had four proposals—from a mechanic, a driller, an electrician, and a clerk in the mine office. Her heart vibrated with delicious indecision.

In the General Store, Pearl Pottner felt the call of spring. She turned a blind eye to Bobby's depredations in the cookie barrel, she extended credit a day longer than usual to those who begged hardest, and in a moment of truly vernal madness she sent to Phoenix for three boxes of California strawberries, which Lydia Mablett eventually bought. Lydia was planning another collation. These affairs usually took place monthly, but had been delayed now since the January fiasco, because of the extreme difficulty of deciding whether to ask the Dartlands or not. She had now decided to do so. The Empress of Lodestone could afford to be merciful.

At the Company hospital Hugh Slater reacted to the coming of spring and decrease of tension at the mine. . . . Professionally, since he had fewer patients, often none—and personally, since the season made him uneasy. And an incident one night gave him a far stronger emotion. He had dropped in to see the Dartlands after supper, and was riffling through some new magazines Amanda's mother had sent, when a face leaped out at him from the glossy pages of *Vanity Fair*. He caught his breath so sharply that Amanda stared at him, and he turned it into a coughing spell. He pretended no interest in the magazine, and waited until both Dartlands were in the kitchen, then he tore out two pages and hid them in his pocket. He knew that Amanda had not looked at *Vanity Fair* yet, and she would think there was some mistake in the printing.

At home again he locked himself in his office, and stared at the photograph. It was of an extremely beautiful woman, her tender wistful mouth smiling a little, her heart-shaped face and tranquil brow just touched by a new assurance and maturity. "Viola Vinton, who is starring in the *Russian Empress*, one of Broadway's most successful plays."

Hugh read the accompanying text, slowly. "An interview with Viola Vinton. . . . From her suite at the St. Regis . . . the exquisite star . . . room banked with white orchids—glowing mysterious type of loveliness—many admirers—but never yet married—she says she believes in love though—but dedicated to her art. Always wears a single priceless pearl ring, no matter what other jewels—says it brings her luck. Laughingly admits she came from simple background in Baltimore—many successful screen rôles to her credit . . . often compared since this new stage success to Duse. . . ."

Hugh stopped reading. He stared for a long time at the photograph, and the wide soft eyes looked up at him as they had once looked up in his arms. He locked the photograph in his desk drawer.

Then he entered upon a three-day binge, beat Maria unmercifully, and emerged with a sense of self-loathing and a black depression. Maria in no way resented the beating, which she found more comprehensible than the savage verbal assaults, especially as she was convinced that the Doc's violence, this time sprang from jealousy.

There was a travelling salesman for mine supplies putting up at Mrs. Zuckowski's hotel, and Maria found opportunity for dalliance. A swell car the guy had, too, and he was a free spender. Him and her had passed an agreeable evening together at "The Laundry" drinking tequila and dancing. Doc had seen her there, too, so you couldn't hardly blame him for getting mad. In fact, Maria examined her bruises with considerable satisfaction. They were a good sign. Get a guy edgy and jealous enough and anything might happen. Even marriage. Mrs. Doc Slater, that'd be one in the eye for that Dartland tart, too. She couldn't swish by the Doc's *wife* with her nose in the air like she smelled a stink. There was another good sign, too. The old picture of that movie actress was gone from among the pile of Doc's shirts. She'd seen the charred edge of it in the stove where he must have burned it up. So he wasn't mooning over *her* any more.

Thus in her way Maria shared in the springtime felicity.

Nor was Amanda impervious to the general lift of spirits. In the middle of March she awoke to one of those days when all goes easily and well. She had Dart's lunch-box packed in plenty of time, and included his favourite egg-salad sandwiches. They kissed each other good-bye with warmth and gaiety, laughing about their invitation to Lydia Mablett's next collation. This time they would avoid all controversy, fortify themselves first with a couple of stiff drinks cadged from Hugh, and treat the ordeal with objective amusement. "Free meal, too," said Amanda giggling, "that'll help."

She stood on the step in the warm sunshine and waved good-bye to Dart, watching the Lizzie chug patiently away up the mine road. She attacked with vim all the unpleasant chores, which she did not usually perform without rebellion: the trip across the yard to the outhouse and the pouring of disinfectant down the earth closet, the transportation of the garbage to a galvanized-iron can under a mesquite tree behind the outhouse, where it would await weekly disposal by Dart, who burned what he could and carried the rest to the town dump a mile down the canyon. She made the bed, swept the house, washed the dishes, cleaned the kerosene lamps, and prepared potatoes, carrots, and prunes for tonight's supper. There would be kidneys too; fortunately, they both liked them and they were cheap. For tomorrow night, Amanda thought with satisfaction, Tessie had promised to give her a Cornish pasty, and some saffron buns to try, so with the help of the Mablett party, Friday, they could just squeak by until pay-night without buying anything.

Tessie was sweet; she had made many friendly gestures, and it bothered Amanda that she could not repay in kind. But Tessie was comparatively well off, Tom Rubrick's pay as shift boss was little below Dart's, and then, besides, Tessie had the post office and the little store.

The thought of the post office momentarily dimmed Amanda's zest, for there had been no letters from home in two weeks. Tessie, as always, had been comforting. "It'll be nought but some delay along the way, or likely one of those planes down; if 'twas anything grave they'd telly-graph." Which was true, of course, and no use fretting until Roy's next trip in from Hayden tomorrow.

The house cleaned and garnished, Amanda found her energy still unslaked, and she debated several ways of passing the time, though the possibilities were strictly limited. She decided to call on Hugh, whom she had not seen for several days, and then take a walk up the canyon, maybe go see Mrs. Cunningham, though here she felt a reluctance. The Cunningham mansion had for her become inextricably associated with the discovery she had made there, the memory of her excitement and exaltation; painful now, since she had forbidden herself to think of it, and all frustrated emotions become painful and rather shameful in retrospect.

She walked back towards the Company hospital dressed just as she was, in levis and a cotton shirt. It had finally dawned on her that the trousseau clothes would have to last a long while, and she had bought the levis in Pottner's store for $2.98 and found them sufficiently comfortable and becoming. The ladies of Lodestone did not wear pants; that aberration was reserved for dudes and little girls, and Amanda's new costume shocked them as much as had her Scottish tweeds and cashmere sweaters and pearls, but this never occurred to her.

Hugh was at home, hunched over the desk in the consulting-room, and in no hospitable mood. "My God, what do *you* want?" he growled at her as she appeared in the doorway. His eyes were bloodshot, and under the little moustache his mouth twitched spasmodically.

"Nothing," she said. "Just wondered how you were; we haven't seen you in ages." She sat down, ignoring his glare with the assurance of a pretty woman, certain of masculine welcome when she deigns to court it.

Hugh made an angry noise in his throat. With his square freckled hand he covered something he had been looking at. "You haven't seen me because I've been drunk, and I'd still be drunk if I hadn't run out of my goddam alcohol allotment."

"Well," she said, lighting herself a cigarette, "there'll be plenty of real liquor soon, I guess; you won't have to drink alcohol."

"Government going to give it away free, too? Or restore my credit at the local bars? Go away, Andy. I don't want to chit-chat."

"It's a beautiful day," she said, smiling indulgently. "Come for a walk with me. It'll do you good."

His little green eyes sharpened with malice, his muscles tensed to rise, then he slumped in the chair again. He gave a curt laugh. "Unfortunately, I like Dart."

"Why, Dart wouldn't care," she said, staring at him. "What kind of a crack was that?"

"No, Dart wouldn't care, you little dope, but it would be all over Lodestone in half an hour.—'Oh, look at those two sneaking off together while poor Mr. Dartland's up at the mine.'"

"Nonsense," she said, flushing. "You've got a filthy mind."

Hugh wheeled in his chair, and spoke towards a crack in the door which led to the kitchen. "Have I got a filthy mind, Maria? Come on out from behind the door and tell the lady."

Amanda suppressed a gasp, then waited with tightened lips while the door slowly opened, and Maria appeared in her dishevelled whitish uniform. Her limpid dark eyes surveyed Amanda insolently through thick lashes, her full red lips were drawn into a pout. "I was just going to boil up your knives and things," she said sulkily, "I wasn't listening."

"Of course not," said Hugh. He slipped the article about Viola under the blotter, and leaned back in his chair, watching the two women with sardonic malice: Maria's suspicious baffled jealousy and Amanda's discomfiture and resentment. For a second this comedy pleased him, stopped the pounding in his head and the gnawing blackness in his soul, then the pounding and the gnawing resumed. He lifted his hand and banged it on the desk. "Get out, both of you," he shouted. "Leave me alone!"

Amanda left, her face flaming, but as she strode up the canyon road, mentally hurling epithets at Hugh, some pity began to seep in and undermine the anger. For she had recognized the look in his eyes while he shouted at them to get out. They had betrayed an emotion which she had never seen in her life before, and yet she knew, with that universal intuition which lies in all of us—that it was the look of utter and hopeless despair.

But what can anyone do? she thought; nobody can help him, even if one knew how to, he wouldn't let them. She sighed and put the thought of Hugh from her, determined not to let it mar the brightness of the day. And her attention was soon distracted by an encounter.

She heard the jingle of a bell, the thud of little hoofs behind her, and a short bark, and turned to see Old Larky on his burro plodding up the hill. Susan, of course, was waddling alongside.

"Good day, ma'am," said Old Larky, lifting his greasy felt hat and bowing. "Agreeable spring weather, isn't it?" He emitted a strong smell of bootleg whisky, but Amanda was startled again, as she had been in the post office, by the cultivated English voice that emerged from this old wreck, and she suddenly remembered the question Roy had asked him: "Found your lost mine yet, Larky?"

She smiled, agreed that it was a lovely day, and fell into step beside the burro. "Do you mind if I walk along with you a bit?"

"Indeed not, I should be honoured—down, Susan!" he added tenderly as the spaniel made one half-hearted exploratory jump at Amanda's legs.

"Where are the puppies?" she asked.

"We left them at home today. This was merely a quick trip down, because I broke my pick and had to replace it."

"Do you do much digging up there in the mountains?"

He nodded. "Quite a lot. I'm searching for my lost mine, you know." Her heart gave an unexpected little jump.

"Do you mind, I mean, could you tell me anything about it?" she said. "Lost mines are so interesting."

Larky nodded again. He was used to this. People were always inquiring about his lost mine, sometimes seriously, sometimes humorously, and sometimes with purpose to defraud, and find it first for themselves.

"It's either in these mountains or across the Gila in the Mescals," he said. "My partner was a very ignorant man, and he wasn't certain, but I spent twelve years searching in the Mescals, so I don't imagine it's there."

"Twelve years!"

He waggled his head, and his bleary eyes looked down at her solemnly. "And four years here in the Dripping Springs, but I believe I have a fresh clue: I made an error in the map."

"What sort of a map?" she asked diffidently.

"Oh, I drew it myself from directions my partner gave me before he died. He was the one who found the mine in the first place, only he fell down a cliff and got hurt so badly that he never could go back."

"What sort of a mine was it?" she asked after walking along a minute in silence.

"Silver. Richer even than the first strike at the Old Dominion in Globe. My partner said he saw a boulder of pure silver so heavy he couldn't lift it, but he brought a few pieces of ore back."

"And you believed his story?" asked Amanda, softening the question with a smile.

"Certainly, he was an honest man and a good prospector. It's merely a matter of locating the mine again."

See, thought Amanda to Dart, here's an educated man and he believes in a lost mine; he's willing to spend most of his life hunting for it. The idea's not so silly."

"You come from England?" she ventured, hoping that he would say some more about the mine. "I was there last summer; I loved it."

"Were you indeed?" said Larky politely. "I haven't seen England in over forty years." He turned on the saddle blanket to look for Susan, who had lumbered into the creosote bushes to investigate an interesting smell. He whistled and she reappeared. "Did you happen to visit Oxford?" he asked, turning around again.

"Oh yes. I was fascinated." She stared up at the hunched figure on the burro, the dirty levis, the flapping hat over stringy grey hair. "Did you—I mean, by any chance did you——"

He gave a wheezy chuckle. "I went to Magdalen."

Amanda had an instant recollection of the beautiful old college by the stone bridge, of elegant young men in emblazoned jackets, of a sherry party in an oak-panelled room with mullioned windows made in the time of Henry the Eighth. And she

dared not ask the questions which she longed to ask. Then
how in the world did you get here into this crude wilderness of
rocks? What transformed you from one of these fine-drawn
aristocratic youths, "the flower of Old England" as the guide-
book said, into a filthy old scarecrow of an Arizona prospector?

"Do you ever get homesick?" she ventured at last.

"Never," said Old Larky with conviction. "This country
suits me. One becomes a part of it. And there is freedom to do
as one pleases."

He pulled up the burro and turned its head towards the south.
"Here's my trail," he said, lifting his hat. "It's been a pleasure
talking with you."

She murmured a good-bye, and stood on the dusty road
watching the burro with its slouched rider, and Susan, all amble
down a dry wash. The burro's bell tinkled peacefully in the still
air. She could still hear it even after they veered left for the
climb up switchbacks towards a gap between two of the low,
mesquite-tufted mountains. How strangely self-sufficient they
were, some of these people she had met, she thought with both
contempt and envy. There was no other similarity between
Calise Cunningham and this old British reprobate who called
himself Larky, and yet they both exuded a maddening atmosphere of indifference to the normal world, to comforts and
companionship and the enjoyment of all the benefits civilization
had painfully evolved for mankind.

If Larky finally found his lost mine, I bet he wouldn't know
what to do with it, she thought; he'd never change his way of
living, never go back to the grace and the refinement that must
have once been his. He and Mrs. Cunningham were both escap-
ists, she thought, visionaries, and she found comfort in relegat-
ing them to a certain psychological category. For by contrast
she felt herself practical and determined. There might be those
who could be happy wandering through life communing with
nature and ignoring the material values which the majority of
mankind thought essential, but she was not one of them. She
might be romantic, as Dart said, but she also knew the necessity
of a definite goal.

You get what you go after in this world, she thought, and she
must manage Dart, since he would not do it for himself. Her
thoughts reverted to the Pueblo Encantado. Maybe there was
no gold there, but surely it was only common sense to find out.

It was ridiculous to pay too much attention to Dart's prohibition. Her mistake with him had been over-emotionalism, and no wonder Dart had been annoyed. With time, however, and logic and tact, his mind could be changed for him.

She would begin tonight, she decided, using a new and casual approach.

But there was no chance to talk to Dart that night. A far more immediate matter claimed them both.

CHAPTER SEVEN

AMANDA turned towards home after her encounter with Old
Larky, completely abandoning the half-formed project of visiting Mrs. Cunningham. She found that the memory of her hour
with Calise had lost all its magic. The atmosphere of singular
purity in that orderly room, her own involuntary frankness, and
Calise's talk of God and content and mountain flowers, all
seemed slightly ridiculous in retrospect. Perhaps this was in
part due to Luther Mablett's comments on Calise in the mine
office, "batty as a March hare, sees ghosts and stuff," but it was
largely due to Amanda's fear that she might again betray her
thoughts, and that mention of her preoccupation with the
Pueblo Encantado would elicit from Calise even less approval
than it had from Dart. She had no reason for this conviction,
but it was nevertheless a certainty.

She reached home again about one o'clock, ate some bread
and jam and drank some tea, then looked longingly at *Anthony
Adverse*, the last book Jean had sent her. She had already been
entranced by its opening pages, and the atmosphere of romantic
passion and derring-do. There was, however, a pile of Dart's
shirts to be pressed, and there was mending, and at both tasks
she continued to be remarkably inept.

"When duty whispers low, *Thou must*, the youth replies, *I
can*," she thought, flinging the heavy black sad-iron on the
stove. Except I don't *want* to. What do you do about that,
stern daughter of the voice of God?

So Amanda compromised. She ironed three shirts, mended
two pairs of Dart's socks, hoping that the puckered darns would
not give him blisters, and then she threw herself across the bed
on her stomach, and propped up *Anthony Adverse*. She became
so engrossed that she did not at first hear a knock on the door.
The second one roused her, and she shut the book reluctantly,
and walked across the room still in a daze of emotion with the
lovers and the cruel Don Luis.

A plump, copper-skinned Indian with ear-length hair, a black felt hat, red plaid shirt and faded levis stood on her doorstep looking up at her with a grave scrutiny.

Amanda stared down at him blankly.

"You Dartland's woman?" asked the Indian, examining her in one glance, then averting his eyes.

"Why, yes. I'm Mrs. Dartland. What is it you wanted?"

The Indian had a round, good-natured face, though he did not respond to her tentative smile, nor did he answer her question at once. He simply stood there by the doorstep, his unwinking black eyes fixed upon the giant saguaro at the corner.

That these ceremonious moments of silence between speeches were Apache etiquette Amanda naturally did not know, and she repeated with some impatience, "What is it you want?"

He moved his gaze to a small grey brittle bush which grew by the path and said, "I have message for Dartland."

"Well, he's up at the mine," said Amanda. "You could find him up there. Or give me the message."

There was another silence, then the Apache said, "I don't go to the mine. I wait here for him." He pulled a bent cigarette from his pants pocket, lit it, and sat down on the doorstep.

Amanda quelled a desire to laugh. She stared down at the stolid red-shirted back. "But you can't sit there for an hour or two! Who are you, and what do you want?"

The Indian puffed on his cigarette, and the smoke drifted out of his broad nostrils. "I have message for Dartland," he repeated with an air of remote patience. "I wait here."

Nor until Dart came home did Amanda get any further satisfaction. The Indian sat upon her doorstep and smoked. He would not come inside, he would not accept a cup of coffee, he would not amplify his one remark.

When at six o'clock the Lizzie chugged into the yard and Dart got out, Amanda rushed to the door and watched, as Dart showed pleased surprise. "Why, hello, Cleve," he cried, holding out his hand to the Indian who advanced to meet him. "I thought you were at San Carlos. Have you come for your old job back at the mine?"

Cleve shook Dart's hand solemnly. "No, Nantan," he said. "Never while Burton is there. He is a very bad man. He is too dangerous."

Burton? thought Amanda. Wasn't that the name of that rat-faced little pip-squeak in Mablett's office that day? How funny.

Dart seemed to think it funny too, for he laughed. "Oh, Burton's okay. I'm surprised you let him get your goat. What *are* you here for then?"

"To see you, Nantan." And then to Amanda's annoyance the Indian continued in Apache. She listened to the explosive guttural sounds, and watched Dart's face anxiously, because after the first minute, the colour seeped out of it, leaving a greyish hue under the tan. His lips tightened, and she could see the pupils of his eyes dilate, but he made no sound until the Indian stopped speaking.

Then he nodded his head and said a few incomprehensible words.

This, the first time that Amanda had heard her husband speaking Apache, gave her a strange sensation, and she rushed up to the men, clutching at Dart's arm. "Oh, what is it?" she cried. "What's he been telling you?"

She saw that Dart had forgotten her, and it took a moment for his eyes to focus on her face, then he said, "It's my mother; she's dying. Cleve has come from the reservation to tell me."

She stared up at him stricken. "Oh, darling," she breathed, "how dreadful. I'm so sorry. What shall we do?"

"Leave just as soon as I tell them at the mine that I'm going!"

He saw the question which she did not quite dare ask, and he said, "Yes. You, too. She wants to see you. It'll be a tough experience for you, but I guess you can take it."

"Of course I can. I've always wanted to see Saba, and I want to be with you—to help you. . . ." Her eyes filled with tears.

"Good girl," he said, and bent down and kissed her, while the Indian turned away.

Later Amanda never could remember much of that wild ride through the night to the reservation. Dart drove back along the dizzy mountain roads which had so frightened her on her first arrival in Lodestone. He drove at a speed which felt to her like eighty, though she knew very well the car was not capable of anything like that. She was too inexperienced to realize that, despite their break-neck pace, Dart's judgment and split-second decisions were always right. But Cleve, the Indian, knew, and though he bounced around on the back seat in utter silence, as they did on the front, he viewed Dart's performances with admiration. The Nantan was a real man and showed his warrior

blood, for what else had made the fibre of the great Apaches but
cool courage and the ability to judge risks correctly?

There had been no rain for many days, and the washes were
all providentially dry, so that it was only nine o'clock when they
emerged from the mountains, crossed U.S. Highway No. 70 at
Cutter on the reservation, and finished the next thirteen miles
of comparatively flat but extremely poor road into the San
Carlos Agency. Here there were stone pillars and a well-lighted
avenue of substantial-looking buildings, all new, for the Agency
had only last year been moved from its old site called Rice, down
by the Gila River. That site now lay deep under the blue
waters impounded by the Coolidge Dam. These new buildings
of stucco and tufa stone along the tree-shaded avenue included
the homes, offices, school, hospital, and churches lived in and
provided by the white man for the soul and body nurture of
the Government's wards. The effect was of comfortable suburbia,
most surprising to Amanda.

But Dart did not pause at the stone pillars nor enter the
avenue, he drove straight on past the island of civilization
and into darkness again; then he spoke for the first time, turning his head towards Cleve. "Do I turn left here? I've forgotten."

Cleve grunted assent. "Up Blue River," he said.

"Hang on tight, Andy," said Dart. "This'll be pretty rough,
but we'll make it if the wheels stay on."

They were running up a dry creek-bed, hurtling over small
stones and bushes, skirting boulders and larger holes, until at
last they rounded a little curve and the Indian muttered something. At once Dart turned the car right and plunged up the
bank into an apparent wall of desert broom and burro brush.
They emerged, however, on to a road of sorts, which ran along
the desert towards a clump of tall mesquite. And clustered near
the trees, Amanda saw the dim beehive shapes of Apache dwellings—the wickiups.

"I get off here," said Cleve. "You go little way on."

"Yes, I know now." Dart stopped the car. "Thanks, Cleve."

The Indian said something brief in Apache and Dart answered
him. The noise of the car had attracted several figures, who
materialized silently from the darkness and came up peering and
murmuring. They were women. Amanda saw the long flowing
hair and the billowing flounced skirts. Cleve, who had been

half-way out of the car, uttered a sharp exclamation and clambered back in the car and slammed the door. One of the women gave a little cry, half mirth, half dismay, then they all turned and scuttled into the darkness. Dart started the car and drove on.

"Why didn't Cleve get out?" asked Amanda, glancing back towards the Indian. "What upset him?"

"Those were some of his wife's relatives," answered Dart hurriedly. "He must never see them. They practise avoidance. It's the old custom."

"Oh," she said. This was no time to question, no time to bother Dart with curiosity, or timidity, or the need for reassurance in this setting which seemed to her increasingly fantastic. The stars were there, the desert scenery, the distant mountains, the familiar car, and Dart whom she loved; but she felt herself increasingly alone and disoriented, surrounded by enigmas to which she might not bring the patronizing amusement of the tourist, but in which she would soon be required in some measure to share. Without preparation, without understanding, she must now accept her husband in the one aspect she had come to dread, as part of an alien and hostile race; and in her veins she felt the stirring of the ancient atavistic fear.

The car had jounced a mile or so farther along the rutted tracks when another grove of trees appeared, taller than the last, for here there was water from a spring, and willows grew among the arrow-weed and broom.

There were several wickiups, and Dart stopped the car near the farthest one. Smoke curled up through the brush-thatched roof and out of the open door where firelight flickered.

The instant the motor stopped, a half-dozen Indians emerged from the wickiups. They surrounded the car, four men and two women, the women stared silently, then dropped their eyes, but the men greeted Dart with low cries. "Shiki!" My friend. And one who was taller than the rest, nearly as tall as Dart, rested his hand for an instant on Dart's shoulder and called him by his boyhood nickname, "Ish-kin-azi."

Amanda stood uncertainly in the shadows, waiting. She was faint with hunger and very tired; the Apache voices, the dark faces, and the silent domed wickiups swirled round her in a vague menacing dream.

It was only an instant, though, before Dart came and drew

her forward. "These are my relatives, Andy," he said. "Second cousins, descended from Tanosay's brothers."

"How do you do," she murmured, and the six pairs of black eyes rested without expression on the girl's white face and the short wind-blown fair hair. "How do you do," answered several voices, and one male voice added, "Welcome."

Dart turned in the direction of that voice and smiled. He indicated the tall young Indian who had greeted him most warmly and said, "This one I grew up with—we were close as brothers when I was here on the reservation———" He hesitated, knowing that he must name him for Amanda, but observant of the inviolable taboo. The real name is sacred and may not be mentioned; many nicknames are discarded, and he could not say to Amanda, "This is my grandfather's nephew," as he would to an Apache.

The young Indian solved the problem himself. "I'm John Whitman," he said to Amanda, giving his Agency name, and his eyes smiled a little.

She held out her hand impulsively, hearing in the voice a slight resemblance to Dart's, feeling some kindliness at last, but the Indian hesitated and she drew her hand back, flushing.

"We . . . they don't go in much for handshaking," said Dart. "John means no offence."

"I know—it's all right," she murmured, and she looked up at Dart anxiously. Why, when they had pelted through the night to get here, was there now this delay at Saba's doorstep? Why didn't Dart rush in to her?

He understood her question and answered it. "One of my cousins has gone to prepare Shi-Ma, my mother. When you go in, Andy, it will make her happy if you call her Shi-Ma too. They say she's wandering a bit. It may be hard for her to place you."

Amanda nodded and leaned silently against the car, staring at nothing.

The group of Indians had dispersed as noiselessly as they had appeared, all except John. He stood with Dart, and they conversed in Apache, while John gave Dart much information which had been lacking from Cleve's knowledge. During the last months, Saba had been growing very thin and tired. She no longer took interest in anything, even her basketry. Soon she almost ceased eating and lay all day on her blankets, looking out through the open door towards the Natanes Mountains, where she had spent her youth. The women had all taken turns caring for her most tenderly, but she had not grown better, though they had summoned the shaman from Bylas, the one whose power came from the Mountain Spirits. He had performed his special curing ceremony, and they had held the sacred masked dance for her too, but it had done no permanent good, only for a little while.

"Why didn't you let me know sooner?" said Dart sadly, for he knew the answer.

"She did not wish it. You understand that. She knows that you must follow the white trail for ever now. That no man can ride two horses."

"What else has been done for her?" asked Dart. "If she can travel, I mean to take her at once to the Agency hospital."

"No," said the Indian. "She will not go." And John went on to explain that the superintendent of the Agency himself had heard of Saba's illness, and he had come to visit her, bringing the doctor with him. But the white doctor had said at once that it was hopeless. That she had a growth that was eating up her stomach and the hospital could do nothing.

And then the Lutheran minister had come to pray with her. Saba was no church member, but all the Indians liked this minister who spoke Apache almost as well as they did themselves. So they had let him into the wickiup, and Saba had listened peacefully while the minister read to her from the white Bible, and prayed for her. So everything had been done. Both the white man's and the Indian's medicines for body and spirit had been invoked, and now all was in readiness for her going-away.

Dart bowed his head, and the two young men stood together in silence, until John's young wife, Rowena, a pretty girl in blue calico, glided out from the wickiup and touched Dart on the arm. He nodded and said, "Come," to Amanda, who followed them through the low door into the bark and canvas dwelling.

At first Amanda's eyes were so blinded by smoke that she saw nothing clearly, but she heard the low choking voice cry out, "Shi-ja-yeh! My son!" and a kindly hand pulled Amanda to the far end of the wickiup. Here, where the smoke was thinner, Amanda stood confused and uncertain, looking down at Dart and his mother.

Saba lay propped on a pile of blankets, which were protected from the dirt by a cowhide rug. Her iron-grey hair, cut square above the eyebrows, flowed loose in strands over the shoulders of her faded cotton blouse. Her emaciated face with the skin stretched tight over her high cheekbones, straight nose, and sharp jawline was the colour of old ivory, and on her chin there were six blue tattoo marks. Her hair and shoulders were dusted yellow with the sacred life-giving pollen the shaman had sprinkled on her.

Dart knelt beside her pallet, and from the hollow eye-sockets her brilliant black eyes caressed his bent head with an expression of burning love. Her hand, knotted and veined, but small as that of all Apaches, lay lightly on his shoulder, and from her lips there came a soft crooning murmur, nearly formless words in both English and Apache—of lullaby, of greeting, and of farewell.

It was Saba who first realized that Amanda stood there. She turned her head and looked up at the frightened girl, and the shadow of a smile came into the burning eyes. "So it is you, my son's—wife," she said in a clear voice. "Come here to me."

Amanda knelt on the cowhide beside Dart, her heart beat thickly and her eyes were blinded with tears. "Yes, Shi-Ma——" she whispered. "I am here."

Saba lifted her hand from Dart's shoulder and touched Amanda's cheek. She took Dart's right hand and Amanda's left and clasped them together. "It is well," she said, and the words drifted through her pale lips like the sighing of the wind. Her hand dropped from theirs, and she sank back on the blankets. "Now leave me with Shi-ja-yeh—with my son."

"My cousins'll take care of you, Andy," said Dart very low, then he turned back to his mother.

Amanda rose, and at once the young Indian girl Rowena, John's wife, came forward. "Come with me——" and she led Amanda from the wickiup, and through the darkness to her own dwelling. In here there was a smaller fire, and a rickety camp cot, as well as a pile of red and grey store-bought blankets. Seeing that Amanda looked dazed and very pale, the Indian girl pushed her gently down on the coat. "Sit here. I'll give you some tulapai. You'll feel better." She went out to the ramada, an open twig and branch lean-to, to fetch the tulapai jug.

Amanda sat on the cot and gazed around the wickiup. It was made of willow saplings, laced with yucca leaves, and thatched with bear grass. Strips of canvas and old flour-bags insulated the outside, where in the old days they would have used deer-hides.

Inside, on the stamped earth-floor, there was no furniture except the cot, and an obsolete treadle sewing-machine. An iron pot, bought in Globe, hung on a tripod over the fire, and emitted a rank odour which mingled with the smell of stale sweat from the blankets. A faint noise attracted Amanda's attention, and upon examining its source in the shadows by the doorway, she discovered a plump baby, tight-swaddled and strapped on a cradle-board, propped against the brush wall. The baby was thus sleeping bolt upright, with a contented smile on its face.

His mother reappeared with a gallon can of tulapai, and giggled when she saw Amanda. "You like my baby? Pretty soon you have one too, mebbe so?"

Amanda smiled faintly. "Some day. I hope so." She could think of nothing but food and sleep, and she did not know how either was to be obtained. Her hostess offered her an enamel cup full of tulapai, which turned out to be a strange greyish concoction made of fermented corn and mesquite beans, with the addition of yeast and raisins to make it strong, and a dash of tobacco juice for flavour. Amanda, fearful of offending, gulped down a little of it, and the heat in her stomach revived her and gave her the courage to say, "Could I beg a little something to eat from you? And do you know where I could rest for a while?"

"Sure," said Rowena. "You sleep here with me and my little sister. John go some place else." She picked up the cradle-board from which there had come a snuffling cry. She went outside a minute and came back with a cold tortilla and a strip of jerky in her hand. She held them out to Amanda. "Here," she said, smiling. "Eat. Drink more tulapai. It will make you not so sad. Then rest on the cot."

She squatted down on the pile of blankets, holding the cradle-board flat on her lap. She raised the short blue Mother Hubbard blouse and began to nurse the baby.

Amanda nibbled a little at the clammy tortilla and the tough salty beef. She docilely sipped the tulapai. She had had nothing to eat since the bread and jam at home after her walk up the canyon. Twelve hours ago according to her wrist-watch, and it felt like weeks. This Amanda, who sat in an Apache wickiup while her husband kept vigil with a dying mother, seemed disembodied from all the other familiar Amandas; the one who was Dart's passionate and responsive mate or the discontented little Lodestone housewife. These seemed as remote as did the earlier Amandas of New York and Greenwich and Vassar and Europe.

If Tim could see me now, she thought, but not with amusement, rather with a remote wonder that life, which had always seemed all of a piece, could offer such extraordinarily disjointed contrasts. What sure continuity was there but ego?—and love perhaps. It was because of love that she was here. She had thought, during the wild ride through the night, that there might be another link. Deep down, suppressed beneath the sympathy for Dart and the sadness of their mission, there had been a hope that if Saba were not too sick, she might ask her about the lost mine—about the Pueblo Encantado. For Saba, who had put the relics in the basket, might feel differently from her son about the search. But during those minutes in the other wickiup she had felt shame for her thoughts, and she had known that even if Saba were well she could never ask her.

There was a soft pad of footsteps at the door, and a little girl of twelve slid in and stopped dead at the sight of Amanda. The child flung up her hands to cover her mouth, and her round fawn eyes grew black as dewberries. Rowena said something quick in Apache, but the little girl shook her head and backed out of the wickiup.

Rowena laughed a little, lowering her blouse and propping the baby against the wall. "That was my sister. She is afraid because you are here. She will not come in."

"I'm sorry," said Amanda softly. "Is there any other place I can go?"

The Indian girl shook her head. "They wouldn't let you in. We don't like white people to come into our homes, especially those of us who live in the old way. But for John and me it's different. He is blood brother to Ish-kin-azi—to your husband, and we're not afraid of white people. We went many years to the Indian school."

"You hate us . . ." said Amanda, sighing.

"No. Not all. Only those who want to change us, only those who came asking rude questions, and taking photographs, and laughing at us behind their hands. Only those who make us ashamed because we could no longer feed ourselves and must take charity. But it's better now." Rowena got up and brought a blanket from the pile over to Amanda. "Now we have the cattle. Our own herds to sell for ourselves. Our clan here at Blue Springs," she added, her eyes shining, "owns many fine head of cattle. . . . Sleep now, our cousin's wife," she said, putting the blanket over Amanda. "The tulapai will make you sleep."

Amanda tried to say something, but her weighted lips drooped. She stretched her legs out on the hard canvas cot, and the flickering firelight on the grass and brush ceiling dissolved into darkness.

She awoke at six to see Dart's face bending close to hers, his grey eyes looking down at her with anxious affection and some humour. Forgetting where she was, she gave a soft cry of welcome, and put her arms around his neck. He kissed her and said, "How're you doing? I gather you got some sleep."

She struggled up on her elbow, staring around the dim, deserted wickiup. She looked down at the rumpled grey blanket, at her camel-hair top coat in which she had slept. Then she remembered."

"Oh, Dart—your mother . . .?"

"She's much weaker but peaceful. The women're tending her. She says that she will go away as the sun sets. I think she knows." Instinctively he used the Apache euphemism for death.

"Come along," he said briskly. "I've rustled up some coffee for us. Then I'll take you downstream a bit. We could both use a wash."

She clambered stiffly off her cot and shook herself. She took her pocket comb and compact from her purse. "Holy heaven, what a mess," she murmured, trying to comb her hair. "Dart, I itch all over." She looked up at him startled, scratching vigorously at her stomach. "Fiery itches. What's the matter with me?"

He bent over, pulled up her cotton shirt, and examined her

stomach. "Fleas—my love." He grinned at her expression. "Maybe one or two other bugs as well. I'll delouse you as soon as we've eaten."

She moistened her lips, her eyes moved from his amused face to the blanket, and it seemed to her that all her flesh crawled. "Disgusting," she whispered. Filthy savages, she thought. Nothing would induce me to spend another night in this horrible place. And Dart could laugh. Could laugh because he was really . . . She clamped her lips tight over the sudden bitter words that rushed against them.

"Come, get your coffee," Dart said. Her thoughts were transparent enough and he was no longer smiling. "I can get someone to take you back to the superintendent's house at the Agency. They have modern plumbing and all the comforts. They'll let you stay there until—until I can come."

She said nothing. She followed him out to the outdoor cooking fire, and accepted the tin mug of coffee he poured for her. She ate one from Rowena's stack of cold tortillas, and some small cakes like hamburgers made from acorns, and the dried sticky fruit of the giant saguaro, all of which Dart handed her silently. She found that she was so ravenous that the strange flavours were unimportant.

While they ate nobody came near them. Rowena was in with Saba. John had ridden off into the hills with the other men to look for newborn calves among their clan herd. There were people around the more distant wickiups, women walking in and out of the ramadas in their flounced, bright-coloured dresses, and children playing, but nobody even glanced in their direction.

As Amanda finished the last bite of tortilla, there was a commotion on the rutted road, and a horse-drawn wagon appeared by the side of the farthest wickiup. Some of the children began to climb up the wheels and jump into the wagon. Dart watched them a moment, then poured himself another cup of coffee. "The kids are going to drive to the Agency school," he said. "You can go into San Carlos with them."

She glanced at his impassive face, withdrawn from her as completely as her anger and physical revulsion had withdrawn her from him. And why shouldn't she go? She thought of the avenue of trees and lights at the Agency, the neat stone houses, the grass plots in front of them, the sidewalks. She thought of

the stone pillars at the entrance which marked the gateway between two worlds. There were lights and baths and telephones
in there at the Agency. There would, in fact, be more actual
comfort than Dart had ever given her since their marriage. . . .
And here, what was she but an alien intruder, tolerated only
because of Dart? Why then should she hesitate? Why should
there well up from the depths of her soul a cold and secret spring
of conviction that this was no trivial choice which confronted
her. No logical matter of cleanliness, or even of contrast between two ways of life. For one instant only, there sitting by
the morning side in an Apache rancheria, she saw clearly, then
the insight faded as arrow-swift as it came, leaving only an unconscious decision for her guidance.

"You better hurry," said Dart, putting his cup down on the
ground. "They're about ready to start."

"I'm not going," and she added in the sad contrite voice of a
child who has been scolded without knowing why, "I don't *want*
to run away."

Dart drew in his breath. He looked at the slender little figure
sitting hunched on the packing-case in the crumpled camel-
hair coat, at the delicate fair skin, blotched red in two places
and filmed with dust, and at the wide blue eyes which did not
meet his, but rested their gaze on the distant mountains. Her
sense of values was so different from his that he found it difficult to be aware of her inward and recurring battles. But his
love for her partly bridged the gap, and he put aside his own
deep sorrow to treat her with the protective tenderness she best
understood from him.

He led her down to the little stream that flowed beneath Blue
Spring, and there in the cold mountain water they bathed together, until both their beautiful young bodies tingled with
vigour and renewed zest.

He assuaged her flea-bites with a herbal Indian ointment he
had borrowed from Rowena as they passed Saba's wickiup, and
forbore to smile at Amanda's continuing disgust. He showed
her how to shake and brush her clothes with a handful of leafy
twigs, and he promised her that he would scour the camp for a
clean blanket that night, but he was too honest to promise her
exemption from renewed attack.

"I know," she said, making a wry face. "What can't be cured
must be endured. But I'm not crazy about endurance. It's such

a wishy-washy virtue when you can get anything you want with a little gumption."

Dart looked at her sharply. Something in her voice reminded him of one of the arguments she had used during that idiotic fight they had had about searching for the lost mine. But she had taken her compact out, and was frowning over the exact line of her lipstick, oblivious to anything else, so he answered lightly. "I'm afraid Indians don't think a few assorted bugs worth spending gumption on. . . . I've got to get back to my mother now, Andy. I don't know what you'll do with yourself, poor kid."

She smiled at him. "I'll be all right. I'll manage."

He left her, swinging up the trail with his light quick step. She sat on by the stream awhile, watching the water purl by over the rose and white pebbles. The sun grew warm on her back, though a breeze rustled through the willows and the cottonwoods, and stirred the silvery white blooms on the desert broom. A large red-tailed hawk, uttering a sharp "Quee-quee," flew over her head to perch in a cottonwood. She sighed and got up, wishing she had brought a book. That would have passed the time. She wandered back to the camp, and saw Rowena on her knees outside her wickiup pounding corn in a stone metate. The Indian girl called a low greeting and Amanda went over to her.

"What are you doing?" she asked idly, smiling at the baby who was wide awake, strapped in the cradle-board on his mother's back, and gazing wide-eyed at a rattle and a tiny bell which were hung in the basketry hood and dangled just before his eyes.

"I grind for meal," said Rowena. She surveyed the disconsolate girl, and her black eyes lighted mischievously. "Try it," she said. She put the oblong stone mano in Amanda's hand. "It's good for women to work together. You can help me."

"Of course," agreed Amanda with all the enthusiasm she could muster. She squatted down by the trough-shaped metate and attacked the parched corn. The task took more strength and skill than she expected, but gradually she discovered a pleasurable sensation of a type she had never known. Not only the joy of working outdoors, but a satisfaction generally denied to white women in the modern world—the satisfaction of companionship —of shared tasks.

The simple act of pounding corn in the metate seemed to provide her with a sort of passport and admit her into the free-masonry of women. She looked up, to hear soft laughter behind the ramada, and to see Susie, Rowena's little sister, standing there round-eyed beside an old woman who held a half-made tray basket in her hand. Rowena turned from a pot of beef stew she had been stirring and said something to them in Apache. The woman and the little girl came nearer, whispering. They watched Amanda for a moment, and then they squatted down near the fire. The woman's nimble fingers began to weave yucca strands back and forth between curving sumac withes. She was making a ceremonial basket for Susie, whose sponsor she would be in the little girl's imminent puberty rite. Susie and Rowena dragged a fresh cowhide out of the pile on the ramada, and spreading it on the ground began to scrape the hair from it with a toothed metal blade.

After they had worked in silence for a while, they began to smile shyly at Amanda and they began to talk. Rowena, with instinctive tact, included the white girl in their conversation by keeping most of it in English, which Susie, who had been away five years to the Indian school, spoke as well as she did. The older woman, whose Agency name was Lizzie Canning, did not speak much, but she understood, and gradually as the hours went by Amanda learned a good deal about their lives.

Here at Blue Springs they were all of the clan which had once been Tanosay's. And though many of the Indians had taken on the white man's ways, here they liked to live pretty much in the old way, keeping the customs. It made one happier. True it also made more work, but it was good work, and the Indians who bought or begged all their food from stores, and got drunk on stolen whisky, and slept in Agency-built houses also seemed to be the ones who spent a lot of time in jail.

They talked of Susie's coming-out party, which would be given next month, even if Saba had "gone away," for Saba had requested this. These puberty rites were very important to ensure little Susie's happy life and health. There would be four days of feasting and ceremonies and dancing, and Susie would be in the centre of it all, living in a special sacred wig-wam and called "White Painted Woman," who was a kind of goddess who dwelt in the sky, but who would mingle and be-come one with Susie during the time of the ceremony. Here the child, who had been listening with a rapt expression, forgot her shyness and asked Amanda if she would like to see the ceremonial costume.

Amanda admired the exquisite buckskin dress with genuine awe. It was soft as yellow velvet, embroidered with jewelled beadwork and symbolic figures, and along the swaying front fringes there was a row of tiny metal amulets which tinkled like bells. The costume had just been finished and not yet blessed by the shaman, so Susie might still try it on. She disappeared modestly into the wickiup, and came back dressed in the costume and glowing with pride. Her soft fawn eyes shone with a mystical exaltation very touching to Amanda, who could think of nothing in her own girlhood that had given her any such obvious feeling of dedication and importance.

Amanda listened to plans for the community expeditions the women would go on soon. First the journey south into the mountains to gather mescal, and a gay few days of picnic and temporary camp during the roasting of the succulent portions of mescal in great pits. Then later expeditions into the high Pinals to gather acorns, and trips to the lower deserts for yucca and cactus fruit and mesquite pods. These trips and the sun-drying and preserving of their harvests were all women's work, as were the building of shelters, and tanning of hides, besides the many operations necessary for any household's smooth management, and the rearing of children. But Amanda saw that the conventional white view of lazy buck and downtrodden overworked squaw had little foundation among these Indians.

The women were on equal footing with their men; they held positions of dignity, their work was of equal importance in the structure of the clan, and the men—though no longer able to win glory and material gain in warfare—still went hunting, and were now at last regaining their independence and self-respect through a belated recognition of their problems by the Government. Neither heavy-handed suppression, nor the attempt to force the men into agriculture, had produced anything but trouble. But cattle-raising was an acceptable solution, particularly as it meant the restitution of grazing lands on their reservation, lands which had for long been nonchalantly pre-empted by white cattle-men.

But it was of past injustice that the women talked as they worked with Amanda through the spring morning, and shared with her the beef stew thickened with mesquite flour and flavoured with a can of store tomatoes. They gossiped a little, and told jokes about the last social dance near Bylas, and they spoke of their last trip into Globe a month ago; the amusement they had had walking down Broad Street, looking in the shop windows, and finally, after long deliberation, buying a can opener and a rhinestone barrette in the ten-cent store.

They asked Amanda no questions at all, because it is not polite to ask questions, and also because they pitied her. So thin and pale, dressed in trousers like a man, with the restless harried eyes so many white women seemed to have. Perhaps her husband was not good to her, though this seemed unlikely, for Ish-kin-azi, in the old days when he came to them summers, had been well liked. Still, he was not really an Apache, and there was no use trying to understand the peculiar relations between white people.

Nor did they speak of Saba, though they loved her deeply, because an evil spirit, a Tshee-dn, might be hovering near, and it is bad luck to give it encouragement by speaking of those who are going away, or have gone. But the two older women quietly watched the door of Saba's wickiup for a sign, and they saw Dart appear and beckon, when Amanda's less keen eyes could see nothing.

"Your husband calls you," said Rowena. "Go. We come soon."

As Amanda approached the isolated wickiup, the shadows were lengthening, and far to the west above the Pinal Mountains the sun dipped into flaming rose. As she came nearer she heard the muffled beating of a little drum, and softer yet above the drum-beat she heard the sound of chanting. She entered and crept silently to stand beside Dart. In the back of the wickiup near the shaman there were dim silent shapes.

Saba's pallet had been moved, and she lay just within the door where the fading light fell upon her. Her eyes were closed, her hands crossed on her breast which still moved. She lay waiting, listening to the tolling of the drum and the chant of the old shaman as he sang:

"To the East a spring of black water lies on a plain of jet,
    It will cool you.
"To the West a spring of yellow water lies in a sky of coral,
    It will cool you."

For Saba there had been much pain these last months, pain grimly born without lament as befitted those who were of "Dinneh" blood, but now she was at peace. Her son was near and her son's wife; they would go on and away together into that other world to which they belonged, and this was fitting, this was their destiny.

For her there were the springs of cool water of which the shaman sang, the eternal life-giving waters—so precious a concept to desert people, and to other desert dwellers in a different land, too. "As the hart panteth after the water brooks. . . ." The Lutheran minister had read this psalm to her when he came to her bedside. In the spirit there was no cleavage; she in whom two races mingled knew that now. The outward paths were different, the forms, the customs, the shape of body or of thought might be different—but deep inside the soul the yearning and the promise were the same for all.

Her eyelids fluttered, and she looked up at her son and the white girl who stood beside him. Her lips moved as she tried to tell them this, but no sound came. Her dimming gaze moved to the distant mountains—purple in the eastern afterglow. She smiled a little and was still.

The drum-beat hushed. The shaman bowed his head, and from the throats of the Indian women there came a harsh wailing cry.

The Apache burial-rites were simple, and hurried, for all ties must be cut at once. No reminder must hamper the escaped spirit, nor pull it back to earth. The women kept up a chanting dirge as they painted Saba's face with carmine red and dressed her in her own girlhood doeskin costume and the long moccasins with the turned-up tips, the turquoise and shell jewellery she had from Tanosay, and the old garnet and pearl necklace her husband Jonathan had given her also. Her scanty possessions must be destroyed, except those which would accompany her spirit on its journey. They "killed" her earthen cooking pots by driving holes in the bottom, and they piled her beautifully woven baskets—all but one, her favourite—in the centre of the wickiup with her blankets and clothing.

At dawn they placed her body on a pole and yucca stretcher. Dart and John Whitman carried the stretcher, and only three people followed it—Amanda and Rowena and Lizzie Canning. These were Saba's closest relatives. It was not deemed fitting for anyone else to attend.

Saba was buried a mile up a canyon behind the camp, in a hidden spot which the Indians never revisited except at these times. Her grave was dug near Tanosay's, though there was nothing to distinguish where his had been, except his favourite gun, rusted now with the passage of twelve years, and the bleached bones of his horse which had been killed at the grave site, as was the ancient custom.

Saba was buried with her best basket and her purse, which contained many dollars, for she had been frugal with the tiny inheritance left her by Jonathan. Also they put beside her some food and a pot of water and her cooking ladle for her use on the journey. They covered her grave with stones and leafy branches of the manzanita arranged in the shape of a cross.

And then they left her, walking slowly and sadly back, but the women no longer sang their dirge, though their cheeks were wet with tears. Flames leaped high in the smoky air as they returned to camp. Saba's wickiup had been fired by those who remained, and already it was half-consumed, with all its contents.

Amanda and Dart ate a little of the food Rowena offered them, then they turned to the car and prepared to leave. Rowena and John followed them silently. "Good-bye," said Dart in a low voice. "You've been good to us, you were good to her."

John stepped forward, and the tall young Indian looked deep into Dart's eyes. "This is truly farewell, Ish-kin-azi, my brother, is it not?" he said in Apache. "She who has gone away wished it so."

"Yes." Dart bowed his head. The men's hands came together in a long quiet grip, then dropped. "Get in, Andy," said Dart quickly.

She obeyed, climbing into the car, all the conventional expressions of thanks or farewell left unsaid. She and Rowena had smiled at each other once across the quiet barrier. There could be no more.

As they drove away, she looked back and waved. The Indian couple raised their arms once palm upward in response, then turned and moved together out of sight. The smoke from Saba's burning wickiup filled the eastern sky.

CHAPTER EIGHT

THE impression on Amanda made by her visit to the Apache camp faded very soon into a dream. It had brought her closer to Dart and given her more understanding of him, but he quite naturally did not wish to speak of the visit, and became at once immersed in the mine again, working doubly hard to make up for lost time. She was left as before to her own devices and the annoyance of distasteful chores. To these were added a burden of worry. Roy the carrier's Monday and Wednesday trips into Lodestone had brought her no letters from home.

"Telly-phone them collect," suggested Tessie after the Wednesday disappointment in the post office, and that night Amanda had gone to Mattie Thompson's home and waited beside the antique switchboard while Mattie's fat old fingers fumbled with switches and bad connections until Amanda reached her mother's New York number. But there was no answer. Then she tried Jean's house in Greenwich, but there was no answer there either.

She left the call in, and promised to bribe Bobby Pottner who lived across the street from Mattie, if he would run up to the Dartlands' the minute he was signalled, and she waited anxiously all Thursday, but Bobby did not come.

By five o'clock, while she prepared their supper in the hot little kitchen, she was in a state of nervous frenzy, which she tried to calm with the logic of a dozen reasonable explanations. It was well into March and the days were growing very warm. She stood by the sinkboard slicing kidneys and onions, when Hugh stuck his head through the open back door.

"Hello," he said, "you sobbing to yourself in here?"

She put the knife down. "No. It's the onions—but I don't feel too cheerful at that." She gave him a feeble smile, glad to have someone to talk to. "Come on in. I can stop this fiddling. Dart won't be down off the hill for hours, of course. It was eight-thirty last night."

"Conscientious type," said Hugh. "But I gather he's really pretty necessary up there."

She made a wry face. "He's in love with that damn mine. Fixation. . . . You act a bit more amiable than the last time I saw you. I didn't particularly enjoy that little byplay you put on with me and Maria."

Hugh shrugged and sat down on one of the kitchen chairs. "The fair Maria is at this very moment cheating on me with a mine hardware salesman, I believe. She's breaking my heart." He chuckled and lit a cigarette.

"You haven't got a heart. I don't blame the girl. You treat her like—like——"

"A dog is the usual simile. Apt in this case, for I don't like dogs. They bore me. Have you got anything to drink in this shack?"

She walked to the cupboard and pulled out a partly empty bottle. "What's left of that stuff you gave us last month, but we were saving it to drink before the Mablett party tomorrow. We'll need it."

"I'll get some more." He poured himself half a glassful. "Maria can rustle up some tequila over in Mex town. She'll have some money tonight, no doubt."

Amanda stared at him; the square freckled face, the sandy hair receding a little at the temples, the clean white shirt, and well-scrubbed hands. Hugh was always clean, and there was about him an indefinable air of breeding.

"Do you mean you'd take money from her like—that?" she cried, flushing.

"I'd take money from any place." He raised his glass and let the sharp liquid fire run down his throat.

"Money's not all that important," she cried in sudden anger. "You'd have enough if you didn't drink it all up."

"Oh, indeed?" His little green eyes sparkled at her over the edge of the glass. "Have *you* enough?"

Amanda opened her mouth and shut it again. She walked away from him back to the drainboard and resumed slicing the kidneys. "One must learn to be contented with things as they are," she said coldly, "until one's luck turns. Of course, it can turn sometimes."

"Oh, sure, sure," said Hugh, draining the bottle. "Rich uncles can die in Australia, oil-wells can gush out of the back-yard, you can stub your toe on a gold-mine."

She sent him a swift glance over her shoulder, then her eyes moved to the closet which contained her dressing-case and the notes on Pueblo Encantado. The impulse to speak of them faded as soon as it came. Even if it were not for loyalty to Dart, Hugh was no fitting confidant. She could imagine the jeers with which he would puncture her dream.

The thought of the dressing-case, however, reminded her of her immediate worry, and she gave a long sigh.

"Cheer up," said Hugh. "Consider the gaiety in prospect at the Mabletts'. We'll make the welkin ring."

"It's not that. I'm worried about my family, Hugh. I haven't heard from them in three weeks. I can't understand it. Mother always writes."

"Oh, I wouldn't worry," said Hugh after a moment. "Sure to be some good reason." He stared at the empty bottle. The liquor was beginning to work, to bring the fleeting stage when he could take the image of Viola and put her off across the room and examine her objectively.

The Russian Empress—smothered in white orchids and one priceless pearl ring. So you've never married, my dear—that panting, grovelling, threadbare young intern didn't really count as a husband, did he? Did he count as a lover, though? You thought he did, as I remember. And you believe in love, you said so. Right in your suite at the St. Regis, you said so. Maybe you'd like your lover back? A rich, successful lover, of course. We all know you like success. Unless perhaps you have an extra bedroom in that suite. Unless you'd like a gigolo to keep? "I'll whistle and you'll come to me, me lad—but you better come in ermine and fine raiment this time, come wagging your tail if you must, but carry in your mouth for me a little basketful of price-less pearls, too." He stared into the corner of the room, and she stood there behind Amanda. She was wearing the old sherry-coloured velvet, the one good dress he had ever bought her. Above the velvet her white skin and auburn curls were dazzling as they had been on their last night together, but her face was that of the new photograph, with its wistful beckoning smile and its softened eyes.

Hugh's chair scraped on the linoleum and he got up. "Thanks for the rotgut. Regards to Dart." He staggered a little as he pushed past Amanda towards the door. He slammed it after him.

Amanda did not hear him. She was staring through the bedroom windows towards the road. "There's a car stopping," she said. "Surely not Dart yet." She wiped her hands on the towel and went to the front door. She stood frozen by the door as she heard a high familiar voice cry:

"Oh, it couldn't possibly be this dump! We'd better go back and ask again."

Amanda moistened her lips as she peered through the window. Incredulous relief mingled for an instant with an extreme dismay.

She threw open the door, calling gaily, "But it *is* this dump——" She ran down the path. "Oh, Mamma—Jean— how in the world——" She flung her arms around them both and burst into tears. George was there too, red and embarrassed, at the wheel of his Packard sedan.

There was an inarticulate moment of kissings and little choked exclamations, then they got into the house. Mrs. Lawrence threw one horrified glance around her daughter's home, sat down on the bed, and began to chatter fast. "Darling, it's a surprise, of course, that's why we didn't let you know. It all came up quite suddenly, and we've been over ten days driving here."

"God-awful roads," said George, wiping his forehead, "and this last piece is beyond words. I know I've cracked an axle and I had four flats." Through his horn-rimmed sun glasses he stared at his sister-in-law distastefully. "How any civilized person can live here. . . ." He sat down on the only chair, and it creaked and wobbled under him.

"Oh, don't mind George," said his wife. "He's just cross because he didn't want to come in the first place. Give him a drink, Andy." She smiled at her sister.

Jean was crisp and cool as always, not a wrinkle in her beige travelling suit or her white crêpe blouse. Her calfskin pumps and her neat handbag both shone sleekly brown.

"I'm afraid I haven't any liquor. I could make some coffee," faltered Amanda, conscious of her stained levis and that she was wearing an old, torn shirt of Dart's.

"Never mind," said George, heaving himself out of the chair. "I've got a flask in the car. Want to look at that axle, anyway." He stamped out with a relieved air.

The three women on the bed turned to each other in a warmth

of emotion, but for a second nobody spoke. Then Mrs. Lawrence put her hand on Amanda's arm. "You're thin, baby. You're not dieting, are you? You know I disapprove of that at your age."

"Oh, I know I'm a mess—I'll fix up later. But tell me how it *happened*. What made you come? I'm so excited, and I was so anxious."

It took quite a time to get the story straight between Mrs. Lawrence's digressions and Jean's impatient corrections, but it seemed that George was worried about business, especially now that that man was in the White House. George's father felt that they'd have to close down the San Francisco branch. George had meant to go by train to attend to it, but Jean and Mrs. Lawrence had persuaded him to drive and call on Amanda *en route*, since business was so slow, anyway, he could take the time. He hated driving, and he had fussed a bit about expense, but he couldn't deny it hadn't cost much. Mrs. Lawrence had managed to sublet her flat to a friend for a month, so she was able to pay most of her own expenses. They'd parked Sally Lou and her nurse with George's parents, so everything had worked out fine.

"Where's Dart?" asked Jean, looking around the two-room cabin as though he might be concealed under the furniture.

"Still at the mine. He'll be down later." Oh, what am I going to do with them? Amanda thought. What about dinner? What about tonight? Perhaps she hadn't actually lied in her letters home, but she certainly had not prepared them for Lodestone either. She had given the impression of an adorable little bungalow, of quaintness and romance. She had boasted of Dart's exalted position in the mine. She had emphasized intimacy with the great Mr. Tyson, saying how much he admired Dart. She had even built the Mabletts into amusing characters and Tessie Rubrick into a close friend—all with a view to assuring them of standing and success in Lodestone.

"Well, as soon as Dart comes, we'll all go out to dinner together," said Jean, whose sharp eyes had seen the four sliced kidneys on the drainboard, and who was rapidly revising her expectations. "You wrote there was a good hotel, and we'll get rooms there for the night."

Amanda looked, not at Jean, but at her mother, whose plump, pretty middle-aged face was turned on her daughter in barely

concealed dismay. "It's a terrible hotel," said Amanda, trying
to laugh.

"Never mind, dear," said Mrs. Lawrence. "It doesn't
matter."

Jean laughed. "It'll matter plenty to George, but I'll muzzle
him somehow. After all, it's only one night."

"Only one night——" repeated Amanda. She looked at the
two sleek confident women whom she loved, who represented
protection, who had re-created for her at once the lost climate of
cherishing care. "Is that all you're going to stay with me?" Her
lips trembled.

Jean and Mrs. Lawrence exchanged a quick glance. Jean
shook her head, and her lips formed the words "Not yet."

"Oh, we have a plan," said Jean briskly. "You'll like it. Tell
you about it later when Dart gets here. . . . Andy, for pity's sake
do something to yourself. You look like an Okie. Don't they
have any beauty parlours in this dump—in this place?" She
surveyed her sister in stern disapproval; the stained levis and
the torn man's shirt might be condoned as temporary, but
not those reddened hands with broken finger-nails, nor the
dry alkali-stiffened hair dulled to the shade Jean thought of as
"dish-water blonde" without its weekly application of golden
tint.

"No beauty parlours and no drugstore either," said Amanda.
She hesitated, then added, "Nor could I afford them if there
were."

Mrs. Lawrence sighed, and her hand went to the clasp of her
pocket-book. She could squeeze out a little gift later, a few
dollars, but George was so difficult about every penny. Jean,
who knew this fact even better than her mother, wasted no time
on commiseration.

"Well, everyone's poor just now," she said. "It's the fashion.
Everyone, that is, except Tim." Again her glance crossed her
mother's.

"Tim Merrill?" asked Amanda, stepping out of her levis and
fumbling in the dark closet for her good heather suit. "How is
he? Crazy as ever? I had a letter from him quite a while ago.
He seemed to be enjoying life."

"Uhuh," agreed Jean, lighting a cigarette. She got off the
bed and walked over to lean against the wall near her sister.
"He's still very fond of you." Her bright hazel eyes watched

Amanda's face, and were rewarded by a ripple of confusion tinged with satisfaction.

"Oh, nuts," said Amanda, moving into the kitchen to wash at the sink. "He's just putting on an act. Keeps him safe from all the clamouring lassies who'd like to be Mrs. Merrill."

Jean followed her into the kitchen. "Did you tell Dart you'd heard from Tim?"

Amanda scrubbed her face on the all-purpose towel and frowned. "As a matter of fact, I guess I didn't. I meant to—but a lot happened on the same day I got the letter and I forgot." A lot happened? she repeated to herself. That was the day she had visited Mrs. Cunningham, the day she had been so excited over the discoveries in the Apache basket. Jean certainly would not consider these happenings of any moment, would consider them idiotic. "Anyway, the letter wasn't important," she added.

Jean was silent, watching her sister brush her hair and make up her face at the cheap, fly-blown mirror over the sink, watching her emerge into a pale approximation of the brilliant assured young beauty who had been the darling of the Proms, one of that season's most popular débutantes. Thank God, she hadn't *really* lost her looks. All Andy needed was some professional grooming and a different attitude. All she needed, Jean thought competently, was the courage to admit a mistake. That this recognition might take a little time and tact to achieve Jean was prepared to allow, but of the eventual result she had no doubts at all. Jean's incisive mind had scant patience with the fuzzy grey edges of problems which seemed so important to other people, but she had learned diplomacy in the efficient chairmanship of many committees and the management of George. Besides, she was extremely fond of her little sister.

"Would you say Dart was the jealous type?" she asked lightly, leaning over to help Amanda fasten the clasp of her pearl necklace.

"Why, no, I don't think so." The question startled Amanda, who saw no sense to it. But a memory flickered through her mind. On Tuesday, when they had been driving home from Saba's burial and while they were still on the reservation, they had had a flat tyre. An old Apache woman had come wandering down the road and paused to watch Dart change the tyre. Amanda, upon seeing the woman, had not been able to prevent an exclamation of horror. The woman had no nose; in its place there was a jagged hollow and two black nostril pits. "What's the matter with her face?" Amanda asked when the woman had passed on, and Dart replied, "The punishment for adultery in the old days. Her husband mutilated her."

To Amanda's shocked protest that that was barbarous and ghastly, Dart had answered, "Yes, Apaches are a poor benighted lot. They've never heard of the dangers of suppressing the libido. They take adultery very seriously."

But that had no direct bearing on Jean's question. And Dart was certainly not possessive. He was too much of a self-contained individual for that.

"What in the world made you ask such a question?" asked Amanda, twisting around to look at her sister.

"Idle curiosity," said Jean, smiling.

The trend of Jean's remarks became clearer at dinner, which was not dinner, but a greasy platter of ham and dubious eggs and fried potatoes, flung on the table at the hotel by a resentful Mrs. Zuckowski, who detested serving meals after hours. Supper was at six and that was that, nor when the Dartland party appeared at eight o'clock did Mrs. Lawrence's and Amanda's pleading, or Jean's reasoning, or George's infuriated demands move her in the least. It was Dart who drew her quietly aside and managed to reverse her decision. Mrs. Zuckowski, like many another woman in Lodestone whose existence Amanda did not suspect and Dart ignored, had a soft spot for Dart.

They had the dining-room to themselves, and Jean waited only until George had simmered into silence before turning to Dart and circling nearer her plans. "Andy tells me your mother just passed away, Dart. I'm so sorry, we all are. But you hadn't seen much of her these last years, had you?"

"No," said Dart courteously, then returned to his ham and eggs. He did not like Jean or George, though he would never say so to Amanda. For Mrs. Lawrence he felt an amused affection, not unlike the feeling Amanda sometimes called forth.

"Still, it must have been a shock, an ordeal for you and Andy," Jean continued. "Tearing up to the reservation like that on such a mission. You both look quite worn out. A little change would do you good. Diversion."

Dart raised his eyebrows. "Diversion?" he repeated. "Your surprise visit is a diversion, and a great pleasure to Andy—to us both. She's been fretting at not hearing from you."

Jean smiled, momentarily baffled. She had seen little of Dart except at the wedding, but she did not underestimate him. He could not be managed by suggestion as most men could. He erected against subtlety a bland impenetrable wall. He *is* attractive, she thought suddenly, in a crude raw-boned way, terribly male—and that dash of Indian blood adds an exotic fillip. She glanced at George, who had put down his fork and was staring into his coffee cup with an affronted glare. Fat and fussy, maybe, she thought, with the coolness she was always able to bring to bear on George, but safe too and predictable. You knew where you were with him.

"But go on, Jean," urged Mrs. Lawrence, who saw no reason for all this caution about a perfectly simple thing. "Tell them our plan. It'll be such fun."

"Oh, it's nothing much," said Jean airily; "we just want you to have a little vacation. Carry you both off tomorrow for a change of scene. It seems there's a simply divine place near Tucson called 'El Castillo.' Tennis and riding and swimming, and swarms of very nice people."

There was a silence. Amanda stared at Jean, her heart beating fast. Was this El Castillo the place Tim had mentioned? Was there any connection? Jean and Mrs. Lawrence looked at Dart. George was smoking a cigar and gazing at the ceiling. Dart was looking at Amanda. Her thoughts were usually clear to him, and he saw excitement and hope shine in her blue eyes and then give way to doubt.

"It sounds delightful," he said slowly; "but I couldn't possibly take any kind of time off now. I've just been away two days, you know."

Jean nodded; she had expected this. "Oh, too bad. But you wouldn't mind Andy going for a bit, would you? She really needs a rest. She looks worn to a nubbin, and of course you could run down for the week-end."

"Dart doesn't get week-ends," said Amanda in a low voice. "And I wouldn't like leaving him." In spite of herself her voice dragged.

"There's no reason why Andy shouldn't go," said Dart, "but" —he turned with a puzzled frown to George—"the place sounds very expensive, and unfortunately I can't contribute. I hate to have you shelling out like that for Andy. . . ."

George's wandering attention came back with a jerk. "Good

lord, no!" he exclaimed. "It's not *my* party!" He completely
missed Jean's glare and went on, "Timothy Colton Merrill,
you know, son of the millionaire, he's a great friend of ours.
He's at this Castillo place now, and he's invited all of us as his
guests."

"Oh," said Dart. "I see."

There was another silence, broken by Mrs. Lawrence, who got
up saying, "Do let's leave this dreadful dining-room. There
must be some sort of a lounge where we can all sit comfortably
and talk it over."

Amanda left in the Packard with her relatives the next morning. Dart had not only made no objections, he had urged her to
go, meeting her protestations with such calm that she had been
suddenly hurt. "You don't care if I'm here or not. I believe
you'd rather be alone," she had cried in anger born partly from
her conscience. "And do you hate Tim's being our host, or
don't you?—not that he means anything to me, and it's all perfectly proper with Mother and Jean there, but you act so strange
—why don't you tell me what you're thinking!"

He had answered in measured tones, "I think you want to go
very much and that you should. I think that either the bond
between us is strong enough to hold through any situation, or it
isn't. And one might as well find out. Besides, you deserve some
fun."

"Oh, don't be so damn logical! You don't give a damn about
me—that's what it is—and Jean asked me if you were jealous!"
At that moment she had seen a strange look at the back of his
eyes. "Oh, I don't mean that exactly, but darling, if you'd only
come with me. We'd have such a good time. Come for a few
days; surely you could wangle it at the mine."

"No, Andy—you know I can't. I'm sorry."

They had parted quietly when Dart went on shift that morning. He had said little in the way of farewell, except to suggest
that she might phone the mine and leave a message when she
was ready to come back; he would then help arrange transportation. And beneath the phrase, "when you're ready to come
back," she had almost thought she heard a startling echo—an
"if." How had the rift between them boiled up so rapidly, and
why should so simple a thing as a holiday with her family carry
such painful overtones sounding a fundamental discord in their
love? Was it because of Tim, though Dart would not say so?

Was it because of Dart's own stubborn pride and his self-sufficiency? She did not know, but she knew that they had suddenly lost each other, and that she had the unhappy sensation of having stepped down one branch of a crossroads, and that she felt, despite reason, the discomfort of guilt.

Her heart was sore as she sat on the back seat with her mother and watched the sheer rock cliffs go by on the Gila Canyon road to Winkelman.

She listened absently to her mother's little shrieks of terror, to Jean's driving advice, and to George's grunts, but she found that she had lost much of her own fear of these mountain roads, though George was by no means the driver Dart was. Dart. The thought of him gave her an aching emptiness in the pit of her stomach, and a growing resentment too. Iron man, she thought with anger; stoic. Won't show emotion. Doesn't need to relax. It's the Indian in him. This indictment gave her a vicious satisfaction, and she repeated it to herself, though part of her knew it to be unfair. It's the Indian in him. But I'm not an iron woman and I'm not an Indian.

"You look very grim, Andy," said Jean, craning around to the back seat. "If it's George's driving, I don't wonder. When in the name of sweet heaven do we get off this horrible road?"

Amanda relaxed suddenly. What the hell, she thought. Dart will come around all right, and I won't think about him now. I intend to have a good time and I'm going to have it! "Other side of Winkelman, I guess," she said. "I've never been south. But, George, look out for the washes, some of them are probably running."

"My God," said George, "what a country. Never in my whole life have I put in a night like that last night; mattress stuffed with straw, filthy sheets, mice, and every dog in the town yapping beneath the window. Drunks, too, in the next room fighting."

"Well, it's a western mining camp, a real one," said Amanda, laughing. "They're not as romantic as the books say."

Jean chortled. "And that's the truth, little one. You certainly got plunged into something pretty rugged. It'll do my heart good to see you back in—in civilization." She had nearly said "back in circulation," but that would have been too crude as yet. Though Amanda was obviously ripe for rescue from a dreary and incompatible marriage, there was still the force of physical attraction to reckon with, the sex urge that had overpowered the girl in the first place. One could not argue with it—all psychologists agreed on that—but it might be diverted to a more suitable object. Jean herself had never had any trouble diverting her urges, or at least restraining them so that they should not interfere with common sense. Amanda was of weaker clay and must thus be helped by those who were stronger. If I'd only known sooner that Tim was really so serious about Amanda, I never would have let her marry Dart, Jean thought, with a spurt of irritation at her mother, who had not mentioned the true state of affairs in time. Muzzy and sentimental, her mother was often childishly impulsive, like Amanda.

Mrs. Lawrence now corroborated Jean's opinion by saying, "Oh, look, what lovely flowers! I had no idea the desert would be so beautiful. You know, I think the country *is* romantic, even Lodestone. Or could be if one shared it with somebody one loved." And she patted Amanda's hand. Since seeing Dart again, she had been growing vaguely uneasy. The perfectly natural little vacation no longer shone in its earlier light—"young people having fun together, and visiting Tim in Arizona is no different from visiting his family at Palm Beach or South Hampton." It was a great pity Dart could not have come, too. Her thoughts went no further than that. She had long ago become adept at sliding away from unpleasant complications, but she liked and respected Dart, no matter how inadequate a setting he provided for Amanda, and she was uncomfortable. Mrs. Lawrence, unlike her elder daughter, believed in love.

At five o'clock in the afternoon they finally arrived at El Castillo, and Amanda, electrified by impact with the lost world of luxury and play, put aside all disturbing thoughts of Dart or love, and plunged herself determinedly into the present glittering moment.

The enormous hotel was built of pink stucco along the lines of the Alhambra, and in its grounds plentiful irrigation had produced tropical gardens. There were palm-trees and camellia bushes and orange trees and hibiscus, and half an acre of emerald-green lawn. There was a marble swimming-pool, and along its margin a row of pink cabanas with red-tile roofs that sparkled in the aquamarine waters. There were detached cottages, too, set here and there in the grounds beneath the palm-trees and bearing Spanish names like Paloma and Mariposa and Encarnación.

A half-dozen bellboys dressed like toreadors rushed for the car as George drew up under the porte-cochère. They were all ushered into the tiled and gilded lobby by a bowing gentleman in a morning coat who said he was the manager and that Mr. Merrill had made arrangements for them. Mr. Merrill, not knowing their exact arrival time, was playing tennis on the farthest court, but he would be notified at once. In the meantime, perhaps they would like to go to their rooms. They would. Amanda in particular wished very much to make certain repairs to her appearance before seeing Tim. She glimpsed several pretty women playing bridge at the end of the lobby and lying sipping drinks in deck-chairs in the patio, women in pale crêpe de chine pastels, with pearls in their ears, and shining waved hair.

Mrs. Lawrence retired to a room upstairs in the hotel, but Tim, it seemed, had reserved two adjoining cottages for the Walkers and Amanda.

Amanda's was "Mariposa," the butterfly. This theme appeared on the green painted door, and was stencilled on the furniture and seemed to the excited girl to be a charming omen. The minute the door had closed on the toreador bellboy, Amanda shed her twenty-one years of dignity, kicked off her shoes, and danced about the two luxurious rooms. Both the bedroom and sitting-room had fire-places with fires ready laid, both had views of the tropical garden and distant Catalina Mountains, both had telephones—and the bathroom, blue-tiled and crammed with warmed thick fluffy towels! My God, thought Amanda, turning on both taps full tilt, I haven't had a real hot soaking bath since I married!

She enjoyed herself so much and took so long to dress that the phone between the beds rang while she was still fastening the snaps on her powder-blue crêpe dress. She jumped and then giggled. It had been a long time since she had heard a phone ring. She picked up the receiver and said, "Hello."

The once-so-familiar drawling voice said, "Darling, you don't have to get all that beautiful, do you? I've been waiting hours to see you. Can I come right down?"

"Oh, Tim," she said, laughing, "I've been having such fun——" She hesitated, but after all, she had a private sitting-room. "All right, come on. I'm dying to see you, too."

She watched from the window as he came running down her little gravelled path, in white tennis flannels, white silk shirt showing bronzed throat, the straight, sleek, fair hair, narrow cleft chin, exactly as she had seen him a thousand times before. But he looks shorter, she thought suddenly. I suppose because I'm so used to Dart. The thought of Dart was unwelcome. She rushed to the door crying, "Hail," and found herself close in his arms being kissed.

"Hey, wait a minute," she said, backing off and laughing; "I'm married, remember? No more dalliance."

"Force of habit. Pardon, lady." Tim threw himself down on the chaise-longue and stared up at her, smiling. "But as a matter of fact, why not a little dalliance? Here you are and here am I. Besides, I'm your host, *droit du seigneur.*"

"Oh, Tim, don't be difficult, and stop making those heavy-lidded bedroom eyes at me. They don't impress me." This was the sort of thing they had always indulged in, half-playful sparring, with just enough sex in it to be interesting. But he had never stirred her, their kisses had been light and meaningless to her. This kiss he had just given her was no different from the others, but it would be embarrassing if she had nevertheless put herself into an untenable position in coming here. But I can handle him, she thought. I always could.

"You look toothsome as always," said Tim, examining her, "but a trifle blurred, my darling. I prefer the ultra-golden locks, and that's the wrong shade of lipstick, should be darker."

"Thanks." She tried to hide her hands from the impish hazel eyes, which never missed a detail of a woman's appearance. "I always knew you didn't love me for myself, and Jean has already bewailed the lack of beauty parlours in Lodestone, so we can skip that one."

"Well, there's a Vanitie Shoppe here at the hotel. You can go and have fierce feminine fun."

Her lips tightened, and her gaze moved from his face to the floor.

"Have them put it on my bill, Andy," he said with sudden gentleness. "We know each other too well for phony pride."

She sat down in one of the carved upholstered armchairs. "Tim, why are you doing all this? Why have you saddled yourself with the whole raft of us here?"

He shrugged and sat up. "Only way I could get at you,

honourably. I'm a very honourable young man. I even invited Dart, didn't I? Though I'm enchanted that you didn't bring him, my angel."

Her eyes flashed, and she spoke with emphasis. "I tried to. I wanted to. He wouldn't come. He's terribly busy."

"Sure. Sure. I understand." He gave her a winning and impudent grin. "Main thing is *you're* here. Now that's over with, come on up to my patio, we'll have cocktails. I've asked a crowd to join us."

That first cocktail party, under the stars and the palm-trees in Tim's patio, set the tone of the rest of the week. It was gay and noisy, enlivened by several flirtations, and gilded for Amanda by Tim's light and expert love-making. It duplicated many vacation times of her past life, and she slipped back into the mood with ease.

There were only a dozen people, hand-picked by Tim from the sixty-odd hotel guests. Jean and George, of course. Then there were two charming little divorcees, Kitty Stevens and Mimi Todd, who were recuperating here from the Reno "cure" on their way back to Chicago. There was a movie starlet, Lora Morton, and her boy friend, a sloe-eyed Latin gentleman who had perfect manners and spoke perfect English and was vaguely referred to as an actor. There were two youngish married couples from St. Louis, and a pale languid bachelor of thirty named Waterman, who dabbled in the arts and had come from Philadelphia to Arizona for his health. They were all wealthy— one had to be to stay at El Castillo—and though they occasionally alluded gloomily to the depression and speculated with even deeper gloom upon the crackpot course outlined by the new President, it was apparent that none of them was emotionally involved in anything but having a good time. And Amanda, walling off Dart and Lodestone as much as she could, most willingly joined them.

It was not hard to wall off Lodestone, since none of these people had ever heard of it. They hadn't heard of Gila County or Globe. They knew nothing of the present mining industry in Arizona, they had an idea that all that sort of stuff went on up in the Rockies or in Canada. For them Arizona contained the Grand Canyon, a few annoying night-time stops on the Santa Fé's Chief, and Phœnix and Tucson. Nor was anyone in the least curious. Except for horseback rides in the desert and a vague recognition that the air was dry and exhilarating, El Castillo and its inmates might have been transported intact to Florida or California.

Jean kept a contented eye on Amanda's progress, when she was not playing golf with George and the St. Louis couples. She even managed to extract twenty dollars from George as a gift to Amanda, who would not charge her session at the beauty parlour to Tim. Jean at first thought this finespun point of honour was idiotic. "My God, Andy, Tim's crawling with money. It isn't any different from accepting a corsage. . . . But still, I don't know but what you're right. Play it cagey, my girl."

"I'm not playing anything, any way," snapped Amanda. "Don't be disgusting. This is just—just an interlude."

Jean raised her eyebrows. "Have you heard from Dart?"

"I don't expect to. There's no reason why I should." Amanda flushed, for she *had* expected to hear from him, a phone call, a note, something to bridge that chill impersonal chasm which had opened between them.

Jean decided that the time had come for plain speaking. "You might as well face it, dear. Dart just isn't the man for you. It sticks out a mile. And you're not cut out to be a drudge in a hovel in the wilds. Especially not when there's something better in view. A whole lot better."

"I love Dart," said Amanda, but her voice wavered. His image had blurred for her. Riding, playing tennis, dancing with Tim, she managed not to think of Dart. It was only at night, alone in her twin bed, that there would come a pain so sharp that she denied it instantly, and her empty arms would go heavy and her eyes, staring into the darkness, would see his face but not the face of love. She would see him in the other aspect—grimly withdrawn—his grey look ironic and cold.

Mrs. Lawrence, too, kept an eye on the proceedings, but hers was not a contented one. She seldom joined the younger group, but she had found three bridge-playing cronies, and from a nook in the lobby she gained many glimpses of her daughter. Amanda's lovely figure in a white bathing suit borrowed from Jean, as she shrieked and splashed with Tim in the aquamarine pool. Amanda in beige jodhpurs and a tricky little suède jacket borrowed from the movie starlet, looking coquettishly up into Tim's eyes after he had lifted her down from her horse. Amanda at night in her own rose-flowered chiffon dinner dress, dancing with the starlet's boy friend, and flirting over his shoulder with Tim, who was being pursued by little Kitty, the divorcee.

No harm in all this, of course, thought Mrs. Lawrence. Young married people nowadays didn't climb on shelves and cleave only to each other. For that matter, there had been quite a lot of giddiness and carryings-on in the Smart Set of her own early married days before the war. But I didn't *want* to, she thought suddenly. I didn't want to do anything I couldn't share with David, and we were terribly poor, too, after the panic of 1907. I can't remember that it mattered so much, we fought through it together.

And yet there was no denying that Amanda had bloomed into a new vital beauty during her days here. She showed no resemblance to the defensive unkempt little drudge who had so shocked her mother in Lodestone.

If this was what she wanted, why, oh why, didn't she marry Tim in the first place? Mrs. Lawrence asked herself unhappily. If this marriage with Dart was only an infatuation, how could she so have convinced me that it was real love? Ah, no doubt she'd been a sentimental fool, as Jean said. One should have realized how young the girl was and how—spoiled. No, that wasn't quite the word for Amanda. She was intrinsically too sensitive and gallant for that. There was a new phrase used by popular articles on psychology: "Over-protection." Was that the trouble? David and she had loved the child so dearly. The sins of the parents—that was the constant theme of the new books Jean read.

Mrs. Lawrence sighed, then jumped as her partner recalled her to the deal. "Sorry," she said, "I was wool-gathering." She gathered up the cards and pushed Amanda's problem from her mind, but it returned half an hour later when she walked outside for a view of the gorgeous sunset glow on the Catalina Mountains to the north. She wandered to the swimming-pool, deserted now since almost everyone had gone off to dress, and stood beside a clump of oleander to admire the ravishing rose and purple mystery of the desert beyond the oasis.

Then she heard Tim's unmistakable drawl from the other side of the oleander. "Move over, honey, and I'll share my flask with you." There was a murmur and a gurgling sound. Amanda, thought Mrs. Lawrence. I wish she wouldn't.

But it was not Amanda. A higher, lisping voice giggled. "Oh,

Timmy, I didn't think you'd ever have a moment for poor me, you're so taken up with your blonde."

Mrs. Lawrence backed hastily away. Actually, there was no reason why Tim should not flirt with Kitty Stevens if he wanted to. Amanda would be the first to agree, but, but ... Her pleasure in the sunset was spoiled. They should never have come here, put themselves in this—this parasitical position. It was *not* like visiting Tim's parents as equals. If only Jean and George would leave now and Amanda go back where she belonged, or come home to New York, if she was really unhappy. But Jean and George showed no signs of leaving. They were having a wonderful time, and George had wired his father there'd be a slight delay in closing the San Francisco branch. He had even taken to treating Amanda with a jocular respect, since she was the tacit reason for this windfall. It was all wrong, sleazy somewhere, thought Mrs. Lawrence sadly, but what was there she could do about it? One might as well stop fretting.

On the night of Saturday, April first, the hotel was giving its big end of the season ball. It was to be a costume party on the theme "Arizona Pioneers." A hundred appropriate costumes had been sent in from Chicago for the guests, and nobody would be admitted without one.

Tim threw himself whole-heartedly into the plans for the ball. He saw to it that his own guests had first choice, made the rental arrangements, and himself picked out Amanda's costume. It was of black velvet embroidered in pearls and sequins, the bodice cut low across the breasts, and a wide, knee-length skirt over black ruffles. There were also black net stockings and black satin slippers with red heels. This creation represented a "dance-hall girl" of a western mining camp in the 'eighties and Amanda was enchanted. The dress made her feel frivolous and abandoned, and it showed off her beautiful legs. By seven o'clock, when she was just leaving her cottage to join the rest of their group for cocktails, a bellboy tapped at her door and delivered a bulky letter.

As Amanda took it in her hand, her knees went weak and her heart started beating violently. At last, cried a voice inside her. Oh, thank God. . . . And this violent emotion seemed unrelated to her brain or to the pleasant thoughts she had been thinking. From some deep unsuspected lair it jumped on her without warning. Then she looked at the writing on the envelope. It was Tim's.

She sat down on the bed, staring at the envelope.

After a moment, she looked at the phone. She put her hand on the receiver and then her fingers loosened. Her hands fell to her lap.

"Call me if you're ready to come back." No, he had said "*when*," but the "if" had been there. He had put it there, not she. And that night, so long ago in feeling, when they had fought about the lost mine, it was he who had said, "Do you want to go home? Shall we call it quits?" The love she had been so sure of, then it just didn't exist, perhaps it never had. He didn't care enough to lift a finger to keep her. What was the use of trying to fool herself? She sat for a long time staring at the telephone, and it seemed that something tight and hard came into her breast. The hardness flowed over her mobile face and aged it.

She picked up Tim's envelope and ripped it open. There was a sheet of notepaper which said:

> *A bauble for Amanda's hair,*
> *She needs no jewels to make her fair;*
> *But if on her head my heart I see,*
> *I'll know that she will marry me.*

To the paper there was pinned a large heart made of tiny diamonds encircling a ruby.

Amanda laughed—a sharp, bitter sound. "Well, there it is," she said out loud. "Jean'll be so pleased. Unless, of course, it's an April Fool joke." One never knew with Tim. Nor did it matter. He loved her as much as he could love anyone, she knew that. I don't love him, but that doesn't matter either. No doubt Jean was right and there was no such thing as "love." Nothing but various delusive forms of physical desire. She picked up the diamond heart and held it in her hand.

Divorce, she thought quite dispassionately. Reno. Tim will pay for it. Honeymoon abroad. Paris. The Riviera. Cocktails. Tennis, swimming, and riding—just like here. And I'll adore it. We'll be an enchanting couple. Golden girl and Golden boy.

She raised the hand with the diamond heart to her hair, then stopped. She pinned it instead to the black velvet shoulder of her costume.

"What does that mean?" asked Tim, eyeing his jewel when they met in his patio. "My poetic effort certainly stipulated in the hair."

"It means yes and no," said Amanda lightly. "It means thank you very much for your gorgeous heart, but tonight just let's have fun with no commitments. Do you mind, Tim?"

"Why no. I'll bear with your modest backings and fillings until tomorrow and that's sweet of me."

"Very," said Amanda, smiling.

It was nearly dark on the patio, the low-hanging stars not so brilliant as they would be later. The only light streamed from the windows of Tim's cottage, and she peered uncertainly at his costume. He wore high shiny leather boots, navy blue corduroy pants, a checked silk shirt, and a large black felt hat turned up on one side, *à la* Robin Hood. He had pasted a curling black moustache above his mouth, and there was a small gilded pick stuck through his belt.

"Cowboy?" she asked, laughing.

"Good lord, no. Nothing so banal. I'm a hard-rock miner from Tombstone, and I leer at dance-hall girls."

"Oh! Well, leer away. I see there's plenty of us."

Kitty Stevens and the other little divorcee were both dressed like Amanda in short ruffled can-can costumes which exhibited all their charms. Jean and George had come as an aristocratic Spanish couple. Jean looked pretty enough in her satin gown and high-combed mantilla, but George was resplendent in the Chicago costumier's version of a Spanish Don, all velveteen and embroidery, white ruffles, and a round hat with a dashing chin-strap like the ones Valentino used to wear. He looked happy too.

Lora, the movie starlet, and her boy friend were Indians in red-fringed beaded cotton, with quantities of feathers in their hair, and a whole battery of clanking shell wampum around their necks. Lora had been pursuing liquid relaxation all afternoon, and had now reached a stage of exuberance. "Me—Minne-haha——" she kept saying winsomely. "Him Big Chief Ha Ha!" And then she put her little hand over her mouth to emit a ululating series of whoops. These were answered by yodels and yippees from the other men of the party, who were cowboys or prospectors or gamblers. The Martinis flowed fast. Tim kept his phonograph turned on full blast, playing "Shuffle Off to Buffalo" and "Who's Afraid of the Big Bad Wolf?" and "Night and Day." While this last was playing, he came over to Amanda, who had been sitting a little withdrawn from the shrieking group, trying to avoid the advances of one of the St. Louis husbands who had turned suddenly amorous.

"This is our piece, my love," said Tim, pulling her up from her chair. "Remember I wrote you." He put his arms around her and hummed, "Night and day you are the one—it's true, you know." He put his hand over the diamond heart, and pressed it against her shoulder; his hand fumbled downwards to her breast. "We'll get rid of that guy—Dartland. What made you want to go and marry him for anyhow—except to make me find out I couldn't do without you? Was that it, baby? You introduced a little complication—a little setback to excite me——"

"Let me go, Tim," said Amanda quietly. "You're getting pretty tight."

"All right—Andy—anything you say. But you don't have to shove. Everybody knows we two are—are—oh, come on, have another drink. Unlax."

I might as well, she thought. Everybody else is getting plastered. Who am I to be unique?

By ten o'clock the ball was in full swing, and nobody could deny that the management had spared no pains to re-create the atmosphere of the Old West. The ball-room walls were hung with painted canvas to represent the rough board interior of a dance-hall. At one end there was a huge mahogany bar, a mirror behind it, sawdust on the floor, and a moustachioed bar-keep who dispensed set-ups for use with the guests' own flasks. There was a sign over the bar, "Kum 'n' git it, folks! Grub 'n' moonshine fur the axin'!"

At the entrance stood the manager, dressed as a comic Indian with feathers and a fearsome painted mask. His function was to keep out anyone without a costume, and to collect an entrance fee from people who had driven over from Tucson. Above his head there was another large sign: "Park yore cayuse 'n' six-shooter at the door with Chief Running Nose. Him heap good Injun!"

The band, imported from Los Angeles and dressed as Mexican vaqueros, interspersed fox-trots with jigs and reels and

sentimental ballads like "Sweet Betsy from Pike" and "Only a
Bird in a Gilded Cage," sung by the band leader. These bored
Tim, who rushed up to the orchestra at intervals waving a ten-
dollar bill and demanding "Night and Day."

Amanda, though dancing continuously, amidst a murmur of
compliments from all her partners, found that the gaiety everyone else seemed to be enjoying still eluded her, and it was with
an emotion no warmer than resignation that she saw Tim cutting
in for yet another dance. His false black moustache disturbed
her. It gave to his narrow face a ludicrously sinister appearance
under the curving felt hat, and he had reached a stage of exhilaration where he thought it funny to hook at passing shoulder-straps
with his little gilded miner's pick.

He held Amanda so tight she couldn't breathe, and she objected. He rested his cheek on her hair. "Andy doesn't like to
be squeezed? But Kitty likes it. Little Kitty just loves to be
squeezed——"

"I don't give a damn what Kitty likes," snapped Amanda, half
laughing. "Tim, I've never seen you so pie-eyed. Please stop
nuzzling me."

"I'll nuzzle if I want to. I'm the best nuzzler north of the
border. I'm a——"

Amanda did not hear him. She stiffened in his arms, staring
over his shoulder towards the entrance. A tall man in an
ordinary grey suit was leaning against the wall in the shadows
just outside the ticket table.

She gave Tim a sharp push. "I'm sorry, but I want to see
something." She left him expostulating on the middle of the
floor and edged her way among the swirling dancers. The man
did not move until she reached the edge of the floor. Then he
straightened and stood waiting.

"Dart . . ." she whispered. "Oh, thank God!" She ran past
the manager into the hallway. She raised her arms. "Oh, my
darling, you came for me—I've been so unhappy not hearing
from you—so unhappy——"

"Unhappy?" he repeated. His cold grey gaze travelled slowly
over her, rested a moment on the diamond heart on her bodice.
"You astonish me."

Her arms dropped. Terror struck through her, but she spoke
fast. "You've been watching the dancing? That doesn't mean
anything. Tim's just tight, and I thought you didn't care—Dart

—darling—please. . . . Why did you come if you're going to—to——"

"I came because your mother telephoned me and begged me to." After a moment he added without expression, "She *said* you needed me."

"*Mother* . . .!" She stared at him stupefied. She had seen little of her mother during the last days, and tonight Mrs. Lawrence had already gone to bed. "Well, I'm glad she did. . . . I couldn't call you because I thought you didn't want me . . . because . . . Dart, can't we go some place quiet and talk?"

"I like it here. It's an interesting sight. I've never seen anything quite like it."

There was no anger in his voice, no sarcasm. He spoke as though she were a casual intrusive acquaintance. He spoke as he had that first night on the boat when she had tried to persuade him to join their party. Oh, what'll I do? she thought, standing there unnoticed beside him. What'll I do? His dark rugged profile was turned towards her, the parting in his stubborn hair a little crooked as it usually was. Standing there so aloof and tall, in that grey suit, the one he had been married in, he was a stranger.

"Do you want to go in and dance, sir?" asked the manager in the painted Indian mask, leaving the ticket table and walking up to them. "There's still some costumes left in the card-room. Mrs. Dartland can show you where."

"Why, no, thanks," said Dart.

The manager went back to his table.

Amanda stood there rooted beside Dart in a kind of drugged despair. Tim was now dancing with Kitty; they were jigging and kicking their heels, and Kitty was brandishing the miner's gilded pick. Amanda looked at them all in there under the bright lights: the bogus Indian braves and squaws in costumes sent from Chicago, the dance-hall girls, the "prospectors" and synthetic cowboys, the "hard-rock miners" with fake moustaches and papier-mâché picks, and she looked back at Dart—the only hard-rock miner here, and the only one with Indian blood; and not allowed to join them because he had no costume.

"Oh, dear God," she said below her breath, and she began to laugh in small broken sounds.

"Something funny?" asked Dart, glancing at her then back to the ball-room.

"Yes. Funny. Very funny. But don't condemn them, Dart—or me. Don't you see how hard they're all searching for something? Just because you're strong and real, you mustn't be so harsh." She spoke with a desperate earnestness, no longer pleading. As she stood there in the dance-hall costume, she suddenly showed some of Dart's own coolness.

The muscles of his face tightened, and he turned and stared down at her. He started to speak, and he was stopped by Tim, who came stumbling through the barrier into the hallway, having just discovered Amanda's whereabouts. "Good sweet Jesus," whispered Tim, swaying slightly. "Look what blew in! He been making trouble, Andy?" He raised his hand uncertainly, and flung the fake moustache to the floor. "He been—making trouble?" he repeated. "We'll get the boys to throw him out."

"He has not been making trouble," said Amanda. "On the contrary. He seems to be enjoying himself."

"What're you doing here, D-Dartland? Spoiling the fun. You can't have her back, you know. It's all—all settled."

"Oh, but yes, Tim," said Amanda. "He can have me back if he'll take me. I'm sorry." She unpinned the diamond heart, and since Tim, staring at her, made no move to take it, she slipped it in his pocket. "Give it to Kitty," she said.

"But look here, honey——" Tim shook his head, squeezed his eyes shut and opened them. "I'm kind of fried, you know—I don't get this." Suddenly he turned on Dart. "Why in the name of sanity don't *you* say something?"

Dart folded his arms. "Because I've been listening with natural interest to what Amanda's been saying."

Tim licked his lips and stared from one to the other of them. "What's the matter with him," he muttered querulously, "standing there like a graven image? You want to fight for her—is that it. Western stuff, is that what you want?"

Dart laughed. "I'm willing, if you wish it. But I don't see what it would prove. Rather a theatrical gesture. After all, the lady must make her own decision."

Tim frowned; he teetered back and forth, glaring up at Dart from under the curving black felt hat. "I don't get it. You're supposed to be a western he-man, you've even got Apache in you. Why aren't you raising hell?"

Because he's real and you're a phony, thought Amanda, with a blinding insight. Because he has a truer sense of values. He knows what the real issue is, and you don't know anything except to grab like a child for everything you think you want.

"Dart, will you take me back?" She did not look at him. She raised her chin and looked past him into the bright-lit lobby.

"I'm leaving at once. The Ford's outside in the drive. I have to be back to go on shift."

"Yes, I know. I'll pack very fast." It'll all begin again, she thought. All the things I hated. I don't know if I can take it. A part of him is hard and ruthless. But I must go with him. The music dimmed in her ears, Tim's face, the costumed dancers in the ball-room, all dimmed and faded; she felt only Dart standing beside her like a tree, like a tower solid above the floating mists.

"Good-bye, Timmy," she said gently. "Thank you for all you've done. I'm so sorry to leave like this." She put her hand on his arm a minute.

He looked from her to Dart, then suddenly he shrugged. He picked the moustache up off the floor and stuck it back above his mouth. "Two turndowns is too much, even from you, Andy," he said. "You're a little fool."

He swivelled on his heel and walked, not without dignity, past the ticket table and into the ball-room.

Amanda packed fast, throwing her things into the suitcases, while Dart stood silently by the door of Mariposa watching her. At last he spoke. "This is indeed a comfortable little nest Merrill provided for you. Did the twin beds come in handy, too?"

She raised her head from the suitcase. She straightened her back and her blue eyes held his steadily. "You know better than that, Dart."

His eyes returned the gaze for a long moment and then he nodded. "Yes, I do. Or I wouldn't have come."

They were silent again. She closed the suitcases. "I'm going up to say good-bye to Mother. I'll be right down to the car."

He picked up her two bags and the fitted dressing-case and preceded her from the cottage.

She ran across the main patio, glancing up at the shrouded windows of the ball-room. The music floated out upon the still air, and the thud of stamping feet. She hurried across the deserted lobby and up the main stairs, knocked on her mother's door.

Mrs. Lawrence was in bed, reading. She put her book down and stared at her daughter anxiously. "Oh, what is it—darling?"

"Why didn't you tell me you'd called Dart? Why did you do it?"

Mrs. Lawrence sighed. "Because I thought you were drifting into something—something wrong. Because Dart's not the kind of man to wag his tail and beg for scraps. I knew he wouldn't make the first move. Maybe that's wrong, maybe he's too stiff-necked. But he's your husband."

"Yes," said Amanda. She knelt down by the bed and put her arms around her mother. "I don't know if it's going to work. I can't seem to stay all of a piece. I change and I can't help it. But I've got to try."

Her mother stroked the golden head. The struggle for maturity, she thought—never-ending struggle. The courage to lie in your bed after you've made it. "But you love him," she said. "And he loves you. Hold fast to that."

Amanda kissed her mother. "Bless you." She got up and smiled wryly. "Jean will be livid. George, too. I hate to leave you to all the mess."

"Never mind, dear. I'll manage——" She looked at the flushed beautiful girl, seeing the baby toddler with the flaxen ringlets and the trusting blue eyes, holding out a broken toy. "Andy break it, Mommy fix." She and David had not fixed, they had bought her a new perfect one instead.

Mrs. Lawrence's eyes filled with tears. Oh, did I do right to call Dart? Can she possibly be happy? Why isn't love enough to give one wisdom, to make one sure? "Take care of yourself, my dearest child," she said quietly. "I'll be so anxious for your letters."

CHAPTER NINE

By the middle of May Amanda knew that she was going to have a baby. It had been conceived on that strange and violent night of transition when she and Dart drove back from El Castillo to Lodestone. Conceived because both of them had felt the futility of words to break down the wall between them.

They had lain together under the stars, and for a little time had known respite from their separate clamours, united in the rapture that looks neither forward nor back, but exists only for itself. But afterwards there had again been many silences between them. Neither of them mentioned the visit to El Castillo; they tried to treat it as though it had not happened, and picked up their joint life where it had been interrupted. Dart, especially, wiped the whole incident from his mind, disliking memory of the confused hurt and cold anger he had felt during those days of their separation. But there was a cloud on their relation, and for Amanda too, except that another factor temporarily dissipated it.

Amanda's recognition of her pregnancy, after initial dismay—for they had certainly not meant to have children yet—had brought a flood of joy and pride. She had wanted to tell everyone, to boast about it. She told Tessie Rubrick, and basked in that little woman's hearty congratulations. While she was buying stewing lamb in the General Store, she told Pearl Pottner, and was unperturbed by Pearl's shocked silence. She would even have told Mrs. Mablett, except that Lydia had been deeply affronted by Amanda's non-appearance for her party on the Friday night that Amanda had gone to El Castillo. Amanda's tardy, stammered excuses, proffered when they met in the store, in no way thawed Lydia, who received them with frosty disdain.

"One positively feels sorry for Mr. Dartland," she told her friend Pearl. "One can see how she embarrasses him." Dart had attended the Mablett party alone, though only for a short time. He had spoken little and made no trouble.

Pearl passed on Amanda's extraordinary confidence about her condition, and the ladies indulged in head-shaking, also in mental arithmetic.

"When did she say it would be?" asked Lydia.

"January."

They exchanged a long thoughtful look. There had been plenty of speculation about Amanda's sudden unexplained disappearance.

"Of course, she was only gone ten days or so," said Pearl reluctantly. After a moment she added, "D'you suppose she'll have Doctor Slater?"

Lydia nodded. "Yes, that's another thing. They've seen plenty of each other—those two. I don't mean anything wrong exactly, but all I can say is I feel sorry for Mr. Dartland."

"How's he doing up at the mine?"

"Toned down," said Lydia with satisfaction. "Luther feels that Mr. Tyson gave him a good talking-to. I expect that girl was most of the trouble, anyway. Egging him on. Now he's learned better."

"Did you notice how much lighter her hair is, since she came back? If I ever caught Pearline peroxiding her hair I'd tan her backside, old as she is. That Dartland girl acts like a tart."

Amanda did not know the full extent of her continuing unpopularity with Lodestone's leading matrons, but the exaltation of her earlier pregnancy gradually faded. She began to suffer from morning sickness, and from vague aches and fears. Dart was kind; he spared her all the heavy work that he could, but he was also matter-of-fact about her condition. He was glad that they were having a child, and was reasonably sympathetic with her mounting discomforts, but after all, it was a natural process and one which she must endure alone.

Somewhat to his surprise he found that Hugh did not entirely agree with him.

One late July afternoon, when Dart was driving down from the mine, he met Hugh on the road near the ghost town and offered him a lift.

"Yes," said Hugh, climbing into the car, "but don't start off yet. I want to talk to you about Andy."

"Why? Is there anything wrong?" Dart looked anxiously at his friend.

"No. Not now, anyway." Hugh leaned back and crossed his legs. Both men lit cigarettes. "But I'm wondering if you've thought about where she's to go for her confinement."

Dart was startled. Like most men, he had only the haziest idea of obstetrics, and for him these were coloured by memories of births in the Apache rancheria during his boyhood. He remembered no fuss, no special commotion. He had naturally known little about it, for Apache women were intensely modest, but all had been conducted with quiet dignity.

"Well, but isn't she going to stay here?" he asked. "Aren't you going to do the job yourself?"

Hugh smiled. He was fond of Dart, who was the only person in the world for whom he felt respect. And in consequence Hugh usually showed a better side to Dart than to anyone else. "You forget that I get very drunk sometimes," he said. "Most husbands wouldn't consider me the ideal obstetrician."

"You wouldn't get drunk at a time like that."

"Probably not, if I were blessed with foreknowledge of the female glandular system. You don't expect me to keep sober for weeks waiting around for Andy, do you?" He puffed on his cigarette and added, "But it isn't that. She's going to have a difficult birth, measurements doubtful. Might even be a Cæsarean. I can't do that here, drunk *or* sober. She'll have to go to a decent hospital in plenty of time. I'd have said Ray, except it's shut down now along with the mine and the smelter. I guess it'll have to be Tucson."

"Oh," said Dart. He stared, frowning at the distant mountains. "I didn't realize she was—was delicate."

"Not delicate. But she's not as tough as you. Few people are." Hugh looked down at his own slack belly, at the slight tremor of his hands. He looked at Dart, lean as a panther, always in control of his body, which never betrayed inner disquiet by twitchings or nervous mannerisms. Integrated, Dart was, as nearly free from ambivalence as any human could be.

"You think I lack sympathy?" asked Dart, smiling faintly.

"I think that, feeling no need for it yourself, it's hard for you to understand the anguish of neurotic drives, of uncertainty—of just plain loneliness."

Dart was silent, weighing the merits of this criticism. He remembered Amanda's broken voice in the hallway outside the ball-room before Merrill interrupted them. "Don't you see how

hard they're searching for something? Just because you're strong
and real, you mustn't be so harsh." He did not mean to be
harsh, but he was puzzled. What illusion were they all pursuing?
Foxfire, he thought, or the dancing will-o'-the-wisp, the something always ahead and never here. What merit was there in so
futile a waste of effort? He brought his thoughts back to the
immediate problem Hugh had posed.

"Obviously, in view of what you tell me, we must make
arrangements for Andy in Tucson. I'll get the money somehow."

"Yes. That's the next thing. You should allow at least three
hundred. How'll you do it? Borrow from her family?"

Dart's mouth tightened. "No." No personal loans again of
any kind, and certainly not from Amanda's family. He had just
about paid back the two hundred dollars Mr. Tyson had lent
him for the wedding trip, and, released from the embarrassment
of being under obligations, he had made up his mind to tackle
the manager again on the subject of the blind cross-cut in the
Old Shamrock. They'd been coasting long enough.

"No collateral, I suppose, for a bank loan?" asked Hugh.

"No. I tried that before. But we can manage. Save from my
salary what we've been paying back to Tyson, it'll be just the
same."

"Andy's been counting on that little extra to spruce up the
shack, build a room on for the baby," said Hugh.

"I know and I'm sorry. It can't be helped."

"Money doesn't mean a thing to you." Hugh turned on Dart
in sudden fury. "All you want is four walls and some food. You
ask a hell of a lot of Andy! Brought up the way she was! I'm
amazed the girl came back to you."

Dart was astonished at the violence of Hugh's tone, by the
sudden clenching of his hands. He stared at his friend and
answered mildly, "That's true; but Andy isn't being asked to
endure anything worse than nine-tenths of the population endures. And it won't last for ever. I'm a competent mining
engineer. I'll work up in time. What's the matter with you,
anyway?" he added, smiling. "You're not in love with Andy, are
you?"

Hugh exhaled his breath, his hands unclenched. "No," he
said. "No. But I had a wife once who couldn't take it, who
didn't care to wait around until I 'worked up in time.' And she's

made a damn good thing of her life without me, too. She's famous, and she's rich as hell."

"Oh——" said Dart, enlightened and embarrassed. "I see."

He still wants her, he thought. And this seemed strange to Dart. Who would want a wife who preferred other things—or other men? Surely if Amanda had decided to marry Tim Merrill, if she had chosen the glittering frothy type of life which had obviously attracted her so strongly, he would have cut her from him without hesitation. He would have felt great pain, certainly. He had felt pain during the days of their estrangement. But he thought that he would not have allowed himself to yearn for her, or lament her going. One did not punish the straying wife as the Apaches used to, but one could expunge her from one's life. One gave and received freely when there was mutual love, but surely emotional dependence on another human being was a weak and shameful thing.

"Will you start up this goddam piece of junk," shouted Hugh suddenly. "I haven't got all day!" He had exposed himself to Dart as he never had to anyone, and the immediate reaction was rage towards the listener. "Run me down to the 'Laundry,' I want a drink. I suppose you're too damn holy to have one; anyway, you'd better go back to Andy. *She* gets lonely."

"I know she does. I hoped maybe she'd find a friend in Calise Cunningham, but it didn't jell."

"Oh, for Christ's sake—of all the screwy ideas! Of course it didn't jell. You're so simple you seem complex, and the hell with all your little problems. You can God-almighty yourself out of them, any way you like!"

Dart did not answer. He had seen these sudden shifts of mood in Hugh before, though he had never seen the green eyes spark with so much anger, nor heard directed at him quite such a shrill edge in the voice. Was it dope, too? he thought, after he had dropped Hugh at the saloon; had the pupils in those suddenly vicious eyes been unduly contracted? He sighed and stopped the car at the dusty little path before his home.

Dart told Amanda a softened version of Hugh's suggestion about the hospital, and she expressed gratitude and relief. "I was sort of dreading to have the baby here. I guess Hugh'd be all right, but Maria's such a bitch, and the hospital—well . . . I do want our baby to be comfortable!" She smiled at Dart. It was one of her good days. Only a little nausea this morning after breakfast, and hardly any headache. "How soon can we get at the room for him here? I've figured it all out. There's just space enough next to the closet, maybe eight feet, then push it out ten anyway, big enough for a crib, and play-pen, bathinette, everything perfect for young Jonathan."

Dart, true to his usual facing of facts, started to speak, and then checked himself. "Sounds fine," he said cheerfully, and began pumping water into the sink.

"But when can we start? This month'll pay up Tyson, won't it?"

"Uhuh," he said. "Andy, where's the soap?"

"I don't know," she answered slowly, watching him. "I guess it's in the saucepan, I melted some for shampoo. Dart—what is it? Won't we have more money when the loan's paid?"

"Sure. Thirty-five dollars a month more."

"Well, then we can buy lumber and paint—you were going to build it yourself. Oh, I see." She sat down on a kitchen chair, staring at the linoleum pattern on the floor. "We have to save for this Tucson business. Then I'd better stay *here*; it's free."

"Hugh says that wouldn't be very wise," said Dart gently. "Don't worry about it. It'll work out."

Work out how? she thought. Mother? But Mrs. Lawrence had no money to spare. Jean and George? Never. Anyway, we ought to be able to manage a thing like this ourselves, without skimping on the baby. She looked at the wall space she had measured; she thought of the bright sunny nursery she had planned.

"There's always the Chinaman," she said angrily. "Raise something on that dressing-case. Too bad my pearls are fake."

"You wouldn't get ten bucks on the dressing-case from that old yellow-belly," said Dart. "Andy, trust me. We'll have to save now, but I'll do the very best I can. I have a plan, and January's quite a way off."

"You're not counting on a raise? Not with depression and the mine just hanging on—I do know that much."

"Things change. The price of gold is rising, and I've made a careful study of the outcrops around the Shamrock shaft; I'm quite certain——"

She had heard only one word of this, and she jumped to her feet and interrupted him sharply. "Gold. Yes, Dart. I know you won't like this, but I honestly don't care if you get mad or not. Because I'm going to have things right for the baby."

"What in the world are you talking about?" He gazed in some alarm at her flushed face and determined eyes.

"I'm talking about that lost mine. The Pueblo Encantado. I want you to go and hunt for it. Right now. This summer."

"My dear child, you're crazy."

"I'm not. I'm serious, and you'd better be. You've no right to sneer at any chance for us to get money. I believe in that mine. I know there's gold there, something worthwhile, anyway." She didn't know how this certainty had come to her, but during the dormant period since Saba's death and the visit to El Castillo, the thought of the mine had been germinating. It now sprang forth in full bloom, a flower of beckoning light, its perfume infinitely seductive.

"Andy, for Pete's sake——" Dart drew up the other chair and sat down. "We went through all this once. I thought you'd forgotten all about it."

"I haven't," she said, staring at him defiantly. "I made tracings, I copied your father's notes. I got a map. The Mazatzal Wilderness Area isn't so far from here. You've got to go and search. Oh, lord—if I could only do it myself I'd be off like a shot. As it is, you go, right away."

The utter unreason of this silenced Dart for a moment, and because of her condition, and the air she had of an embattled kitten scratching out blindly at a shadow, he was not moved to anger at her persistence as he had been the other time, nor even at her duplicity in copying the papers. He made one more attempt at reasoning with her.

"Andy—leaving everything else aside, I can't take time off to go rambling around the mountains on a wild-goose chase. I have a job, my dear. I'd lose that job and serve me right. And another thing—I'd have to hire a pack mule, get camping equipment, provisions—all cost money."

"You could quit your job. They'd give you two weeks' severance pay. Mr. Tyson likes you."

"That's utter nonsense." Dart got up and poured coffee into a cup. "Here, drink this, and stop being a silly baby. I'm going to put you to bed."

She pushed the cup aside. "In other words, you won't do it."

"No," said Dart. "I won't do it."

All that night she lay stiff and unyielding beside him. Like a trapped animal, her mind scurried here and there in panicky dashes. She was not so foolish that she could not see the logic in Dart's position, but stronger than any common sense was her conviction. The cage would open, the miraculous, the blissful escape to freedom was there for the taking, but how? Who else could help her? There was nobody she could trust. Nobody but Hugh—an unpredictable and slender prop indeed. But better than nothing, even if he laughed, even if he subjected the bright beckoning flower to a blast of scorn, it would be a release to talk, since she could not talk to Dart.

Dart spent no sleepless hours; in his mind there were no panic scurryings. He dismissed Amanda's aberration as a transient symptom, but he proposed to act now in the only possible way that might alleviate the rational part of her distress. He would work harder than ever for the success of the mine, and he would go to Tyson again in the morning.

The next day was the beginning of a heat-wave. Lodestone, hot enough on normal summer days, awoke to a dry baking heat, and a lurid stillness in the air like the inside of an oven.

Dart got his own breakfast and left a listless and silent Amanda in bed, a prey to racking nausea every time she lifted her head.

"I hate to leave you like this," he said. "Do you want me to see if Tessie Rubrick'll sit with you awhile?"

She shook her head. "It'll pass. It always does." She spoke coldly, keeping her eyes shut.

Dart hesitated; he kissed her quickly, then turned and left for work.

On this morning he went down on shift with the men to the thousand-foot level, the deepest part of the mine. It was as yet almost undeveloped. They had just finished the station, and were about to blast a cross-cut towards the feeble and elusive Plymouth vein. Tiger Burton, the shift boss, went down in the cage with Dart, and as usual answered Dart's questions and listened to Dart's opinions saying "Yes, sir. Very true, Mr. Dartland," the paragon of meek acquiescence. To be sure, he never raised his eyes above Dart's shirt, but as there was nearly a foot's difference in their height, that was not surprising. Dart had always found the man too negative to provoke any feeling of like or dislike. Burton was simply an efficient little machine, but this morning, while they stood jammed into the plunging cage together, Dart was conscious of a faint repulsion. The man had a stink, thought Dart, his nostrils quivering, not ordinary sweat and dirt stink, but an acrid odour—like a den of baby rattlers he had once discovered in the Natanes Mountains on the reservation. Maybe, Dart thought, amused, that was why Cleve had taken such a scunner to the man. The Apache nose was very sensitive to certain odours.

As they stepped out of the cage at the lowest level, Dart waited until the crew had gone on ahead and asked on impulse, "Whatever was the trouble between you and the Apache boys, anyway?"

Tiger cocked his head; beneath the shadow of his hard hat his little eyes gleamed and then shifted. "No trouble at all, Mr. Dartland. They just took a notion to quit. You know how they are—slippery as eels—oh, pardon, I forgot."

"Forgot what?" Dart snapped, annoyed by the soft hissing voice.

Tiger scratched a minute piece of mica from the rock wall beside him with his finger-nail. "I shouldn't have mentioned it, sir—I forgot—I better get to the face now, them drillers'll never lift a finger until I make 'em."

"Wait a minute," said Dart. "There isn't any secret about my Apache blood, and I'm not in the least ashamed of it. That clear?"

"Yes, sir," said Tiger, moving away. Something in the obsequious gliding motion provoked Dart's rare anger. "For that matter, I've heard *you* have *Mexican* blood and *do* make a secret of it." He bent his head so that the light of his carbide lamp shot down full on the meagre figure in front of him. The face was averted, but Dart thought he saw a stiffening, an involuntary sideways jerk of the head, and his anger vanished, partly dissipated by the tolerance of a big man for a small one. This cringing, gliding little creature was not a fair target. "But that's your own business," he added cheerfully. "Go on to your drillers. I just want to have a look at the timbering we did yesterday."

He did not see the look that Tiger gave him from under the hooded lips. He could not know that the shift boss's palms were wringing wet, and in the tortured brain the long-smouldering

hatred had burst into a blaze of revenge. "I'll get him for that
crack——" The words screamed like whistles through Tiger's
head, their clamour so shrill that when he was out of Dart's sight
he sank down on a pile of lagging unable to walk on. He had
long been awaiting an opportunity, but now at last, under the
impetus of this new fury, a plan sprang forth crystallized. Nor
did caution desert him, the devious contrivances which had let
him out from the slums of Nogales, a nameless Mexican bastard whose mother had been raped and killed by Geronimo's
band. He had slowly forged himself a new personality, as he had
made himself a new name and nationality. Not again would he
let himself be betrayed by the desperate sweetness of blood-lust
and outward revenge as he had been in his younger days. This
time he would be canny, because this time it would not be a
senseless killing, there was a further object to be gained. Ambition. Promotion. And as he perfected details of his plan, his
chest swelled with a voluptuous pleasure. Smarter than any of
them. The little greaser bastard, smarter than any of them, with
their college degrees and their patronizing contempt. Next
week, he thought, when I'll be on night shift, they'll be blasting
down here. The hoist. . . . Take care of the hoist-man, Bill
Riley—the Thermos full of coffee—that was easy. Half an hour
would do it—less.

He rose from the pile of lagging, and walked to the rock face
where the drillers had finally started the holes for the morning's
blast. They'd just be starting the cross-cut next Monday. He
looked back towards the shaft station—not more than a dozen
feet away. Good.

Dart waited until eleven o'clock, inspecting work in various
parts of the mine, then from the 700 level he signalled the hoist-
man and returned to daylight. He knew from experience that
this would be the best time to find Mr. Tyson. The manager,
however, had not come to the mine office that morning. A clerk
said that he'd heard the old man was sick again.

Dart sighed, hung up his hard hat, and washed his hands in
the change house, then swung down the path which led into the
canyon by the mill and up the other side to the six-room frame
bungalow where Tyson lived.

The house sat in a neat desert garden; chollas and bisnagas
and hedgehog cacti all planted in symmetrical formations and
outlined with brilliant rock specimens. There was an anæmic

orange tree and window pots of geraniums. All these were the
special charge of Manuel, the Filipino houseboy.

Manuel appeared in answer to Dart's ring, and his greeting
was uncordial. "Mr. Tyson not see nobody. He resting. Go
'way, pliss."

"Is he really sick?" demurred Dart. "I don't want to bother
him, but I would like to see him a minute."

"Go 'way, pliss." The houseboy guarded his master with an
obstinate tyranny, and Dart would have been defeated by this
except that a voice was raised from the bedroom. "Who is it,
Manuel?"

Dart pushed past the Filipino and walked to the open door.
"It's me, Mr. Tyson. I'm sorry you're sick again. I just wanted
a word."

The old man sat in his wheel-chair by a table on which were
spread out a quantity of broken sherds, pottery fragments dug
from the prehistoric Indian village down the canyon. He fondled
a piece of glazed red on buff Hohokam painted ware in his thin
veined hand. He looked up slowly, and Dart saw the effort he
made to pull himself back from this hobby which usurped most
of his waning energy.

"Hello, Dartland," he said in a faraway voice; then in a brisker
tone with a shade of embarrassment, "nothing wrong on the hill,
I hope?"

"No, sir. Nothing special." Dart hesitated, checked by respect and the old man's obvious frailty. "But I did hope you
might feel up to going underground soon, down in the Shamrock; you remember we talked about it some months ago."

Tyson nodded; he put the sherd down reluctantly. He turned
on Dart the friendly smile that had kindled the loyalty of many
a man. "Of course. You've got some sort of hunch about the
old vein, you want to jam through a cross-cut."

"It's more than a hunch, really, sir. If you could get down
there you'd see, too. Look, I made a map." He pulled it from
his pocket, pointing with his pencil—slickensides, the direction
of the drift, the fault here, not there as the old engineers had
said, a hidden outcrop above ground beneath a thicket of cactus.

Tyson listened, but his eyes strayed to his specimens. The
exhaustion which plagued him became intensified by all this
youth and energy. Eager young men with ideas—yes, that was
fine. I used to test them all out unless they were too crackpot,

but now it doesn't seem worth while. We're getting by some-how—why doesn't he leave me alone?

"You better tell Mablett about it," he said vaguely. "See what he thinks. That's the proper thing to do."

"But, Mr. Tyson," Dart burst out in dismay, then he lowered his voice. "You *know* Mablett won't listen to me. He doesn't have any knowledge of geology, either, but if he did, he wouldn't see what I asked him to. You know that, sir. Don't you remember we talked about it before? You asked me not to cross Mablett in any way for a while, and I haven't, though I've seen a lot of things that could be bettered. Don't you remember?"

Tyson frowned, his bluish lips tightened. "Of course I remember! I'm not doddering yet. And that's why we've had some peace at the mine lately. You're learning to co-operate."

Dart reddened and swallowed. "You've been good to me," he said. "I don't need to tell you how I appreciated that loan——"

"My dear boy"—the manager raised his hand—"I like to help my young men—plenty helped me. Now, I'll get down to look at your precious cross-cut one of these days, but I'm very tired now and——"

"I know, sir. I'm sorry. Never mind the cross-cut, but there is one thing I've *got* to say"—he spoke desperately against the coldness on the transparent face—"it's a matter of mine safety, or I wouldn't bother you——"

"Well——?"

"There's no telephone connected down to the new thousand-foot level. Mablett won't okay the order for more cable."

Tyson made a brushing-away motion with his outstretched hand. "He's doubtless and very properly cutting costs this month. You don't need the phone immediately, the signals are enough. Now listen, Dart, I backed you up on that timbering job you were worried about, but if you're going to come running to me with every little thing——"

"I don't, sir"—Dart drew himself up and gazed stonily out of the window—"but the generator failed last week, and the signals didn't get through. Then men are blasting right near the shaft, it's close timing."

Tyson checked a sharp rejoinder. Irritation born of guilt jabbed down to the bedrock of fairness which still lay beneath. His hand dropped to his lap. "I'll speak to Mablett," he said after a moment, and then he smiled the warm smile. "Cheer up, young 'un, the troubles of the world aren't *all* on your shoulders!"

Dart plodded back up the canyon to the mine. He was unused to moods of discouragement or depression, and while he breathed deep of the hot shimmering air, drawing from it the comfort that any contact with Nature always gave him, he tried to detach his emotions from the situation and appraise it. Tyson was largely ineffectual, but he was still the boss, and, despite his ill-health and semi-withdrawal from the mine, he still commanded respect. There was nothing to do at present but wait for the inevitable change of one sort or another which life always provided. Once identified with a course which seemed right to him, patience and endurance were as instinctive with Dart as the necessity for determined action when his sense of justice was outraged.

He could accept the defect of his own plan this morning and be content with victory in the matter of the telephone cable, which, no matter how trivial it appeared to Mr. Tyson who had lost contact with the underground world, or to Mablett whose bullheaded economies and lack of imagination made him take the wrong chances, Dart knew to be of immediate importance. In mine management, as in other enterprises, it was the little things that counted, and eternal vigilance was the price of success in an operation so constantly exposed to dangers.

Dart reached the collar at the shaft and waited for the cage in a renewed mood of acceptance. Why then should there be an element of foreboding which no amount of common sense quite dissipated? Somewhere impounded in the deepest recess of his mind there was a fluttering of unease, a quiver of warning. During the rest of that day he inspected every foot of the active mine with doubled concentration, but the compressors and ventilators, the drills, the pumps, the ore trains, the electric power—all the complicated machinery for extracting ore from the reluctant earth were functioning with exemplary smoothness. In the afternoon on the swing shift he even mentioned his disquiet to his friend Tom Rubrick, who laughed at him.

"Gor-blimey, Mr. Dartland, that I should see the day you'd be getting sendings and queasies! Why, me Cousin Jacks ain't even 'eard the Tommyknockers of late. Ye work too 'ard, that's wot it is. There ain't nothing wronger with this mine than normal. Ye shouldna fret."

Dart laughed too. He and the shift boss went off to do a little sampling near the No. 74 stope.

All that morning Amanda lay on the bed, wilted by the heat and the state of her stomach. By noon the nausea had passed, and she dragged herself up, washed her face, and dressed in a loose, brown cotton smock bought at the General Store. Her figure had not thickened much yet, and she might still have squeezed into one of her other dresses, but the smock was cooler. She combed her hair, which clung lankly to her head, and powdered her nose, giving an indifferent glance in the mirror. She killed a scorpion and two stinkbugs with the same stony indifference. There was no keeping them out of the house in summer-time. One got used to things, she thought, even bugs, even heat. But underneath her indifference there lay purpose. She was going to see Hugh.

She extracted the envelope with the material on the lost mine from her dressing-case where it had lain so long undisturbed and walked outside. A hot, dry little wind blew in fitful puffs, raising dust-devils on the road. The desert which had been so brilliant three months ago had now flattened to a dun-coloured monochrome. The giant saguaro on the corner had shrunk into sharp folds, patiently enduring until the rains should fatten it again. Amanda choked on the dust and walked as fast as she could to the Company hospital, praying that Hugh was sober and in a reasonably good mood. She found that he was both, but that it was office hours, and the dingy, stifling waiting-room was full of patients.

Hugh stuck his head out when he saw her and said, "Sit down Andy, you'll have to wait."

She sat down on the wicker bench, squeezed next to a fat old Mexican woman with sore eyes—and a smell. The woman greeted Amanda with a toothy smile, and pointed at her capacious belly. "I got pains," she whined. "Mebbe so I eat too much chili. You think Doc fix?"

"I'm sure he will," said Amanda, drawing as far away as she could. Now that she had made up her mind to consult Hugh, this delay exasperated her. And none of them looked very sick, she thought impatiently. A miner with a bandaged hand. A little boy with ringworm crusts on his head. A blowsy blonde in maroon silk who sat in the far corner on an upended packing-case, one of Big Ruby's girls doubtless come in for monthly inspection.

It would take an hour to get through them all, thought Amanda, and there was nothing to read. She sat and tapped her foot. She thought of the last doctor's waiting-room she had sat in. Two years ago, accompanied by her mother, who was always so anxious over any of Amanda's slightest ailments. It must have been a cold she had had, because the doctor was a Park Avenue nose and throat specialist. She remembered the waiting-room hung in gold brocades, with a moss-coloured rug, all the latest *Vogues* and *Vanity Fairs* and *New Yorkers* on the inlaid central table. She remembered the two soft-voiced smiling nurses, the efficient secretary, the four gleaming white cubicles for the use of the specialist and his assistants. There had been an atmosphere of reassurance and smooth charming warmth.

And did I ever think poverty was romantic? Why shouldn't we cushion ugliness and pain if we can? If we can? Her hand clenched on the envelope until it cracked.

The last patient left at four; it was the blonde crib girl, and as she stumbled out, her slack mouth had dropped open like a gasping fish, tears streaked mascara runnels down her cheeks.

"What's the matter with her?" whispered Amanda as she walked into Hugh's office.

"Lump in her breast," said Hugh curtly. "And no doubt what it is, either. She's let it go too long."

Amanda exhaled her breath, staring at his square emotionless face. "Oh, Hugh, how dreadful. Did you tell her——"

"Of course I told her. She'll have to go to Tucson at once for amputation if she wants a whack at a thousand to one chance of recovery. But it's hardly worth while."

"Would she have the money for an operation?" asked Amanda slowly.

Hugh shrugged. "Probably not. Now, what may I do for you today?"

She looked down at the envelope in her hand. "Hugh, you're so heartless, so callous. . . . I don't know. I'm sorry I came. I wanted to ask your advice about something, but you'd sneer. . . ."

Hugh leaned back and crossed his legs. "Okay, so I'd sneer. I haven't had a really good sneer for ages. What is it, brand-new symptom?"

"No, no. Nothing like that." She fingered the envelope uncertainly. Too precious, too beautiful a dream, and she had no right. . . .

"Ah, I've got it," Hugh cried. "Dart's been writing love-letters to another woman, and you've snitched one!"

The swift angry colour ran up her face. "How dare you!" she cried. "Dart would never do a thing like that!"

Hugh burst into a roar of laughter. "How dare I! How pat the language of hick melodrama flies to the lips of outraged vanity. Do you think you're the only one who can indulge in a little playful adultery on the side?"

"I didn't," she cried, momentarily too stunned for anger. "That isn't fair—you don't understand about that trip." She got up, putting the letter in the pocket of her smock. "I don't know why I was such a fool as to think I could turn to you." Her voice trembled, and helpless, angry tears blinded her. She started towards the door.

"Oh, Jesus——" said Hugh. "Women, tears. My misplaced humour. Sit down, and get it off your chest." He pushed her back into the chair and took the envelope from her pocket.

"No—don't," she faltered, but she stopped her protest, watching him as he read the inscription. "Notes on the Lost Gold Mine, 'Pueblo Encantado'; copies from those made by Dart's father, Prof. Jonathan Dartland."

She waited for his mocking laughter, but the face he raised to hers was blankly astonished. "What in the world," he said; "what in the world have you got here?"

The mildness of his words decided her. "Well, read it." She leaned back in her chair. "Read it aloud, will you? I'd like to get a fresh impression."

Hugh glanced at her, then began to read, in his harsh, clipped voice, the Professor's cautious preamble.

"There exists here in this south-western land an inordinate amount of myths and legends referring to so-called 'lost mines' and buried treasure. I believe the majority of these 'lost mines' to be as illusory and illusive as the various forms of *ignis fatuus* (the will-o'-the-wisp, Jack-o'-lights, or foxfire) which are popularly supposed to guide the gold-seeker to their exact location."

Hugh continued reading through the adventures of the two Franciscan missionaries, and Amanda could tell nothing from his face, but his voice slowed gradually, and dropped lower. He read the sentences, "The next morning they investigated the cliff dwellings which . . . seems to have inspired both men with a great and strange fear. They reported that it glowed in the night 'like an enchantment.' They persisted, however, and holding their crucifixes in front of them they explored the dead city and the reaches of the cave behind it. Here there were corpses (Los Muertos—probably mummies), and here also at the back of the cave they were stunned to see a wall of glittering gold."

Hugh stopped. His lips were tight-compressed beneath the short moustache. She watched him, puzzled, for he got up, strode to the door, opened it sharply, and peered outside. He then slammed it shut. So steeled was she for his derision that she did not understand this action.

"Maria," he explained. "Supposed to be upstairs with the patients, but one never knows. I think I better read the rest to myself."

He's taking it seriously, she thought, in amazement so great that it left no room for triumph.

Silence fell over the little office except for the flick of turning pages and the sound of Hugh's breathing. He finished the notes, examined her tracing of the copper map, and then read the notes again. His green eyes held an expression of intense, painful concentration, more than that, she thought, suddenly a little frightened. His eyes were like those she remembered in a painting of Savonarola—fanatical—then the burning light was veiled. He looked at her intently, and with utmost seriousness he said, "Why did you bring me this? Does Dart know?"

She shook her head. "He doesn't believe in the mine. The whole thing makes him angry. We've had quarrels about it."

"But you've talked about it. What did he tell you?"

She thought back, trying to remember Dart's exact words. "He said the place, the enchanted canyon, was a legend in his grandfather Tanosay's tribe. That the Indians were afraid of it, it's sort of taboo."

"Then he believes the place exists?"

She nodded. "He admitted that, said the details in the notes corresponded to Coyotero tradition."

Hugh leaned forward, eyes narrowed, watching her. "Why did you bring this to me?" he repeated, this time in a harsh whisper that dismayed her still more.

"Because you are the only one I could talk to. Dart won't.

But I thought you'd laugh . . . I didn't think you'd——" Why had she come? Was it an obscure wish to hurt Dart? Had she, after all, half hoped that Hugh would laugh, that his caustic materialism would free her from the obsession? She had not bargained for this terrifying change in him, for the tenseness that galvanized his body, for the danger which she felt flowing across the littered desk.

She rose, attempting to laugh. "But Dart's right, of course; it's just a lot of nonsense, just a fairy-tale——" she said quickly, and she stretched her hand out for the envelope.

"Oh no, you don't, my lady." He put the envelope in his pocket. "I'd like to study this some more. I find it fascinating."

She sank down again, moistening her lips. "Hugh," she said; "Hugh, that doesn't belong to you, it's Dart's. You can't keep it. What have you got in your mind . . .?"

Her hands clenched on a fold of her smock, her heart pounded as he sat silent, staring at her. "You've no right, give it back to me——" She heard her voice rising high and hysterical, and she controlled herself. That wasn't the way with Hugh. Instinct helped her. "It's Dart's," she said quietly. "He's your friend."

Hugh's eyes flickered and slid away from her white face. "This sudden tender loyalty moves me deeply," he said through his teeth, "and I repeat again, then *why* did you bring this to *me*?"

She made a choked sound, and her body slumped. "Oh, I don't know, except we need money so desperately—I thought, I don't know what I thought."

"You thought I'd go searching for the gold, and bring it all back and dump it in your lap? You little damn fool."

She leaned back in her chair, her eyelids drooped, and she listened to the echo of Hugh's words in full agreement, but her panic had passed, and she found herself possessed of calm.

"I suppose you can steal the envelope if you want to," she said. "And you can go off searching for the mine, too, but you'll never find it. Not without Dart. There's not enough facts there, for one thing, and for another, you don't understand this country any better than I do. You couldn't cope with the wilderness."

He looked at her with grudging respect. The frenzy of desire which had leapt at him while he read now receded a little; it withdrew to a subterranean den, where it crouched growling and watchful, but the dispassionate master in his mind regained control.

"Then Dart must go," he said. And he went on in her own previous words, "The Mazatzals aren't so far. If Dart knows where the place is, it wouldn't take us long."

"I know," she said. "But Dart won't go. At least, not for me."

"I'll talk to him," said Hugh.

She sighed and did not answer. Was this not the desired result of her impulse to tell Hugh? Was not his belief in the mine, and co-operation, the reaction she had longed for? Yes, but not like this. Not tarnished by the ugly thing that had been in the room with them for a little while. The Pueblo Encantado, the bright beckoning flower had indeed shrivelled, but not under his scorn, under the far more scorching and dangerous blast of greed. She had unleashed a force far bigger than she had expected, one that she could not long control. But Dart could. He would be angry with her, and justly, but he would deal with Hugh, and Hugh would listen, because the only redeeming feature that she was sure of in his character was his attachment to Dart.

She dragged herself up from the chair. She was exhausted, drained, and no longer knew what she wanted, except rest. Her head ached again, and she thought with yearning of her mother. Somebody to soothe, somebody to wave a magic wand and make things right. Darling, I'll help you, of course; what does my baby want? Whatever it is, I'll get it for you. Had her father or mother said those words once long ago? One of them had. Had this been what she had hoped Hugh would say? Poor little damn fool, indeed.

"I'm going home now," she said faintly. "I don't care what you do about the envelope."

"No," he said, not moving. "You don't carry through very well on your impulses, do you? When you find things don't go as you planned exactly, you give up."

She did not answer. She stumbled out back into the heat and glare of the August afternoon.

Hugh sat on at his desk. He took the envelope from his pocket and spread the notes and map out in front of him. He got up and locked the office door. He looked at the cupboard where he kept a gallon tin of grain alcohol, but for the first time in years the idea of a drink did not appeal to him. After a while he took the photograph of Viola from his inner breast pocket. "Whistle and you'll come to me, my lad," he said out loud. "Come bearing gifts like the Greeks. Come as my prince, my Emperor, that I may see how wrong I was twelve years ago."

He smiled to himself; he put the picture and the envelope back together in his breast pocket. He crossed his legs and lit a cigarette, considering with all the coolness and intelligence at his command the best way to conduct his interview with Dart. For Amanda, so childish and uncertain about many things, was right in this: Dart's help and knowledge were, at least so far, essential.

CHAPTER TEN

HUGH achieved his interview with Dart that night. At nine o'clock he saw Dart striding past the hospital alone and obviously bound down town. This was so unusual that Hugh could guess what had happened. Amanda had told him, they had quarrelled, and Dart was following the normal masculine reaction of flinging out into the night.

Hugh walked on to the hospital porch and called, "Hey, Dartland, wait a minute!"

Dart paused in the road, but his face, plain in the starlight as Hugh came up with him, was dark and implacable.

"You going down for a drink somewhere?" asked Hugh casually.

"No. I'm just walking." And he started off again.

Hugh followed for a block, conscious that he was panting and his shorter legs trotting to keep up with that long effortless stride. "For Christ's sake!" he burst out at last; "I know you won the hundred-yard dash; do we have to prove it here? I want to talk to you, Dart."

"Amanda has already talked to me. And I'm not interested." Dart's stride did not slacken.

"God, I know, you're stubborn, but I've never known you to be unreasonable. You might at least listen for a moment!"

Dart's jaw tightened, and he stopped so abruptly that Hugh bumped into him. "Well," he said, "I'm listening."

Hugh glanced around. They had reached Bosses' Row; there were lights in the Mablett and Rubrick houses, and down the street two drunken miners were lurching towards them and singing.

"Not here," he said. "Down in the canyon a bit, where no one can hear."

"I don't give a damn whether anyone hears or not," said Dart. "If what you have to say concerns the lost mine, I'm fed to the teeth with everything about it. It's an obsession with

Amanda, and if you want to join her mania, that's your business. Go on off and hunt for it, and welcome!"

Hugh mastered an impulse to hit that contemptuous face which had not once turned in his direction, but he said quietly, "You know very well I couldn't find it alone, or I certainly would accept your kindly invitation. Dart, you say Andy has an obsession, but so have you. Are you afraid of the place, that you won't even discuss it?"

Dart made a derisive sound in his throat. "Probably," he said. "Doubtless my regrettable Indian strain lays me open to superstition not shared by the whites."

Again Hugh controlled his temper. "Never mind about me," he said, as persuasively as he could; "but you're not fair to Andy. Don't hold it against her that she showed me those notes. Try to see her side a little."

Dart heard the slightly false ring in this. He had been angered by Amanda's disloyalty, by the conspiracy behind his back, the buzzing and whispering over a sacred concept handed down by Tanosay. And he had been disgusted at the clutching greed he felt in both of them—gold-fever, a disease as mutilating as leprosy. But now his sense of justice spoke in answer to Hugh's words, no matter how venal their motive. And he felt a twinge of pity.

"I don't need your pleas, Hugh, to keep me from being brutal to Andy. And you can keep those copies she made. Brood about Pueblo Encantado all you want to, if it makes you happy. But don't ever mention it to me again."

He turned on his heel and walked away in the opposite direction back up the mine road. Hugh stood still, watching him. That isn't the end of it, my fine arrogant friend! he thought. I'll let you cool off a bit, and then I'll tackle you again. Hugh was now more convinced than ever that Dart knew many details about the location of the mine. And there'd be a way of getting them out of him somehow. Every man had his Achilles heel. . . . Through Amanda, probably . . . she's handled it all wrong so far, but I can show her. And as he thought this, the beast leaped out of hiding and seized upon Hugh again. Through its red eyes, he saw the gleaming of gold, and beneath the walls of gold he saw Viola flattened, crushed, and sobbing for mercy. A sudden exhilaration tingled through his body. I'll *make* Dart, he thought; I can do it, I'll find a way.

But it was through neither Hugh nor Amanda that their desire was fulfilled, and Dart's attitude was changed. It came through evil greater than theirs, through the workings of an ancient racial wrong in which Dart had had no part, but for which he suffered nevertheless.

For the next few days Amanda and Dart lived in a state of abeyance with each other. They were very polite and spoke of trivial things. They saw nothing of Hugh, nor did they mention him.

On Sunday the heat-wave had broken, and the weather was golden crisp and clear. Dart, seeing that the mine was running smoothly, took a day off, and suggested to Amanda that they might go somewhere for a picnic. Amanda was pleased, and repaid this consideration by asking if he would like to picnic in the ghost town and call on Mrs. Cunningham.

"Yes, I would," said Dart thoughtfully. "I haven't seen her in a long time."

So they ate their lunch on the mountain-side, chatted about Mrs. Lawrence's last letter (Jean had not written since Amanda's abrupt departure from El Castillo), about an old grey desert tortoise which waddled by them as they ate, about the possibility of rain that night at last, since thunderheads were forming behind the northern mountains.

"But," said Dart, "no one but a fool or a foreigner ever predicts weather in Arizona."

Amanda smiled, willing enough to join him in fending off the interior tension. They even talked a little about the baby, avoiding all sore spots of its arrival and accommodation later. It would be a boy, she was convinced, and they agreed on its name. Jonathan David, for both fathers. He would have light eyes, grey or blue. "In fact, he has to," said Amanda, laughing, "since we both have—according to Mendelian Law, isn't it?"

And underneath this inconsequential talk there ran the dark river of conflict, a river reflecting in murky flashes the underside of the twofold shield of love and hate.

Calise, when she opened the door of her mansion to them in response to Dart's knock, felt this at once. Her quiveringly sensitive perceptions received the full shock of the hidden turbulence, and she recoiled from the young couple on her doorstep. She was herself but just emerging from the re-enactment of her own tragedy. After months of freedom the frightful

visitation had come upon her again. Again and with a sharpened
horror her shrinking soul had been forced through the obscene,
the grotesque motions of past adultery and murder. Her prayers
were of no avail, the serenity and glimpses of the eternal light
which she had thought to constitute at last the perfect armour
had all dissolved again under the hideous impact. She was not,
then, yet forgiven. Repentance was not enough. There was still
something more required. It must be that more prayer and fast-
ing was required—more searching, more meditation, and for
these the only possible atmosphere was one of untouched
solitude.

"I cannot ask you in," she said to Dart, her silvery voice
hurried and distraught. "I'm sorry, but I cannot see you both."
And in her own mind she added the words, I cannot help you.
For she saw them in need of help. Around them both she saw
dark forces swirling, near Dart she saw through lurid mist an
evil face, and danger, against the shimmering mountain-side
she saw a picture form, an image like the head frame over the
mine. She heard the whir of machinery, and she felt impelled to
warn, but she rejected the impulse, refusing to listen, or believe.
For these people would not heed, their violences and tragedies
they brought on themselves, as everyone did, and they had no
right to burden her with their exigence.

Amanda had been staring with concealed astonishment. Today she saw nothing of the special luminous quality she had
felt before in Mrs. Cunningham. She saw nothing but a nervous
old woman in black, who was acting like an eccentric.

"I'm so sorry we bothered you," said Amanda soothingly.
"We just had a picnic up here, and we thought we'd drop in.
But we'll come some other time."

Calise scarcely heard her. "Forgive me," she said to Dart.
"I must be alone. It's the only way I can regain my strength."
She thrust her long pale hands out as though she would push
the two young people away from her. "I'll pray for you," she
added. And she shut the door.

Amanda laughed a trifle uncomfortably. "Well, that's that.
Nice to be prayed for, anyway. Do we need it?"

"I dare say," said Dart. He was suffering from dismay.
Calise had never shut him off like that before. He partially
understood that it must have to do with her strange tragedy, but
this repudiation was different in quality. She had fended them

off as though they were dangerous or unclean. He had
thought her above all pettiness. He had, in fact, considered
Calise a fountainhead of strength and wisdom, despite her
peculiarities. Her love of solitude and of the mountains had
evoked deep sympathetic response in him. But today the sympathy had been shattered.

True to his instinctive antidote for uncomfortable thoughts,
he now himself longed to go off alone into the mountains, and
when they got home from their fruitless call at four o'clock he
asked Amanda if she would mind being left.

"Oh, Dart, you're *not* going back to that damn mine! Not on
this one day off! I thought you were going to amuse me for
once."

"No," he said slowly, "not to the mine. I was thinking of a
hike across country, maybe towards the Gila. But what would
you like to do, Andy?"

She checked a sharp answer, for what was there to do? They
might play a little cribbage, they might do a crossword puzzle,
but of their real thoughts they could not talk. And she loathed
tramping over these deserts, even if her condition had not made
it unwise. "Oh, go ahead," she said, trying to smile. "I know
you get outdoors so little, always stuck underground. I can
always write to Mother, I suppose."

Dart escaped into the beauty of an Arizona sunset, into the
glory of an enormous sky that rippled into violet and crimson
as it touched the gilded summits of the Tortillas, and reflected
itself like a ribbon of satin on the winding Gila far below. He
forgot all forebodings and disappointments in the rattle of the
woodpeckers, the dusk music of the canyon towhees, and the
whistle of the cardinals from the mesquite.

But for Amanda there was no music, no sound in the shack
but the scratch of her fountain-pen, and the beating of her own
rebellious and discouraged heart.

By Tuesday of the next week, Tiger Burton had perfected his
plan. He was on the swing shift this week, according to the
conventional rotation between the two main-shift bosses. Old
Olaf the Swede remained always on the graveyard.

Tiger's plan seemed to him virtually foolproof, and for the
success of its details he had drawn upon a shrewd knowledge of
psychology. First that of Bill Riley, the anxious, apprehensive

young hoist-man who drank a quart of coffee every night to keep himself alert. For him Tiger had procured an ounce of chloral hydrate. It was not his intention to knock Bill out completely, that would have been suspicious, just render him hazy enough so that he would not interfere.

And for Dart's unconscious co-operation, Tiger relied on the young foreman's well-known conscientiousness. The development work just started on the new 1,000-foot level provided the ideal means.

At 5.30 p.m. Tiger, having spent some time looking over the setting and seeing that all was satisfactory, returned to the surface and waited by the collar until Dart came on top, his day's work presumably finished.

Dart stepped out of the cage to see the shift boss sitting huddled on a pile of timber near the hoist-house. Tiger staggered to his feet when he saw Dart, and stumbled towards him. "I got an awful belly-ache, Mr. Dartland," he gasped, "kind of a colic. I can't finish the shift."

"Why, that's too bad," said Dart. "You better go to the bunkhouse and lie down. Shall I get the doctor up here?"

"Oh no, sir," said Tiger quickly. "I don't need him; I've had these belly-aches before. I just got to take a good dose and wait until they stop. I had my appendix out, it's not that—only thing is I'd ought to be down below to spit the fuses on the thousand tonight. Old Craddock and Pedro don't do so good alone." He waited, his arms clasped around his middle, his eyes downcast to Dart's rubber boots.

"Oh, don't worry about that," said Dart, precisely as Tiger had known he would. "I'll come back after supper, and stay underground with them."

"That's fine, sir," Tiger whispered. Suddenly sweat sprang out on his forehead and glistened on his pallid cheeks. Dart attributed this to illness and thought nothing of it. He watched Tiger's dragging departure towards the bunkhouse long enough to be sure the man would make it all right, then went up to the parking space and his own car.

Amanda was in a happier mood that night. She had received a long affectionate letter from her mother, enclosing ten dollars as a little gift, part of which Amanda had immediately spent on a roasting chicken, a can of sweet potatoes, a jar of jelly, and a store cake for their dinner—all delicacies usually beyond their budget. She had also bought some bottles of legal beer to add to the feast. She had further cause for rejoicing, in that she had this day felt life at last. Now well into her fifth month, but ignorant of the exact course of pregnancy, she had been uncertain about the flutterings she had felt during the last week. But this morning there had been an unmistakable movement, a gentle tapping as though the tiny entity within her were trying to communicate. And this to Amanda had been a revelation. The baby was real, it was there, and the surge of tender excitement awakened Amanda to her motherhood.

There were no words with which to communicate the joy of this private miracle to Dart, but it released her love for him, and weakened all the carking little tensions and conflicts which had been stifling it.

She even forbore to complain when she discovered that he must go back to the mine that night, although she had asked the Rubricks in for beer and to play cards, and this unprecedented little party would represent more gaiety than she had had in a long time.

"All right, dear," she said, smiling at Dart. "I understand that you have to go back. I guess we can play something three-handed. . . . See how good I'm getting?" she said, kissing the top of his stubborn black hair as she walked past, "the perfect miner's wife!"

Dart laughed and caught her around the waist.

"Don't squeeze Jonathan!" she cried. "Oh, Dart, it's going to be such fun having the baby!"

His spirits, too, were higher than they had been in a long time. Amanda's gaiety was infectious. The dinner had been good, and above all he was grateful for the reasonableness she was showing. He had no hint of omen or portent tonight; the uneasiness he had felt last week had entirely gone.

He waited long enough to greet the Rubricks and explain. Tom and Tessie arrived all spruced up in their Sunday best. This little party was unusual for them too—except for Mrs. Mablett's all-inclusive collations, Tessie and Tom were not usually invited to staff houses.

Tom grumbled a bit. "Ye work too 'ard, Mr. Dartland, any'ow; and why would this measly Tiger 'ave to be ailing tonight. . .?" But he could not help but agree to the wisdom of Dart's return. The work on the new level was important, and must go ahead on schedule. And as they were still blasting so near the shaft down there, there was added responsibility for proper timing of the fuses and co-ordination with the hoist. Boss or foreman should be present.

"Ye didna get the telly-phone down there ye've been yammering for!" said Tom, cocking his grizzled head and chuckling, as Dart prepared to leave. "Bull'ead thinks ye're a great mollycoddle fussing so about it. 'E says ye even got at the old man."

Dart flushed. He paused with one hand on the doorknob. "I did. I hope Mr. Tyson gave the order, too."

"Aow. I expect 'e did, since Bull'ead's madder'n a wet hen. Says 'e'll take 'is own good time about getting the cable. 'E said some mighty stiff things about your going over 'is 'ead to the old man."

"Oh, hush now, Tom, do," laughed Tessie, shaking her head. "Ye mustna tease poor Mr. Dartland. He knows what's best; ye've said so yourself time and again."

"For sure I 'ave," agreed Tom, grinning at Dart's frowning face. "It's just me bit o' fun. Ye'll win out, sir, ye always do. Bull'ead's no match for you."

Dart started to speak and then stopped. There was no use explaining to Tom that this matter of the telephone was not a personal feud between himself and Mablett, at least in Dart's eyes. It was a matter of rudimentary mine safety, of improved practice. But Rubrick had worked most of his life in small mines where such refinements had been ignored, and it was clear that he shared Mablett's view that Dart was showing excessive caution. Dart was too sure of his own ground for real annoyance, so he merely shrugged and said, "Well time will tell."

A meaningless phrase which was later to find an unpleasant echo in the shift boss's memory.

Dart kissed Amanda, nodded to the Rubricks, and strode down the path to the car. Tessie and Amanda set out a deck of cards on the kitchen table, opened three bottles of beer, and using matches for chips, were soon immersed in an enthusiastic game of Black Jack. They intended to wait and play until Dart came back off shift at midnight.

Tiger had his own room in the mine bunkhouse, and he watched from the window for the lights of Dart's returning car. As soon as he saw them, he glided downstairs and out into the night. He concealed himself behind a creosote bush near the

shaft and watched the foreman's tall straight figure moving in
the darkness exactly as Tiger had foreseen—disappearing in the
hoist-house for a moment to have a word with the hoist-man,
then walking silhouetted against the sky, until he reached the
waiting cage at the shaft.

Tiger crept near enough to hear what Dart said to the cager.
"Evening, Mike. Boys down below on the thousand okay?
Well, we'll spit the fuses, after you get all the other men up,
then you can go. I'll handle the cage myself." He stepped inside, and the skip clanged downward.

The listener in the bushes squeezed his hands tight together
in an ecstasy of satisfaction. He had no particular reluctance
to eliminate the cager as well as the others, but the satisfaction
came from having foreseen just this decision too. Mastery over
the Apache's brain, smarter in every way than the Apache.

Tiger crept to the window of the hoist-house. He watched the
tense young figure on the high stool by the levers that ran the
hoist. . . . Bill Riley hunched forward, his eyes glued to the
enormous round indicator that showed by means of a revolving
arrow the present location of the descending skip. The hoist
drum thundered and whirred paying off its lengths of oily black
cable. The huge arrow paused on the indicator, the machinery
stopped; then from a horn high overhead on the opposite wall,
there came a sharp buzz, and a red light flashed. The hoist-
man pulled the levers again, and the indicator arrow resumed its
slow revolution.

This routine procedure was not what interested Tiger, he was
watching for something else, and soon he was rewarded. Bill
Riley lifted the Thermos full of coffee and took a long pull.
Tiger nodded to himself. Just enough dope in there to take the
edge off Riley's alertness, just enough to haze his time sense a
little, so he wouldn't get to wondering. But there was small
chance of that, anyway. Riley never took responsibility on his
own, he stood in great awe of Dart, and his anxious mind was
focused on only one thing, precise obedience to the signals.

It can't go wrong, thought Tiger exultantly. His bony fingers
caressed the reassuring bulk of the flashlights in his pocket, and
the twin prongs of the wire-cutter. That was all it needed. So
simple, as though the Lord had planned it. He glanced around
the deserted collar, then slipped behind one of the steel uprights
of the head frame. There it was, the conduit running up out of

the shaft, innocent inches of wire, inconspicuous as they were
accessible. He had already loosened the insulation, he knew
exactly where to cut. It wouldn't take five seconds, the minute
Riley received the alert-for-blasting signal, and acknowledged
it.

After that there would be no more signals. But later, when
someone began to wonder, when indeed he himself perhaps
might start the wondering, the wires would have been spliced
again, the signals in perfect working order. No one would know
what had happened, except that the Apache down below had
somehow made a fatal mistake.

Tiger's eyes glowed like a cat's in the darkness, he clamped
his lips tight over a burst of triumphant laughter. He eased
himself cautiously down the hill below the collar and the abandoned tailings dump. Here in the darkness he would wait until
the moment came.

At eleven o'clock Dart, replacing the absent shift boss, had
checked on work in all parts of the mine, and was now prepared
to go down to the 1,000-foot level, where the two drillers, Old
Craddock and Pedro Ramirez, had been working. He went on
top with the last of the regular shift, dismissed the cager, and
took the skip down again alone. It was well to have as few men
as possible around when the blasting was as close to the shaft
as this would be.

Dart stepped off the cage at the lowest level into a little inferno
of choking heat and rock dust. The ventilation was poor down
here as yet. The two men greeted him eagerly. Old Craddock
was not yet sixty, but he was humped over and wrinkled like a
mummy. His lungs were half-eaten away with silicosis, he
wheezed and coughed constantly, but he held on always just a
bit longer, trying to save enough money to buy a little farm back
East.

Pedro was a burly brute of a Mexican, who had a certain
knack with the jack-hammer and drill, but otherwise the men-
tality of a ten-year-old child.

"All set, mister," said Craddock, limping up to Dart and
coughing. "All ready to spit 'em." He gestured back to the face
of the cross-cut. Dart nodded and walked over to inspect.

The rock chamber in which they stood was about ten feet in
diameter. On one side there was the shaft with the waiting

cage, on the other the beginning of the cross-cut, a tunnel so far but eight feet deep, blocked by the rock wall in which the men had been drilling. Across the face of this rock wall there dangled eight thread-like fuses.

Dart looked at the fuses, and turned frowning to Craddock. "You've trimmed them already!" he said. "I told you I'd do it."

"Gee, mister," answered the old man plaintively, "I been trimmin' 'em for thirty years, I know how they fire best. I want to get out of here fast. Me chest's killing me."

Dart nodded and accepted this. He considered that some of the fuses were pretty short, they'd not burn two minutes, but also at the back of his mind he heard Tom's chuckling quotation of Mablett's "mollycoddle."

"Okay," he said. "We'll signal to Riley."

The two men stood beside him while he turned to the shaft and pulled down the signal cord five times, the alert-for-blasting signal.

It seemed to Dart that the hoist-man's response was slower than usual, but after a moment the waiting cage began to rise slowly thirty feet up the shaft, hovered, and descended back into position by Dart.

This was the proper acknowledgment of the first signal, it showed the hoist-man to be alerted and ready, and that the hoist was under control. Riley would now wait for the one long ring which showed the fuses had been lit, and the men in the cage must be carried at once quickly to the surface.

"You get in," said Dart to the two men. "I'll light them."

Craddock and the Mexican walked into the cage and stood together at the back. Craddock coughed long and rackingly. He wiped some bloodstained spittle off his mouth with his hand.

Dart moved back and forth across the rock face, lighting the fuses, the glow of his carbide lamp dancing methodically in and out of the shadows with his quick controlled motions. The fuses began to sputter and hiss like little snakes, an acrid sweetish odour mingled with the smell of rock dust.

"Okay," said Dart, and he pulled the signal down once sharply and sprang into the cage with the men.

They waited.

"Jesus Maria," said the Mexican, "whassa matter—you no give signal?"

"Of course I did, you fool!" Dart reached around the wall of the cage, and pulled it again. He waited a second, and then added seven convulsive jerks—the alarm signal!

A thousand feet above them in the hoist-house Bill Riley sat waiting, staring at the horn on the wall which would presently buzz, at the red light which would flash. He was sleepy, couldn't seem to think straight. How long did it usually take between the alert and the blasting signal? But Mr. Dartland was in charge, so there was no use speculating. Probably last-minute change in trimming the fuses. His eyes shut and he opened them with a jerk. He reached for more coffee. Never let Mr. Dartland catch you nodding like this, be right out on your ear in nothing flat, and then how about Mary and the baby, with decent jobs so hard to get, any jobs—you got to be alert—alert—how long was it since that alert signal, maybe only a second: I don't know what's the matter with me I'm so dopy; I don't want to do anything wrong. His hand went to the lever, and then fell back. Can't raise the cage without the signal—what's the matter with you. . . .

Outside, behind the head frame, Tiger crouched near the broken signal wires. Fifteen minutes would do it for sure, then he could splice again. He laid his ear to the shaft, listening, but you couldn't tell from that far down. There were some dull, shaking thuds from somewhere under the earth, but might be from other parts of the mine. Anyway, it was foolproof. The Apache blown into a dozen mangled pieces, like my mother was mangled, and again he had to clamp his lips tight over wild laughter.

Below in the cage the three still stood. The eight writhing fuses sputtered and hissed inexorably.

"My God—my God——" whispered Craddock, staring at them. Suddenly and louder, he cried in a thin whine, "My God, my God, my God——" He gave a sharp bubbling gasp, and fell forward on to his face across the floor of the cage.

In the same instant Dart jumped out of the cage. He flashed to the rock face, his jack-knife opened in his hand. Already the character of sputter from the three shortest fuses had changed.

The hissing red fire had crawled up into the rock holes which led to the caps. Dart took a deep gasping breath. He dug with his knife into the holes beneath the tamping and cut the fuses.

He pulled the burning ends out with his fingers and threw them to the ground. Then he cut steadily with precise motion the remaining five fuses which still protruded. He stamped out all the burning ends with his heavy boots. Then he released his breath and swayed against the wet rocky wall, staring at the eight black holes in the face of the rock. He unclenched his jaws, and a warm soft trickle ran down his chin from his bitten lip.

Pedro, the Mexican lumbered out of the cage and came over to him. "Brav' hombre," he said, peering at Dart. "You cut fuse? We no blow up?" There was a foolish uncertain grin on his slack mouth.

Dart straightened slowly. "No," he said. "No. I guess we don't blow up." He looked down at his right hand, the first two fingers and thumb were charred black, beginning to ooze a bloody serum, but he felt nothing.

"Somesing go wrong wid Craddock——" said the Mexican. "He fall down."

Dart walked back to the cage. The old miner lay crumpled at the back on the planks. By the sharp yellow circle of his lamp Dart saw that the shrunken face had turned grey-blue, but the man still breathed.

"Give me a hand here——" snapped Dart to the Mexican, who sluggishly obeyed. They lifted the unconscious man out of the cage and laid him on the wet ground.

Dart stared down at Craddock, then pulled the signal again. Seven sharp jerks. He waited, but there was no response. What in God's name has happened, he thought, and he looked at the wall by the shaft where the telephone should have been.

Craddock gave a feeble sighing moan, his hands fluttered, then dropped to his side.

He's dying, thought Dart. We've got to get him out of here—decent air—doctor.

"Take his feet again," he said to the Mexican, and he knelt down scooping his right arm under Craddock's shoulders and around the bony chest.

"Wha' for?" said Pedro, staring. "Where you goin'?"

"Up the manway," said Dart impatiently. "Hurry up."

Pedro's jaw dropped. He stared at the perpendicular iron ladder which ran up the side of the shaft. The spindle rungs a foot apart were slippery as eels from the constant drip of water.

He wagged his head. "No can go up with him——" He hunched towards Craddock. "We fall."

"Shut up!" shouted Dart. His blazing eyes glared at the Mexican. "Do as I tell you."

Pedro gave a rebellious mutter, but he picked up Craddock's legs.

Dart hauled the inert hundred-and-fifty-pound body up a few rungs, then rested the feet on Pedro's shoulders while the Mexican stood below. They began to crawl up the ladder one rung at a time, grunting and heaving. Dart felt his injured right hand go numb, and tried to shift Craddock's weight to the other arm, but his right hand was even more useless for grasping the rungs above his head, and he had to shift back.

During this manœuvre Pedro's rubber boots slipped off the slick rungs, and he gave a frightened bellow, thrashing wildly in the darkness beneath, while Dart, his ears bursting and his heart thundering, supported the whole weight, then Pedro regained his balance on the rung.

They resumed the agonizing crawl, heave, rest—crawl, heave, rest—up the hundred and fifty feet to the next level.

When they reached this next station, Dart stumbled off the ladder, laid his burden carefully down, and collapsed, panting, on a pile of lagging. He waited only long enough to regain his breath, and until the trembling of his muscles subsided, then he sprang to the telephone.

He thought for several seconds that this too would not answer, and he tried to calculate their chances of hauling Craddock the remaining 850 feet up the manway to the top.

Then he heard a click, and Riley's voice said, "Hello—yes, sir? Hello?"

"Christ in Heaven!" cried Dart. "What's happening? Why didn't you answer the signals?"

"You didn't signal, Mr. Dartland," said the thin voice plaintively, a trifle aggrieved, "not after the alert. I've been watching."

"You damn fool, you're drunk——" began Dart, and stopped. He knew that Riley would not be drunk—there was something wrong with the signal wires then. He reached over and jerked the handle.

"There's your signal now," said Riley through the phone. "You didn't give it before."

"I *did*—but never mind now. There's a man hurt—Craddock. Bring the cage up to this level and then get us out of here fast."

From the time they reached the surface and the blessed cool night air, the scene became blurred for Dart, though the judgment which had told him to a split second when he must stop making fruitless signals to the top and start cutting fuses did not fail him.

As he got off the cage he saw Olaf and the graveyard crew lounging by the collar and smoking, unconcernedly waiting to go on shift. It was not yet midnight. The whole episode underground, from alert signal to the reaching of Riley by telephone from the next level, had taken but twenty-five minutes. Dart pushed through the men, who started to murmur and exclaim as they saw Craddock. He walked into the hoist-house, and pulled down the lever that set off the siren. The high throbbing warning of disaster screamed through the night, into the sleeping bunkhouse, down the quiet canyon.

"What're you doing that for!" cried Riley from the hoist-man's chair. "There's nothing wrong!"

"There's plenty wrong," said Dart, "and a dying man."

Riley twisted around to see two of the miners carrying the inert form into the hoist-house, laying it down on piled coats as Dart directed them. Dart turned to one of the silent miners. "Take my car and bring the doctor back, while I telephone." The man nodded and ran down the hill.

At the sound of the siren Tiger jumped up in his hiding-place by the tailings dump. A wild exultation possessed him. Now they all knew, now he might reappear innocently, as though roused from the bunkhouse, mingle with the others, and savour the delicious success.

He circled around so as to arrive from the proper direction, and walked towards the hoist-house. And then against the lighted doorway he saw the outline of Dart's tall figure. He stopped dead, reeling—staring unbelieving. Dart raised his left arm in the air, a commanding characteristic gesture.

"No," Tiger whispered. "It can't be him." As he stared, shaking sobs rose in his throat.

One of the miners from the bunkhouse ran past him crying, "What's up, Burton, d'you know? What's happened?"

At once the hysteria left him, and the habits of years came

back to his support. "Don't know," he answered in his soft colourless voice. "Just going to find out."

He walked on unobtrusively to the hoist-house and slipped among the murmuring crowd, watching and listening. There might still be a way to turn the fiasco to advantage.

Down in the Dartland cabin Tessie and Amanda had just gathered up the cards, and were rinsing out the beer glasses.

Tom, tilting back his chair, thumbs in armholes, and contemplating his pile of matches, chuckled. "A bit rough on the fair sex, that's wot I am—but you ladies couldn't expect to win against an old——" He brought his chair down with a thud. "'Ark! Wot's that!"

Tessie swivelled from the sink, white-faced; she stared at her husband. "The sireen——" she whispered. Again they heard it faintly borne by the west wind down the canyon.

"Cripes!" Tom jumped to his feet. "Summat's gone wrong on the 'ill!"

Amanda gave a low choking cry.

"Naow, dear," said Tessie quickly, putting her arm around the girl. "It'll be all right. Ye mustna let yourself get dithery."

Tom grabbed his coat. "I'm running back for me car, must get up there. Stay with Mrs. Dartland, Tess!"

"No," cried Amanda, "I've got to go with you. I've got to go——"

Tessie gave her an anxious look. "We best take her, Tom—it'd be worse for her waiting—I know."

He ran outside and back towards the town. The women stood together by the roadside. Tessie went back into the house and brought out Amanda's coat, and put it over the girl's shoulders. As they stood there they saw the flickering lights of a car pelting down the mine road, it streaked past them.

"That's *our* car!" whispered Amanda, clutching at Tessie's arm. "But that isn't Dart driving. . . ."

"That means nought, dearie," said Tessie staunchly. "See they're getting the doctor, that's all."

Down by the Company hospital they could see Hugh running towards the car. As it passed again, Amanda called out, "Stop, Hugh—tell me——" But he did not stop; he shouted something from which only two words came back to them, "accident" and "Dart."

Oh, dear God, thought Tessie. She kept her arm around the girl, but Amanda stood rigid as a stone statue, she made no sound.

Tom came up at once in his car, and the girl remained rigid and silent in her corner of the seat, though Tessie tried to manufacture soothing chatter.

There was a crowd outside the hoist-house as they came up to it, other cars parked by the collar—and miners streaming up, gaping through the windows, questioning each other.

Tom hailed one of them who stood nearest. "God blast it, wot's 'appened, Mac!"

"Something underground, on the thousand with Dartland," answered the young miner.

"Is Mr. Dartland——?" began Tom, glancing at Amanda.

"Oh, *he's* okay," said the miner. "It's old Craddock what's hurt."

Amanda made a small mewing sound; she slipped down and forward through Tessie's quick grasp.

"Naow, naow, dear," cried Tessie, shaking her a little, "your man's all right, didn't you hear? Bear up naow, do. Think o' the baby!"

A long shiver ran through the girl's body and she stood up straight. She walked resolutely ahead of Tessie and into the hoist-house. The outside ring of miners gave way for her, staring curiously.

She saw Dart standing alone against the wall, near a cleared space where Hugh bent over the quiet figure of Craddock on the floor. She saw that Dart's jacket was hanging in ribbons from his shoulders. She saw blood on his dirt-blackened chin, and a purple lump on his forehead where it had hit one of the rungs. She saw that he looked dazed; his bloodshot eyes passed over her with momentary recognition, and then returned to the huge indicator by the hoist-man. Then she saw his right hand, and she gave a sharp cry. "Dart—your hand!"

Hugh looked up from his examination of the still form on the floor, and followed the direction of her horrified gaze. Then he removed the stethoscope from his neck and threw it in his bag.

"Well, Craddock's gone all right," he announced, getting up off his knees. "Nothing to be done. Better take him away, boys."

Two of the miners shambled forward, and at the same time there was a commotion around the door. Mablett strode in, and behind him glided Tiger Burton, who had, during the last few minutes, been waiting outside for Mablett's arrival.

Mablett cast a quick glance at Craddock's body while the men bore it off, then turned on Dart. "*Now* what in hell've you been up to! What's the meaning of all this? This time you've gone too far, my lad—you've killed a man with your goddam crazy——"

"Hold on a minute, Mablett!" cried Hugh sharply, pushing him aside as a gasp went up from the men. "You can sound off when I've fixed that hand."

He walked up to Dart and lifted the injured hand. It was swollen to the size of a baseball, from which the thumb and first finger dangled in a bloody pulp. "Pretty thing," said Hugh, rummaging in his black bag. "Just what were you doing with it? Looks like burns."

Dart stared down at his hand and then he raised his head and looked at Mablett. "I cut the fuses," he said, "when the last signal wasn't answered."

"You never gave it, sir——" Riley pushed forward his anxious face peering from the foreman to the superintendent. "I never *got* it, sir," he said plaintively to Mablett.

"Pedro Ramirez!" cried Dart, turning towards the assembled miners.

Pedro came forward shuffling, the foolish grin on his face. He had no idea what the foreman wanted now, but he nodded amiably. "Sí, sí—brav' hombre. He cut fuses so we not blow up. Then we climb manway with Craddock; bad climb, Craddock too heavy."

"Did you see Mr. Dartland give the blast signal?" It was a new voice from the back of the room. Amanda wheeled around with the others to see Tyson limping towards them, leaning on his Filipino's shoulder.

"Oh, thank God! she thought. He'll straighten this out. She did not understand what was happening, nor what it was that was forcing Dart on the defensive. She saw that Mablett was hostile, but she discounted that. She had not seen Tiger Burton, who stood just behind Mablett's bulk, and whose whispers completed the work he had started when he greeted Mablett at his car.

Tyson limped wearily into the open circle by Dart, and repeated his question to Pedro. "Did you see Mr. Dartland give the signal?"

Pedro was frightened now. Here was the big boss himself asking questions. He licked his lips. "I dunno," he said. "I was in the cage. He *say* he did."

Mablett exploded into a roar, he lunged forward, shaking his fist at Dart, and yelling at the general manager, "Goddam bastard! You can't be blind to *this*, Mr. Tyson! Don't you see what he's done? Never gave the signal, showing off, make the men think he's a hero, cutting fuses, wasting all that work, hauling that poor Craddock up the manway, responsible for his death —all to prove his point—to get the better of me about that goddam telephone cable!"

Tyson shook his head. "Wait—quiet—keep quiet, Lute. Riley, come here."

Tyson questioned the hoist-man in a low voice. Dart stood in the same position against the wall, staring out over the heads of the hushed crowd. He seemed unconscious of Hugh, who was dressing and bandaging his injuries.

Tyson dismissed Riley. He turned and looked over the group until his tired eyes lighted with relief on Tom Rubrick. Here was a man friendly to Dart, one whose word might be trusted. "Tom," he said, "go down to the thousand-foot level now and try the signal while we watch."

"Yes, sir," said Tom slowly. "There might be a break in the line just that last hundred and fifty feet, that would explain why it didn't come through." And as he went off to the shaft, he prayed that the signal would not work. And he tried not to think of the conversation with Dart earlier in the evening about the fight with Mablett over the telephone cable, and of Dart's farewell remark—"Well, time will tell."

Riley back at his post pulled the lever, the great hoist drum roared, the cable played out, and every eye watched the indicator as it crawled downward to the white number marked 1,000. It stopped. There was silence. Then the light bulb on the wall flashed scarlet, and the sound of the horn rasped across the room.

All heads turned in Dart's direction, but on his face there was no change, not a muscle quivered.

"You better go home now, Dartland," said Tyson. "Get some rest and take care of that hand."

The manager spoke very quietly, but not a man who heard him doubted what his opinion was. It showed in the sadness of his eyes as he looked at the young foreman, and it showed in the way he allowed Mablett to accompany him outside and listened to his furious indictment.

The men scattered without talking much. They watched Dartland and his wife and the doctor get into the car, and those three did not say anything either to each other. The men were puzzled and uncertain, many sympathetic with Dartland, who had shown a hell of a lot of guts whatever the reason. But you couldn't get around it, there'd been an accident in the mine and a man had died from it.

CHAPTER ELEVEN

The next day Amanda suffered deeply for her husband. Though he was running some fever and his hand was in a condition that moved Hugh to violent profanity, Dart insisted on going back to the mine and facing his detractors.

Tom Rubrick drove him to the mine, since Dart could not drive, and tried to reason with him. "Ye should've stayed in bed, lad, like the doctor says. Give 'em time to cool off up there. They'll overlook a bit of a mistake, when they've cooled off. Ye meant no 'arm, I know."

Dart twisted around and gave Tom a strange look.

"Such a look as I ever seen," Tom told Tessie later, "like 'e was King George 'imself and I was a mad dog yapping at 'im. Yet I was fair sorry for 'im. It's bad for 'im all right, and that poor young wife o' 'is. They was all against 'im up on the 'ill."

"Oh dear. Oh dear," said Tessie. "What will they do?"

"I fear the old man'll fire 'im. Mablett's 'ot for it. Keeps yammering that Dartland's dangerous. Tiger Burton's acting foreman already."

Dart's interview with Tyson and Mablett in the general office that morning had been doomed from the start. Tyson, forced into a distressing muddle he had neither will nor strength to cope with, had already made up his mind, and Dart's attitude did nothing to change it.

Dart stood before the manager and the superintendent, looking down at them with remote contempt. He offered no defence except the monotonous reiteration that he had given the signal and the hoist-man had not answered.

It was his word against Riley's, and Tyson, led by Mablett and reinforced by his own questionings of Riley and that young man's excellent record, felt that he had no choice but to believe that Dart lied. That Dart had carried his insubordination to Mablett too far at last, and indulged in a foolhardy, melodramatic attempt to prove his own superiority, and thereby cost the life of a man. Indirectly, it was true—everyone knew of Craddock's poor state of health—but the shock and fear of that moment waiting for the blast had been the death of the old miner.

So Dart left the hill in disgrace. He came home again at noon, and Amanda suppressed a frightened cry when she saw his face. It was set in an iron mask, grim, relentless, the lines from his nose grooved to his indrawn mouth. It was, in fact, the face of Tanosay when he set out to avenge injustice. But for Dart, product of a more complicated civilization, there could be no quick release into revenge. There was no object that he knew of to wreak revenge upon. There was no explanation for the circumstance which had made of him a laughing-stock.

"Oh, Dart—tell me. Talk about it——" Amanda pleaded, for since he had come home he had sat silent for hours, staring at the floor. She knelt down beside him, looking up into his face. "Please speak to me. Don't shut me out. Maybe I can help."

"There's nothing to say," he answered, not looking at her. "They think I lied."

"You've never lied in your life," she cried hotly. "That much I know about you, though I know so little."

He moved his bandaged hand and seemed to withdraw from her. He did not speak.

But still she tried again. "Dart—I don't understand it very well—but could you—might you be wrong about giving the signal? Could you have had a sort of an—an hallucination?"

He looked at her then, and his eyes were black as winter ice. "I'm sure of no one else in the world," he said, "but I *am* sure of myself."

She got up from the floor, and turned from him. Yes, that's true, she thought, and maybe that's the trouble, too. He needs nobody. He doesn't need me. But during those moments of terror the night before, when she had been in mortal fear for him, she had tasted the agony of loss—and love.

Because of this she tried again. "Dart, you saved two lives, the Mexican's and your own, by a great act of courage, and you tried to save Craddock's. Hugh explained that to me. Doesn't the thought of that help?"

He gave a sharp laugh. "They think I staged it all. Leave me alone. I don't want to talk."

She sighed, baffled and unhappy, then suddenly a memory came to her. Big Ruby's cryptic warning last February—"There's a guy at the mine's got it in for your husband—just put a flea in hubby's ear."

"You have an enemy, Dart—Mablett—could he have engineered something, something to hurt you?"

Dart shrugged. "I've plenty of enemies, it seems, and Tyson too." He rose violently. "Leave me alone, I tell you!" He plunged his injured hand through the sleeve of his jacket, and flung open the door.

"Dart, you're not going off like that, not with that hand! Dart, please!" But he was gone.

Amanda threw herself across the bed. No help. No one to turn to. No way to help Dart, either. He would not be helped. And he had no job! This was the realization she had not yet faced. How often had she thought of this with longing, "I wish he *would* lose his job here." But not like this, not in this way that hurt him more than anything else could have, reflecting on his competence, shaking the deepest structure of his pride.

What could she do for him—for them—and for the baby?

After a while she got up and washed her face, and she walked out of the house towards town, turning past Bosses' Row down Back Lane. The lane was deserted in the afternoon heat, and she knocked on Big Ruby's door.

An angry voice called from inside. "Who's there? What do you want? I'm busy."

Amanda knocked again.

Ruby's flushed face appeared in the crack of the door. She had been drinking heavily, and she had a client inside, one of the miners from the graveyard shift. "What the hell d'you mean by bothering me?" she shouted.

The girl drew herself up and spoke fast. "My husband's in trouble, no fault of his. I want to know what you meant by telling me there was a man at the mine had it in for him. I want to know who it was. Please——"

"Shut up, you little fool!" Ruby hissed, casting a quick glance behind her. She had already heard the story of the mine accident from her client. "I don't know what you're talking about except your precious husband's been fired, and good riddance, I guess."

"But you *said*, when I talked to you last spring——"Amanda began. The door slammed in her face. She heard the sound of a bolt being shot.

Amanda walked back up the lane. She had now no plan. Her mind held no thoughts, she simply walked. She felt no emotion but a formless longing, for what, she did not know. For rest, perhaps—for peace, for communion with something. Her mind floated in this longing, and her body continued to walk. It took her, without her conscious knowledge, to the ghost town and up the avenue of vanished palms to Calise's mansion. And in this state that was close to somnambulism, she knocked on still another door. And this one was, after a little while, opened to her.

"*Ma chére enfant!*" cried Calise, shocked out of her own pre-occupation when she saw the girl. "What is it?" She came out on to the porch beside Amanda, who shook her head in a dazed way.

"I don't know why I came, Mrs. Cunningham, or just how I got here. But Dart's in trouble. You must have heard the siren last night. Bad trouble. He's been fired from the mine. Something happened, I don't know exactly what. I went to Big Ruby——"

"Wait, child—you went to Big Ruby—who is she?"

"She's one of the crib girls down in town. She knows something, something about a man who had it in for Dart. She won't tell me. Dart's gone off to the mountains, I guess, and he's hurt. He won't let anybody help him. I had to talk to someone. I don't know why I came. I'll go now. I just had to talk."

And before Calise could speak, Amanda turned and walked down the steps.

Calise did not try to stop her. She watched the little figure walk down the trail and disappear around the corner of the opera house, then she herself went back into her sanctuary.

There were two candles lit on the prie-dieu where she had been praying. On the piano there lay open a Bach cantata which she would presently sing in the twilight, releasing her soul in the pure melody untouched by human passion. *Untouched by human passion*; was it not towards this that her whole life was directed? Cleansing herself from human passion into purity. She stood beside her prie-dieu, and the light streamed on her, light that did not come from the candles, and mingling with the light as perfume mingles with the rose, she heard a voice speaking.

She sank to her knees holding her face up to the light; but it brought her no joy, for the light grew terrible and blinding, and it seemed that it asked of her what she could not do.

I cannot, she whispered in her heart, I can stand no more than I already have to bear. Surely at last I am forgiven.

The light faded, leaving her in darkness.

She bowed her head and tears ran down her cheeks, for she felt the dreaded drumming along her nerves, a thickness and a coarsening. Memories began to assault her helpless mind. Raoul's face bent over hers with lust. The smell of the heavy scent she had worn. The smell of blood. Ah, not so soon again, she cried out in terror. What have I done that it should come so soon again. . . .

And faintly beneath the din of her despair a different question chimed. "What have I *not* done?" But to this she would not listen.

Amanda's pace slowed as she left the ghost town. The energy which had sent her on the two impulsive visits drained away. She became suddenly very tired, and when she reached home again her feet dragged in the dust, it seemed more than she could manage to get up the steps into the shack. The familiar room had suddenly taken on the menacing quality of a dream not quite nightmare, but removed from it only by a thick veil which deadened sharp perception. She closed her eyes and, a sudden sleep fell on her.

It was pain that woke her up, though she did not at first recognize it. She opened her eyes and stared up at the shadows beneath the dim rafters, waiting for a repetition of that strange summons. It was dark now in the room, and she wondered vaguely how late it was. She heard the fretful buzzing of some insect in the kitchen, and the distant barking of a dog.

Her attention was pulled downward to her body; a formless ache in her back, which had not reached the first level of her attention, seemed to be gathering insistence. What's that? she thought, still without identification. Did I hurt my back— walked too far?—and she turned over on to her side. At once the bed and the room dissolved into a reeling merry-go-round, bitter liquid rose in her mouth and she retched violently. The nausea passed and the pain passed. She sat up on the edge of the bed and groped for the matches. Then she lit the kerosene lamp, and by its yellow flickering light she saw a dark stain on the bed where she had lain.

"Dart!" she called wildly, staring at the stain. "Dart!" She sat on the edge of the bed for a long time, while the pain, like a summons from far outside herself, came back and called her and ebbed away. "Stop it," she whispered. "Make it stop—please," and plainly she saw her mother's face bending over her—"Why, its' all right, baby, just a bad dream—my silly baby, to be frightened."

And for a few minutes Amanda believed this. The incantation had worked. Then the pain came back again, and the nausea.

She tottered to the kitchen sink and vomited. She heard herself whimpering, and the feeble, mindless sound shocked her into full awareness.

She set her jaw and straightened up as best she could. She crept out of the back door, and down the road to the hospital.

There was nobody in the waiting-room, where one feeble electric light flickered incessantly.

"Hugh!" cried Amanda, sinking on to the rattan couch, and gasping while a pain seized her. When it passed, she was too weak to search farther; she slipped off her shoe and hammered with its heel on the floor, then lay panting.

She did not hear shuffling steps approach, but she opened her eyes to see Maria peering down at her.

"Whassa matter with you? You sick?" Maria was dressed in a sleazy red satin frock and rhinestone ear-rings. Her hair was slick with brilliantine. She had been sneaking out to a baile in Mex town.

"Where's the doctor——?" whispered Amanda.

"Doc's pretty drunk." Maria hunched her shoulder in the direction of Hugh's quarters. "All afternoon he drink mebbe so a bottle of hooch."

"Get him somehow—make him come to me. . . ."

Maria showed her beautiful teeth in a faintly pitying smile. She enjoyed drama. She particularly enjoyed the abasement of the snooty blonde girl on the couch. Just like everyone else, scared and messy when this happened. "You're having a miss," she said, shrugging. "Doc can't do anything."

"Maria—for God's sake!" Amanda struggled up on her elbow "Get the doctor—I can't—— I can't stay here—I——"

Maria was suddenly frightened by the glistening pallor, the dilated staring eyes. She muttered something, and going back to Hugh's bedroom she shook his shoulder violently. "Wake up, Doc! Wake up! Emergency."

Hugh had taught her to use this word, and it penetrated through his stupor. He got on his feet cursing. He slapped water over his face with a wet towel. His vision cleared, and the formless rage that welled up in him focused on Maria in the red dress—sneaking out again—the bitch—and he lunged for her, his fist clenched.

She side-stepped quickly, and past her, through the open door, Hugh saw the huddled figure on the couch, and heard a long moan.

"Goddamn it!" he muttered, and staggered through into the waiting-room. "How long has this been going on?" he growled to Amanda, his shaking fingers digging into her pulse.

She looked up at him through the haze of fear and pain. His eyes were bloodshot and half-closed, his breath stank of bootleg liquor.

"I don't know—about an hour, I guess. Hugh—help me—make it stop."

"How the hell can I make it stop! Come on, get upstairs to bed."

"I can't. I can't walk any more."

"I'm certainly not going to carry you. Buck up, Andy. You're not the first and you won't be the last. Here, you bitch," he added to Maria, who had been gaping, fascinated. "Take her arm."

Hugh took Amanda's other arm, and they dragged her up the stairs and into one of the vacant rooms.

"Dart——" whispered Amanda when she lay on the cot. Her voice rose high and thin, and she began to throw herself from side to side. "Dart—Dart, I want Dart!" She felt Maria's rough hands on her shoulders holding her down. "Lay still now—whassa matter with you hollering like that. You'd ought to be shamed." She heard Hugh's voice thick and angry, swearing about something.

Then she felt the sharp prick of a needle in her arm. Alone, alone—she heard the words tolling like a funeral bell. "Alone—

alone on a wide, wide sea, and never a saint took pity on . . ."
Nobody took pity on. There was no answer.

Amanda lost her baby during the dawn hours, and after that
she was unconscious from exhaustion and the whiffs of ether
Hugh had given her. She did not know that Dart had come in
at five, and had sat silently by her bed for an hour while she
slept. Then, in response to Hugh's call, he had gone downstairs
to the hospital kitchen for coffee.

"She'll do now," said Hugh, shoving a steaming cup across
the table to Dart. "Be okay in a week or so, unless there's
infection."

"Infection?" repeated Dart.

Hugh shrugged. Amanda had been threatened with gross
hæmorrhage, and it had been necessary to curette and then
pack. "Depends upon how sterile the instruments were; my
technique was sketchy, near as I remember."

He spoke with a weary contempt. His head pounded, and he
had already finished the remains of the whisky bottle.

"Poor kid," said Dart, twisting the cup around with his left
hand and staring into it. "Poor kid—it's tough."

Hugh gave a derisive laugh. "Tough nothing. Mighty lucky,
I'd say, with you bounced right out of your job. At least there
won't be *three* of you to live on grasshoppers and acorns."

Dart raised his head and sent the doctor a long speculative
look, as though he were going to speak. But he did not speak.

"Suppose I've got to dress that goddam hand of yours," Hugh
said. "Boy wonder—little Rollo and his daring rescue act, half
a hand cheap at the price."

"It doesn't need dressing," said Dart. "Go to bed and sleep
your drunk off. I'm grateful for what you did for Amanda. Now
shut up."

"What d'you mean, it doesn't need dressing?" Hugh stared at
Dart's hand. "What the hell is that yellow stuff you've got on
there?"

"A poultice made from one of the spurges."

"My God—Indian stuff!"

"Exactly." Level and expressionless, Dart's grey eyes rested
on Hugh's disgusted face. Hugh's next words died on his lips.
He turned his head away. He walked out of the kitchen to his
own room and slammed the door.

Dart returned to Amanda. He sat down beside the bed and waited.

When Amanda struggled up at last through layers of consciousness to blinding August sunlight, she saw Dart sitting there. But she gave him no welcome. She twisted her head away from him and stared at the scabrous papered wall beside the bed.

"Andy——" he said softly, and he bent over and kissed her on her moist forehead where dishevelled hair stuck in sweat-dampened whorls. "I'm sorry," he said. "Terribly sorry."

She did not answer. Painfully she moved her bruised body so that her back was towards him. She lay very quiet, staring at the wall.

This repudiation shocked him more than the loss of the baby had. Always she had been the one to cling, to beg, to assault his own self-contained inviolability.

"I didn't mean to fail you—I couldn't know. I had to be alone—you understand that——" He heard his own anxious voice with astonishment. Never complain, never explain—the motto which seemed to him most admirable was not then all inclusive.

"Andy, dear," he said very low, "don't turn from me like that. I know things are bad for us now—but we'll fight through together, somehow."

She spoke then, her lips barely moving, so that he had to bend down to hear. " 'Together.' When you need nobody but yourself. When you've never done a single thing I wanted. When you've put everything else ahead of me—your profession, your Indian memories, even rocks and desert."

He sank back on the chair, looking at the back of her small, tousled head, the tender, childish line of her neck. "That's not quite fair," he said quietly. "I love you——"

"I doubt it——" She closed her eyes so that she might not see the peeling wall. It seemed to her that she no longer knew what love was, but only hate. This loathsome place which had killed her baby, the evil of foul minds and tongues and disgrace, sordid and besmirching all it touched. And this man who had failed her.

There was silence in the tiny hospital room. Down the road there came a rumble and the grinding of gears. Dart glanced out of the window to see one of the ore trucks from the mill carrying the concentrates to Hayden Junction. A miner, Gus Kravenko, was sitting beside the driver and laughing. What's he doing off shift at this hour? Dart thought. I'll have to check —— He averted his eyes from the window, and a black curtain descended in his mind.

He turned sharply back to the bed. "Andy—do you still want me to search for the Pueblo Encantado?"

His harsh question did not at first reach her through the heavy mists where she now drifted. Pueblo Encantado? The Enchanted City, the bright flower which had once beckoned so seductively. How strange that Dart should ask that.

"I don't know . . ." she whispered. "So far away . . . I'm tired, nothing's real . . . you're not real. . . ." Her voice trailed into an incoherent murmur.

Dart sat on quietly beside the cot. He had in that moment made up his mind, though there had been forerunners of his decision while he wandered over the mountains during the night. The values on which his life had been based were torn from him by injustice. His profession had repudiated him. And had not in fact his Indian heritage repudiated him, too? With Saba's death the last link was broken, as she had wished it. Why, then, cling to a superstitious fear of taboo?

If the lust for gold were in fact a disease, as he had always felt, then he would now forcibly inoculate it into his own blood. Gold meant power. It was for this the white men loved it. He would now act as white men did, using, as they did for their own ends, whatever help they could extort from the Indian. And further than that, there was Amanda. If there were truth in her complaint that he had never done a single thing she wanted, it would be true no longer.

He turned all his concentration and all his practical knowledge upon the problem. He reached in his pocket for pencil and paper, impatient at the awkwardness of his injured hand. The search must wait until it healed, of course. That would make the expedition probably the first week in September. An excellent time for the mountains. His salary would be paid for another month, Tyson had said. This would buy the necessary supplies. Supplies for how many? It was then that he debated the problem of taking Hugh. There would be advantage in having a companion, another gun, another pair of hands. Disadvantages, too, inherent in Hugh's nature. Still, Dart decided finally in the affirmative. They'd have no whisky with them, and Hugh, whatever his peculiarities, deserved a break. It never occurred to him to take Amanda.

Amanda recovered rapidly. Hugh's dire predictions as to infection were not realized. In a week she was up and around, heartily tired of Maria's grudging ministrations, but she continued to stay on in the hospital. She found in herself a great reluctance to return home to Dart. She had suffered too much in that cabin, and, too, there was fear—fear of being overwhelmed again by passion. The baby's death and that night of anguish had hardened her. She, too, felt betrayed as Dart did, though for different reasons, and she walled herself against him. She was sick of emotion, sick of love. There was one channel left for all her thoughts. The Pueblo Encantado.

For, as she recovered strength, she also recovered her interest in the search. Thanks to Dart's change of mind this search was now at last within the bounds of realization. But the character of her interest had changed. Too late—she thought during many night hours on her hospital cot—too late for the soft beautiful things it had promised her once. Too late for augmenting the baby's comfort, too late for softening the harshness of her life with Dart, for bringing to their marriage the grace of luxury.

The gold that must be there—for still she had this certainty that it was there—now meant for her but one thing: escape. By means of her share she would be able to return to that other life. Independent of such men as Tim Merrill, independent of anyone's bounty, she might do as she pleased. Travel around the world with her mother; perhaps a year in Paris. A new life in which all pain and failure would be forgotten.

Hugh had taken Dart's capitulation in astounded silence, for it came just as Hugh was preparing for renewed attack. Then, as he listened to Dart's carefully thought-out plans, Hugh could not hide his exultation. Dart, as Amanda had earlier, saw the green eyes gleam with a greedy light which revolted him, despite his decision to inoculate himself with the same disease. And he said coldly, "You're quite aware that we may find nothing, and if we do find anything, your share will be exactly one-third. Also there'll be no boozing on this expedition, and I suggest you get yourself in some kind of training before we start."

"Yes, my lord," said Hugh.

Dart looked at him keenly. A foreboding came to him, and he dismissed it, though it prompted him to say, "There'll be danger, Hugh. You know that, don't you? We might not come back. Are you sure you know what you're getting into?"

Hugh's lips tightened and he jerked his head. "You needn't think you can frighten me out of it, Dartland. I'm going."

So, it appeared, was Amanda. To all of Dart's objections she presented an impervious front.

"The whole search was my idea in the first place, as you very well know, and I most certainly intend to be part of it."

"But you'll hold us up, Andy. You're not strong enough for a thing like this, and my God, think what a fuss you made over a few bugs at the rancheria!"

"I've changed since then."

Yes, she had changed, Dart thought. She smiled seldom during those three weeks of preparation, her blue eyes had lost their eager friendliness and avoided his. She seemed to have encased herself in a brittle skin of ice, and he could no longer read her thoughts.

Whether this was the sign of increased emotional maturity, or the sulky withdrawal of a hurt child, he did not know, though he was more acutely conscious of her than he had ever been. She lived on in the hospital, helping a little with the other patients, while he resumed the old familiar bachelor's life in their shack. He made no further attempt to woo her back, after the first morning. He had come to believe that her attitude sprang from contempt. That she shared in the general Lodestone attitude that he had made a pernicious fool of himself, and it was resentment that finally quelled his objections to including Amanda on the expedition.

"Okay," he said angrily. "Have it your own way, but you'll be treated like another man. No quarter, no coddling. You apparently don't wish me to consider you my wife any more, so you won't be."

"I know," she said. She looked at his lean tanned face, the stubborn black hair, the bandaged hand, and she turned away, denying the pain in her heart. "All I want is my share of the gold, then we can go our separate ways." Her voice wavered, but she added at once firmly, "That's what we both seem to want, isn't it?"

"So it seems," answered Dart with equal coldness. They did not look at each other.

The three of them had drawn up an agreement in triplicate, apportioning whatever they might find into thirds. They had each signed it and retained a copy. Hugh put his in a locked desk drawer with Viola's photograph. Amanda put hers in the fitted dressing-case which she had moved to the hospital and kept under her cot. Dart carried his out to the Cunningham mansion and put it in his old trunk, when he went to retrieve Saba's basket and the original Pueblo Encantado data.

He did not see Calise on this trip, nor did he wish to. He went up the back staircase into the servants' quarters without disturbing her.

She saw him, however, as he walked back down the trail, and though he held himself as straight as ever, and his effortless walk was as rapid, she saw an indefinable change, a diminishing of the clear honesty she had always known in him. Again, and more imperiously, she received an impression of what she must do, and this time she did not quite deny it. "*Bientôt, bientôt,*" she murmured, "*quand j'aurais plus de force——*" And she knelt down to pray.

So isolated were the Dartlands and Hugh from the life of Lodestone now that they had no difficulty in hiding their plans. Hugh, who alone still had contact with the mine, telephoned Mr. Tyson one day and abruptly announced that he was taking a vacation the beginning of September. Tyson protested that that was most inconsiderate at short notice, to which Hugh replied that he didn't give a damn, that he didn't expect to practise much longer in this rat hole in any case. They might do what they liked about it.

Tyson sighed. "Well—I suppose we can use a Globe doctor until you get back. By the way, Slater, how's Mrs. Dartland? I heard she'd been sick."

"She had a miscarriage. She's okay now."

"Too bad. Too bad. That whole Dartland business was most unfortunate—it bothers me—I used to be able to trust my judgment about men——"

"Well, you can stop bothering," cut in Hugh. "The Dartlands are pulling out of here next week."

So people knew that they were leaving, but nobody came near them except Tessie and Tom Rubrick.

Tom got no satisfaction from his farewell interview with Dart, who answered the shift boss's clumsy sympathy in mono-syllables.

"Did ye get another job then?" inquired Tom anxiously. "Did Mr. Tyson write a decent letter o' recommendation for ye?"

"No," said Dart.

"But I 'eard 'im fighting it out with Bull'ead; 'e said 'e was going to. A most o' the men're for ye, Dart; they think ye 'ad a raw deal, no matter wot ye did."

"Thanks," said Dart.

"I wish ye was back m'self, I do. Tiger don't do so good boss-ing the 'ole show, gets flustered-like, and the men're grumbling a good bit. We're running into 'eavy ground on the thousand, too, let alone 'alf me Cousin Jacks won't work there on account o' Craddock dying there."

Dart stood up and walked to the door. "Good-bye, Tom. Thanks for coming."

From her visits to Amanda Tessie got no satisfaction either. The girl seemed glad to see her, and her eyes filled with tears when Tessie tried to comfort her about the baby. "It was nought but the shock o' that dreadful night at the mine, dear—you'll likely never have trouble again. Start another one soon, that's the best way to forget——" But Amanda answered all sympathetic questions with silence.

Tessie's warm heart ached for the Dartlands. She could feel that something was very wrong between the two of them, let alone the troubles you could see like losing the baby and Mr. Dartland losing his job and leaving town under a cloud. But it certainly was queer the way the girl stayed on in the hospital after she was well—though Tessie almost alone in Lodestone did not impute this behaviour to a guilty passion between Amanda and the doctor. She was wiser than this, and shrewder, too. Amanda's was the behaviour of extreme innocence, not intrigue.

"It's just that those two young Dartlands hasn't learned how to get along yet," she said to Tom. "When trouble comes they draw apart and think about themselves, instead o' finding com-fort in each other." She patted her husband's hand, and he responded with an affectionate grunt.

"All the same," added Tessie thoughtfully, "I wonder where they're off to next week? It seems very strange."

How strange Tessie could not know. Nor would she ever have understood the illusion that danced on the horizon for the three disparate human beings who were linked together in the quest. For each the foxlight that lured them to the lost treasure took a different form, but for each the cold beckoning gleam sprang from the ashes of disillusion and bitterness.

CHAPTER TWELVE

They left Lodestone at five o'clock on Saturday morning, September second, Amanda and Dart on the front seat of the Lizzie, and Hugh squeezed behind with their bags, knapsacks, blankets, and two guns. They intended to get supplies and a pack burro later, at Staghorn, a tiny trading post and ranch on the edge of the Mazatzal Mountains.

Dart, after consultation with Geological Survey quadrangles for the region, and comparison with the nearly unintelligible copper map made by the Mimbreño Indian a hundred years ago, nad settled on the general location most likely to contain the Pueblo Encantado: the wild northern reaches of the Mazatzals, east of the Verde River. In this decision he was aided by memory. On that day in the Apache rancheria, when Tanosay had confided the map and the legend to an awed boy of fifteen, he had said, in speaking of the lost valley, that it was "maybe four days' journey from the great bridge that held the earth on its back." This would be the natural bridge near Payson.

Four days' journey to an Indian afoot in rough country probably meant about fifty miles, and Dart considered this a sufficient clue, combined with the others, to use as a basis for exploration.

He did not, however, share Amanda's and Hugh's optimism. They saw only a square inch on the map with a road of sorts leading towards this inch where Dart said they would search. Both felt immediate certainty that the thing would be easy, and they were annoyed with Dart for his refusal to admit it. He, who knew his south-western mountains and the conditions they would find in a wilderness of volcanic malpais, box-canyons, and uncertain water supply, did not bother to argue with them.

They were all three silent as they left Lodestone that morning. Amanda looked back on the sleeping town, rose-grey and quiet in the dawn light, while a peculiar sensation oppressed her heart. Not regret, exactly—for her whole soul was focused on escape. Not shame—for surely the failures there had been none of her doing, and yet it seemed that her oppression contained something of both, of shame and regret. She moved as far as possible from Dart on the seat, then broke the silence with a casual remark. "I hope it isn't going to be as hot today as yesterday."

During this period that she and Dart were still bound together by their common aim, it was obvious that the strain must be relieved and the failure between them ignored, as all the passion they had shared must be ignored. They were now simply members of an impersonal expedition.

"It'll be hot all right until we pick up some altitude," said Dart, slowing for the turn on to the highway to Globe, and she knew from the tone of his response that he shared her decision. But then, when had it ever been hard for Dart to be impersonal?

At eight-thirty they stopped at the Dominion Hotel in Globe for a cup of coffee. A party of breakfasting tourists stared at the trio with interest as they filed into the dining-room. Hugh and Dart wore laced leather boots, levis, worn leather jackets, and carried stetsons in their hands. Amanda wore her levis, the cashmere sweater, and a brown twill cap with a sun visor.

"They cowboys, Ma?" shrilled a young voice from the tourists' table, and a woman's voice replied complacently, "Yes, dear."

Amanda giggled suddenly. We're much more exciting than that, if you only knew it, you tenderfeet, she thought. We're treasure-seekers. Her spirits rose. She was young, and strong again. She was quit of Lodestone for ever. She was embarked on a great adventure. What did anything else matter? She fished in her pocket, and bringing out her compact she applied powder and lipstick, and fluffed her hair out over her cheeks beneath the cap.

Hugh and Dart both watched her. "Effect of the return to civilization, I gather," said Hugh morosely. "I wish to God you'd stay here and not louse up this expedition for us."

"Well, I won't stay here," she cried, smiling. "I can't wait to lay my own two pretty little hands on the——"

"Shut up!" Hugh banged his fist down on the table, drowning out her last word. "You damn fool, haven't you got sense enough not to go blabbing all over the place!" He threw a quick glance around the dining-room.

Indignant colour flooded her cheeks. "Heavens, we don't

have to be *this* grim, do we! You sound like a dime novel. 'Hist,' he snarled, and two more redskins bit the dust.''

"I don't give a goddam what I sound like. You keep your trap shut.''

Instinctively she looked at Dart. He was the one to give orders, he was the one to arbitrate. But Dart was gazing out of the window at the busy life that passed in the town's main street; he seemed quite withdrawn from them, though the instant she put down her empty coffee cup, he spoke without turning his head. "Okay, let's go.'' He put a quarter on the table, and stood up.

They walked out through the dark Victorian lobby decorated with cholla cactus chandeliers, elk heads, and cuspidors, into the Saturday morning bustle of Broad Street. They clambered back into the flivver and waited, for this was one of its temperamental moments when the starter failed and Dart had to crank.

"D'you want help?'' Hugh called reluctantly from the back seat. "Can you manage with that hand?'' But the injured fingers had healed perfectly, only pink, crinkled scars remained, and Hugh was not surprised at Dart's refusal.

Just as the engine started they heard a clear hail, "Ola! Dartland!'' They all swivelled round to the street. The Apaches were streaming into town from the reservation, as they always did on Saturdays. There were half a dozen of them sitting on boards in an open pick-up truck, and it was the driver who had hailed Dart.

Dart straightened up slowly as the truck pulled alongside and the driver jumped out. It was John Whitman, dressed in his best yellow satin shirt, silver belt, and turquoise ear-rings. He advanced grinning, while the truckful of Indians peered over and laughed. Amanda saw Rowena and waved. The Apache girl waved back.

"Well, my friend,'' cried John Whitman, pumping Dart's hand. "It's good to see you again. You come to town for the day, too?''

Dart shook his head. He could not smile. How little he wanted to see this young man who had been his boyhood companion, who shared with him memories of Tanosay, and Saba.

"What is it, Ish-kin-azi?'' asked the young Indian in Apache, instantly perceptive; "trouble?''

Dart let silence answer. They stood together on the sidewalk,

Dart offered John a cigarette and they both smoked awhile. Hugh and Amanda, in the car, waited impatiently.

"Where do you go, then?" asked the Indian at last.

"North," said Dart. Both men turned and looked up Broad Street to the northern sky, an azure bowl cupping great mounds of thick white cumulus clouds.

"To Holbrook, maybe?" suggested the Indian. "To the rail-road? You are leaving our country?"

Dart knew that this unusual persistence sprang from friend-ship, and perhaps something more. Apache intuition is very keen. But he could not lie.

"No. We go north to the Mazatzal Mountains." He met the other's eyes, then turned away.

The Apache's lids flickered, his smile disappeared, and he took a long drag on his cigarette. In the pick-up truck the other Indians were murmuring and laughing with each other. Rowena had slung the cradle-board around on her lap and was modestly nursing the baby under her blue Mother Hubbard blouse. They were content to wait until John should be ready to drive them to Pinal Ranch on the road to Superior. There at the Ranch some of the tribe had been encamped while gathering acorns. There would be a festive meeting.

Hugh, however, was fidgeting. "For Christ's sake, Dart," he shouted above the rattle of the Ford's engine, "you going to lounge there all day with that guy? Tell him to go back to his squaw."

John Whitman glanced around very briefly at the doctor. Apaches do not like the term "squaw."

"I must go," said Dart. "Good-bye again. Good luck."

"Wait!" The Indian threw his cigarette butt on the sidewalk and crushed it with his heel. "Something has changed you, Ish-kin-azi. You have become all white. I see it in your eyes as you look at me. That is well, no doubt. It is what she-who-has-gone-away wished for you."

He paused, then went on in a lower voice, each guttural Apache word taut with meaning. "Yet I hope you have not for-gotten that you were once a member of our clan. Not forgotten that you were much *trusted* and beloved by he who was your grandfather and our chief?" He paused again, staring gravely at Dart's averted face. "As *I* was also," he added very slowly, with meaning.

Dart raised his head. He looked steadily into the black un-winking eyes that were nearly on a level with his own. "I *have* forgotten," he said. "I have become, as you say, wholly white, for no man can ride two horses."

Their long expressionless gaze held for a second, then the two young men separated in silence. John returned to the truck and swung himself up on the seat. Dart stepped into the Ford. Both vehicles pulled away from the kerb, and started up Broad Street, past the shops and the movie theatre and the courthouse, past the enormous tailing dumps of the once so productive Old Dominion Mine.

They continued together on the highway for four more miles, then Dart turned north on a broad dirt road. The truckful of Indians went onward through Miami towards the summit of the Pinals. There was no gesture of farewell as the two vehicles parted company. Again the black curtain descended in Dart's mind, shutting off a new foreboding which he did not wish to analyse, and for which there was no plausible basis.

All that day the sun beat down on their heads, for the Ford's top had long since disintegrated into tatters. The heat rose, searing, fierce, from the desert floor, a fitful wind raised dust devils to writhe among the saguaros and the cholla, and when they passed the infrequent cars, dust enveloped them like a yellow fog, sifting grit into eyes and nostrils and between the teeth.

Amanda grew dizzy from the baking heat and the lurching of the little car around interminable curves, but she made no com-plaint. I can stand it, she thought proudly, I can stand anything; even the sight of her first rattler, limp and dead on the road, crushed by an earlier car. At least she had learned during her months in Lodestone that the tenderfoot fear of rattlesnakes was largely unnecessary. Tessie Rubrick had lived in Arizona fifteen years and never seen a rattler. Besides, they had anti-venom in the medical kit which Hugh had provided.

This isn't so bad, she thought, pleased that familiarity had vanquished so many of her earlier fears. How this road would have terrified her a few months ago, and now she scarcely noticed its dangers. There were, besides, compensations. A glimpse of the Tonto cliff dwellings high in a cave on a moun-tain-side; the first unexpected view of blue water at Roosevelt

Lake, sparkling beneath the white-capped Sierra Anchas. The white patches on the mountains were not snow, Dart said in answer to her exclamation; they were the tailings from asbestos mines.

"Mines, way up there!" she cried in astonishment. "It doesn't seem possible. I thought this was the wilds."

"I don't suppose there are many square feet anywhere in this country that some man hasn't trodden at some time," said Dart.

"Yes, damn it," interposed Hugh, leaning forward. "I hope to God nobody but Indians have trodden this place we're going. Might be sheepherders, wandering cow-punchers—gives me the jitters to think of it."

"I don't think you need worry," said Dart dryly. "Look, there're the Four Peaks; those are the Mazatzals."

His passengers stared far to the west, where four jagged crests and a fifth tiny one reared sharp against the cloud-banked sky. Seven and a half thousand feet tall, they towered above the lower Superstitions to the south. Since the beginning of mankind these peaks had been guardians to the desert peoples. They had marked the end of the world, and beyond them one might not venture. They had been given many names by their beholders; some had tried to minimize their majesty and called them "Four brothers and little sister"; the first American pioneers, a matter-of-fact race disinclined to imagery, had named them the Four Peaks; some of the Apache tribes had called them the "four terrible horns of the Thunder Gods," seeing in them portentous embodiment of their own sacred number; but few had ever beheld them without awe. Nor did Amanda.

"Is it near those peaks that we search?" she asked faintly.

"No," said Dart, "beyond them to the north."

They paused at the little hamlet of Roosevelt to buy cold drinks and petrol, then they wound along the shores of the vast lake until they reached the dam, and they crossed it, leaving behind the Apache trail which they had been following. The trail continued through magnificent scenery towards Phœnix, and was a popular tourist route for the adventurous. But the road they now followed became far worse, narrow and dangerous, as it clung to the precipitous indented sides of the lake.

For hours they saw nobody, they were alone on the road, and Dart, moved by an interior pressure of his own, suddenly began to speak of the history of this Tonto Basin. Hugh did not listen; he had covered his mouth with a bandanna and gone to sleep.

But Amanda, at first indifferent though surprised that Dart could be so talkative, soon found her interest fastened. Only sixty years ago this wide, pleasant valley had been Arizona's "dark and bloody ground." Here over and over again man had killed man in fear and in greed. The Graham–Tewkesbury feud had been a struggle between white men for the land. It had started ludicrously enough in the classic conflict between sheep-herders and cattle-men, and finished in an orgy of purposeless killing, still inexplicable to those who had watched in horror from the outside.

"How queer," said Amanda, "that that should happen; where there's so much land, surely there is room for everybody."

"Do we white men ever believe there's enough of anything?" said Dart.

She looked at him curiously. This did not sound like him. She thought of the sidewalk encounter with John Whitman this morning. It had seemed to her no more than a trifling incident, and one more proof of Dart's different reactions from other people. Perhaps it had been more than that. But she had put away from her the struggle to understand him.

Dart began to speak again, in a detached and musing voice, as though he wished to fill space with inconsequential sound, and the story he told was again of violence. He spoke of the Battle of the Caves which had taken place not far from Roosevelt Dam, which they had recently crossed, but long before the dam had been built, when the Salt River still pursued its ancient course. This battle had been one of the decisive victories in General Crook's campaign against the Apaches. Here 320 United States soldiers had trapped 76 Apache men, women, and children in a cave and caused their massacre.

Tanosay's aunt had been trapped in that cave too, but this Dart did not say. Instead he commented in the same judicial voice, "It was of course necessary to subjugate and subdue the Indians in any way possible. They were vicious and treacherous, and there wasn't room in this country for both races."

Again she was startled, for his tone was serious. How often she had heard him make a remark like that in sarcasm, in irony, but now there was no irony. He's siding with *us*, she thought, how strange, but the realization gave her no warmth.

"Do you think we'll make Staghorn all right tonight?" she asked.

Dart glanced up at the north-western sky. During the last hour thunderheads had been piling up on the Mazatzals. "If the road doesn't get so slick we can't stay on it. We've got to cross the range yet."

They made it across the mountains to Staghorn by one o'clock that night, and long before they drew up beside the two dark log cabins in a clearing of pines, Amanda had lost much of her new-found confidence. It had duly rained, a brief shower, but they had skidded down switchbacks and into culverts. The staunch little Ford had failed twice, once by blowing out a tyre, and again by jarring loose the ignition. Both these emergencies had been fixed by Dart while Hugh stood by holding the flash-light and cursing and shivering, for it had turned freezing cold. While they were fixing the tyre a great black form had loomed out of the woods, reared up, and stared at them. Amanda had screamed, and Hugh, dropping the flash-light, whipped out his Colt ·44 from the holster and fired. But the great form lumbered away.

"Bear," said Dart, watching, then turned back to the tyre.

Amanda made no further sound, steeling herself to realize that the true ordeal had not yet begun. She set her jaw and endured the rest of that ride.

Staghorn consisted of a one-room general store and a cabin behind it, both made of rough yellow pine. It was run by a corpulent old-timer known as Payson Pete, because he had lived in Payson most of his sixty years. He had, however, been born farther north under the shadow of the Mogollon Rim, to Mormon pioneers. He had lived in and around Gila County all his life, nor wished to go farther afield. In truth, there was no need to, for Gila Country contained an example of every type of western attraction—desert, valleys, mountains, mining, and the open range—everything but a city, and for cities Pete had no use.

He had once been a hell-raising cow-puncher, a maverick among sober, industrious Mormons, but of late years, since setting up the isolated little store which catered to an occasional prospector, sheepherd, or hunter, he had grown both fat and placid. His wife Molly was as fat as himself, for they lived on baked beans, canned spaghetti, smoked pork, and pies. Eating

had become a satisfactory pastime for the many days and sometimes weeks when no customers came near Staghorn.

Pete and Molly slept well, too. After the arrival of the Dartland Ford, neither the barking of the little terrier nor the men's
shouts awakened them. Dart finally pounded on the cabin door
until Pete waddled out in his night-shirt, clutching a blanket
around him with one hand and a candle in the other.

"Howdy, folks," he called, yawning. "You lost? You took
the wrong turn matter of fifteen miles back off the Bush Highway, that's what it is."

"We're not tourists," said Dart impatiently, "and we're not
lost. We aim to do a little camping over towards the Verde. We
hoped you could outfit us."

Pete was startled. He had been fooled by Dart's cultivated
eastern accent, and he couldn't see the three very clearly in the
darkness. "Reckon I could," he said dubiously, "if your wants
ain't too fancy. We'll see in the morning. You kin sleep in the
store. The stove's going. Make yourselves t'home, folks." He
yawned and retired to his cabin.

The Dartlands and Hugh took their host at his word. They
hauled an old bearskin and a couple of cheap saddle blankets
down from the shelves in the store, wrapped themselves in
separate cocoons, and settled down on the floor by the stove.
And they slept heavily.

When Amanda awoke the store was filled with dazzling sunlight, the exhilaration of pine-scented air, and the smell of coffee
from the cabin behind.

Amanda stretched, pleased that she was scarcely stiff despite
six hours on the floor, and that her zeal for the adventure had
returned. She sat up and looked across the store to the place
where Dart had lain, but he was already gone, had folded his
bearskin, returned it to the shelf, and removed his own blanket.
Behind the stove Hugh still snored. She got up and glanced at
Hugh as she passed him, then turned away embarrassed. In the
nakedness of sleep she found him repellent and yet almost
pathetic. He frowned as he slept, his bristling brows drawn together as though in pain. His slack lips twitched spasmodically.
Above the pasty, freckled skin of his forehead she saw his scalp
through the thinning sandy hair. He looked more than his
thirty-eight years, and yet she could see for the first time the
sort of little boy Hugh must have been. A tough, cruel little

boy, sullenly impervious to authority, careful always to hit first lest he be hit, and perhaps very insecure once, long ago before he had learned to transmute fear into aggression.

Had any woman ever really loved him? she wondered. But then, what is love?

> Love's but a frailty of the mind,
> When 'tis not with ambition joined. . . .

As she paused on the doorstep of Staghorn's general store in the wilds of central Arizona, this couplet flashed through Amanda's mind. She saw the blue book which had contained it, *Restoration Dramatists*; she saw the whiteness of the page, and the black underscorings and exclamation marks put around the couplet by a girl's enthusiastic pencil. But it wasn't Amanda who had so approvingly underscored that cynical passage. It was Jean, years earlier.

And when Amanda in her turn had used the book at Vassar, she had violently disagreed with Jean's markings. What a romantic little fool I was! Then Amanda thought of Tim Merrill, deliberately re-evaluating the decision she had made that night at El Castillo when she returned to Dart. No, Tim was not the answer either. Her disenchantment had been complete. It was independence that she wanted, beholden to no man. An island unto myself, like Dart.

Dart was already eating at the rough table in the cabin when Amanda entered. He said "Hello" coolly, then returned at once to his consultation with Pete, who sat at the head of the table gorging on flapjacks.

Molly had cooked breakfast for them: coffee with condensed milk, sourdough bread, and a mountain of flapjacks drowned in corn syrup. She trundled her bulk back and forth between cook-stove and table heaping the plates, and urging in a thick comfortable voice, "Eat hearty now, folks. Don't be bashful. You need plenty of vittles in the stummick if you're going to hit the trail."

Molly was curious about the party, not because the tall young man offered no special explanation for the camping trip—folks who turned up in this neck of the woods were often reticent about their business—but because there was a girl with them. This was almost unprecedented, and Molly hadn't figured it out yet. A pretty girl, too, with big eyes, blue as cornflowers, though awful quiet, and much too skinny for Molly's taste. She had a wedding-ring, so she must belong to one or the other of the men, but Molly was jiggered if she could make out which, even after the older sandy-haired one came in and sat down grumpy as a bear to his breakfast. Because none of the three said anything to the others. The girl didn't say anything at all, the sandy-haired fellow just grunted from time to time, and the tall young one who was nice-looking in a way, and seemed to be the boss, just talked with Pete about supplies. They didn't want many supplies, either. Pete's moon-face began to look crestfallen. He'd decided they must be some queer kind of dude after all, maybe artists or rock-hounds, and he could unload a lot of fools' stuff on them which had been gathering dust on the shelves for a dog's age. But he couldn't. The young fellow said right out they were short of cash, and it seemed he knew exactly what he needed.

The first thing was a pack burro. Pete had a couple of those, grazing in the corral down by the creek. They were kind of wild since Pete had got too heavy to use them much, but the young fellow said that didn't matter, and paid five dollars for one, with rope and pack bags thrown in. He sure knew his way around.

"You'll need horses, of course," Pete said hopefully. "You can get some over at the Seven-Bar Ranch down by Sunflower; I'll fix it for you so they'll be here by tomorrow."

But the young fellow didn't want horses, and didn't want to wait till tomorrow. They were going to start right away, as soon as they'd stocked up.

"But there's a fair trail down to the Verde, kind o' rough through Deadman's Creek, but you could make it on horseback," objected Pete, who had the usual western horror of going anywhere on foot. "Them horses wouldn't cost much to hire."

The young fellow still said no. Pete shrugged his fat shoulders and gave up, contenting himself with what he could sell them: flour, bacon, jerky, baked beans, coffee, canned tomatoes, condensed milk, a box of Hershey bars, and matches. They'd brought cigarettes with them from Globe. They bought cartridges and canteens too, and they borrowed an empty five-gallon can for water.

"They're never fixin' to just go down to the Verde," said Pete in an aside to his wife, as he viewed Dart's expert loading of the burro. "They're aiming for a lot rougher country than that." He noted the miner's pick that Dart was slinging on the pack, and he lumbered over, heavily jocular.

"Say, you folks—if you wasn't headin' into the wrong mountains I'd say you was after the 'Lost Dutchman'!" He wheezed and chuckled, prodding Hugh in the ribs. "*That* mine's down in the Superstitions, they say, leastwise, a hull lot of suckers're for ever huntin' it. You won't find nothin' in the Matazals."

"Don't expect to," said Hugh curtly, moving away from the jovial finger. Dart continued loading the burro.

Pete, nothing daunted, turned to Amanda, who stood silently watching. "Say, ma'am," he said, chuckling again, "d'you know why these here mountains're called the Matazals?"

She knew that they were not spelled that way on the map, but even Dart gave them that local pronunciation. She shook her head repressively, dreading further curiosity.

"They say that once, mebbe two, three hundred years ago there was a great Injun pow-pow up in them mountains up north. Now it's turrible rough country; I ain't ever been up in there myself, and I don't know anyone who has, but them 'Paches went, except they had an old chief was purty feeble, he wanted to go too, awful bad, but he couldn't make it. They had to leave him behind down in the valley. And the old chief was 'Mad-as-hell,' begging your pardon, lady—d'you get it?" he asked, anxiously, for the girl looked startled, her blue eyes wide, and the two men by the burro had both stopped and turned towards him as though this stock joke was something important, and like they expected something more.

Then Dart laughed. "Sure we get it." He pulled the rope again under the burro's belly and fastened it in a diamond hitch. "D'you ever see any Apaches round about here?" he asked casually.

Pete shook his head. "Naw. They's a few near Payson, but you want to see plenty 'Paches you got to go over to the reservation. *That* ain't what you're after, is it?" Six years ago there'd been a couple fellows from the East got lost off the Highway and wandered into Staghorn. From something called the Smithsonian in Washington they'd said they'd come, and they was making a study of "modern Apache living conditions," and they'd asked a lot of damfool questions nobody could answer but an Indian, and ten to one *he* wouldn't. "There ain't *nothin'*

up beyond here, mister," said Pete firmly to Dart, "exceptin' a
mess of granite and malapie; ain't even been surveyed exceptin'
from an aireoplane, and I don't advise you to go into it. Especially with a young lady."

"Oh, we'll be very careful," interjected Amanda, smiling at
him. "This is just a little camping trip. Just for fun." She was
in a fever to be off, but the charming smile she had given Pete
to shut him up had the opposite effect, for it awakened chivalry
in his massive bosom, and he examined Dart's preparation with
a new and disapproving eye.

"Yore travellin' turrible light for 'fun,' " he said. "What's
the lady goin' to sleep in? They ain't enough beddin' for a gel."

"Oh, I can manage as well as the men can," said Amanda
hastily. She had agreed to no quarter, no special consideration.

But Dart paused and turned. He did not look at Amanda, but
he gave Pete a considering gaze, weighing the justice of his
objection, then he said, "Maybe you're right. You got a heavy
blanket for sale, and a poncho?"

"You bet!" Pete waddled happily back to the store.

"Oh but Dart—you don't have to—we shouldn't spend the
money." She almost put her hand on his arm, then drew it
back.

"As long as you insist on coming, it'd be foolish to take a
chance of your getting sick, nuisance for all of us," said Dart.
He walked over to the Ford, which was parked behind the store
to await their return, and began to stow away the gear that they
were not taking.

Hugh snorted, looking up from his cartridge belt which he
had been filling. "At least I won't have to be nauseated by the
cooing of lovebirds on this expedition," he said. "That's always
something."

She flushed, and walking up to the burro tried to pat it. The
animal bared yellow teeth and whickered unpleasantly, backing
off. But it had stood perfectly quiet for Dart.

Damn Dart, she thought violently, resenting this further proof
of their helplessness without him. She set her jaw and approached the burro again, but he laid his ears back and snapped
his teeth two inches from her hand.

"Tonto ain't used to women," observed Pete, advancing from
the store. "You'd best keep away from him, ma'am."

Lovely, she thought. A happy little trip into the mountains

with three male animals who don't want me along. But I'm going to do it, and I'm going to get back, and I'm going to be rich. Pockets full of gold, and then get out of this hellish country for ever.

"All set?" said Dart, coming up to them from the car. "Let's get going." He unhitched the burro and held the lead rope in his hand. "So long," he said cordially to Pete, and to Molly who had come out of the cabin to join her husband. "We'll be back when you see us." He started off towards the edge of the clearing and the trail through the chaparral growth of manzanita and scrub oak. The burro followed, his bell tinkling.

"Good-bye," cried Amanda warmly, suddenly seeing reassurance in the two solid figures by the log cabin. "Thanks for everything. You've been swell." She followed Dart and the burro at a respectful distance from the latter's heels.

Hugh made no farewells. He did not look back. His head throbbed, and despite the water he had drunk that morning, his mouth and throat were dry as cotton. He had a quart of grain alcohol in his knapsack, and a filled flask in his left hip pocket, but they would have to be rationed until he craved a drink even worse than now.

He'd had another bottle of hooch hidden in the car, and had tried to slip it into his blanket roll so that Dart wouldn't notice it when he was loading the burro. But Dart had known at once, and put the bottle back into the car, saying pleasantly enough, "No dice, Hugh. We'll have enough trouble hauling water without bothering with this stuff."

Like a goddam drill sergeant. Wish to God I'd gone into this thing on my own. I could have figured out the map. He always thinks he knows it all. You'd think he'd come off his high horse after the fool he made of himself at the mine, but he's worse than ever.

So the three of them plodded along the easy, well-marked trail.

Dart had closed his disciplined mind to all resentments past or present. His faculties were concentrated on the task ahead. His nostrils sniffed the high pungent mountain air, and he fell into a long easy stride while his eyes instinctively noted old friends along the trail: the jojoba bush, rich with oil-bearing berries like olives; piñons, the delicious nuts not ripe enough yet for use; the algerita, whose berries would yield an agreeable jelly. He was happy as he had not been in weeks. His soul breathed deep and felt at home. He was again master of his fate, freed from the turmoil of people and their inexplicable stupidities—except, of course, for the two who trailed along behind him. For them he felt a remote tolerance, and the responsibility of a leader to those in his charge. They were a nuisance, undoubtedly, greenhorns were always a nuisance to the mountain-wise, but they must be accepted as they were, in the frame in which they now all found themselves. Amanda had rejected him as a man, as a lover—so be it. He could look upon her without desire, repudiating all that they had been to each other, as she wished it repudiated.

He was no squaw man, to be dependent on her softness and her childish whims. The words "squaw man" came into his thoughts, not because they were Apache, but quite the opposite —as an echo from a sentimentalized play he had seen in Boston as a boy and thought very silly—but they also reminded him of Hugh's use of the term "squaw" yesterday morning in Globe, and of the conversation with John Whitman.

This reminder held considerable pain. Did it also hold the threat of danger? He tried to remember the look in the Indian's eyes, to remember the exact words they had both spoken, but his memory was clouded by the emotion he had felt. And he dismissed his uneasiness as ridiculous. What threat could there be from a young Indian cow-puncher bound on a Saturday outing with his family!

Dart shrugged his shoulders, pulled out his map and studied it. The trail down to Deadman's Creek was clearly marked, then they should leave it where it turned west to the Verde. They must cross to the other side and branch north-east into uncharted country.

The next three days seemed interminable to Amanda. They blurred into a jumble of plodding climbs up, and stumbling, sliding descents, all additionally hazed by discomforts. Her feet swelled, and blisters rubbed off her heels despite Hugh's grudging first-aid. He was having trouble with his own feet, and was none too sympathetic.

While they were in the lower altitudes down in the canyons, the vicious cat's-claw and wait-a-bit bushes scratched her groping hands and tore shreds from her levis. On the tops of mesas a biting wind rushed at them and she shivered miserably, being usually wet to the knees from splashing through whatever little creek had run through the bottom of the previous canyon. There was still plenty of water—too much, since each evening at sundown it showered, while Amanda sat huddled in the poncho under a brush shelter Dart would cut for them. The only moments of respite came after the rain stopped and they ate their supper while warming themselves by the campfire. But she was too tired to stay awake long, and the first nights she fell asleep as she chewed the last mouthful of rank bacon, or of half-cooked bloody rabbit Hugh had shot.

Hugh suffered, too, though not in silence. His slack muscles ached, his wind was bad, and he kept up a continuous *sotto voce* swearing while they were on the trail, occasionally taking a surreptitious pull from his flask when Dart was not looking. Neither Hugh nor Amanda was particularly useful with camp chores, though the girl made feeble efforts, but Dart had expected nothing better, and he left his charges pretty much alone to break themselves in. They'd toughen up all right. They'd have to, for they had not yet reached the base of the granite peaks they now saw to the north, and for which Dart was heading. He was sure that these were the mountains indicated on the Mimbreño's copper map, for the two peaks seen from this angle tilted slightly together at the top, like an inverted V, and the Mimbreño had made an arrow beneath this symbol pointing upward to it.

He explained this to Hugh and Amanda on the fourth night, as they lay on their blankets around the campfire.

"Christ," said Hugh, staring across shadowed canyons and a stand of yellow pines towards the mountains Dart indicated. "D'you mean to say we've got to get over to those damn things? I should think we'd be *some place* by now." He rubbed his swollen feet gloomily.

Dart laughed. "You want to turn back?"

Hugh scowled, staring out to the far horizon. "No."

"Well, I wouldn't turn back if you wanted to," said Dart, stretching and yawning. "I'm going to see what's up there."

"Gold——" said Amanda softly, as though to reassure herself, and she tried to visualize a glittering wall of gold somewhere beneath those tilted mountains.

"I'm pretty sure that's the place." Dart squinted his keen eyes and pointed. "See that darkish blur below the peaks?

That's volcanic—the malpais they all mentioned, the hatchings marked on the Mimbreño's map too, I guess. We'll have to cross it."

The other two craned and peered through the swift-descending twilight, but they could not see what Dart saw.

They were silent, all smoking.

The campfire of piñons crackled aromatically, sending out little sparks. The western sky became streaked with mauve and ruby red, and the evening star sprang out in trembling yellow light.

Fifty feet beyond their camp site Tonto the burro cropped rhythmically, browsing on the dense prickly forage, and his bell, tingled from time to time. The night wind blew gently past their shelter, and Amanda was conscious of peace. Her young body had adjusted itself to discomfort, and she was aware of an entirely new sensation. For the first time she felt without resistance the insidious beauty and the mystery of the wilderness.

And then an owl hooted, a hollow, eerie sound from the gathering darkness behind them. Dart jumped. Wheeling sharply around he leapt to his feet.

The other two gazed at him in astonishment. "What the hell!" said Hugh, sitting up. "What's the matter?"

Dart stooped in one lightning motion and snatched his gun from the top of his bedroll. He stood holding the gun and staring into the darkness.

Then the owl hooted again from farther off, and soared, flapping its great wings, into the sky.

Dart released his breath audibly. He put the gun down beside him and sat down again on the blanket. Then he laughed. "Atavistic reaction," he said in apology to the two startled faces. "The Apaches consider owls very bad luck. It took me by surprise."

Hugh made a disgusted noise and resumed rubbing his feet. "I'm glad something can take you by surprise, Superman. My God, I thought, from the way you acted, you expected a howling band of redskins to jump at us. Grade B Westerns, that's the way you looked."

"I suppose I did, at that," said Dart, laughing. He was annoyed with himself for that blind reaction, though it had not entirely sprung from childhood superstition and Saba's fear of owls, which were supposed to be the spirits of the unquiet dead. There had been a further memory awakened by that owl's hoot. Hoots like that had been one of the rallying cries of Apaches before a raid, and Tanosay, in telling tales of the old days, had often reproduced the sound for a listening grandson.

Dart glanced again at his gun, and then at the brilliant camp-fire. Its glow and the white smoke rising from it against the night sky could certainly be seen for miles. Wiser, after this, to camp in lower, more hidden, spots—and yet, what nonsense! That was a real owl.

"We'd better turn in now," he said, his voice harsh and peremptory. "There's plenty of tough going ahead."

When Amanda lay rolled in her blankets, her head on her knapsack, she thought about the owl incident, and a warmer feeling for Dart came back to her heart. She had never before seen him discomfited or truly apologetic—except, said the sudden voice of truth, the morning she had lost the baby and he had sat by her bed. She had been frozen to him then, deaf to what he said, fathoms deep in her own resentment that he had failed her, and that he had not somehow divined that her frantic efforts to help him by visiting Big Ruby, by rushing to Calise, had been contributing factors to the baby's loss.

"That's not quite fair. . . . I love you." His words came back to her now, as she had not heard them then. She raised her head and looked across the ashes of the campfire to Dart's long, dark form. It lay quiet, and she heard even breathing.

She nestled down into her cocoon, and lay awake for a little while staring up at the brilliant starlit sky.

It took them three more days to creep up and down the savagely indented country to the base of the tilted peaks, and many were their vicissitudes. Earlier they had seen dried sheep-dung and fragments of wool caught on bushes, and had known that at least some solitary sheepherder had once passed this way. But now they entered a desolate land where it seemed no man had ever been or would wish to go. Even Dart quailed before the precipitous box canyon that they must cross, and they lost hours while he reconnoitred back and forth on the rim seeking the easiest way. They pushed and hauled the burro over slide rock and up boulder-strewn creek beds, for Dart did not dare leave their pack carrier behind unless they were forced to.

Dart during the first days had had no trouble finding springs or filling their five-gallon can from the creeks they forded, but after they entered the waste of dead lava, they found no more water. Bare and grey as the mountains of the moon, the malpais stretched ahead of them in massive crenellations and rounded pits that looked as soft as the ashes they had once been, but were actually as hard and sharp as knives. The human beings' tough leather soles and the burro's unshod hoofs were soon criss-crossed with myriad tiny cuts.

The night they were forced to camp on the lava waste was a night of dismal foreboding, and there was no firewood to warm them or cook their supper. They huddled down into a partial shelter formed by a semicircle of black rocks as silent and sinister as the Druidic circle Amanda had seen at Stonehenge. She ate cold beans from a can and chewed the tough salt jerky, shivering in her blankets, for they had reached an altitude of 7,000 feet. She thought with growing amazement of the date. It was Saturday night again, it must be September 9, and a year ago she and Dart were on the *Bremen*. In a kaleidoscope of swirling lights, she saw the dance floor and the balloons and champagne and the German orchestra playing selections from *Fledermaus*; tara *dum* da da, *dum* da da, she heard Peggy Gordon singing, and the creaking of the ship and the waves swishing by. The kaleidoscope twirled again, its coloured pieces flashing, and then it fell apart, splintering into darkness and the deathly quiet of the black volcanic rocks.

How is it that I'm here? So far from all I know—dislocated into a world where none of the emotions I have ever had return to give me guidance?

She looked at Dart, and thought for a second of leaping hope that he met her eyes in answer. But she wasn't sure; there was not enough light to see for sure. Still held in the dream-like suspension, she might have spoken to him, she might have said, not in appeal but with grave confidence, "Do you remember——?" But Hugh shattered the weird silence.

"Jesus, what swill!" he cried, flinging his empty bean can far into the darkness, where it clattered and cannonaded over the naked rocks. "Where do we go from here, dear Captain, or do we just sit here for eternity, mouldering on the malapie? . . . That's good," he said viciously, "mouldering on the malapie. I like that." He raised his flask and took a long gurgling pull.

"I trust there's water in that flask," said Dart grimly.

"Well, you trust wrong, my lad. . . . Here, have a swig," he said to Amanda, "it'll warm you up." He thrust the flask at her.

She sniffed it and pushed it back. "Oh, Hugh, I can't drink straight alcohol, and I wish *you* wouldn't."

Hugh shrugged and took another pull.

"Cut it out, Hugh," said Dart. "We've got to get out of here soon as it's light, and I can't haul any drunks along."

That they were in a situation of considerable danger tonight Dart knew very well, though he had not impressed it on the others. Everything depended on their finding the lost valley soon, and its water and game to supplement the provisions the burro carried. Prudence demanded that he ration these for the trip back, at least as far as the lower country, where they might hunt again, and where there was water. But they must get over this wilderness of dead lava. Already they had finished their canteens, and one could not count on rain, which never came when it was needed. The emergency can would not go far among three humans and an animal. And worse than that, the burro had gone lame today after his hind leg had slipped between two boulders. Fortunately, burros were the toughest little beasts in the world. They could exist on any kind of browse, but here on the malpais there was nothing. As if in affirmation, Tonto that moment stuck his head around the rocks and brayed mournfully.

"Hee-haw!" said Hugh. "Hee-haw. That's what I think too. Now, Dart dear, I've been a very good boy on this jaunt, but there're limits. I don't like this God-blasted place we're in, an' I'm going to get drunk." He had finished the flask, and forgetting concealment he began to fumble in his knapsack for the spare bottle.

He found his wrists held in a vice-like grip, and the knapsack was taken away from him. "I'm sorry," said Dart. He extracted the bottle, pulled the cork, and the fumes of grain alcohol floated through the chill air.

It took a moment for Hugh to understand, then he stumbled to his feet and lunged across the lava hollow. "Goddam you," he whispered: "goddam you!" His wavering fist crashed past Dart's head in the darkness.

"Oh, sit down, Hugh," said Dart impatiently, giving him a slight push. Hugh collapsed back on his bedroll, breathing hard.

Amanda shrank away from him until she felt the harsh pitted lava pressing through her blankets against her back, but she watched Hugh unconsciously, still frightened by the ugly moment, and then she thought she saw his hand gleaming white against the darkness of his clothes, and moving slowly. She watched uncomprehending, and then gasped:

"Hugh! What are you doing?"

The white spot stopped moving.

"What is it, Andy?" asked Dart from across the hollow.

"Nothing, I guess," she answered, trying to laugh. "This place is spooky. I'm seeing things." Hugh was half drunk and full of the violent temper he often showed, but he was Dart's friend. It had been her own foolishness or a trick of the dim light that had given her the impression that his hand was creeping stealthily back towards his revolver. I'm nuts, she thought, but the two rough little words did not reassure her. This witches' sabbath of amorphous black rocks and echoing space had little to do with sanity.

"Dart," she said very low, half hoping that he wouldn't hear; "I'm frightened. I thought I'd got over my fear of the mountains, but this——"

He did hear her, and across the darkness he said, "Don't be frightened, Andy. You've done magnificently, better than I ever thought possible."

A warm pleasure suffused her. He had never praised her like that before, never treated her with the dignity of an equal.

"Dart," she said softly, "do you think we'll find it soon, the lost valley? It seems farther away here than it did in Lodestone."

"Well, I hope it isn't," said Dart, laughing a little.

"It's queer," she went on, emboldened by the greater ease between them, "I don't seem to care about it the way I did in Lodestone. I can't seem to remember the gold. I don't mean I want to turn back, of course——"

Hugh stirred suddenly, and his voice, harsh and thickened, exploded between them. "You've got to remember the gold! It's the only thing. The only thing. Viola knew that, didn't you, darling!"

The two Dartlands started and turned. Amanda's heart began to pound. That sudden coarse voice exploding the silence frightened her nearly as much as the motion she thought she had seen.

"He's just pie-eyed," said Dart quietly. "God knows how much straight alcohol he's had. Better come over here, Andy."

Amanda obeyed thankfully, picking up her blankets and settling near Dart away from that lumpish, heavy-breathing figure. It went on muttering, and then the voice broke out again on a shriller key. "The Russian Empress wants her gold. Waiting at the St. Regis for her gold. Hughie'll bring the gold, darling—this time he'll bring it and you'll be stretching out your white arms and smiling like the night we—we——" The voice trailed off into incoherence.

Amanda drew nearer to Dart. "How horrible," she whispered, appalled by that shrill, unfamiliar voice. "What can he be talking about, or is he—he completely off?"

For a time Dart did not answer, then he broke through his first instinct of reticence. "I think he's talking about his wife, poor guy."

"His wife——"she repeated in astonishment, but she did not question Dart as she once would have; neither feminine curiosity nor the old annoyance that Dart told her so little seemed important here in the lost primeval world of rocks and silence.

The muttering figure across the lava pit subsided after a while, and they all slept a little until the shadows beneath the cliffs turned grey, and a blood-red glow tipped the wall of granite peaks ahead of them.

CHAPTER THIRTEEN

DART left their encampment in the lava pit as soon as there was light enough for him to pick his way among the pitted jumble of rocks. He told Amanda not to worry if he were delayed in returning. It was imperative that he find some clue to their proper direction before starting out with a partially crippled burro. Not to speak of Hugh, who was still snoring, huddled in his blankets.

"If he comes to, try to get some water down him," added Dart grimly, "but for God's sake don't waste any."

She nodded, too dispirited at his leaving her alone for speech. She watched his tall form merge into the dead volcanic greyness. She sipped a little water from her canteen, ate a dry, crumbling piece of pilot biscuit, lit a cigarette, and settled down to wait.

Dart climbed steadily, skirting glazed crevasses and fire-blackened ridges where the lava had buckled and cooled æons ago. He headed for the granite barrier to the east. Here, from this close view, the peaks could no longer be seen as separated; they reared up, one unbroken and apparently impenetrable stone expanse, into the sky. And yet somewhere along this expanse he hoped to find the crevice or portal which led into the lost valley.

After an hour of scrambling he reached the edge of the lava flow, and was relieved to see a fringe of grama-grass struggling up from a seam between the black glass-like obsidian and the sharp granite wall. Here at least would be browse for the burro, but Dart could see no sign of water.

A tumbled mass of pinkish diorite jutted out from the rest of the granite, and Dart clambered to the top of it. On this vantage-point he shaded his eyes with his hand and took a quiet, concentrated survey. Far off to the north-east there jutted up an abrupt purple shelf rising a thousand feet above the tops of the pines in the plain below. That was the Mogollon Rim. To the west, perhaps only twenty miles by air, though three times that on foot, he caught thin blue glimpses of the Verde's convulsions as it meandered southward to merge eventually with the chain of man-made lakes on the Salt River.

He turned and scanned the granite wall behind as far as his eye could reach. Then he laid his compass and the official contour map and the Mimbreño's copper disc on the sliced surface of the diorite rock beside him and squinted at each in turn, checking his calculations. There was no doubt as to their general location, and if indeed the valley existed at all, it must be in there behind the granite. But where? In which direction. The rough cliffs stretched for many miles. He gazed again at the Mimbreño's map, at the arrow which pointed towards the tilted peaks that were no longer visible, at the jumbled cross-hatchings which he had assumed to represent the malpais. There were other faint symbols scratched apparently at random on the copper; wavy lines and dots, and a tiny round object with outstretched legs like a beetle, and for these he had no interpretation at all.

Doubt came to him then, and a wash of black discouragement. What rational basis had he after all for belief in this fantastic project? Nothing but Indian legends, Spanish legends, and an emotional desire for escape as immature in essence as the motives he had once derided in Hugh and Amanda.

He looked back across the malpais in the direction of the lava pit where he had left them waiting, and he shook his head. He scrambled down from the diorite and retraced his steps around the crevasses and ridges, shouting out as he drew nearer until Amanda's clear answering hail guided him to the hollow. It was now full morning, and the lava waste had grown blazing hot.

"I'm so *glad* you're back," Amanda cried, running to meet him. "I was getting worried. Dart, did you find anything?"

He shook his head. "I'm beginning to wonder if there's anything to find." He looked at Hugh, who sat hunched over, his head in his hands, and had not moved as Dart approached. He looked at the lame burro which was leaning against a rock, its ears drooping. "I think we'd better try to turn back," Dart said, smiling a little.

Amanda swallowed, staring at him with round unbelieving eyes. "Dart! You can't mean that! Not when we're so near. We couldn't turn back now."

She stood there on the edge of the hollow; slender and valiant in her frayed levis and her dirty cotton shirt, with her little head

held high, her ruffled curls glinting in the pitiless sunlight. The
unconscious gallantry of her carriage and the limpid honesty of
her sea-blue eyes reminded him of that moment on the boat
when he had first really seen her.

"It would be wiser to turn back, Andy," he said slowly. "I
don't want to risk—risk serious trouble for you—and Hugh. Not
for a mirage."

"It isn't a mirage," she cried. "I know it, I feel it. We're
very near. It isn't like you to give up."

Dart bent his head, looking deep into her eyes. "You still
believe I can get you there, to this place you want so much?"

"Oh yes!" she cried, surprised that he should ask this or feel
doubt of her trust in him regardless of what other doubts she
might have.

"For Christ's sake, you two—why don't you get moving?"
snarled Hugh, raising his head from his hands. "You haven't
even loaded the donkey yet!" He opened his medical kit with
shaking fingers, and pouring three white pills from a vial, he
swallowed them with water from the canteen.

"Okay," said Dart suddenly. "We'll go on. Only, the burro
can't carry his usual load, and no matter *how* you feel, you'll
have to do some toting yourself. And you're not going to like
what's ahead, either of you."

The moment of reluctance and indecision had passed. He
was, in fact, ashamed of it, especially as he did not quite understand it. The reluctance had been partly born of disbelief in
their mission, of course, partly of genuine concern for the safety
of his charges, but there was another ingredient which he did not
wish to examine.

After they finally got going across the malpais again there
were hours of sweating and straining, each one of them carrying
some of the provisions to lighten the pack on the disabled burro,
and even so they had to leave a pile of heavy cans behind in
the lava pit. Hugh stumbled and fell often, and the sweat poured
from his body, until the effects of the alcohol passed off, but he
endured grimly, and when they reached the granite barrier and
the strip of grama-grass, he flung himself headlong, and closed
his eyes.

The little burro brayed with excitement when he saw the
grama, and began to crop it voraciously, but it was fairly dry
browse, and soon even a burro would need water. The canteens

were still full, but the emergency can contained scarcely a gallon. Dart searched the sky anxiously—there were thunderheads far to the north near the Mogollon Rim, but above their heads only a cloudless greenish sky fading into dusk. Except for the burro's forage, they were no better off than they had been the night before. There was still nothing with which to make a fire. He opened a can of tomatoes for himself and Amanda, and they sucked the semi-liquid fruit down thirstily. Hugh would not stir.

Amanda, needing privacy, wandered off a little way from the two men. Suddenly Dart heard her voice calling out in wild excitement. "Dart! Come here! Dart!"

He grabbed his gun and ran around the rocks towards her.

"Look!" she cried. "What's that?"

He cocked his gun, peering, expecting a rattler.

"No, higher—on the rock itself—something's drawn there!"

He followed her pointing finger, gave a smothered exclamation, and pulled out his flash-light. The yellow beam illumined a round object with feelers like a beetle, and an arrow to the left of it.

"Yes, it seems to be an Indian pictograph," he said after a moment. He took out the Mimbreño's copper disc and compared the two symbols, while Amanda craned over his arm breathing hard. "They're the same!" she cried. "We *are* on the right track. I *knew* we were."

He played the flash-light beam again on the rock. The figures had been incised, probably with an obsidian chip, deep into the surface of the granite, and there were faint traces of black pigment at the bottom of the grooves. It was clear enough now that the beetle-like object was really a sun with rays, the ancient symbol for a goodly place, a land with water and game. And the arrow next to it pointed north. "Yes, we're on the right track," Dart said. And in that moment it seemed to him that a chill wind blew across his neck, and the hieroglyph above his head spared down at him malevolently, neither beetle nor sun, but an unwinking, baleful eye. He recognized then the other factor in his earlier desire to turn back.

Am I after all a coward, he thought? Could it be that for all his education and practical Yankee intelligence, and despite his repudiation of the other racial strain, that superstition and taboo could still overpower him with the dark magic of fear!

He stood there by the pictograph, denying this fear, and disgusted to find that it did not lessen, that, instead, it seeped and spread like oily black water and mingled with another type of fear. He wheeled around suddenly, turning the flash-light on the slope below them, playing it from side to side along the granite wall.

"What is it?" said Amanda. "Why do you do that?"

He snapped off the flash-light. "Oh, it's nothing. Come on, let's get back to Hugh and tell him the news." That sensation of being watched by eyes in the night was a common one in the wilderness. I'm turning jittery as an old woman, he thought, more than ever annoyed with himself, and into the rousing of Hugh and the narration of their discovery he put by way of compensation an uncharacteristic amount of enthusiasm.

And this Hugh, whose head was clearer now, did not fail to note.

"So all you needed after all, my dear Dart, was a tiny bit of confirmation to get as gold-bit as the rest of us," he said disagreeably. "I've never seen you so gushing."

"But, Hugh!" cried Amanda, half laughing, "it's so thrilling. It's the first real certainty we've had."

"I'm quite aware of that." There was such venom in his tone that Amanda was silenced. She thought with some dismay that Hugh's extreme ill-temper had not faded with his drunkenness as it usually did, and she wondered if he remembered anything of what he had said last night—the ramblings about Viola.

Hugh did know, the tiny watcher that never quite slept in him had known, and he hated the Dartlands for having listened.

During the night, while they slept, Hugh got up and made his way down behind the rocks to see the pictograph for himself, but he could not find it in the darkness, not knowing just where to look, and as he clambered among the rocks his foot slipped and his ankle suffered a nasty wrench. Tears came to his eyes from the sudden pain, and from rage at his impotence. He limped back to camp, sat down on his bedroll, and examined his ankle. Nothing broken, anyway. He bound it up savagely with the ace bandage he had brought for emergencies. Just like that goddam burro, he thought, both of us crippled. He stared through the darkness at the sleeping Dartlands.

His body ached for a drink, as the pain in his ankle screamed for anodyne. He glared towards Dart again. Goddam him to hell. He rummaged in the medical kit, and brought out a hypodermic syringe and a little bottle of clear liquid. He sterilized the needle in a match flame, and punctured his arm. Not too much, just enough to dull the edge of pain and increase clarity of thought. He had no intention of again dimming his faculties.

All the next day they hunted along the base of the granite cliffs in the direction of the arrow, and Hugh limped along with them, refusing any help from either Dart or Amanda. By four o'clock it seemed that they must give up and struggle back to the strip of grama-grass where they had left the burro and their dwindling supplies.

The sun had beaten down all day from a flaming copper sky on to their sweating backs, and both Hugh and Amanda, heedless of Dart's objections, had before noon finished the last drops of water in their canteens. During the afternoon hours Amanda learned the first terrifying forerunners of the tortures of thirst. Her tongue grew thick, and her lips, already dried from days of exposure, cracked in two places. She moistened her mouth with water from Dart's canteen, ashamed that she should have to accept it from him, and sucked as he directed on a dried raisin which he gave her. And none of them mentioned the scanty quart of water which was all that was left in the can back with the burro.

So this is what it's like, Amanda thought; this is what I've read about a hundred times. And yet she felt little fear. That was because of Dart. As long as he was with her she felt safe. That's a funny thing, she thought, becoming a little lightheaded; I must tell him he's safe and cool as water, a still, safe lake the wind can't ruffle, deep and never changing, I must tell him. But she could not tell him, she could not see him anywhere, nor call him, for her thickened tongue clogged in her mouth. She sat down on a stone and leaned her head against the granite.

"Andy!"

She opened her eyes to Dart's urgent voice. He held her head back and poured the rest of the water from his canteen into her mouth. "I've found it! Come!"

She jumped to her feet, instantly revived, and Hugh came shuffling after them sullenly. They went only a little way farther, to an enormous diorite boulder that seemed to be part of the great cliff barrier and was not, for it was possible to squeeze behind it and up a slide rock slope to a crevice in the granite— a crevice wide enough for a man to pass through with out- stretched arms.

It seemed to be a tunnel leading into blackness, but as they came up flush with the entrance they saw a glimpse of slanting light twenty feet ahead.

"The 'portal'——" whispered Amanda, and she clutched Dart's arm. He stopped as she did, staring into the narrow rocky passage to the oblong of light at the far end.

Hugh came up to them, panting; it had taken him longer to climb up the slope behind the diorite boulder. He muttered something as he saw the two hesitate before the passage. He shoved roughly by them and limped through the darkness ahead. And they followed.

This crack in the igneous rocks had been made a million years ago when the volcano still poured its lava down the mountain- side, but the crack had been widened in places by the hand of man. There were the marks of flint axes along the walls.

The passage twisted and then widened. The three stepped out upon a ledge into the daylight.

"Ah——" whispered Amanda. Her knees weakened and her hands grew as cold as the rock she sank down on.

The forbidden valley lay below them, green and dark like jasper in the shadow of the overhanging cliffs. It was a tiny grassy park fringed with pines, stunted junipers, and golden aspens. At the far northern end a silver-white veil dropped down the canyon side, splashing crystal sparks into the shimmering air. Across the little canyon on the eastern wall, so near it seemed that she might reach across and touch it, a cavern yawned like a great mouth, enclosing a little city of stone. The slanting sun rays touched the square-piled buildings with rose and violet shadows. The buildings floated in a mist of enchantment in- finitely still and awesome, breathing the solemnity of a past which still endures, frozen into sleep, yet ever awaiting the enchanter's wand.

During the time that they all stood silent on the ledge, the impact of the lost canyon engulfed them each in emotion. For Amanda it was the magic of the fairy-tale, of nostalgic beauty yearned for and found, at the end of the rainbow—and she knew a moment of pure æsthetic joy.

Dart felt no joy, except fleeting relief that here was water at last. He gazed across the canyon at the frozen city of the Ancient Ones, and he thought, then it *is* here, and if it is really here, it is also forbidden, as Tanosay told me. And he was wearied of the conflict in his heart, he who had never before known conflict.

Hugh examined the valley and the pueblo in one quick, gleaming glance, and he jerked his head and smiled for the first time since they had left Lodestone. "Well, there's the cliff dwelling sure enough. How the hell do we get off this ledge and down to water? I never thought I'd think of water before gold!"

Both Dartlands started and turned towards him. Dart gave himself an interior shake. His brooding eyes lightened.

"Yes, of course," he said briskly. "Here, I think this must be the old trail."

He picked a path down among the great boulders fallen from the cliffs, until they reached the sparse fringe of ponderosa pines, and a few junipers and aspens. Beyond the trees lay a clearing in which grew grasses and mountain flowers; the scarlet phlox still blooming in patches like flame, and in the moistest spots near the creek bed the pale orchid of iris waved.

The fertile canyon, not half a mile long, was watered throughout most of its length, until the creek, fed by a spring above the waterfall, disappeared underground to trickle into some subterranean flow beneath the mountain.

Amanda and Dart and Hugh made for the nearest point on the creek. They threw themselves down on the bank and snuffled up the water like animals until they were satisfied, then Dart lit a cigarette and said with decision, "I'm going back to get that wretched burro, we need the bedding and grub, too. I should be able to do it in a couple of hours now I know the way. You two make a fire and wait here."

"Good God," cried Hugh, "you're nuts if you think I'm going to sit around on my can, with the gold so near. I'm going up there"—he jerked his chin down the canyon towards the cliff dwelling.

"With that ankle?" asked Dart quietly. Hugh had unbound his leg and was bathing it in the stream. The foot and ankle were bright purple and swollen to twice normal size. "You give it a rest until tomorrow, Hugh, the gold won't run away. It's

been there quite a while. Besides, there's apt to be plenty of
rattlers in a place like that. You don't want to explore in the
dark."

Hugh knew that Dart was right. He muttered angrily, but he
subsided, nursing his ankle and staring up towards the cliff
dwelling four hundred feet above and straight up a precipitous
slope of slide rock.

"I'll find some firewood," said Amanda, at once uneasy when
Dart had left them. "It'll be nice to have a fire again." She
walked quickly up and down the banks of the creek, picking up
pieces of dried juniper and twigs. As the shadows fell heavier on
the valley and the warm colours lent by the sun disappeared,
she lost the sensation of magical beauty. The cliff dwelling became a jumble of grotesque square teeth on the lower jaw of the
cavernous black maw. She avoided looking at it. She gathered
wood enough and started a fire beside Hugh, but she could not
settle down to enjoy the warmth. She chewed dried raisins
and jerky and ate two of the Hershey bars from her knapsack,
drank more water, and still the gnawing discomfort did not
cease.

She wandered farther up the canyon in nervous search for
more firewood and saw ahead, near a clump of buckbrush, what
seemed to be a cluster of white sticks and a round white stone,
glimmering in the half light. She came nearer, staring curiously,
and bent over to pull up one of the smooth sticks. It was
attached to its fellows, and as she pulled, all the other curving
sticks moved with it, and the round stone rolled off a little distance on the grass.

Then Amanda saw what she held in her hand, and she jumped
back, giving a sharp cry. It was the bleached rib cage of a
skeleton at which she had been tugging, and the round stone
was the skull.

She rubbed her hand violently back and forth against her
levis, still feeling the chalky rough surface she had touched.
Panic waves washed over her, and receded.

Stupid to be so frightened. The bleached skeleton must have
been there a long, long time. She crept back presently to stare
down at the bones in fascinated horror. She saw a small, dark
object wedged between two of the ribs near the crumbling spine.
She hesitated, then snapped on her little flash-light and bent
nearer. The dark object was a flint arrowhead, and near it, on

the ground beneath the rib cage, she saw a dull gleam and a flash of shiny black.

She reached down, careful not to touch the bones, and drew up the second object. It was a heavy onyx crucifix, with the figure of the Christ carved in elaborate, tarnished silver.

She put the crucifix in her pocket and walked slowly back to camp. Her legs were trembling. She sat down by the fire, gazing into the bright flames. "I didn't really believe it before——" she whispered to herself.

"What are you mumbling about?" Hugh snapped, closing the medical kit. He had just given himself another hypodermic.

She raised her hand in almost helpless gesture, then let it drop again on her knee. "I've just found the skeleton of Padre Rodriguez," she said, "the one who was slain by an arrow from the skies. It did happen like that. It *all* happened. . . ."

"Well, bully for us! What the hell do you think we're doing here anyway unless we believed the story, you little dope? I've always believed it and so most certainly did you." He snapped a match and lit himself another cigarette.

"I don't know——" she said, still gazing into the fire. "I believed in a dream; I was in love with the bright beckoning flower —it's a strange thing when a dream comes true; I don't think they're meant to—at least not here—not like this."

She shivered, and glanced quickly towards the black cave high on the cliff side, and she thought of the words in Professor Dartland's quotation from the Spanish: ". . . seems to have inspired both men with a great and strange fear . . . 'like an enchantment.'"

"I never heard such a bunch of crap," said Hugh almost amiably. The hypo. was beginning to work, and a clear, thrilling euphoria ran along his veins. "If all your metaphysical hashings means you're no longer interested in your share of the gold mine, I assure you I couldn't be more charmed."

She did not answer. She scarcely heard him.

The canyon walls pushed close around her. The valley grew murmurous with unquiet shadows, and she was afraid. Even when Dart came back, leading the stumbling burro and carrying much of the pack himself, she could not rouse herself from the numbing weight. She followed the familiar routine of making a proper camp at last, helping Dart boil water for the coffee, frying bacon, laying out the bedrolls on pine boughs beneath the pine

shelter which he cut, and none of the homely chores seemed
real. It was as though she performed them under water, struggling through dense resistance.

She showed Dart the crucifix and told him of her discovery,
and wondered that he could take it so lightly, brushing it off,
barely answering her or glancing at the crucifix. He needed no
confirmatory evidence, not after the moment he had stood on
the ledge and seen the lost pueblo of his ancestors. He was withdrawn from her now, as brusque as Hugh; the tentative close-
ness which had lately returned to them had gone again.

She tried to sleep that night, but she could not. The soughing
of the great pines and the rippling of the little creek brought no
comfort, for underneath their gentle music she heard a deeper
note of warning, and of doom.

Turning and tossing in her blankets, she tried to reason with
herself, tried to recapture the first mystic joy she had felt as she
stood upon the ledge, telling herself that of course physical
exhaustion gave one morbid fancies, that the valley was beautiful, and the little stone city. But she dared not open her eyes for
fear of seeing the little city in the cavern. Earlier, before they
went to bed, she had looked at it and seen it gleaming like a
pearl against the black mountain-side. There was no moon, and
yet the cave glowed with an unearthly luminescence. She had
finally pointed this out to the two men, and felt Dart stiffen
beside her. Then he laughed and said gruffly, "Phosphorescence
from the old rotting beams. Nothing but foxfire!"

And Hugh had laughed too. "Andy's positively oozing
psychic whimsies tonight. Here, take this." And he'd given her
a sedative. But still she couldn't sleep.

Nor did Dart sleep, though he lay quiet. His gun lay cocked
and near to his right hand. His senses all alert, he lay thinking.
Downstream, where he had led the exhausted burro, there was
a narrow strip of sand. He had noted the flashing of a tiny
puddle of wetness in that sand. The mark of some kind of foot-
print. It could have been made by mountain lion or bear, yet
how could there be big game in this tiny rock-girdled valley? It
could have been made by the ball of a man's foot.

Hugh did sleep, at least his body did, but his mind projected
him into dreams as sharp and vivid as surrealist paintings. He
saw Viola's face bent down to his in adoring welcome. He saw
the separate hairs in her auburn curls as they sprang up from

her white forehead. He saw the shining texture of her blood-red mouth, the down on her cheeks, the black mole beneath her left eye. He felt her warm breath on his face, and smelt her carnation perfume. She wore a crown of golden bay-leaves, and as he knelt before her, she reached up to take the crown from her own head and place it on his.

"I knew you'd come, Hughie," she said, bending closer, "because you're famous now." And as she said this to him, her face changed; it grew sharp and sly as a fox, her lips drew back in a sneering grin. Her skin darkened, and her eyes became muddy and full of hate—Maria's eyes, and Maria's voice burst into a mocking cackle of laughter. . . .

He held a dagger in his hand, and he plunged the dagger into the sneering, cackling mouth, but it met no resistance. The dagger fell impotently into space and faded away.

And yet someone was dead. He stood at the edge of a great chamber and watched a figure laid out on a bier, draped with black velvet. He could not see who the corpse was. But he heard the far-off sound of sobbing, and he knew that he, too, should mourn for the unknown dead upon the bier.

Daylight brought calm to the three who had spent the night in the lost valley, a tacit return to normal. The sun was shining, there was breakfast, and even water to bathe in. Dart and Amanda separately went up the canyon and refreshed themselves under the icy waterfall. On the way back from his trip to the fall, Dart, hearing a fluttering among the bushes, had the luck to shoot a wild turkey, and bore it triumphantly back to camp. Fresh meat at last.

"We'll cook him for dinner when we get back from up there," said Dart, nodding towards the cliff dwelling.

Amanda laughed. "When we get back from up there we'll all be rich, I guess." Her fears and tremors of the night before seemed very silly in the sunlight.

"How much gold ore do you figure we can carry back on this trip?" asked Hugh. "Thank God that damn burro's leg seems better." They all looked at Tonto, who was frisking clumsily on the grass. Hugh went on, "Of course, there'll be free gold, too, the account said so. We can get a hell of a lot of that in our knapsacks, and pack the rest on the burro."

Dart glanced at him. Hugh's voice was faster than usual,

louder and more clipped, the pupils of his eyes were contracted
to black specks in a blinding green; but his ankle was certainly
better, and excitement was natural under the circumstances.
Dart turned his mind to practical considerations. He had not
bothered to pan the gravel in the creek bed, for there seemed to
be no sign of the black sand which meant gold; nor had he
seen any evidence of float anywhere in the canyon. Still, that did
not prove much, and he could see that the cave which contained
the cliff city was made of quartzite, which sometimes accompanied gold. He had no more doubt than the others that they
were about to make a very lucky strike, and for the first time
Dart allowed himself to wonder what he would do with his
share. The logical thing would be to put it right back here to
develop this mine into a going concern. The expenses of development in so remote a place would be enormous. Still, man
had surmounted worse difficulties than this—why, even at Lodestone. . . . His mouth tightened.

He hooked to his belt the carbide miner's lamp he had brought
in the burro's pack, slung his pick over his shoulder, and turned
to the others. "All set?" He hesitated, then made the final
practical decision. "We won't bother with the guns, Hugh.
Nothing to shoot except maybe snakes, and you've got your
Colt."

Hugh nodded. Dart glanced at him keenly again. Hugh's face
glistened with fine sweat, and he was lighting one cigarette from
off the last. A circle of still smoking butts lay on the grass
around him.

Dart walked over and stamped the butts out with his heel.
"You'll cut your wind and we'll soon run out of cigarettes, too,
if you smoke like that," he observed mildly.

"You mind your own goddam business!" The green eyes
were hard and blank as jade, the tremor of the freckled hands
grew more pronounced.

I hope to God he doesn't crack up, thought Dart; this thing
means too much to him, poor guy. . . . And did it mean so
much to Andy, too? He usually avoided looking at the girl, but
he did so now.

She stood on the bank of the creek, breasting the gentle wind
like a young Niké, waiting for him to give the signal to start.
Her eyes were fastened on the cliff dwelling, and he could not
see their expression, but her cheeks were pink and her lips

parted. She seemed very young and very eager. She'll have her chance, Dart thought. Chance to get away from me and all the things she hates.

It took them over an hour to zigzag through the talus of coarse, broken rock and up the tiny trail that clung to the edge of the cliff. A trail hewn eight hundred years ago from the living rock and worn by generations of patient feet plodding down to the valley floor for water, and to cultivate the corn and pumpkin patches which had once fringed the creek.

Several times Dart and Amanda had to pause and wait for Hugh to get his breath. Dart offered to pull him up the steepest places, but Hugh stubbornly refused, as he shrugged off Amanda's concern about the ankle. He wanted no patronizing sympathy which might be held against him later. They might say he had no right to the gold, might say they'd dragged him along on sufferance, might try to cut his share. Though there was the document they'd drawn up with their signatures. Make that stick in a law court. But you need all your wits about you. Got to watch out.

The cliff city grew larger as they approached it. There were some fifty dwellings and squat towers all flung inside the giant cave like a tumbled pile of children's blocks. They were built of flat stones and mortared with adobe, and in full sunlight the soft, tawny hues alternated with black shadows.

It was the *hush* that Amanda felt as they pulled up the last stone steps and stood on the brink of the cavern before many low doorways. Not the quiet of the wilderness or the mountains, but an expectant hush, as though voices had but that minute stopped.

She moved off quietly from the two men, and walking to one of the doorways she stooped and gazed into a low room, raftered with round cedar beams. A ray of sunlight slanted down through the one tiny window and illumined the age-old dust on the earthern floor. The centre fire pit still held the remnants of charred embers, and a rough brown corrugated cooking pot stood upright beside the dead fire. Next to the cooking pot a smaller, finer pot lay fallen on its side. The pot was a brilliant buff polychrome in tiny red and black geometric figures under high glaze, and from its gently flaring mouth a stream of spilled corn still trailed out on the ground.

Amanda stepped over the high sill and stood just within the quiet room. She saw a stone metate with the mano resting in it, like those she herself had used in the rancheria on the morning of Saba's death. In the corner beneath the window there had been a bed, with a woven turkey-feather blanket, rumpled a little—as though someone had lately lain there. Beside the bed on the ground there was a string of rough turquoises half-buried in the dust, and near to them two little yucca straw sandals, shredded and crumbling, but waiting there as they had throughout the centuries for their owner to come back.

Pueblo Encantado, she thought. And her eyes filled with sudden tears.

She heard Dart's voice calling to her, and she stepped back over the sill into the bright light of the open cave.

He saw the tears in her eyes, and his brows raised in surprise. She gestured towards the room, "They must have gone so quickly—everything just as they left it—waiting for them—the woman's pots—her jewellery—the child's sandals. . . ."

His astonishment grew, and he stuck his head through the door. He straightened up slowly, "Yes, the Anasazi fled in fear, the legend says." He spoke in a repressive, curt tone, but then he added as though against his will, "You didn't touch anything . . . ?"

"Oh no," she said, smiling a little; "they wouldn't like it."

He bent down to her, looking into her face, questioning, "Andy——?"

The hush deepened around them. It was shattered by Hugh's shout from the top of a watch tower just above where they stood. "What the hell are you two doing? I've been crawling through this labyrinth, but I haven't found anything promising. Where in the name of God would they put their inner cave?"

Amanda and Dart moved apart. The softness left his eyes, and he answered Hugh dryly. "Well, they certainly wouldn't put it up there by the roof. Come down and we'll hunt."

They joined forces again. Led by Dart, they stooped and crawled through the high-silled doorways, up and down levels among the many still rooms, penetrating ever back and south into the cavern. Some of the chambers had served as middens, or granaries—desiccated corncobs and the tiny bones of small game lay shin-deep on the floor. In others, where the Anasazi had lived, there were the same evidences of panic flight as in the first room Amanda had entered. Stone knives and hatchets lay strewn pell-mell among shreds of yucca-fibre clothing, feather blankets, and many exquisitely painted pots and bowls and dishes.

"I suppose all this trash'd make a field day for an archæologist," said Hugh viciously, "but we're not getting anywhere."

"Yes, we are," said Dart. "I've been looking for the great kiva, and I'm sure this is it." He stopped at the edge of a circular pit at the south-eastern corner of the cavern. This he recognized as probably the main ceremonial chamber of the Ancient Ones, a place of secret rites, for in the centre of the pit floor six feet below there was a sipapu, the hole made for quick passage of the spirits between the underworld and earth, and at the back of the kiva, interrupting the stone bench which encircled it, there was an opening into a cave behind, as Dart had expected.

He jumped down into the kiva, and Hugh and Amanda followed. He turned on his carbide lamp and said, "Flash-lights!" to the others. They snapped them on. But they had not far to go. The cave behind the kiva opened into a great rock chamber so vast that margins were lost in shadowy ledges and boulders. The circles of their lights showed them many dim forms lying at measured intervals, some on the ground, some raised a little on piles of rubble. They saw the gleam of polished brown skulls shining through the feather and yucca shrouds which once had covered them. They all lay, the quiet dead, drawn up in the fœtal position as they had once been born, and around each grave clustered jewellery and weapons and their most beautiful utensils for comfort on the journey.

Dart stopped, the beam of his lamp wavered.

But Hugh pushed forward. "They're nothing but a bunch of mummies—corpses are no treat to me—my God, look!" His shrill voice echoed through the cavern.

Hugh ran forward, stumbling over one of the mummies. He kicked it savagely out of his way, and it disintegrated into bones and dust. Dart set his teeth and followed, staring, as Amanda did, at the face of the rock beyond the graves. From the floor to the low roof in a strip four feet wide the rock sparkled and glinted in the lights.

Dart picked his way carefully between the mummies, and Amanda followed, shrinking, hypnotized. "Oh, don't," she murmured, "don't——" But she did not know that she spoke.

They passed beyond the places of burial and came up to Hugh. He was digging into the wall with his knife, picking with his finger-nails, and his breath came in sobbing gasps.

Dart stood rooted behind him, staring at the glittering rock. He put his hand on Hugh's shoulder. "That's pyrites, Hugh," he said very quietly. "That isn't gold. You know that. You know enough about mining for that."

Hugh swung around, and he stared down at the flakes of brassy mineral in his hands. "But there's *got* to be gold," he said in a hoarse, shaking voice, "they said there was gold. . . ."

"There is," said Dart, more quietly yet. "Here." He moved his light again from the wall of glittering pyrites to a recess to the left. Here the light showed a rounded mass of white quartz streaked with the unmistakable dull richness of free gold stains and specks.

"Thank God—that's it!" cried Hugh his voice breaking. "We've got it, then——"

Dart put the carbide lamp on a rock, and by its light examined the quartz, while Hugh's breath rasped through the cavern.

"It's only a small pocket, Hugh," said Dart at last. He swung his pick along the margins. "It's high grade all right, but there's mighty little of it, a few hundred dollars maybe, that's all."

Hugh reached his hands forward, clutching the rough speckled quartz, and twisted his head over his shoulder. "You're crazy," he whispered. "There's a mine here. This is a vein. It's bonanza. . . ."

"No." Dart shook his head. "I'm sorry, old boy, but you'll have to face it. I can tell by the country rock, by the formation, there's nothing here but what you see—a small pocket."

"You lie, you bastard, you lie. . . ." Hugh backed against the lump of quartz, throwing his arms out as though he protected it. "You lie," he hissed again; "you want it all for yourself. I knew it. I knew this would happen. . . ." The green eyes glaring up at Dart were like eyes under sea water, submerging, drowning.

"Hugh," pleaded Dart on a long breath, "you know I'm not lying, it's——" He stopped, standing there tall and helpless in the bright light of Hugh's torch, while Hugh, with one clumsy, fumbling motion drew out his revolver and fired.

Amanda screamed, and in the echo of her scream a second shot detonated from the shadows in the back of the cave. Hugh gave a bubbling gasp and fell prone beside the glittering wall of pyrites.

In the confusion of blinding smoke and terror, Amanda ran to Dart, who had fallen to his knees, his head hanging forward on his chest. He was struggling to get up, and a stream of blood spurted from a hole in his leather jacket and ran down on to the ground.

"Darling—my darling," she sobbed, kneeling beside him and holding him frantically against her breast as though to staunch that spurting blood with her own body. "Dart—my God—what happened——?"

"Hugh shot me," murmured Dart in a vague dreaming voice. "But I didn't shoot him. . . . How could I—unarmed?" He struggled once more to get up, the blood spurted again, and he slumped against her into her arms. "Be careful, Andy——" he whispered, and his eyes shut.

She did not understand him. She laid him down on the ground and wadded her sweater under his head; she pushed back his jacket and looked at the hole in the cotton shirt, high up, thank God, near his armpit. Tourniquet, she thought—no, too high. She took her bandanna and stuffed it over the hole, pressing down hard.

There was a soft thud of leaping footfalls behind her in the darkness of the cave; she heard them, but she was beyond all fear, concentrated on the pressure she was applying, and praying underneath steadily, "Dear God, don't let Dart die, don't—don't——"

She saw a shadow approach from the darkness, the figure of a man who came and stood over them. She looked up and saw who it was, uncomprehending but without surprise. In this cave of nightmare and death there was no place for surprise. "John Whitman," she cried on a low pleading note, "oh, thank God, you're here—Dart's hurt—help me."

The Apache stiffened; behind his unwavering black eyes there flickered a strange expression. He rested the stock of his gun on the ground, staring down at Dart's white face, ignoring the woman.

Dart opened his eyes, and looked at his boyhood friend. "So it *was* you——" The words drifted from his mouth like dry leaves on the wind.

"Eheu—Ish-kin-azi," answered the Indian in Apache, bowing

his head. "You have betrayed. I've followed many days, and watched. The secret of this valley was known to me also and better than to you. Did you in your white arrogance not think of that?"

"Yes," whispered Dart. "I thought of that."

Beneath the pressure of her hands on the wound Amanda felt Dart's big body strain and gather itself together, the muscles tensing. She cried out in protest, but he stumbled to his feet and stood swaying, leaning on her a little. The Indian's hand tightened on his gun barrel, but he made no move.

"I'm weak as a child," said Dart. "I cannot fight you. You will shoot if you like. Finish what the other started, but I beg you, by all the friendship we once had, by the same blood that flows in both our veins—do not hurt *her*."

The Indian was silent. He turned his head and looked at the shattered mummy. He glided to the pyrite wall, and he kicked Hugh's body over with his foot. "This pig is dead," he said. "I killed him to avenge the desecrated spirit of our ancestors. Let him lie by the shining wall he slobbered over with such greed."

He picked up his gun, cradling it in his arm. He glanced at Amanda, and saw horrified comprehension dawning in her face. He spat on the floor and continued in English. "As for you, Ish-kin-azi, and your woman——" His narrowed eyes glinted. "You bleed fast, it may be that your wound will kill you. I do not know. But I leave you to the Mountain Spirits, whose hiding-place you betrayed. I leave you to Usen, who is the Giver of Life and Death."

And he was gone, sliding swift as a panther between the graves and out of the cave.

Dart's body slumped, falling against Amanda so hard that she staggered. "No," he said through his teeth, straightening himself painfully, "we've got to get out of here." He put his good arm around her shoulders.

He felt his wound. "Is there blood in the back too?"

"Yes," she whispered, "not so much."

"I think the bullet went right through, missed the lung. Bleeding's the main—press here, Andy." He guided her fingers to the hollow of his neck. The spurts lessened and thinned to a ooze.

They staggered slowly forward together, she supporting half his weight on her shoulders and pressing on the artery. They stumbled out of the burial cave and up through the kiva and the dozen deserted rooms in the silent city they had traversed with Hugh an hour ago.

When they stood again on the terraced ledge by the brink of the great cavern, she cried, "Darling—lie down here; don't try to go farther. I'll get food and water up here from the camp."

His lips were grey, and cold sweat dripped down his forehead, but he said, "No. Not here. We've disturbed them enough."

They made their slow agonizing way together down the trail, and back across the creek to their little camp. Then he collapsed on his blankets beneath the brush shelter. Under weighted lids his grey eyes were full of light, and he smiled faintly.

"My poor Andy," he said, as she bent lower to hear, "I'm in your hands—I'm not going to be much use to you for a while —no good at all. This isn't the way it was supposed to turn out, is it——?" His lids fluttered and fell.

CHAPTER FOURTEEN

AMANDA knelt beside her wounded unconscious husband. Flickering light filtered through the leafy roof of the brush shelter. There was no sound but Dart's quick, shallow breathing and the gurgling of the little creek. She was alone in the lost valley, face to face with the fear she had glimpsed and desperately warded off with anger and self-pity on the night she lost the baby.

No one at all to turn to now. No one to help you but yourself. And not only yourself in need of help this time. Relentless implacability that sneeringly demands a wisdom and a strength that is not there, that waits in ambush, laughing at your destruction.

Dart shuddered, and his body shook again with chills, though already he was wrapped in all their blankets. Her own heart shuddered and seemed to stop. She crept under the blankets with him, trying to warm him with her own body. On her breast, through the cotton shirt, she felt the sticky thickness of his blood. He muttered something and turned towards her a little, as though to pull her closer, but his arm slipped back. He sighed, and she felt with terror the faintness of the hurried tapping in his chest.

My love, my love, she whispered. Her words filled the shelter. They filled the valley. Nothing beyond the valley, nothing in the valley but love and death.

She had no ritual to guide her, no certainty of faith, and yet her soul obeyed the ultimate eternal instinct it hears when all else has failed. Her mind, her body, and her spirit rushed together like surging water, channelled into a formless, desperate prayer.

It seemed there was no answer. Dart's shuddering continued, the shallow, sighing breaths became more rapid.

Amanda's agony of tension snapped into a sudden deep exhaustion. She dozed for a few seconds. Behind her lids the reflection of the chequered light and shadow in the shelter dissolved into blackness. The blackness faded and became a crystal mist. The mist was cool and passionless, as though it floated from behind the stars. Woven through it, floating in a nimbus of cool light like a white flower, she saw a woman's face looking down at her with an expression of tenderness and comfort. The dark, tender eyes were like those of Calise, yet the light and the peace that flowed around and through them was infinitely greater than Calise, for the crystal mist was but a thin and gauzy veil across the shining land beyond.

Dart stirred and murmured, "Water. . . ."

She awoke at once, completely alert. The dream vanished, leaving no memory behind. She felt only refreshment and a keen competence of mind.

She slid carefully out from the blankets. Her brain, released from paralysing fear, took command. It presented her with concrete remembrance and a plan of action through the practical medium of a first-aid course she had taken at camp when she was sixteen.

She added a little salt to the water she brought Dart, and holding his head and murmuring encouragement, she coaxed him to drink many cups. She made a fire, and put round stones in it to heat, and she put on the coffee-pot.

Very gently, so that he did not waken, she cut the stiff, blood-sodden shirt from around his wounds, both back and front, under his left collar-bone. She debated, to the best of her knowledge, the dangers of starting up the bleeding again by removing the fragments of shirt which had coagulated into the wound, as against the dangers of infection. She decided to compromise. She opened Hugh's medical kit. She stared at the label pasted inside the lid. "Dr. Hugh Slater, Lodestone, Arizona." The words swam before her eyes. A spasm of realization translated into actual nausea, her stomach heaved. She controlled herself, forcefully turning her mind back to the contents of the kit. She took out the bottle of mercurochrome, set her jaw, and poured it over the wounds and the embedded pieces of cotton shirt.

Dart gasped.

"It's all right, darling," she said, kissing his forehead. "Lie still." Her voice was soothing and firm.

He looked up at her and tried to smile, then his lids fell again.

She took sterile compresses from the kit and placed them over the wounds, fastening them with adhesive tape, tightly so as to exert some pressure. She brought warmed stones from the fire, and wrapping them in Dart's and Hugh's and her own extra sweaters, she put them at Dart's feet and alongside his body. And she gave him a cupful of strong hot coffee. His shivering stopped.

When she went back to the fire he was breathing more deeply, his pulse was stronger. She sat down on the grass by the turkey he had shot that morning, and began to pluck it, wrenching out great handfuls of feathers, and allowing them to float down the canyon on the freshening twilight breeze.

Her mind continued to function with clear precision. She could take it up like a reading glass and stand apart with it to view their situation with as much objectivity as though she were examining a photograph.

John Whitman was gone. He had left the valley, his mission ended. He had left them to Fate, to the mercy of the Mountain Spirits he believed in. Had he also killed or taken the burro? This, now that Dart was as comfortable as she could make him, was her next practical consideration. The little beast was nowhere in sight.

She finished plucking the turkey, and went to the shelter for Dart's hunting knife. She cut off the turkey's feet and head, slit and disembowelled it, as she had seen butchers do. She cut and peeled an aspen branch, thrust it through the turkey, and suspended it above the fire on two piles of flat stones. Then she went up and down the creek looking for the burro, but she could not find him, and she did not dare leave Dart alone for long.

It will be bad if Tonto's gone, she thought calmly; we'll have to carry extra water ourselves to cross the malpais. But when and how were they to leave this valley? She did not know, and she ceased to think of it.

The only thing that matters is Dart, to make him well and strong again.

The turkey fat and juices fell hissing into the flames, while she turned the bird from side to side, watching the skin brown and crackle. How many unknown skills attention and necessity called forth.

The turkey was tough and pungent, but it satisfied her hunger. She ate a pilot biscuit with it, and drank quantities of the pure sparkling creek water. She dared touch none of their few remaining cans, or the flour, for Dart would need the fullest diet she could provide. How much blood did he lose, she thought? Enough for shock and ghastly weakness. But he was strong, and if the bleeding did not start again, if the bullet had done no greater internal damage than appeared from the hole's position, if there was no infection. . . .

She washed up her few utensils and doused the campfire. She made Dart drink again, rousing him only enough to swallow, and she gave him a sedative from the vial so marked. She took his gun and laid it beside her, then she crept close to him again under the blankets.

The shadows fell once more deep into the canyon, and the Pueblo Encantado glowed on the dark cliff-side with its strange luminescence. But Amanda saw neither the shadows nor the Pueblo, she saw and felt only Dart.

The next morning he seemed a trifle better, his mouth was not so pinched, a faint colour showed in the ash-grey of his cheeks above the stubble of black beard. She fed him coffee cream-thick with condensed milk, and bacon and pan bread. His wounded shoulder had stiffened in the night and throbbed violently. He was still dizzy and too weak to move, but his eyes followed her as she nursed him. "Thank you——" he whispered.

"Hush!" she said, smiling. "Don't talk. Everything's fine. Don't worry if you hear a shot, I'm going to practise."

She took Hugh's 20-20 and went outside. Long ago she had gone duck-hunting with her father in South Carolina and fired a few shots, but never since. On this expedition it had not occurred to her to shoot, and neither of the men had suggested it. She had, however, watched Hugh. She knew his gun was loaded, and she intended to see if she could get a rabbit. The brush was teeming with curious jacks, remarkably tame, for they had never seen human beings before. She did not manage to shoot any, and she fired only twice, being afraid of wasting ammunition, but the shots produced an even better result.

She heard a startled bray, and a scuttling noise. The burro stuck his long mournful face around a clump of red-berried algerita.

"Tonto!" she cried joyfully. "It's a good thing I didn't shoot you. Come here, you little devil!"

But Tonto would not; he scampered off to the side of the

canyon. Well, she thought, at least he's here, and he certainly can't get away. It's a good omen. Contentment filled her.

A strange new happiness came to her during those days of nursing Dart in the lost valley, watching him grow slowly stronger. As his strength returned, he told her how to find various foods to supplement their diet.

She ranged the little canyon, bringing in finds for his inspection: the soft inner bark of the yellow pine, the cliff rose or quinine bush which made a strengthening tonic, algerita berries to stew into jelly, acorns from Gambel's oak, and a low green plant for which he did not know the English name, but whose tender shoots could be cooked like spinach, and it was a prime Apache blood builder.

When he spoke to her during those days of the first recovery, it was in few words, and only of matters pertaining to their immediate joint welfare, but his voice had a humble, hesitating note she had never heard before, and he watched her lithe, graceful motions constantly, but averted his eyes if she chanced to look at him.

After the first night when his chills had passed, she no longer lay under the blankets with him, but slept across the shelter. Yet to her this was no hostile separation as it had been before. Her love demanded nothing now but his happiness and full recovery. She was content to respect his reticences and the special exigencies of his nature, and to wait.

On the fourth morning she shot a rabbit and bore it back to him in triumph. "Change of menu," she cried gaily. "I'm getting sick of turkey soup, aren't you?"

Dart was sitting in the sun by their fire, frying bacon. He was still too weak to walk more than a few steps. He looked up at her and smiled. "Swell. Give it to me—I'll skin it."

"Oh, no," she said, shaking her head. "You can't use that arm yet."

"I can use the hand enough to hold the rabbit, while I flay him with the other. Give it to me, Andy; it's all I'm good for. Woman's work."

He said this, not bitterly, but in the wondering, hesitant voice which was new from him.

She laughed and gave him the rabbit. "Well, you don't look like a woman, my bearded monster. Black Teach the pirate, more like."

He grinned, rubbing his chin ruefully. "I'll hack some of this off tomorrow," he said. "I'm sorry; I must be a repulsive sight."

"Good Lord, no," said Amanda, turning the bacon. "I don't mind." Nor did she. And yet there had been a time when she minded very much, when she had nagged him into shaving twice a day, resentful that he was indifferent to her smooth, sophisticated standards. Effeminate standards, perhaps. She thought suddenly of Calise Cunningham and their first conversation together. Calise had asked why she had married Dart, and she had answered something to the effect that it was because he was big, strong, very male, and different, and Calise had replied, "Then you must not at the same time resent the qualities you love."

She had repudiated Calise's remark with blank anger. But she understood better now. For had she not after all been for ever trying to change Dart, dissatisfied with the uncompromising strength she had also admired?

"What are you thinking of?" asked Dart quietly.

"About Calise," she said, startled into the truth. She wanted no reminders for either of them of the past yet, of the world beyond the enchanted valley.

"Ah," said Dart, and a shadow crossed his face, as she had feared it would.

"No!" she cried. "Don't think back, not of anything."

She glanced unconsciously to the cliff dwelling down the canyon. The frozen city hung there as aloof and separate as the moon, withdrawn again into the perfect quiet which they had violated.

He skinned the rabbit in silence for a moment. "We must face it all soon, though," he said at last very low. "There's much to be said between us."

"Not now," she cried, "not until you're strong enough."

He raised his head and looked at her. There was sadness and question in his eyes. "You saved my life, Andy," he said; "I'm still helpless without you. How can I deny anything you ask?"

She rose impulsively. She would have gone to him, telling him that when there is love there is no debt on either side, that she did not wish him humbled and uncertain, that his pride was now as dear to her as her own. But a wiser instinct stopped her. Too often in the past she had assaulted the citadel of his personality, battering her way with coarse and blunted weapons, trying to hurry him, trying to change him to a preconceived mould. She knew how painful, how deep a dislocation of all his character was the admission he had just made, and that she must take no advantage of it.

She sank back again, and picked up a handful of green shoots from off a tin plate. "I'm too hungry for deep discussion," she said lightly, as though she had not heard him. "Shall I fry these wild onions in the bacon grease for the rabbit? And you go back to bed now, that's quite enough exertion for a convalescent."

Dart gave her a puzzled look, but he finished preparing the rabbit, and did as she suggested. His body would not obey his commands. He loathed the waves of blank exhaustion and the dizziness which still swept over him and which he could not ignore as he did the pain in his healing wounds, as he had always ignored the few discomforts and ailments of his healthy lifetime. He lay down on his blankets, and just as sleep overpowered him he heard Amanda singing softly out by the campfire, a plaintive waltz tune.

Her voice was small and low and pure, it lulled him and gave him pleasure. Yet he had never heard her sing before. He had not known she ever sang.

Five more days passed in the enchanted valley, and except for the stiffness of his wounds, Dart was nearly well. He could walk the length of the canyon now, he had managed to shoot for them another smaller and more tender wild turkey. He had bathed in the waterfall, and duly shaved off his beard. During these days of his returning strength, when she no longer nursed him, they had been oddly shy with each other, like the shyness of early courtship. They spoke little and left sentences unfinished, an unexpected touch on hand or arm left them both confused and stammering. And like a golden current, a newborn tenuous magic flowed between them. It was as though they had never known each other, or been together before.

On the ninth evening since the tragedy in the cave, they sat beside their campfire having dined on dried turkey breasts, stewed greens, coffee, and a whole panful of sourdough bread topped with wild honey, discovered by Dart in a hollow tree when he shot the turkey.

There were no stars tonight studding the narrow strip of sky above the canyon; great mounded clouds floated and caught on the overhanging rim, and a waxing moon peered through the clouds fitfully.

"Thunder in the air," said Dart, lighting a cigarette. "We're about due for a storm."

"Yes," she said. There was a hot tension in the still air.

Dart got up and fastened her poncho over the top of the shelter. He had already woven and fortified the pine-bough roof. "At least we won't get drenched in there when it comes," he said, returning to the fire.

They were both silent, both smoking and staring at the flames. Then Dart stretched out his long legs, leaned back against a tree-trunk and deliberately gazed up at the cliff city. It shone tonight, not by its own phosphorescence, but by the wan light of the fitful moon.

"We've got to face it, Andy," he said. "We've got to talk about Hugh."

She sat up straight, clenching her hands. "*Hugh!*" she repeated on a breaking voice. "He was evil—horrible. He tried to kill you."

Dart shook his head, his face turned upwards to the cliff city. "He wasn't altogether sane. He tried to kill the thing he thought stood between him and—and his last chance."

The last chance, the fabulous wealth that wasn't there, and if it had been, Hugh must have known in his soul that it would not buy back his wife; no gold would have reversed the long disintegration, or given him self-respect.

"But he was your *friend*," cried Amanda violently. "That was one thing I always felt, was sure of."

"Yes," answered Dart, sighing. "And yet I was no friend. I gave him nothing. There were times way back when I might have listened to him. He tried once to tell me about his wife. I was embarrassed and I shut him out."

She was silent, wondering. What had they found in the Lost Valley? Nothing that they had set out for. Ugliness and murder and the smell of blood and death had hidden in the bright beckoning flower, but beyond that there had been a bridge for two of them leading out of fear and into gentleness and pity.

"The Mountain Spirits had mercy on us," she said at last. "We two were protected—and, I think, forgiven."

He had been going on to speak of other things pertaining to Hugh, to speak of plans and arrangements they must face in the world beyond the valley, but hearing her low dreaming voice he could not. He looked across the firelight at her, seeing the beauty and the strength which he had so long denied. Not boyish, not a pretty child's face under bright curls, but the face of a warm and understanding woman.

He got up and came around the fire beside her, and he knelt by her, gazing up into her wide and darkening eyes. "Am I too forgiven?" he whispered. "For I cannot live without you now."

Her breath came through her lips and touched his cheek as gently as the first fluttering of the storm wind in the pines. She leaned close to him. "There's no thought of forgiveness between us, Dart. There's only love."

He picked her up in his arms and carried her into the pine-bough bed. The storm came. The thunder and the lightning roared and flashed in the canyon, but for the two inside the shelter there was no fear. The majesty of the storm mingled with the awe of their own fulfilment. Not only the union of their bodies in passion and release as it had been before, but the deeper union of the spirit as it had never been; the blinding bliss of communication when two beings for the brief, unbearable instant that is allowed, merge into one.

The storm passed, and the moon came out unhindered, flooding the canyon with silver. Silver darkened to grey, and dawn filled the canyon with murmurous mist. The birds awoke, and pale cinnamon light spread through the leafy roof over the two who lay in each other's arms.

Amanda stirred; she raised herself on her elbow and looked down at him. His eyes were open as she had known they would be. They looked into each other's souls with recognition and deep awareness, and they smiled at each other. The smile was more beautiful than the ecstatic merging of their bodies had been.

She dropped her head and kissed his naked arm. He held her hard against his body, and they listened together to the music of the dawn. They were one with the mystery of all creation, and there was peace.

A mountain thrush called his clear song from the summit of a great yellow pine, and the great symphony to which they had listened diminished, as it always must, into quieter, simpler melody.

Ah, stay with us for ever—but it may not stay, yet it will leave behind an echo of vibration, never silenced, though sometimes in the deafening crashes of the outer life it may go unheard. And then there is still the thrush's song.

The sun mounted the overhanging cliffs and burst in red-gold challenge through the doorway of their shelter, bringing, even to the enchanted canyon, inexorable return to system, to the exigencies of the material world.

Amanda and Dart rose together, and she shivered a little in the chill mountain air. She looked at his big, lean, hard-muscled body, and she cried, in contrition and in tender laughter, "Oh, my darling—I had forgotten your wounds."

He glanced down at his left shoulder and laughed. "So had I."

"Do they hurt?" She touched the bandage anxiously.

"No, they don't hurt, silly one." He pulled her to him and kissed her softly on the mouth. "Here," he said, "you're cold——" He picked up a blanket and wrapped it around her. "I'll make the fire while you get dressed." He pulled on his pants and a sweater, and she heard him whistling as he laid their breakfast fire.

After breakfast they bathed together in the waterfall, and they laughed much, scrubbing their glowing bodies with the remnants of their soap, swimming in the tiny pool, splashing beneath the icy spray, and all the time, beneath the love and the laughter, a shadow deepened, and the knowledge of the question that she dreaded.

She voiced it at last after they had dressed again. She sat down on a rock beside the little pool, and, gazing down the sunny valley towards their camp, she said, "When, Dart?"

The pain and the yearning in her heart were reflected in his own eyes. He touched her shining hair, but he answered with quiet firmness. "Tomorrow."

"If we could stay——" she said, her voice faint above the sound of the waterfall. "If we could stay a little while——"

"No, Andy. Very soon the snows will come. But, anyway, we could not stay. You know that."

She bowed her head. "Yes, I know that."

"This isn't life," he said. "This is the lost valley of the Ancient Ones. It's a dream that we forced ourselves into and where we found both tragedy and great beauty. But it's not enough. It could never be enough."

"No," she said. "I know."

"You must wonder what we're going back to." His tone hardened. "It's better to speak of these things now, here—while we are still—protected." He took her hand and kissed it. "I know now that we have each other, and we always will; our love will give us both strength——" He stopped.

But love is not all, she thought. There are other needs. For a man like Dart there is work, his profession, and honour. And this must be so, it was inherent in his virility, in the tough masculinity which she no longer wished to soften or to cloy.

"I have no job," he said. "I was fired under circumstances of—of peculiar ignominy. Made to look a fool. An incompetent, exhibitionistic fool."

"No, no," she cried. "It isn't true."

"You didn't believe it?" he asked, looking at her suddenly with startled eyes.

"Of course, I didn't believe it. I thought Big Ruby knew something that would help. I went to her. I went to Calise—on the day before the baby . . . but it didn't do any good."

Dart shut his eyes. He raised the soft, brown little hand he held and put it against his cheek. "My dear," he said, "I didn't know. In everything that had to do with you I *was* a fool."

"And I was a grasping, spoiled brat. Oh, Dart, you talk of the hard things out beyond this valley, but they still seem far away and unimportant. When we get back, we can forget Lodestone for ever. Wipe it off the slate."

"Perhaps we might," said Dart slowly. "Except for one thing. I'll have to report Hugh's death to Mr. Tyson."

At first she did not understand the meaning of his words, and then shock spiralled through her, and a terrified recoil.

"No, Dart—no. They didn't believe you before; they might think . . ." She shuddered. "You don't have to tell anything. Nobody cared what happened to Hugh."

"Hush—darling," he said, and the endearment she had never heard from him cut through her panic. She listened, knowing that he spoke the truth. "His death must be reported. Tyson must know who should be notified. The thing happened, and we can't pretend that it's never been. I was responsible for Hugh on this expedition, and I must see it through."

Yes, it was for this of many reasons that she loved him. She would not let fear strike down into her heart again, not yet. . . . Not while they were yet cradled in the enchantment, not while the sun shone through the pines, and the cascade rippled out its music.

"We still have today," she whispered, and Dart, understanding, smiled, and jumped up. "Come, let's search for the lotus-eating burro. I'll bet by this time he thinks he's Oberon disguised, with myrtle and with roses twined. You'll have to be Titania and lure him."

"He doesn't lure easy," she said with a choking laugh. They ran together down the pine-scented trail into the canyon, still guarded by the magic of the lost valley.

The next day at seven they stood again upon the ledge beside the crevice in the rock which led outside, and they looked back for the last time at the green valley, fairyland of whispering trees and cool, life-giving waters. There was nothing left to show that they had been there. Dart had taken down the shelter and scattered the pine boughs back among the primeval carpet with their fellows. The ashes of their fires were buried under clean, sweet earth where the grass would soon grow. And they had taken nothing from the valley except the onyx and silver crucifix which had belonged to the Spanish padre.

All was as though they had never dared the forbidden journey, except that something of their spirits would remain with the other spirits of the long-ago and happy people who had once lived there.

They raised their eyes to the Pueblo Encantado. The frozen little city of stone floated blue and still in its shadow eastern cave, hushed in mystery, guarding one more of the quiet and passionless dead.

Amanda's heart whispered farewell, her eyes burned, but the compassion and the yearning were too deep for tears.

She heard Dart's quivering breath as he stood beside her, and knew that it was the same for him.

They turned together and walked through the darkness of the little tunnel, leading their burro, back to the sharp, cruel light of the barren waste of rocks—the malpais.

They travelled fast, down, ever downward over the trail they had so painfully struggled up, as Dart's unerring memory retraced their steps. They found the hollow pit in the lava, and the store of cans they had had to leave behind to traverse the terrible country beyond with the lame burro.

Dart saw at a glance that three of the cans were gone, and on the edge of the lava pit there was a pile of interlocking small stones.

"What's that?" asked Amanda. "It wasn't here before."

"No," he said quietly. "John Whitman stopped here. He must have left this message for me." He bent over and examined the position of the stones.

"What does it say, Dart?"

He straightened up, his mouth constricted. "It says, 'Friend.' He left it here in case we should ever get away alive. It's the Apache stone language we learned together as boys."

She asked no further questions. He must always do as he thought right, and her love for him accepted him now as he was, with many things she would never entirely understand, though always she could trust his sense of justice. But what was justice in the case of John Whitman? She thought of John at the rancheria at San Carlos—of Rowena and the baby, and the kindness they all had shown to her. She thought of the cruel Apache face in the Cave of the Dead, vindictive, sneering, as he kicked the body of the man he had shot. But, then, he had shown mercy according to his code. He had spared the two he might also have slaughtered, leaving them to the dispositions of Fate. He had killed, not from blood lust, but for the preservation of an ideal. And yet he had murdered. . . . And she did not know what Dart would do.

As they descended the mountains and the canyons, she felt their troubles crowding up to meet them ever thicker and more dense. They never spoke of it, it was not necessary to speak of it, but when at last they descended the easy trail from Deadman's Creek towards the Verde, and saw in the distance the smoke of Payson Pete's General Store at Staghorn, she saw what awaited them with a cold and unshrinking clarity.

They had no money and no job, and in this year of 1933 jobs would be hard to find for a young engineer who had been fired in disgrace. Moreover, they must report a murder under circumstances which would probably not be believed.

Payson Pete waddled forth to meet them when he heard the tinkle of the burro's bell through the trees. "Howdy, folks," he called, waving his fat arm. "D'you have a nice outing? Molly and me was kinda gettin' to wonderin' how you was makin' out. Been gone so long."

He surveyed them shrewdly. Nice-looking pair for all they were grown lean, and tough as a couple of young lions. The fellow's dark hair was longer, and he moved easy and lithe like an Indian runner Pete had known in his youth. He might almost have been an Indian with that iron-quiet look about him that you knew there was a lot going on inside you'd never find out —except he was so tall and his eyes were grey. As for the girl, she was prettier than ever with a kind of glow in her pink cheeks under the tan. There was something straight and shining about the two of them that hadn't been there before, when they took off. The mountains did that sometimes, changed people one way or the other.

Pete glanced back up the trail behind Amanda and Dart. "Where's the other fellow?" he asked, leaning over the burro to help Dart untie the pack ropes.

Dart did not answer at once, and Amanda spoke in the brief silence. "He went—by another way."

Dart glanced at her quickly. She saw doubt in his eyes, then he accepted her decision. This inquisitive old store-keeper was not the man to make a report to.

"You don't say," said Pete quizzically. He had no doubt they'd had a fight over the girl, and the other man had had to clear out. Which was okay. He and Molly hadn't liked the other guy, anyhow. "D'you make any luck strikes?" he asked, chuckling. While he helped Dart unhitch, he had managed to feel over the nearly empty packs, just in case. And there sure wasn't any ore in them any place.

"No, we didn't," said Dart, smiling. "But we certainly hit some rough country, as you said." He smiled, but there was a cool dignity about him which made it impossible for Pete to question further. So he acquiesced cheerfully, saying, "You bet. Them Matazals're rough as hell," and added, "What're you aimin' to do with the burro? I'll buy him back for six bits." Pete might be curious about the few wayfarers that turned up at Staghorn, but he was also an old-timer bred to a country where everybody's business was his own, and it wasn't polite to get too nosy.

The Dartlands spent that night again on the floor of Pete's store, but this time not on different sides of the old pot-bellied stove. They slept close together on the bearskin, with Amanda's head on her husband's shoulder. The next morning at six o'clock they bade final farewell to Staghorn, and set off in the Ford. The faithful flivver coughed and snorted and bucked as usual before starting, but Dart persuaded it into action. "Like Tonto," said Amanda, laughing. "There's a resemblance between them, though even that burro must be considerably younger."

She had given the battered, dilapidated car a rueful greeting when she saw it again, waiting patiently in Pete's back-yard. Dart was an excellent mechanic, but the Ford was about worn out, and even Dart could not manufacture new parts. This problem was again on top of them like so many others.

They drove back over the crest of the mountain pass and down into the Tonto basin, then Amanda said, "How much money have we got exactly, Dart?"

He grinned wryly, jerking his chin towards his hip pocket. "I don't know. Count it."

She complied, piling the heavy silver dollars and the four tens on her knees. "Sixty-three bucks," she said. "Definitely a fortune."

"Sure. And it'll have to last quite a while," said Dart mildly. "Maybe I can get a W.P.A. job pretty soon, if nothing else."

"Of course you can. Something'll turn up. Dart——" She paused, looking out at the flowing landscape. Cactus again, and mesquite. "Maybe you'll feel this is crazy, but I think we might stop in Globe tonight at the hotel, blow ourselves to a room and bath and a real dinner—pull ourselves together before, well— tackling Lodestone, and Mr. Tyson." She spoke nervously, knowing well Dart's indifference to creature comforts, wondering herself if her idea were an idiotic extravagance.

"I think you're absolutely right," said Dart; he glanced at her expression of relief, and said, "Lord, Andy, did you really think I was going to make you sleep in the car? Have I been that much of a tyrant? And I'm in no hurry to get into the Lodestone mess, either."

So they had a large room and bath at the Dominion Hotel, Dart bought a haircut in the barber-shop, they changed their clothes, and Amanda put on a skirt for the first time since they had left Lodestone—the heather tweed suit, and a clean, though rumpled, white shirtwaist.

They drank some beer and ordered a large meal, but neither of them could eat much when it came. And when they left the dining-room, Dart said abruptly, "I guess I better phone Tyson, just to let him know we're coming. He might refuse to see me at all unless he knew why."

She nodded, but her heart sank. She sat in the lobby, with her hands clenched together while Dart was in the telephone booth.

He came out across the lobby, walking slowly and frowning. He sat down on the sofa beside her, and stared unseeing at a vase full of pampas grass.

She moistened her lips and said, "What is it? Was it bad?"

He shook his head, and answered in a puzzled voice, "I don't know. The connection was lousy, but the old boy sounded sort of hysterical. You'd almost think he was drunk. He kept saying for God's sake to hurry back. I tried to tell him about Hugh, that he was dead, and he just kept saying, 'Come back here at once,' and something about an investigation. He wouldn't listen to me."

"Oh," she said. Investigation into the mine accident, no doubt, or had they cooked up some new thing with which to bedevil Dart? "Did he sound—pleasant?" she asked anxiously.

"Damned if I know. But he *won't* sound pleasant when he's really heard about Hugh. I told him we'd be there tomorrow morning by ten o'clock."

They came down into the canyon off the Lodestone road and entered the town at a quarter to ten the next morning. The Ford rattled through the quiet main street past the bridge to Mexican town and the false fronts and arcades before the post office and saloons and Miners' Union Hall. They passed the General Store, and Amanda saw Pearl Pottner's bulky, white-aproned figure just within the door. Amanda looked the other way; she had hoped never to see any of them again, or Lodestone. Then she heard a shout, and she glanced back. Pearl stood outside on the sidewalk, waving her fat arm in vigorous greeting, and she was smiling.

"That's funny," said Amanda, but Dart had not noticed. His jaw was tight, and he stared straight ahead through the cracked windshield.

They passed the Company hospital. She could see people inside in the waiting-room, and there were new white curtains at the upstairs windows. A man was painting the side of the house a bright, fresh yellow. She stared uncomprehending at the hospital. Then they passed their own shack. It was unchanged, the front door still sagged, the kitchen stove-pipe, though repeatedly fixed by Dart, lay on the ground as usual, blown off by some recent wind. All the misunderstanding and the suffering and rebellion she had felt in that cabin struck out at her as she saw it. I couldn't stand it again, she thought. I couldn't. But then she looked up at her husband's tense face, so dearly loved now, and she put her hand on his arm. He did not move his head, but he covered her hand with his. "It's a tough moment, Andy," he said very low, "but we'll fight through it."

They climbed the mine road past the cut-off to the ghost town, and drew up in the parking-place near the change house.

There were a lot of men hanging around the steps of the mine office. Dart noted them with astonishment. What were they doing there at that hour when the shift was in full swing? Strike? The hoist was running, anyway, the great greased cable spinning down from the sheave above, and he heard the roar of cascading ore from the skip to the bin. And what difference does it make to you what happens here, anyway, he thought angrily.

"May I come too, Dart?" said Amanda, as he opened the car door. He was startled. It was true that women were discouraged at the mine, and that for a difficult interview like this it might be far better not to further annoy Tyson and Mablett. But she had become so much a part of him since their days in the lost valley that it had never occurred to him not to take her. "Yes, of course," he said. "Come."

They walked across the stones and dust towards the mine office, and the lounging men all stood up, forming lines up the steps and on to the porch. There was a commotion around the open door, and a nudging and whispering. Some large whitish object seemed to be passing from hand to hand.

"What the hell goes on?" said Dart, hesitating. The men were advancing in a solid phalanx down the steps. Suddenly a figure emerged in front and came marching towards them. It was Tom Rubrick, and his grizzled little monkey face was split with a grin from ear to ear. He held a white sign straight-armed out in front of him, and shoved it at Dart. The sign said "Welcome!" in

large block letters, and it was decorated with garlands of decalco-
mania roses.

Dart drew in his breath and stepped back, staring.

"It's for you, lad! It's for you!" cried Tom, waving the sign,
and the men behind crowded forward, laughing.

The Dartlands stood rooted. A dull red flush crept up Dart's
neck and face. He tried to speak, and emitted a muffled sound.
He fumbled in his pocket, pulled out a handkerchief, and blew
his nose. "Thanks," he muttered. "Thanks."

Tom clapped him on the back. "It's good to see ye, sir! And
the little lady. The boys're all tickled pink, everyone in town'll
be glad!"

"I don't understand——" said Dart in a humble, groping voice.

"Well, ye will, lad—Mr. Tyson's waiting for ye—in there."
Tom propelled Dart through the grinning, sympathetic miners.
Amanda followed close.

Mr. Tyson sat in the General Manager's office in his wheel-
chair. He was wrapped in a blanket, and he looked as fragile as
ever, but when he saw them approach he called out in a hearty
voice, "Here, Dart! Come here. Hurry up, I want to shake your
hand. Good Lord, we've tried every way we know to get in
touch with you, but you vanished into thin air." He pumped
Dart's hand with surprising vigour, and then Amanda's. "My,
but I'm glad to see you!"

"Well, thank you——" said Dart, moistening his lips and
swallowing. "But just exactly why?" Vivid in his memory was
the scene the last time he'd stood in this office, with Tyson's and
Mablett's suspicious, angry faces glaring at him.

"Sit down, you two, and I'll tell you," said the old man. They
obeyed, wondering. Tom Rubrick chuckled delightedly to himself, and could not forbear giving Dart's shoulder a pat as he
passed towards the door. He shut it behind him.

"I was a doddering old fool, I guess," said Tyson, leaning forward, "and I ask you to forgive me, Dart. All the same, I never
was quite easy in my mind, no matter what Mablett said. I
didn't think I could be *that* wrong in my early judgment about
you. I've always been a fair picker of men."

"Yes, sir," said Dart slowly. The sudden readjustment of all
his expectations dumbfounded him. He frowned, trying to
understand. "It was Mablett, then, I take it—who engineered
the mine accident?"

"Mablett?" repeated the General Manager in astonishment, and then he smiled. "Oh, I see. Certainly Mablett hated you and is a pigheaded ass sometimes, but he's not a criminal. No, it wasn't Mablett, it was Tiger Burton, and Mablett knew nothing about it."

"Ah——" said Dart on a long breath. He pulled out a cigarette and lit it automatically, thinking. Not really so surprising; there had been that forgotten scene down at the 1,000 station, that nonsense about Apaches, and yet . . . "But I don't see how —the guy was sick that day, in bed in the bunkhouse. He looked sick, too, and how could he—what did he do?"

Tyson laughed. "So damnably simple that none of us fancy engineers thought of it. He wasn't sick, at least not his body, but he was a fine actor. When you were underground he just hid in the old tailings dump, cut the signal wires outside the shaft, did a neat piece of timing, spliced them up again, and scuttled back to bed in the bunkhouse thinking he'd blown you and, quite incidentally, the two drillers into smithereens. He was terribly disappointed that he hadn't."

"You mean he confessed?" asked Dart in amazement. "When I left he'd got my job. I can't imagine him with pangs of conscience."

"No," said Tyson, leaning back in his chair. "He didn't confess. That is, not spontaneously. When he knew he was discovered he went into fits of screaming hysterics and disclosed his whole plot. He is right now, as a matter of fact, in the State Asylum in Phœnix."

"So," said Dart after a moment, "it *was* simple. I suppose I should have suspected him, but he was so insignificant, mealymouthed. How in the world did you find out if he didn't confess?"

Tyson straightened up. He cocked his head, and his tired old eyes brightened with enthusiasm. "Mrs. Cunningham!" he said, smiling.

Both Amanda and Dart cried "WHAT!" in one voice, staring at the old man, who enjoyed his sensation.

"Yes," he said, nodding solemnly. "She did it for you, my boy. She was magnificent, like an avenging angel. I never was so startled in my life. She went down into town about a week after you left, she commandeered somebody's car, and dragged that crib girl up to my home—what's her name——"

"Big Ruby," whispered Amanda.

"That's right. Big Ruby, who was terrified. She knew about Burton all right, and she surely didn't want to talk, either, but Mrs. Cunningham made her."

"Mrs. Cunningham came *here*?" said Dart. And this seemed to him more astonishing than anything he had heard yet. Calise, with her pale silver hair and her transparent, mystical face, over-awing a frightened prostitute, dragging her to the mine, con-fronting Tyson. "She never leaves her home, never sees people."

"Well, she certainly did this time. She talked to Mablett, and she talked to some of the men. And it was she herself who handled Burton, or we'd never have got the proof. A lot of the men still think she's crazy—you know that old story—but she's not. She has power, spiritual power, and she used it like—like a Joan of Arc. I've never seen anything like it! She even gal-vanized *me*. I swear she sent a sort of thrill through the whole mine—of good-will and optimism."

Tyson paused, remembering again the awe which Mrs. Cun-ningham had inspired in all of them. Even Mablett had been reduced to red-faced gulping silence.

"We must go to her at once——" said Amanda brokenly. "Thank her."

"Yes, you must. Nobody's seen her since that day, and I wouldn't dream of invading her privacy. But she loves you two." He stopped and he looked at Dart, a mischievous and kindly gleam in his eyes. "You'll be mine superintendent now, my boy," he said. "You can jam through that cross-cut in the Old Shamrock you were always nagging me about."

For the second time in the hour Dart flushed a dull brick-red, and his voice betrayed him. "But what about Mablett?" he said, trying to clear his throat.

"Oh, Mablett's being transferred—to Colorado. Company's got a little mine there they want opened up, now the price of gold's jumped again. It *did*, you know, while you were gone. The Lord bless and preserve F. D. R.—Mablett and the estim-able Lydia are pleased as punch about it—seems she has a niece in Denver."

Amanda looked at her husband, and her heart filled with un-selfish joy. His face was aglow, and his eyes gazed out of the window towards the great head frame over the shaft with an expression of dawning excitement. And then his face darkened, his nostrils indented sharply—he turned back to Tyson.

"Everything's been so swell," he said, "I'd forgotten why we came back—what I have to tell you——"

Oh no, she thought, darling, don't. Don't spoil it all now just when you're so happy. She looked at the floor, ashamed of her cowardice, but unable to stop it.

"Mr. Tyson, Hugh Slater went with us to the mountains. The doctor."

"Yes, I know," said Tyson impatiently. "He told me; left us in the lurch here. As a matter of fact, I got a very good man from Globe to substitute. He's got a nice young wife, too, girl about your age," he said to Amanda. "I think you'll like her."

"You don't understand, sir," said Dart. "Slater's never coming back. He's dead."

There was silence in the mine office. The wall clock ticked ponderously a dozen times. Then Tyson spoke.

"Accident?"

"He was shot."

The old man examined the young man's stern face across from him, he noted Amanda's involuntary movement, heard her quivering breath.

"Did you shoot him, Dart?"

Dart raised his head and looked back steadily into the wise, searching eyes. "No—he——" Dart stopped.

Tyson clasped his hands and turned a little, gazing out of the window towards the mine-shaft, as Dart had done. "I guess you better tell me the whole thing," he said quietly.

"Yes," said Dart. "That's why I came back to Lodestone."

Amanda saw the grim lines deepen around his mouth. She held her breath and her heart pounded.

Dart told the story of their journey to the enchanted pueblo with scrupulous exactness. He told of the tragedy in the cave, using factual words devoid of emotion, and the old man listened intently, his face as grave and expressionless as Dart's voice.

When Dart had finished there was another long silence, then Tyson spoke. "So the Apache shot Hugh Slater and thereby saved your life. Slater would have shot you again."

Dart bowed his head. "I suppose so."

"Do you think the Apache, your cousin, should be prosecuted, Dart?" asked the old man gently. "Do you think the sacred canyon should be again invaded—by those in search of legal proof, by journalists, by curiosity and treasure-seekers? Would you lead them there again?"

"Oh no!" whispered Amanda. "That's horrible——"

"Hush," said Dart. He raised his head and looked steadily at Tyson. "I'll do what's right, and I'll tell the truth."

The old man smiled. "I know, Dart—and you have. You've reported the doctor's death to me. I'm a deputy sheriff, and I believe you. The responsibility is now all mine. From now on you can keep your mouth shut."

Dart frowned. He started to speak, and the old man stopped him with an upraised hand. "Listen, Dart," he said, "I've lived a long time, my boy, and I've seen a lot of things that won't fit the textbooks. Some things are better not talked about, they can't be without starting a lot of new harm, a lot more harm than is called for. I think this doctor's death is one of those things."

There was quiet. The dingy mine office gathered itself into a waiting pool, and muffled through the windows they could hear the hum of the compressors and hoist engines.

As Dart did not speak, Tyson went on sternly, "These are orders, Dart, and I'm your boss. I'm taking the entire responsibility, and you've discharged your duty in full. You children have been through a lot, and mostly my fault. I'm not going to let you head into unnecessary trouble again. *Un-necessary*," he repeated, and turning at a sound from Amanda, saw a blaze of joy in the girl's eyes.

"Listen to him, Dart——" she whispered. "Please——"

Dart looked at her and then at Tyson. "But don't you know someone who should be notified—about Hugh?" he asked slowly, and as Tyson shook his head, Amanda, watching her husband, saw the grimness leave his face and his tense body relax.

"No," said Tyson. "There is no one. And I know he didn't have a penny in the world. In fact, he was in debt to me. I'm sorry he's dead, I suppose. He had some good points, but I'm glad he's gone. The new doctor's fine, and I think he'll stay here."

Oh, Hugh, thought Amanda. This then, is all the requiem for you. The waters close over so quickly, with no ripple to show that you've ever been.

"I'm not heartless," said Tyson, feeling the tenuous impact of her thought. "But Slater was nothing but a drunken bum, dishonest, too, and worse because he had the makings of a brilliant doctor—and as for that half-breed whore he kept—excuse frank speaking, Mrs. Dartland—well, this new man, Doctor Jones, got rid of her in jig time. She's left town, I hear, with some man or other."

So even Maria will not mourn, Amanda thought. Nor Viola, whom he loved and who will never know. Then for Hugh there must be pity, since there was nothing else. Pity, and remembrance sometimes. Companionship there had been at times, the sympathy he had once had for Dart, and once for her on the night he had worked in vain to save the baby.

She sighed, and returned her attention to the two men. Tyson was speaking of the mine, technical matters she did not understand, shoving graphs and reports across the desk to Dart. Take over from Mablett in the morning. Mablett would be leaving at once now that Dart was back and on the job.

"He's sorry about the whole business. I mean, the way we treated you," said Tyson ruefully, "but I dare say he won't admit it."

"Good God, no!" Dart laughed. "I wouldn't expect him to. I'll keep the peace till he goes."

Tyson raised his eyebrows, and smiled. "You've learned a thing or two, I think. Your camping trip did you good."

Dart turned and looked at Amanda. Their eyes met. Then they both rose. Dart shook Tyson's hand again, and left him contentedly wheeling his chair over to a shelf where he kept his office collection of Indian sherds.

They went down the narrow hall out on to the porch. The miners had all gone back to the boarding-house for dinner, but Tom Rubrick was waiting for them, smoking his pipe by the water-cooler. He rushed up, beaming. "So now ye move into Bosses' Row, me lad!" he cried, clapping Dart on the back. "Tessie's that pleased about it all, ye wouldn't believe."

"And I'll be so glad to see her," said Amanda, smiling; then she checked herself and repeated, "Bosses' Row?"

Tom chuckled. "Why, ye'll be moving into Bull'ead's 'ouse, o' course. Goes with the job. Didn't ye think o' that?"

"No," said Amanda, sitting down on a bench. "I haven't had time to think of anything." She had an instant vision of the

Mabletts' four-room cottage as she had seen it on the night of
the disastrous party. The overstuffed furniture, the antimacas-
sars and Nottingham lace curtains, the sulphur-yellow wallpaper
dotted with lithographs and chromos and framed photos of the
Mablett family. And she began to laugh. "We'll give collations
—Dart——" She choked. "We can have collations, too!"

He sat down beside her on the bench, and he put his arm
around her. Tom drew away tactfully to the side of the porch.

"Andy, I know. I know how you feel about Lodestone. I've
been waiting to talk to you. I don't have to take this offer. I can
find something else now my name's clear. And from your point
of view my promotion here isn't so much help. Salary's bigger,
but not so much. And as for the Mablett house——"

"Oh, darling, darling," she said, shaking her head and looking at him with tender and still mirthful eyes. "The Mablett
house is heaven. It has a *bathroom*. Don't you know I can be
happy anywhere now, if you're happy?"

Tom watched them from the corner of his eye. Something's
'appened to them two, he thought; they're pulling together at
last. They'll 'ave rough times again, o' course, like all married
folks, but I believe they'll stick it.

Dart and Amanda drove down the mine road again towards
Lodestone, and Dart turned left on the cut-off to the ghost town
and parked the car near the dry creek bed, by the farthest of the
half-demolished shanties. They walked up the dusty road, past
the opera house and the fallen sign, through the rubble of
foundations and among tiny darting lizards.

They turned silently up the trail that led to the great empty
mansion on the mountain-side. And Amanda thought of another trail which had led upward through the hush of the past
and brooding things to a stone city on a mountain-side—and in
the poignancy and longing, in the beauty that came to her,
almost she understood the single note which throbbed through
both these feelings, and then it slipped away before she could
grasp it.

They mounted the broken steps to the huge front door with
the silver shamrock knocker. Dart listened for the sound of the
piano, as he had so often heard it. The crystalline notes of
Mozart, and her voice rising clear and bell-like in "Il Mio
Tesoro"—"Take my beloved in your keeping, console her, drive
away her fears——"

How can I thank Calise? he thought. And it seemed to him that gratitude was an emotion he had never known, strangely ambient, compounded of love and pain.

"The door is open," Amanda cried. "Oh, Dart, the door is open. What does that mean? It never has been."

They looked at each other in quick and fearful surmise. They went through the open door into the hall, calling to her softly. The door of her own suite was open, too. The two rooms were as they had always been, of a shining, ordered purity, and faintly perfumed with dried mountain flowers in the terra-cotta bowl.

Amanda looked at the rose-grey froth of delicate flowers and thought of those she had seen here the first time with Calise. She had not understood then how beauty could grow among the "prickles and the violence" of the desert, and Calise had smiled at her with compassion. I understand now, Amanda thought, I must tell her. But the rooms were empty.

Then they saw a folded piece of white paper on the table. And written in a delicate European script it said, "For Dart and Amanda." They carried the paper to the window and stood together reading.

"*Mes chers enfants*—No, you will not find me, for I have gone into the mountains—from them I shall never return. I am very ill. My summons has come at last, and my release. You must not be sad for me, or think with sorrow that you would have liked to say Adieu, for my release came through you. It is I who am grateful. And I am happy.

"I know something of the strange journey you two went on together. You went seeking for illusion, *les faux follets*, that beckon on but to destroy, and tragedy walked with you. I have held you both in my heart and prayed for you constantly, and I know my prayers were answered. You will come back.

"I leave what material things I am possessed of to you. As long as one lives in the material world one must be practical, also this I had too long forgotten. So my will is in order. It is in the brass chest beneath my bed with my jewels and a little money. The house, I think, you will not care to live in, it is too full of ghosts and long-spent passions. But sell the contents, and be happy, my children, whatever you do. As I am, now. *Que Dieu vous bénisse.* CALISE CUNNINGHAM."

They raised their eyes from the letter, and stood silently side by side looking out of the window to the mountains, studded with cactus and mesquite and paloverdes, and for Amanda at last these, too, had beauty. She would never again see the other terrible mountains to the north, girdling the lost valley, but the enchantment would endure. She looked down the canyon towards Lodestone. Yes, one must be practical, too. One lives in the material world—of people and work and striving and accomplishment. And the only true enchantment is love.

CATCH CORONET IN YOUR READING NET

ANYA SETON

☐ 15701 1	Katherine	40p
☐ 15693 7	Devil Water	40p
☐ 01401 6	My Theodosia	35p
☐ 15700 3	The Turquoise	35p
☐ 15699 6	The Hearth and Eagle	35p
☐ 02713 4	Avalon	35p
☐ 01951 4	The Winthrop Woman	40p
☐ 02469 0	Dragonwyck	35p
☐ 15683 X	The Mistletoe and Sword	30p
☐ 17857 4	Green Darkness	50p

MARY STEWART

☐ 15133 1	The Crystal Cave	40p

CATHERINE GAVIN

☐ 12946 8	The Devil in Harbour	40p
☐ 02317 1	The Cactus and the Crown	40p
☐ 04354 7	The Moon Into Blood	40p

MARTHA ROFHEART

☐ 16530 8	Cry 'God For Harry'	50p

JANE AIKEN HODGE

☐ 02892 0	Watch the Wall My Darling	35p
☐ 10759 6	The Adventures	35p

NORAH LOFTS

☐ 15111 0	The King's Pleasure	35p
☐ 16216 3	Lovers All Untrue	30p

All these books are available at your bookshop or newsagent, or can be ordered direct from the publisher. Just tick the titles you want and fill in the form below.

CORONET BOOKS, P.O. Box 11, Falmouth, Cornwall.

Please send cheque or postal order. No currency, and allow the following for postage and packing:
1 book—7p per copy, 2–4 books—5p per copy, 5–8 books—4p per copy, 9–15 books—2½p per copy, 16–30 books—2p per copy in U.K., 7p per copy overseas.

Name ....

Address ....

....